THE ASHEN WAR

THE ASHEN WAR

DAN LE FEVER

ISBN: 979-8-9850368-0-0 (print)

ISBN: 979-8-9850368-1-7 (ebook)

First Printing, 2022

PROLOGUE

The Daily Telegraph, London
28 February 1901
Forty years have passed since the plague began to spread across the American continent after the battle of Shiloh in the American state of Tennessee. Forty years since Queen Victoria the Great, to protect her subjects, declared herself the absolute monarch of England and suspended Parliamentary procedure. Forty years since her decrees built the Great Blockade and the Northern Wall to seal off our nation from the ravages of the pestilence that silenced America. It has been forty years of war within our country, when those who would be so selfish as to call the Queen a tyrant and take up arms against her, putting us all in danger. But now, after forty years, we finally have Victory in England! King Edward VII has utterly defeated the rebels after decades of war. In accordance with his decree, His Royal Majesty had welcomed the former rebellion leaders to the Palace of Westminster as a show of faith in opening the country to elections. An overwhelming force awaited the leaders and their lieutenants inside while additional Crown soldiers seized the remaining rebel forces at their camps. His Royal Majesty gives credit to his mother, Queen Victoria the Great, who, on her deathbed, devised

this plan. The King, in his infinite kindness, declared that the rebel faction not be executed. Instead, they will work to rebuild the country that he loves so dearly. . .

THE PRISONER

Newgate Prison
London, England
April 1910

A whistled tune cut through the prisoner's dreams, too joyous to be anyone locked within the cold, damp cells. He lay on the smooth stone floor and shivered, hoping to find sleep again. With a sigh, he accepted his fate and opened his eyes. A small square of light crept through the tiny window above him. Footsteps accompanied the approaching whistle. The prisoner hoped they would pass right by, but then a loud bang shook his cell door. "James Barlow, prisoner one-two-five-seven-c, stand and put your hands on the wall," the guard, McDonnell, commanded. There was a hint of an Irish accent buried in his voice. His family must have been trapped here by the dead Queen's laws.

"Bloody hell, McDonnell, it isn't even breakfast yet," James said, staring at the ceiling.

"Just do what you're told, James. Let's make this easy."

"Fuck. People are trying to sleep here," someone yelled from another cell. Angry shouts broke out along the prison block.

"You lot can get your rest once James gets his lazy arse up," McDonnell said. The shouting grew louder in response. "You see, James? Everyone agrees you're a lazy arse. Let's go. Up with you."

Letting out another sigh, James did as he was told. Hunched over, with his hands on the wall, he looked at the silhouette of McDonnell's head in the torch-lit hallway. McDonnell grunted in satisfaction and jingled the keys, looking for the right one.

"What's this about?" James asked.

"Someone's come to talk with you."

The guard refused to tell him who while fumbling with the keys. James looked back to the wall. The moisture that seeped along the cracks chilled his hands. Over a hundred years of scrawl was carved into the rough stone. After almost ten years in this cell, his name was all he'd added to this tapestry of sadness and anger.

Finally, McDonnell found the right key and unlocked the cell. He walked in with a set of chains. "Let's do this easy, now. Place your right hand behind your back…"

James nodded and didn't put up a fight. He wanted to know who had come to this hell hole just to see him.

When the last shackle was locked around his ankle, he was led out into the hallway, where the acrid stench of human waste was more pungent. After so long, James had grown used to it. Groaning, he stood to his full height, a good head and shoulders above most men. The Irish guard beside him barely reached his chest.

McDonnell looked up at James. "Don't get any ideas there, boy-o." To remind him who was in charge, the guard struck him in the stomach with his Billy club. James bent over from the pain, but not wanting to give the Crownsman the satisfaction, he gritted his teeth and held the gasp in his throat. And with a rough push, McDonnell followed behind the prisoner, whistling his tune once more.

It wasn't a long walk to the end of the hall, where they came to a small room with narrow vertical slit openings that allowed the guards to look out into the cell blocks. Inside, torches burned in sconces along the wall. A well-used wooden table and several iron-framed chairs were in the center of the room. Like everything else in the old debtor's prison, the walls were stone.

Even though the public had called for executions, King Edward VII decided to imprison the leaders throughout England and force the remaining rebels to perform manual labor. James was just lucky enough to end up in London, where anti-democracy sentiment was highest. When he'd been dragged to the prison, the first thing he saw was a guard holding a sign that read "Death to Traitors." James had called the guard the real traitor and earned himself a concussion and three months in a dark, windowless cell.

Two guards and an older man were waiting in the room when James entered. The older man, in his mid-fifties, was dressed in a clean, brown suit with a starchy white shirt. As McDonnell was securing him, James studied the well-dressed man. The Irish guard latched James's handcuffs to a ring embedded in the wall, then nodded, and the three Crownsmen guards headed for the door.

Before he left, McDonnell turned to the older man. "Begging your pardon, Your Excellency, but you sure you don't want one of us in here? For your protection, of course."

"No, that is quite all right. I believe even a man of his size couldn't break those chains," the older man said in a nasally, aristocratic voice. McDonnell nodded before giving James one last glare and then shut the guard room door with a resounding *clang.*

Alone, the aristocrat stood for several moments, eying him. James felt like a pig being appraised for market. He knew prisoners were enslaved around England, but this man didn't seem like a slaver. *McDonnell called him Your Excellency. The stink of nobility is all over him. Probably a duke. Duke Butterbottom or something pretentious like that,* he thought.

"I'm Lord Robert Reid, servant of the King," the older man said as if he could see within James's head.

James mulled over how he would respond for a few seconds and finally settled on, "All right."

The Lord waved a soft, well-manicured hand in his direction. "You are James Barlow, aged thirty, son of George Barlow, a former cell leader for the so-called resistance to our Queen's rule, am I correct?"

The vision of his father standing on top of a wagon, calling for the rebels to advance before disappearing under the bombardment of mortar fire, was forever burned into James's memory. "We called ourselves squads, but the rest of that is spot on. Of course, now it would be resistance to the King's rule, if we're going for accuracy."

Lord Reid sniffed in disgust. "Squads would imply military organization. That rabble was anything but organized."

James took a step toward Reid, but his restraints kept him from strangling the Lord with his chains. "Us *rabble* managed to fight against your *organized military* for forty years."

Reid, with a smug smile, said, "Yes. Well, we know how that turned out, don't we?"

Sneering, James said, "People, whose only crime was wanting a say in how the country was run, are held in chains, while the King rules with an iron fist."

The older man's face twisted in anger. "King Edward continues to protect—" Lord Reid began to shout but composed himself. He straightened his tie and continued quietly, "I'd been warned that you were an insufferable goad. It seems you're always quick to start a fight."

"You don't know anything about me."

"Ah, but I do." Reid smiled cooly. He picked up a leather pouch from the ground next to him and placed it on the table. "Everything about you is right in here. Shall we give it a look?"

James shrugged. "It must be light reading. I've been in here since I was twenty."

Lord Reid slowly pulled a chair over to the table. The screeching sound of metal scraping against stone sent a chill down James's spine. Before sitting, Reid brushed off the seat, then reached into his suit jacket and pulled out a pair of glasses. Leaning back against the wall, James tried to cross his arms but found it impossible to do so while chained. Reid removed some papers from the satchel and thumbed several pages before setting them aside.

Clearing his throat with a wet cough, Reid found what he was looking for and said, "Now let's see here, as I mentioned, you were born to George Barlow and Catherine Clarkson, both deceased. Your brother, Michael Barlow, aged twenty-five, is held in the Bedford worker's camp. And your sister, Julia Barlow, aged eighteen, it says here her whereabouts remains unknown, it seems." Reid arched an eyebrow and looked up from the page, giving James a curious look.

James hoped the relief didn't show on his face, even as he could feel his heart race. "I've been in here. How am I supposed to keep track of her?"

"Ah, well, I'm sure we'll find her, eventually. Continuing, it appears you took over your *squad*, as you call it, after your father was killed during a battle in Bristol. Afterward, you managed to get everyone back to whatever hole you called home. My, my. A young man of eighteen, leading his own squad. I bet your mother must have been proud. That is, until she was caught and executed after attempting to blow up a bridge." Reid chuckled and glanced at him as he turned the page over.

James felt cold as he recalled that day. The proud woman looked out at the jeering crowd; her dark hair brushed back by the noose. She caught his eye as he was slowly headed toward the gallows and gave an almost imperceptible shake of her head. He obeyed his mother, and she smiled just before the floor dropped from under her feet.

Reid must have seen the pain in James's eyes because he smiled in satisfaction. "Still a bit sore, I take it? Keep in mind, if she had succeeded, many civilians would have also been killed."

"And you'd have lost the entire battalion marching in that parade." How many rebels would those soldiers have killed the following day? Even to James, the argument was weak. There had been children among the crowd, but he'd made a choice, and now he has to live with its outcome. He swallowed hard and stared icily back at Reid. "We would have taken out a thousand Crownsmen. It was acceptable losses."

"Who gave her the order? Ah, yes. I believe *you* were the one who sent your mother to her death. You can't blame the Crown for all of your poor decisions." Reid held a hand up before James could respond. "Let's keep going, shall we? You remained active in your efforts for two more years before your brother joined when he turned fifteen. And then your squad became less active. Afraid of losing more family?"

"My family's been fighting you lot since your Queen took away our rights and stole our livelihoods. So, no, I wasn't afraid of losing more family." *Don't let them know you couldn't sacrifice your brother. You weren't ready to take care of Julia alone, not when there was still so much left to do.*

Reid raised an eyebrow. "Livelihood? Ah, you were fishermen. That goes all the way back to the beginning, doesn't it?"

"My grandfather was. Don't have that in your pile of papers there?" James nodded at the small stack.

"Well, a lot has been lost during the war, you see, and . . . Why am I explaining this to a prisoner?" The annoyance, mixed with confusion, on Reid's face was almost worth the ten years in prison. "No. I will not be baited." Reid's hand brushed at a wrinkle on a page as he looked down again. "And then we come to nineteen-hundred and one and the year of victory."

"Year of betrayal," mumbled James, looking down at his bare feet. It was hard to tell the difference between dirt and bruises.

"Look at how it ended. No more civil war. No more fighting. We are all grateful for Queen Victoria's victory." Lord Reid had a look of smug pride on his face. "It brought peace to our great nation."

The chains suddenly felt heavier. "A one-sided peace, birthed by treachery. Now is there a point to all this? Or am I just part of the tour?"

"Yes, well, we are getting to that." Lord Reid stood and began gathering the papers. "How would you like to go for a ride? I understand you haven't left these walls since you first entered."

James's eyes narrowed. "Why? Where are we going?"

Lord Reid picked up a final piece of paper. He walked closer to James, still well out of reach, and held the page up. "I trust you can read?"

Looking past the document to Lord Reid, James replied dryly, "Mother made sure her children had an education. How else would we be able to read intercepted communications?" He turned back to the paper, looking at the finely printed lettering.

Immediate Prisoner Transfer
The prisoner 1257-C, James Barlow, will be transferred into the
care of Lord Chancellor Robert Reid, 1ˢᵗ Earl of Loreburn. All care
will be taken to protect the Lord Chancellor from harm during
the prisoner transfer, and any failure in this regard will result in the
execution of those involved.
This transfer is authorized by proxy of the Crown, His Royal
Highness, George, Prince of Wales.

James had to read it three more times before asking, "The Prince of Wales? What is this about?"

"Oh, I'm not at liberty to say. But, His Royal Highness will certainly be able to answer most of your questions, I assume." Lord Reid turned to the door and shouted, "Guard, prepare to move this prisoner. I'd rather like to leave this God-awful place."

"Me too," James muttered under his breath, the wheels in his head turning as he tried to figure out what the Crown had in store.

The guards came in and unchained him from the wall. McDonnell escorted James and the Chancellor down the wide hallway toward the prison gate. James's heart was pounding. "I don't even get to say goodbye to anyone?"

McDonnell prodded James with his club and asked, "What makes you think you won't be coming back?"

"Just a feeling," James said.

"I'll give everyone your fondest farewells, then." McDonnell chuckled.

The gate opened to a busy street and James's first view of the outside in many years. It was jarring and over quickly. He was shoved into the back of a waiting prison carriage where the windows were covered with heavy fabric. Behind him, the doors were locked. Sitting on a hard bench, he went over the brief glimpse of the street, just as his father had trained him. Armed soldiers stood on the corner across from the prison, and civilians walked freely along the roads. However, James had noticed a mother holding tightly to her son as they passed by the Crownsmen, with her head down. He also had to admit it was a rather lovely Spring morning.

One crucial detail stood out more than anything, however. The look on the faces of the soldiers. They looked anxious. As if they were waiting for something. Something they dreaded. James also noticed the rough state of their uniforms. Even during the war, the soldiers had kept their red coats clean and presentable. The uniforms out there, just now, were wrinkled, and one had brown stains on his white trousers. "Getting sloppy," James said to himself. Discipline was slacking.

The carriage rocked as it got underway, and the window coverings swayed. This gave him quick flashes of their journey. He saw the Thames briefly. A small number of ships, mainly military, chugged along the river. At armed checkpoints, soldiers were inspecting people's belongings. Large placards hung from buildings with slogans such as "The Crown Protects," "King Edward's Peace Delivered from Queen Victoria's Victory," and "Safety in isolation: The World fell, we did not!" Civilians played football, with soldiers looking on, in a vacant lot that used to be a bank before being blown up about twenty-five years before. Even street vendors were out, selling various items along the road, and each had an official Crown-authorized peddler sign on their stalls. The one thing James didn't see was anyone smiling. The same nervousness he saw on the soldiers outside the prison was reflected on everyone. Maybe, it's because, not too long ago, this had been a battlefield.

***

During an attempt to get a foothold within London and thus strike a blow against the Crown, James had led multiple squads across the Thames and into the city's heart. His mission was to seize the Tower and establish a forward command post. On one of several rowboats in the middle of the river, James waited for their people on Blackfriars Bridge to create the distraction they needed. With him were a few older rebels, along with his brother, Michael. Also, James's second-in-command and best friend, Ryan Lloyd. Tai Navrange, another squad leader, sat across from him. A flash of light lit up the bridge before he heard the explosion. Moments later, a section of wrought iron arches fell into the water. Bells rang out along the London bank, and voices, running toward Blackfriars, called out.

In a whisper, James said, "Quickly, but quietly." He nodded to Tai, picked up an oar, and together, they paddled downriver, away from the explosion and beneath London Bridge. A second massive fireball lit up the night as they neared a pier. It had exploded in the middle of the bridge a hundred yards behind them.

"Goddamn!" Ryan exclaimed loudly. James hissed at him before turning his attention to the street above the pier. Nothing but shouting and more alarm bells. He turned back as London Bridge crumbled, sending stone blocks into the dark river.

"I knew Uncle packed too much powder in those crates," James said.

Tai slapped her thigh. "How are our reinforcements getting across the river now? We'll be trapped on this side of the river with those bridges down." She pushed a few loose strands of dark hair behind her ear. The fire on the bridge reflected in her wide brown eyes. Most wouldn't think the almond-skinned woman could hold her own in a battle with her slight build, but James had seen her take down quite a few Crownsmen in the few short years he'd known her.

"Ah, Cautious Tai. We'll figure that out when we have to. Let's stay focused and do what we came to do." James then hopped out of the boat with a rifle strapped to his back.

"Don't like that nickname," Tai grunted as she stepped onto the dock.

"Then don't be so cautious." He winked as more boats arrived.

Everyone carried a rifle, but ammunition was at a minimum. Most of the gunpowder they had left was used for the bombings. Like everything else these days, powder was hard to come by, and the resistance had learned to improvise when arming themselves. James double-checked the axe hanging from his belt. He'd found it a few months back when he'd been hiding in a museum. The weight and balance just felt right, so he kept it. Most of the rebels had blades, and a few carried clubs. There was even a man wielding a flail. *We're going right back to the Dark Ages. And here I thought the Queen was trying to save civilization?*

James turned to his brother just as he was climbing onto the dock. "Stay with the boats."

"W-what? W-w-why?" Michael asked. The stutter was always worse when he got nervous.

Ryan, his shaggy red hair tied back behind his broad shoulders, smirked as he stepped off the boat and into a family squabble. "Told you, yeah? You shouldn't have gotten the kid's hopes up," he whispered to James.

"Shut it," James said, then to Michael, "I need you here to guard our escape if this doesn't work. Also, it's an order." And smiled at him.

"I c-c-can fight t-t-too." Michael's face was contorted with frustration, magnifying his boyish features. He looked like a child who had had his favorite toy taken away. Michael had his dark hair swept back with the help of some oil. The first faint wisps of a patchy beard did little to hide an ugly scar that ran from his neck to his right ear—the result of not keeping his head down during heavy shelling. Michael was a bit shorter than James but, like him, stood a head above most of the men and women in the resistance. And, unlike James, he was still growing.

With a hand on his brother's shoulder, James said, "I know you can fight, but I need you to trust me. Stay here and watch the boats." He pointed at one of the other men and told him to stay behind as well. The man let out a long breath, then nodded. Once everyone was off the boats, James ordered them to move out.

The street along the Thames was empty, just as they'd hoped. Old gaslights stood at attention on either side, but the only light they gave off these days was from the torches tied near their base. The next part of the plan relied on sheer luck. *Probably why the rebel council put me in charge of this*. The Tower was usually defended by a small garrison, about a hundred. In all the years of this war, the resistance had never assaulted London in such a way. Sure, there were random bombings and ambushes, but nothing to this scale. They could only hope the soldiers at the Tower had grown complacent.

Keeping to the shadows, they moved toward their target. A tin whistle shrilled out ahead of them. James signaled for everyone to press back against the darkened buildings. From around the corner, a small company of Crownsmen came running down the street in formation, rifles in hand. Just as he'd hoped, the soldiers appeared to have been caught off guard. Most were barely in uniform. Even so, James had to admit that maybe they should have brought more people with them. A couple of dozen rebels looked tiny in comparison.

The soldiers passed by, unaware of their presence. When they were out of sight, Tai came up beside him. "That's about half the garrison. It means we're still outnumbered two to one."

James avoided looking at her so she couldn't see the worry on his face and replied, "We've still got the element of surprise. Now, let's just hope they left the door open for us." He then turned and gave her a reassuring smile.

She gave James a scolding look. Tai often reminded him that she wasn't fond of his jokes during life-or-death missions.

Keeping the smile in place, he said, "Head back down the line and tell the others to get ready. We'll need to take care of those torches quickly once we're at the Tower." Tai didn't reply but did as he said.

When they reached the corner, James was relieved to see the Tower's main entrance was wide open, with only two guards on either side of the gate. Additional guards were gathered on the ramparts, but their attention was on the river. A stone bridge crossed a rock-filled moat from the street to the entrance. Sandbag fortifications were laid out on the road, but they were unmanned.

Torches burned on the street side entrance of the bridge. James signaled two men to move quickly ahead. Keeping low, the men dashed between the shadows. James held his breath. But when they made it across unseen, he let it out slowly. They removed the torches quickly, then threw them down into the moat, casting the street in darkness.

Up in the rampart, a guard shouted, "Torches out!"

"I can see that, Claridge," replied a guard by the entrance. The two went back and forth several times until someone pulled rank and ordered the guards on the bridge to relight the torches. During the exchange, the rebels had moved up the bridge and crouched below the short wall on either side.

As they walked across the bridge to the street, a guard said, "My father never had to deal with this. Gas lamps would stay lit the whole night, they did."

Before the other guard could say anything, James grabbed the closest by his legs and pulled. The guard fell, his head cracking against the cobblestones. Tai put a hand over the guard's mouth and slit his throat. Air escaped from the slit, giving off a gurgling sound as blood poured from the gash. The familiar smell of bitter copper wafted over to James. The guard twitched, his eyes wide, then he grew slack.

James waited a few moments, then let go of the body. He nodded over to Ryan. He and another rebel had brought down the other guard. Ryan returned the nod as he rummaged around in the dead man's powder bag. He found a few rounds and slipped them into his pockets. James did the same but passed what he'd found down the line, ensuring everyone had at least an extra shot each.

They made their way along the bridge, shrouded in darkness, with no guards between them and the entrance. They were halfway across when a bright red glow bathed them in light. Looking up, James saw a flare soaring in the sky.

"Did you lose your way, Hunter? Or have you forgotten how to light a torch?" a guard from atop the rampart called out, and a few men laughed. The laughing stopped as the guards spotted the rebels. The two groups stared at each other for a few seconds, then one of the guards ran to the alarm bell and pulled at it frantically.

"Fuck," James said and made a mad dash for the entrance, followed by the others. Shots rang out from above, and he heard a few cries behind him. James saw at least ten soldiers in the courtyard, unsure of what was going on. *It could still work.* He tried to convince himself they still had the element of surprise.

As the rebels stormed through the gate, the soldiers seemed to catch on. A Crownsman barely had time to raise his rifle before James buried the axe in his skull. Stomping on the dead man's chest, James wrenched the weapon free and turned to the next soldier, who swung his rifle at him and struck his shoulder. More annoyed than hurt, James raised his axe, but Ryan tackled the soldier before he could get his payback. Straddling the Crownsmen's chest, Ryan proceeded to club the man's head in.

Soldiers were filing out of the Tower by then. Glancing back to the gate, James could see even more coming up the street, probably called back by either the flare or the alarm bells. He hated to admit it, but Tai might be right. There was no way they'd be able to hold the Tower. Not without support. He reached down and pulled Ryan to his feet. "We're falling back. Get everyone to the river!"

A disappointed look crossed Ryan's face, but he nodded and shouted to retreat as the soldiers opened fire. The rebels returned fire through the gates to cover those still trying to escape from the court-yard. They were trapped on the footbridge between the soldiers in the Tower and those returning in the street. Tai shouted as she ducked below a hail of bullets, "That Barlow luck giving you any ideas on how we get out of this?"

With only one place left for them to go, James shouted for every-one to jump into the moat. He grabbed Ryan and Tai and tossed them over the side of the bridge, then jumped down after them. He waited as long as possible to make sure everyone left alive had made it down before sprinting over the rocky, uneven ground for the Thames.

It was chaos as he ran, bullets whizzing by. The faster rebels were already pulling themselves out of the moat and heading for the river. He saw the first of them dive in as he climbed out. He looked down the ten-foot drop to the water below. Gunfire erupted again behind him, and he felt explosive pain in his leg as a bullet grazed him, but he gritted his teeth and jumped.

***

James hit his head against the ceiling when the carriage stopped without warning and was dragged from his memory. He heard muf-fled conversations through the small, covered window while rubbing the pain away. After a loud clang, the carriage door swung open, and the sunlight momentarily blinded him. Hands grabbed at him, drag-ging him out of the carriage.

A voice, less nasally than Lord Reid's but still irritatingly pomp-ous, said, "Now, now. This is no way to treat our guest."

As he turned to look at the speaker, the chains that bound James's legs scrapped against the hardpacked dirt road. Blinking until his eyesight cleared, James saw a gaudily dressed man in a military uniform covered in medals. Beneath his black cap, the man's brown hair looked neat and clean, and his mustache and short beard were well-groomed. To the man's right stood Lord Reid. But it was the person in chains on his left that caught James by surprise. After ten years, the once-great mane was nothing more than stubby red hair, cut close to his scalp. But he was still built like a barroom brawler, and he wore that old, familiar smirk.

"Oh, right, introductions are in order, I suppose," said the bearded man. "I am George, the Prince of Wales. You've already met Lord Reid." He then motioned to the other man in chains. "And you know Ryan Lloyd, here. A friend from the old days, as they say."

James grinned at Ryan. "Funny. I was just thinking about you."

"Good thoughts, yeah?" Ryan said.

James nodded, unable to say more as emotions suddenly overtook him. He thought he'd never see his friend again. Breathing deeply, James fought back the tears stinging his eyes. All these years, James hadn't known if Ryan was even alive. The King's betrayal had separated more than just the rebels, it had separated families.

James didn't want to remember that day. It was too painful. Looking away from Ryan, he took in his surroundings. The carriage had brought him to a shipyard on the bank of the Thames. Guards lined the street, blocking any escape. A warehouse rose above the prince, and more guards lined the way to its entrance. Finally, feeling more in control of his emotions, James asked, "Why am I here?"

"Well, where are my manners? I apologize." The prince turned and extended his arm to the warehouse. "Come in. Breakfast is about to be served."

BREAKFAST WITH ROYALTY

The building was on the brink of collapse. Hastily constructed struts had been added recently to reinforce the roof and cracked brick walls. Most of the windows were smashed, and the rancid smell of river runoff permeated the air. The cement floor had a slimy look to it, even after efforts had been made to clean it up. James wondered why anyone, let alone a prince, would come here. Then it struck him. *Guess they didn't want to parade us into one of the palaces. Imagine the scandal!*

A long table, decorated with fine dinnerware and a floral centerpiece, had been set up in the center of the warehouse. Empty chairs waited for them along the sides and at each end. Two male servants, both in impeccably clean suits, stood nearby. James must have gawked too long at the ridiculousness of it all because a guard shoved him and growled, "Move it, traitor."

Prince George had gone right over to the table and taken a seat at one end. He was flanked by guards, who stared daggers at him as they gripped their rifles. Led to the chair opposite the prince at the other end of the table, James had thought it would have been reserved for the Lord High Chancellor, not some rebel prisoner. One of the servants held the chair for him, and after he sat, a guard knelt and attached James's leg shackles to a large cement block beside the chair. After double-checking to make sure James was secure, the guard stood and removed the manacles from his wrists.

"We apologize for the chains, but one can never be too careful," Prince George said from the other end of the table.

James grunted in response as Ryan was seated to his left. Soldiers marched in from the street, filling up the warehouse but leaving a ten-foot perimeter around the table. Lord Reid sat to the prince's right, and the two began to have a whispered conversation.

After several minutes, Prince George looked up. "We are expecting a few more guests, and then we'll begin. You may talk with your friend if you'd like. I doubt you'd be able to overthrow the Crown with some light chatter." The guards laughed at the prince's joke.

James eyed the empty chairs, then he leaned over to Ryan and cupped his hand over his mouth. In a whisper, he asked, "Where are they keeping you?"

Ryan followed suit, keeping his voice low. "Bedford. A few of our friends are there with me."

"You've seen Michael?" James asked quickly.

"Once or twice. They don't let us mingle much. I think they're afraid of a riot, yeah? I saw him a few months ago. He looked tired but all right. Where'd you end up?"

"Newgate."

Ryan gave a low whistle. "They must have thought you were a big deal to end up there, yeah?"

James shrugged. "Have you heard anything about Julia?"

Leaning in closer, practically mouthing the words, Ryan said, "She went north with Uncle before the arrests. Nothing more."

For the first time in years, James felt relief. "If she's with Uncle, she's safe."

Ryan nodded and sat back as a servant came over with a steaming pot and poured tea into their cups. It was strange to smell tea after all these years. It wasn't often available during the war, but the rebels were still English after all.

While James smelled the rich aroma, boots clicked as soldiers stepped aside, making a show of it as they let a group of people pass between them. James looked up from his cup and eyed the newcomers. An old man, face wrinkled, his scalp pockmarked with liver spots beneath a few wispy hairs, hobbled along with the aid of an auburn-haired woman, dressed similarly to him in gray trousers and a brown sweater. A bit behind them came an African man. His broad chest stretched the fabric of his heavily mended shirt. Half of the African's right ear was missing, and lines of pinkish scars snaked along his forearms. Following him, a skinny man with brown hair and glasses clutched at a large backpack he carried while looking nervously at the guards. The last people to pass through were two men with identical features, tight lips, and military uniforms.

"Ah, yes. Here are our guests now," the prince announced. He waved the newcomers over to the table. The men and woman looked curiously at James and Ryan before they sat. All except for the old man; he just sat with his eyes on the empty plate before him and fidgeted with the silverware.

Lord Reid stood. "More so now than before, introductions are truly in order." He moved to stand behind each person as he introduced them, starting with the old man. "First, we have Captain Peter Stillman. That is, a ship captain, mind you. Next is his granddaughter, Elizabeth Stillman. This fine dark-skinned gentleman is Stuart Okeny. Here we have Reginald Belmont. How are you, sir?" Reid didn't wait for the nervous man to answer before moving on. "And lastly, we have outstanding members of England's grand army, Privates Richard and Nathaniel Kitts." Reid returned to his seat and pointed down the table. "This is James Barlow and Ryan Lloyd, convicted traitors. Mind your forks and knives around them." A few guards let out some polite laughter.

Servants—carrying trays of fish, eggs, and ham—came next. James's stomach growled when a thick slab of ham was slapped onto his plate. It had been years since he'd smelled cooked meat. In prison, they were primarily fed a thick, brown porridge, and no one wanted to guess what the lumps in it were. James looked at Ryan just to be sure this wasn't a dream. His friend's mouth was already full of fish and ham with his eyes closed, moaning. That was all he needed to see, and James dug in. He ate quickly, using the tea to help push the food down. Grease dripped down his chin. He wiped it off with his hands and then licked his fingers clean. While sucking on his thumb, he noticed the others staring. And none had touched their food.

"Were we waiting for something?" James asked, flecks of meat escaping his lips.

Reid, his brow furrowed in anger, was on his feet. He slammed a hand on the table and said, "One must wait for the prince's permission before one can eat. This is a civilized country with manners…" The rest was lost in stammers as if Reid's anger had taken his ability to speak.

"It is quite all right, Lord Reid," said Prince George, patting the Chancellor's arm. He turned to the other guests. "By all means, please eat and enjoy."

After everyone had their fill, Prince George stood and placed his hands on the table. He leaned forward and said, "I believe it is time we explain why you are all here."

The guests around the table did their best not to look at James, but a few couldn't help themselves. Feeling fuller than he'd ever been, James patted his stomach before crossing his arms. Ryan gave furtive glances at the guards.

"Relax," James said. "They need us for something."

"Quite right." The prince nodded before continuing. "England is at a bit of a crossroads, you see. By the Crown's might, we've been protected from the ravages of the outside world. But that power does have a limit. And I'm afraid to say, we've almost reached it."

"You mean the food and ammunition are running out," James said.

His face beet red, Lord Reid stood and pounded a fist on the table. George once again patted the chancellor's arm. Reid sat down in a huff, and George turned back to James. "What makes you say that?" he asked.

Feigning boredom, James sighed and leaned back in his chair. "First, your patrols look nervous, and their ammo pouches should have been sagging a few more inches if they were full. Secondly, the way these blokes watching us have been salivating since the food came out. I'd say it's been a while since they've had a decent meal."

"Rat has nutritional value. There've been studies…," said Reginald, the man with the glasses, before he wilted under the burning gaze of Lord Reid.

Prince George's applause was either sincere or mocking. James couldn't really tell. "My word. I was told you were an observant fellow."

Digging a nail into the wood of an armrest, James said, "I also don't like long speeches. So why, exactly, did you bring us here?"

"We're here to establish an expedition company. To explore outside of England," the prince said.

James sat up straight. He suddenly had a bad feeling about where the conversation was headed. "An expedition? To the continent?"

"Oh, no. From what our captains have seen at the Southern Blockade, Europe is still in turmoil. They've heard cannon fire along the French coast. Nothing to worry about, mind you. The Blockade remains perfectly capable of thwarting anyone from reaching our shores. Have you ever been to the Channel?"

"Once, with my father," James said. "Ships as far as the eye can see, surrounded by cannon platforms and naval mines. Some say it's a real show of British military might. I always thought it made us look scared. We're hiding here on this island, afraid of the rest of the world."

"The world is gone," said the old man, Peter.

"Oh, grandfather, don't be so apocalyptic," Elizabeth said. "History has shown that the world can be reborn from small pockets of civilization. Look to the Byzantines, the monks during those dark ages of Europe, and even the Moors. All it takes is for someone to remember."

"Here, here," cheered Prince George and raised his cup of tea to her.

Elizabeth smiled brightly and held her grandfather's hand. The old man gently worked his hand free. "I'm not so sure about this time, Liz."

"Is there going to be a point to this anytime soon?" Ryan said. He was resting his head on his fist. "Because, mate, I have a cell to get back to that needs a good scrubbing, yeah?"

Prince George placed a steady hand on Lord Reid's shoulder, keeping the chancellor in his seat. He then said, "The point, if you're in such a hurry, Mr. Lloyd, is that we're sending you to America."

James's eyes narrowed. "Why us?"

Ryan nodded. "Right. And why there?"

"Do you know why we first colonized America?" Prince George asked, looking at all his guests. "Wood, iron, farmland, coal. Everything your insufferable insurrection has drained from our country is all right there. The king, my father, wants to use the riches of our lost colonies to strengthen our people once more. And in doing so, take back what was lost to begin with."

"What about the people still there? They may not like your plan," James said.

"As you know, the plague began in America. It was the source of all this chaos. We have reason to believe that what the plague did not kill, the descent into barbarism did. Fifty years have passed since any messages have come across the telegraph. Either no one knows how to operate the machines, or there's no one to use them. Either way, the Crown has stored enough ammunition to make our point. If there's anyone left to argue, that is."

"That explains the uneasiness on your soldiers' faces. Your recruits thought they'd be spending their careers on the street corners or guarding a pompous asshole. Now, they have to deal with being sent out into the unknown." James noticed a twitch in the eye of one of the twins, Nathaniel, if he remembered correctly. Lord Reid appeared ready to explode. James continued, "But before you send in the troops, you want to send Ryan and me?"

"Yes, along with this fine group of volunteers," George said. He gave them a reassuring smile.

James tilted his head and raised an eyebrow. "And why do you think I'd ever help you? Unless you've forgotten, the Crown killed my friends and family. Then it threw me in prison. Do you want me to get into the atrocities, or do you get my point?"

"Yes, well, aside from our current disagreements, I'm sure there is something we can do to convince you." Prince George made a show of pacing back and forth at the end of the table, deep in thought. "Ahh, yes!" He held up his finger. "We have your brother."

James gripped his chair's armrests tightly, fought back a wave of anger, and calmly said, "That isn't something new."

Prince George said, "Indeed, you are right. But as we discussed, we are running out of vital resources, such as food. We may have to consider culling the herd, as they say, so those loyal to the Crown can survive."

James felt cold. "You mean mass executions."

"Why should we continue to let the traitors feed off our dwindling food supplies when all they contribute is growing old inside their cells? Granted, some of you are contributing more than the rest with our work programs—"

"Slavery," James interrupted.

"Call it what you will." Prince George waved it off. "Now, if you succeed in your mission, we'll open the jails and let them all go. You can do whatever you want with what's left. Have your Parliament back if you'd be so inclined." George gave Lord Reid a sidelong look. "We won't be here to care."

Ryan sounded skeptical. "Wait. You're going to leave England?"

"There isn't much of an England left, I'm afraid. We've stripped the forests bare to fuel the war. And then, of course, the farmlands," Prince George said, the barest hint of remorse in his voice.

James remembered his father arguing with the squad leaders. He had tried to stop them from retaliating after discovering the wilted crops on their farms. The food they relied on to feed themselves, and their children, had been destroyed. But back then, it was an eye for an eye, and with Uncle's help, they did the same thing to the Crown's crops. Only the wealthy nobles and the Royals themselves still had access to viable land and animals by the end of the war.

I probably just ate the king's pig, James thought as he looked back up from his empty plate and asked, "Aren't you the least bit afraid we'll come after you?"

The prince waved off the question. "There'll be an ocean between us. We plan to scuttle the remaining ships."

"So, let me try to understand what you're proposing. You want us to do what exactly? See if America is safe for you to settle? All without considering if the locals will even let you? Remind me how that worked out for England in the past. And if we go through with this, you'll grant the rebels our freedom so long as we don't sail back and kick your teeth in?" James laughed.

The prince looked away for a moment, and when he turned back, his face was almost as red as Reid's. But Prince George was better at keeping his composure. "We are quite aware of our history, and we have learned much from our previous mistakes. Don't you want to help the world rebuild? Aren't you tired of the fighting? Don't you want to make something better for future generations? The Crown can do that, with your help."

This speech wasn't new, and James had grown tired of hearing it long ago. He said, "You never did answer my first question. Why us?"

"Because, Mr. Barlow, you have a knack for leadership and deal-ing with difficult situations. We discovered that out of all the squads we'd arrested, yours had the fewest casualties in the two years you were in charge. We need a good leader who will look after this ex-pedition. And we thought it might be easier if you had a familiar face going with you, hence Mr. Lloyd. All this will demonstrate that if we work together, we can create something truly wonderful in this world." When the prince was finished, his gaze was distant, looking past James with a giant smile across his bearded face.

The spikey hairs on his neck stood up as James got a bad feeling. Even with the pomp and circumstance, he knew the real reason he was here. *The bastards don't want to waste their own people on a suicide mission.*

Ryan asked the other guests, "And what's your stake in this? Did that speech work on you?"

Lord Reid stood quickly and spoke before anyone had a chance to answer. "You will be crossing the ocean on Captain Stillman's ship. He agreed only if his granddaughter could serve as his first mate. Highly against protocol, mind you, but she has worked on the Blockade for a few years. The others know that what is good for the Crown is good for all of England."

Around the table, the men and woman nodded but didn't look an-yone in the eye.

Reid continued, "I suppose I should go into a little more detail about who will be going along with you. Not many know this, but

Captain Stillman is one of the last few still alive who has ever been to America. He used to deliver cargo there as a young man. Isn't that right, captain?"

The old man nodded.

"Mr. Okeny has trained extensively in wilderness survival. We can only assume that nature has taken back most of the continent, and we want to be sure you don't eat the wrong berries." Reid chuckled.

"Reginald is an engineer. He'll be there to assess what infrastructure you may discover and find the best possible location to land our fleet." The skinny man was shaking so severely that he almost dropped his cup of tea. He gave up and placed his hand back in his lap. "He appears a bit out of sorts at the moment, but trust me, he's brilliant at his work.

"The Kitts are here for your protection. They are good and loyal Crown soldiers." Reid sat when he finished.

James eyed the two soldiers at the table. *Most likely been given orders to kill Ryan or me if we do anything they deem suspicious. I'll have to keep an eye on them. Wait. Why am I talking like I'm going along with this?*

"If I agree to this plan, you have to do something for me first."

"And that would be?" The prince asked, an eyebrow arched.

"I want to see my brother," James said.

Prince George nodded. He waved over a guard and whispered into his ear. The guard ran off quickly afterward. "It has been arranged."

James let out a slow breath, trying to ease the tenseness in his back. "How long until we leave?"

"Lord Reid has all the information you will need." The prince pulled a watch from his pocket, checked it, and grumbled quietly as he placed the clock back. "I'm afraid I'm late for another meeting. May the Crown watch over you and Godspeed."

Everyone except James and Ryan stood as the prince hurried out of the warehouse, flanked by two guards.

Lord Reid took the Royal heir's place at the head of the table and said, "I believe you will be leaving this morning. Isn't that right, Captain Stillman?"

The elderly captain nodded. "Yes, sir. Ship's ready."

A sudden rush of panic sent James's heart beating. He had hoped for a couple of days at least. He needed time for him and Ryan to figure out their escape. "Do we have all the equipment we'll need? Supplies? Weapons?"

Lord Reid did nothing to hide his disdain for James. "We've prepared for this expedition for nearly a year. Believe us when we say you have everything you'll need."

James shook his head. "You want me to lead this thing? I'll decide if we're ready."

"You are insufferable," Lord Reid sneered. "Guards, take him to the ship. Everyone else, please feel free to accompany him at your leisure. There may be some more tiresome questions." Lord Reid turned on his heels and passed through the ranks of soldiers.

After the restraints were locked on once more, James was pulled roughly to his feet and shoved out the opposite side of the warehouse.

"There isn't a need to be so rough with them," Okeny said. He and the others were walking behind James and Ryan.

A guard said without looking back, "If you knew what they've done, you wouldn't be saying that."

"Don't worry," James said, "I'll be sure to fill them in along the way."

THE OPHELIA

An old paddle steamer waited for them outside, lashed to a dock. It had an open deck with the wheelhouse at the back. James guessed it was about two hundred feet long. Someone had put a fresh coat of blue and yellow paint on the ship. At the prow, in red letters, was the name *The Ophelia*.

"Like Hamlet's girlfriend?" Ryan said.

James lifted an eyebrow. The guards had kept them separate from the others in the expedition. "I didn't know you read Shakespeare. In fact, I didn't know you could read."

Ryan stuck an elbow in his side, then gave him a playful grin. "You're in a right good mood." He chuckled.

Rubbing his ribs, James said, "I'm out of that bloody cell and about to go on a boat ride. What's not to be happy about?"

"It isn't going to be as simple as all that."

Both men turned as one of the Kitts approached the circle of guards. The rest of the group remained back, talking amongst themselves. "We've a duty to perform. This is not a reprieve." After a short pause, the private shook his head and added, "I don't understand why they're sending rebels with us, let alone *lead* the expedition. It doesn't make a bit of sense."

"And I'm sure you think you could do it better," Ryan said.

The Crownsman didn't bother looking at Ryan. "Not I, but certainly someone else from the Crown's guard. We have the country's best interest in mind. You and your kind only want to tear it apart."

"We want freedom—" Ryan made for the twin, and the guards moved to intercept him.

James used his large frame to get between Ryan and the guards. He gave Ryan the same stern expression he often used during the war, and his friend eased back with a bitter scowl. Ignoring the guards between them, James made an effort not to appear imposing, which was hard to do when you stood a foot taller than the other person.

"Look, Richard, isn't it?"

The Crownsman's nodded after a brief look of surprise.

"If we're going to do this, and I mean *really* do this, then I don't think insulting one another is a good way to start. Ryan's a good man. A bit hot-headed sometimes, but if anyone is going to save your skin out there, it'll be him. And I'll be honest. I don't understand why I'm here any more than you do. But I do know one thing—I don't want to go back to my cell. If that means I have to go to America and get the king some chocolate, so be it. Do I have to like working for the people I've fought against my entire life? No. But if it means keeping my brother and the rest of my kind alive, so be it. And maybe we end up doing some good for the world, just as your prince said."

Richard looked into James's eyes for a few seconds. Apparently satisfied with what he saw, he nodded and left to rejoin the others.

When James turned back to Ryan, his friend whispered, "Laying it on a bit thick, don't you think? We're not going through with this, yeah?"

James whispered back, "Wait on my order. If I see an opportunity, we'll take it."

Almost an hour had passed before a prison carriage arrived. James and Ryan had been catching up as much as they could when the sound of the wheels grinding against the dirt drew their attention. The soldiers driving the wagon hopped down as soon as it stopped, went around the back, and started barking orders until a tall man emerged and came around to the front. The tall man's childhood scar stuck out even more with his head shaved. But what stood out was the thick muscles of his arms and neck. He looked suspicious at his surroundings as he shuffled past the wagon, his legs shackled like the other prisoners.

"I thought you said he looked weak when you last saw him?" James said, staring at his brother Michael.

"I said tired, never said weak. The boy looks like he could tear a bloody cannon from its mounting, yeah?" Ryan said.

The guards prodded Michael to get him moving faster. Michael studied the group of volunteers, unsure of what was going on, then he stopped in his tracks when he looked at the ring of guards, and he let out a roar of laughter. James felt his throat tighten, and he tried to push through the guards to embrace his younger brother, but they held him back. The boy his mother had sworn him to protect was just out of James's reach. He saw her, their father, and their sister in that scarred face. All the pain and loss that had dulled into a manageable ache over the years came rushing back, stronger than ever.

Still laughing, Michael said, "D-don't g-get too c-close. I've been out splitting rock. I d-don't smell t-too nice."

"Too true, mate. I can smell you from here," Ryan joked, waving a hand in front of his nose.

"Been a long time, Michael. I heard you're in Bedford with Ryan?" James said when the tightness in his throat abated.

Michael scratched at his nose and nodded. He blinked away tears that he didn't want the guards to see. "Yeah, I was f-for a t-time. They g-got me at a camp s-south of the river now."

"Well, it's nice to know you've been getting fresh air. They've kept me locked up all this time," James said, rubbing the sores on his wrists around the manacles.

Michael said, "I c-can tell. You need to get s-some sun." And grinned in a way that looked all too much like their father.

Fighting back his emotions and forcing a smile on his face, James said, "Don't fret. I'll be getting plenty soon."

The two men looked at each other uncomfortably for a few moments. Having been incarcerated for so long, James had very little to tell his brother.

Michael was the first to break the silence. "W-what's this about anyway? They t-took me from the camp without t-telling me why." Michael looked around and let his eyes linger on the group of volunteers, who were trying their best to act like they hadn't noticed Michael's arrival.

"This is about freedom," James said. He nodded at the ship. "They've got a job for me to do. And if I'm a good boy, they'll let us all go."

Michael tilted his head. "What k-kind of job?"

"That's quite enough of that. Time's up," a guard escorting Michael said. He started to pull on Michael's chains to get him back to the wagon.

"Wait a bloody minute," James said in a voice just shy of shouting. "Can I at least hug my brother before you bastards take him away? I haven't seen him in ten years."

Just as the guard was about to answer, Elizabeth called from the others, "What harm could it do, guardsman?" Her grandfather was tugging at her arm, trying to quiet her, but Elizabeth glared at the guard, her hands on her hips.

Okeny, the African man, nodded. "They're chained up, private. How far do you think they'd get if they overpowered you?" James noted the commanding tone of his voice.

The nasty look the guard gave Okeny wasn't lost to James either. "Fine. Be quick about it," the guard said gruffly. He released some slack on Michael's restraints.

The two men moved closer to each other, and after several awkward attempts, they figured out how to embrace with chains on. Leaning in close, James whispered into Michael's ear, "Not sure what their game is yet, but spread the word. I'll be back." He then pulled away.

Michael gave him a grim nod, and the guards took him away.

James watched the carriage until it was out of sight, then he nodded to the red-coated guards. "Guess that's it then."

After a few more seconds, he added, "Are you waiting for permission to go aboard or something? I'm not sure about the proper etiquette, but the captain *is* right there."

A club jabbed James roughly in the same spot as Ryan's elbow, and the two rebels were pushed up the ship's ramp.

Once they were all on the deck of *The Ophelia*, a guard handed keys to Nathaniel Kitts. "Unlock them only when you're out on the ocean, private. No sooner. We don't need them jumping ship and causing trouble now, do we?"

Nathaniel nodded and fixed the ring of keys to his belt.

"What about equipment? I need to see what we're taking with us," James asked the guard. But the Crownsman ignored him and headed for the ramp.

James reached for the guard and said, "Hey, I'm talking to you—" He didn't get to finish as something struck him in the head, and everything went black.

***

Softness, real softness. James woke up on a cloud. He rolled onto his back and pulled the blanket to his chin, which made his toes cold. Grudgingly, he opened his eyes and, through slightly blurred vision, saw that his feet were dangling off the edge and that it wasn't actually a bed after all. It was a suspended cot attached to the bulkhead. Still, it was more than he'd ever had in Newgate. Soon, his eyesight cleared, and he took in the rest of his surroundings. White paint did its best to hide the harshness of the metal walls and rivets of the small room.

"Sorry, but they didn't tell us you were so, uh, large," said a woman's voice from beside him.

Pulse racing, James hoped it would be Tai sitting in the chair, but it was only Elizabeth. Her hair was amber, not black, and she kept it neatly contained in a tight bun. They had the same brown eyes, though. And looking into them only reminded James that Tai was lost to him somewhere in the Crown's prisons. *Maybe Michael can get word to her. Let her know I'm still alive.* Something had been blossoming between Tai and him before the arrests, and the fact he never had the chance to tell her how he felt was just another on his long list of regrets.

James realized he'd been staring at Elizabeth for far too long. She got to her feet, placing the book she'd been reading down on a small table. Worried that he'd made her uncomfortable, he asked, "What happened?"

Elizabeth picked up a glass of water from the same table and handed it to him. "Stupidly, you tried to grab one of the guards. You'll have to thank your friend later. He managed to convince them not to kill you. Then we carried you down here."

"Charming bedside manner," James mumbled quietly to himself. He took a sip of the water and asked her, "How long was I out?"

"About a half-hour. We set off soon after. Grandfather was eager to be underway."

James winced when he sat up and touched the sore lump on the back of his head. "He didn't seem so eager at breakfast."

"He's *eager* to have his ship back and sail her on open water again after all these years." A brief smile crossed her lips.

"Is it true that he'd been in America when the plague began?" He placed the glass back on the table next to her book and read the title, *Experimental Researches in Electricity* by Michael Faraday.

"No. Truthfully, he warned before he ever reached port," she said with a shake of her head. "Another ship signaled to him to stay away. But my grandfather is still a hero. He brought that story back with him to England. The telegraphs had gone quiet before he got back, so his story was all justification the Queen needed to seal off England. If it hadn't been for him, England would have ended up like all the other countries. Dead and gone."

"We don't know the rest of the world is gone," James said. "That's what the Crown wants us to think. But I've been on the other side of their lies before. Remember that."

It looked like she was mulling his words for several seconds, but then she said, "My grandfather told me about how it was before the plague, how ships used to go back and forth between the Channel and the continent. I've never seen a ship sailing out beyond the blockade. It's empty out there. The Queen saved us from something terrible."

James laughed bitterly. "And then she took away our rights and our property. Then she enslaved those willing enough to stand up and demand them back. And that outcome was better?"

"At least you're alive to complain about it." She turned and opened the cabin door. "Everyone is still on deck, and you probably have many more grievances to get off your chest. I'm sure one of them would be willing to listen."

"Look, I'm sorry…" he started, but she was gone. He swung his legs around to stand and realized he was still in chains. The manacles had rubbed the skin raw and left his ankles sore and bleeding. Even his toes were bruised from stubbing them against the metal links. The chains hit the floor with a resounding *thud*. They clanked and rattled as he crossed over to the door.

With the ring of keys still on his belt, Nathaniel stood guard next to his door. The Crown soldier nodded down the hall toward a set of stairs leading up. "That way," he said. Like the cabin, the hallway was painted white. Pipes ran across the low ceiling, which forced James to hunch down. Iron doors lined the short hallway in both directions before it reached another set of stairs leading down, from which he heard a rhythmic thrumming and guessed that was where the engine room was.

"You know, mate, it'd be easier for me to get around if you'd unlock these." James banged the chains against the floor for emphasis.

"We're not out on the ocean yet," Nathaniel said, avoiding eye contact with James.

Smirking, James asked, "You take orders from prison guards?"

Nathaniel's jaw tightened, but his voice remained emotionless. "I wouldn't want to be responsible for you blowing up something important, like Westminster Palace."

"That wouldn't be my first target." Nathaniel stiffened, and James saw the same slight tremor in his eye from breakfast. "Relax, Crownie. It's only a joke." *Or is it?*

With Nathaniel trailing behind him at a distance, James made his way for the stairs. "But it's good to know you follow orders. I'll remember that." He tapped his temple.

The whole ship probably heard him climb up the stairs. A propped open hatch led outside, and a cool breeze was blowing back into

James's face. Peering through the gap, he watched as the outskirts of London passed by. It was a view he thought he'd never see again. Blasted buildings and crumbling stone walls lined the river—the scars of war left to fester far from London's center. James wondered what the Crown was even rebuilding with their forced labor projects.

Ryan's voice came from across the deck, and James pushed the hatch open and exited the stairs. Together at the railing, Ryan was talking to Okeny and Richard. From the way he was nodding without really looking, James could tell Okeny wasn't paying attention but wanted Ryan to get whatever he had to say out of his system. Richard had his rifle close at hand as he watched James approach.

"We were trying to get away from a platoon along the river there, yeah?" Ryan said excitedly. "My mate pointed out a cannon position beside a carriage with what I thought had to be barrels of gunpowder sitting on top of it. I took my shot." Pretending to point a rifle, Ryan continued, "Bang! The damned thing blew up, taking the cannon with it. The Crownies shat themselves. Never seen so many red-coated cowards before."

A scowl crossed Richard's pinched face while Okeny continued to nod along, but James could see the muscles bulging in the Black man's neck. After all these years, Ryan had never learned to read a room.

"It blew up? Just like that?" James said with a forced smile, hoping to clear some of the tension in the air. "Ryan tends to exaggerate a bit. I remember the carriage had already been on fire before you even noticed it."

"I, well…I might have mixed up a detail or two. But I do remember the river and an explosion…," Ryan's voice trailed off. Face reddening, he scratched the back of his head.

The corded muscles of Okeny's neck relaxed, and then he began to chuckle. The chuckle grew until he laughed so hard that James couldn't help but join in. Soon, he was holding onto the railing and wiping tears from his eyes. Okeny slapped a snickering Ryan on the back.

Sucking in the moist river air, James felt surprisingly good. It had been so long since he'd laughed or felt the wind in his face. He knew he should be looking for a way to escape, but he wanted to enjoy the cruise a little longer.

Nathaniel, who had followed James up to the deck, crossed over to stand with his brother. The two soldiers eyed the prisoners with contempt. The threads of an idea wormed their way into his brain as he stared back at the armed men. Perhaps it was time for the cruise to end. *If we can get their guns, we could force the ship to take us wherever we want.*

Before James continued that train of thought, Okeny clapped him on the arm. "Ah, been a long time since I'd laughed that hard," he said. "Cheers for that."

"Sure," James said, peeling his eyes off the rifles the twins carried.

"Good to know you aren't the ruthless animal they warned us about," Okeny said, moving to the rail and placing himself between James and the soldiers.

James said, "I'm sure you've been told not to trust us."

"At least they trust us enough to give us our hands back, yeah?" Ryan said, holding up his arms. "But not enough to keep us from drowning if we jump ship." He kicked at the chain between his legs.

"We're not—" Nathaniel started.

"Out on the ocean yet," James finished for him. "I've been paying attention."

James didn't look back to see if Nathaniel could take a joke. Instead, he decided to take in the rest of the ship. This was, after all, the first time he'd been on anything larger than a rowboat. He found it curious that a steam-powered ship had two masts rigged with sails, but he also knew very little about boats to begin with. The hatch they came out of was just below the wheelhouse, about ten feet off the deck. A narrow set of metal stairs led up from the deck to a door at the side where the captain piloted the craft. And that's where Peter was, a smile splitting his wrinkled face. Elizabeth was beside him, but she wasn't watching where the ship was headed. She was looking down at the deck. After catching James's eye, she leaned over to Peter and pointed down at him. The captain nodded but didn't take his gaze off the water, and Elizabeth disappeared until she came down the steps to join them.

"Pardon me, gentlemen, but seeing as this will be your home for the next six weeks or so, I believe it might be best that I show you where you should and shouldn't go. For your own safety, of course," Elizabeth said.

She led them back to the stairs James had just so valiantly contended with. Nathaniel went ahead of him and Ryan while Okeny followed behind them. The chains made even more noise going down than they did going up. Elizabeth paused at the bottom of the steps and said to Nathaniel, "Take those blasted things off. They're bound to give me a headache."

"I can't—" Nathaniel began.

"You will." She cut him off. "On this ship, I'm the first mate, and you will obey *my* orders." She continued further down the short hallway, muttering to herself, and James could hear the annoyance in her voice. It made him smile.

Ryan leaned over to Nathaniel, and out of the corner of his mouth, he loudly whispered, "Might want to do what the lady says. Otherwise, she'll likely make you walk the plank, yeah?"

Nathaniel shoved Ryan back with his rifle, then stuck a finger in his face. "Never get that close to me again, traitor. And I don't take orders from you or any civilian. I serve the Crown and only the Crown." He turned and continued down the stairs.

At the end of the hallway, Elizabeth waited with a withering look.

Angrily, Nathaniel took the keys from his belt. "Not one word," he said coldly and crouched as he tried to find the right key for Ryan's chains.

When the key slid home, Nathaniel looked over his shoulder at Elizabeth. "I want it on record that I'm doing this under protest. You'll be responsible if anything happens."

Elizabeth gave a dismissive wave, and Nathaniel turned the key, releasing the first manacle from Ryan's ankle.

As the soldier went to work unlocking James's legs, Ryan rubbed his hands together and locked eyes with his friend. James knew that look—he was waiting for the order to fight. Behind them, Okeny blocked the stairwell, and his eyes practically pleaded with James as he shook his head slowly.

He knows.

They stared at each other, and Okeny's foot braced against the stair. James gave Okeny a quick nod and turned away, heading down the stairs. He'd have to keep an eye on Okeny in the future. There was a mystery about him, and James wouldn't want to kill him without first solving it. James hated mysteries. A mystery meant he lacked a piece of knowledge, which could be fatal when you're fighting for your life.

The tour began with the cabins. Each man had their own. Elizabeth explained that a ship like this usually housed a crew of sixty men, but they could only support fifteen because of supply issues. That meant double shifts and hard work to make up for the loss of manpower. As they continued through the ship, they passed by the boiler room. Pistons hammered in the steam-filled room. Unaware of their passing, the crewmen inside were focused on dials and turning valves.

They passed an open door to a room filled with tools of all kinds on the walls, and among them was the scrawny engineer, Reginald. He stood at a table, pulling a wooden case from his pack. It was the size of a large jewelry box with wires coming out of two holes below the hinge. Pushing his glasses back up his nose, Reginald looked up to find James staring. The engineer quickly shoved the box back inside the pack. James wanted to stop to speak with him, but Elizabeth hurried them to the cargo hold.

Aside from a few crates, the hold was empty. Metal bars lined the floor and walls where boxes and other goods could be secured. In the past, Elizabeth's voice echoed as she pointed to the crates and said, "You wanted to see what the Crown has supplied us with? Have a look."

A pry bar was sitting on top of a crate, just waiting for him. James went over and worked off one of the lids. Inside, he found bundles of bread and meat, but the box was only half full.

"Is this all the food we have?" he asked. During the war, food rationing had become a part of life, and he knew this wasn't enough with just a glance.

"We have fishing nets and rods. We'll be fine," Elizabeth said with a slight eye roll. James recognized her tone. His mother had often used it when she'd been tired of his questions.

Ryan gave a low whistle as he looked inside another open crate. James went over to see a few long guns fastened to a rack on the side, ammunition boxes, pistols, knives, and swords. But what caught James's breath was nestled right in the center: a big, bearded axe.

At first, he thought it was the one he'd found in the museum. His pulse quickened as he examined the nicked handle and worn blade. But after he studied it, he realized it wasn't. His had been seized when he was arrested. But someone must have kept good records to include a similar one with the rest of the weapons.

Slowly, his hand was inching toward the crate when the lid slammed shut, almost taking his fingers off. Nathaniel was next to him, his hand on top of the wooden box. "This remains closed until we are very far from England." The soldier looked around the cargo hold. "I'll be sleeping here. Someone needs to make sure everything here stays safe." He looked James in the eye as he stressed the word *safe*.

"Yes. Good idea. I don't know any of the crew, and we don't want anything important to suddenly turn up missing," James said, keeping eye contact with Nathaniel.

"Gentlemen," Elizabeth said from the doorway. "If you're quite done, I can show you the engine room."

"We haven't seen what's in the rest of the crates," Ryan said.

"I'm sure it's more of the same," James said. "Let's not keep her waiting."

While Elizabeth led them further into the ship, James noted that Nathaniel had stayed behind. The Crownsman was cautious, which might be good, considering where they're supposed to be headed. But James needed to find a way to get rid of him.

Lost in thought, he was unaware they'd arrived at the engine room until he was engulfed in sweltering heat. Startled, he nearly tripped over Ryan. His friend was swearing about almost losing his eyebrows. Somehow Reginald had made it to the engine room before them and was appraising the coal furnace when they walked in. Around the engineer, five crewmen were working on various tasks. Some were shoveling coal. Others read dials and yelled at the men digging.

"I'll just wait out here, yeah?" Ryan said and stepped out of James's way. Ryan didn't like heat. During the scorching summers, he'd spent most of his time in a river or pond if he could find one that wasn't too polluted.

Sweating already, James chuckled and patted him on the shoulder, then continued into the room. Reginald and Elizabeth were talking over the roar of the furnace. The engineer smiled as he pointed out parts of the machine while Elizabeth answered his questions. Reginald nodded along as she spoke.

It wasn't a large room. Most of it was taken up by the furnace, but in one corner was a pile of coal, and while James wasn't an expert, he was sure it wasn't enough for a six-week journey. And he wasn't the only one who noticed. Okeny had circled around to get a better look, then asked, "Where is the rest of the fuel stored?"

The smile on Elizabeth's face slipped at the question. She patted Reginald on the arm and took a few short steps over to the two men. "This is all we have to work with."

"This isn't enough to get us there, is it?" James said.

"We'll be relying on our sails once we're out of the Blockade. This is just to get us there and in case of any emergencies."

James nodded, not so sure. He caught one of the crew members looking over at them. A short, balding man with arms coated in coal dust and sweat. He looked at the engine, then at the coal, and shook his head. "If it's emergencies you're worried about, we'll be lucky to make it a day with this," the man said.

"Eugene, that is enough!" Elizabeth shouted.

"Sorry, Miss," the crewman said and went back to work.

"This is sounding more like a one-way trip," James said.

"The port officials said this was all they could spare," Elizabeth said quietly, barely audible over the pounding of the engine.

At the furnace, Reginald said, "For millennia, man has sailed the oceans. It was only in the last century did we have the engine."

Elizabeth gave him an appreciative nod, but the engineer was still looking up at the machine powering the ship.

"What's everyone worried about? There's coal in America," Ryan shouted from the doorway. "Isn't that why we're going? Might as well help ourselves, yeah?"

With the tour over, Elizabeth led the group back out the way they came. While they had been below deck, the ship had left the mouth of the Thames toward Margate and, ultimately, south to the Channel. Off the port side was the Great Blockade that protected England. A massive wall of ships made up of all makes and sizes. The protective barrier was ten ships deep in some places, chained together.

During the initial panic caused by the threat of plague, cannons had lined the shore to keep ships from landing. But the military deemed it wasn't enough, and the Queen agreed. The order was given, and every vessel was seized to construct the Blockade. It was the largest military operation in British history, and it had worked. Not one ship ever broke through.

Of course, even with all the country's ships, there weren't enough to surround the entire island nation, so sacrifices had to be made. Queen Victoria had commanded the construction of a large wall atop the ruins of what Hadrian had built. The Scottish army guarded the northern coastline while the stones were being laid. The assumption was that they'd be recalled before the wall was finished, but, in the end, they were abandoned along with everyone else.

The Scots tried to mount an attack, but the plague had arrived and ravaged their numbers. The last anyone had heard from north of the wall was a single, frail man begging to be let in. He'd screamed himself hoarse until night fell, and his voice faded away.

The smell of the salty water brought back the memory of the time James's father had taken him to see the Channel when he was a boy. *Somewhere, among the thousands of ships, is your grandfather's,* George Barlow had said with his big hand on James's shoulder. *They took it from him, from* us. James had never met his grandfather Andrew Barlow; he had died a few years before James was born. But the same anger his grandfather had burned inside his chest, so in a way, a part of him was always with James.

"If you've got a plan, we should do it soon, yeah? Don't think there's a good chance of us getting away if we're on the other side of the Blockade," Ryan said quietly. Leaning on the rail, he looked down at the once blue water, now a sickly green and brown from years of runoff.

James rubbed the bridge of his nose. "Nathaniel's guarding the weapons. Without them, there isn't much we can do."

Angrily, Ryan said, "So, that's it then? We're not even going to try? There's two of us and one of him. Last I checked, those were good odds."

"Twenty-one."

"What?" Ryan looked up from the water.

"There are twenty-one other people on this ship, and just the two of us. None of them seem to be on our side, so I don't think they'd let us take the ship without a fight." James sighed, turned his back to the Blockade, and stared at the English coast. "I don't see any other way. After sitting in a cell for years, I'm not as strong as I used to be. Even if we jumped ship, I doubt I could make it to shore. As I see it, I'm stuck on this boat."

Ryan grunted and slapped the rail. Almost sulking, he studied the deck once more. Elizabeth and Reginald had gone up to the wheel-house. Richard and Okeny were having a private conversation by the ship's bow. And Nathaniel was nowhere in sight. "What about that rowboat over there? Couldn't we use that?"

"See the red box with the heavy padlock on the winch? That's an emergency alarm. As soon as we pull that lever, the bell will go off."

After a moment's pause, James said, "But just because I can't make the swim doesn't mean you can't try."

As if he hadn't heard James, Ryan sighed and said, "Damn it. Well, I always wanted to travel the world." He left James and headed over to where Okeny and Richard were talking.

James smiled and looked back at the Blockade. Once past the ships and weapons platforms, there was no Crown. Out there was the rest of the world. And no matter what danger was out there, it wouldn't be wearing red coats and waving Union Jacks. For the first time in his life, James felt a glimmer of freedom.

BEYOND THE BLOCKADE

"Have a look. It might give you some appreciation for what the Crown has done for us." Richard had come over, most likely to escape one of Ryan's boisterous tales, and held a pair of binoculars out to him.

James held his tongue, even though every fiber of his being wanted to argue that point with the soldier. After all, the man was holding a rifle, and James wasn't too keen on having his body dumped into the ocean. He took the binoculars, peered through the lenses, and had his first glimpse of another country. Through the lenses, he saw a rocky beach. Past that was what remained of a seaside village. Cottages and larger homes had weathered to the brink of collapse after years of neglect, but nature was retaking the ruin. Young trees grew from fallen roofs, and grass pushed through the cracked stone block paths. The destruction didn't bother James. He'd seen worse. But he was shocked by the crosses. He counted at least twenty erected along the short wall between the beach and the village. Skeletal arms dangled from the few where the ropes hadn't rotted away.

"Savagery. I never saw it firsthand, mind you, but I've seen the early sketches sent back from the Blockade," The soldier shook his head. "I had hoped to never see such a sight as this." Richard sighed. "But here we are."

Handing the binoculars back, James asked, "If that bothers you, why *are* you here?"

Richard placed the binoculars neatly in the pouch at his waist. "Nate and I volunteered for the expedition." Brushing some lint from his sleeve, Richard said, "Our father always filled our heads with glorious tales of war. Nate always wanted to make him proud, and he somehow convinced me to follow along. 'We'll be the first Kitts to set foot on foreign soil in a hundred years. Imagine the stories we'll get to tell.'" Richard smiled wistfully, then continued, "I believe he's more interested in the women who flock to such fool-hearty men."

"And what convinced you to come then, the stories or the women?"

Richard shook his head. "Respect."

James lifted an eyebrow. "From who?"

Richard looked away. "I don't care to talk about it."

James could see Richard was walling off a painful memory. He'd seen it many times before. Changing the subject, he asked, "How about Okeny? Did he come for the same reasons as your brother?"

Richard was still busy building his wall, but he said, "We met only this morning. Perhaps you should ask him yourself?" The soldier gave the French coast one last glance before standing at the door to the lower decks.

After no longer seeing him at the bow, James searched until he found Okeny on the other side of the wheelhouse at the ship's stern, watching the waves created by the ship's wake. As James came over, Okeny asked, "Need something, sir?"

James raised an eyebrow. "Sir?"

Okeny shrugged. "The Crown put you in charge."

Stroking his chin, James said, "I don't think Elizabeth heard that bit…" He gave Okeny a wink.

Okeny's laugh was genuine and lighthearted.

He's in a good mood. You might as well get right to the point.

"Why are you here, Okeny?"

"I'm the wilderness survival expert. Or hadn't you heard that?" Okeny grinned.

James leaned against the rail and crossed his arms. "I heard. But why didn't they send a Crownie?"

The grin fell. "I was in the military. For many years."

"Oh," James said.

"Then I was told to resign."

"Why?"

In a bitter, formal voice, Okeny said, "Fraternizing with an officer's sister. A *White* officer's sister."

James wished Okeny's story was unique, but it wasn't. Shaking his head, he asked, "Where were you stationed?"

"I bounced back and forth between the Wall and a garrison in Lincoln. I spent most of my career hunting and tracking rebels."

Taking in Okeny's scars and the mutilated right ear, James was surprised he hadn't put two and two together. Here was a battle-hardened veteran.

"The Kitts were still children when the war ended, but you and I were on opposite sides ten years ago. I wonder if they ever sent you after me?"

"I doubt it."

"Oh? What makes you so certain?"

Quite matter-of-factly, Okeny said, "You're still alive."

James looked down at the Black man, feeling the old hatred begin to simmer. But then he saw the sadness in Okeny's eyes. An apology he couldn't put into words. This was a man whose regret bubbled right beneath the surface.

James let out a slow breath and fought to keep his anger in check. When he felt more in control, he asked, "Are you capable of taking orders from a rebel?"

Okeny closed his eyes, nodded, and then turned to the rolling waves. "The war's over. People change. Ideas change."

Not always. But his words seemed genuine. James rubbed his face, then watched the waves with Okeny. "So, wilderness survival?"

"Wasn't my choice," Okeny said. "They were having a laugh. African jungles, and all that. But who was I going to complain to?" Okeny spat over the side of the ship.

"And now you're helping them again. Why?"

"An old regiment buddy of mine recommended me to a higher up. The army said they would clear me of any wrongdoing and give me my pension. I couldn't say no to that."

Okeny looked at James. "Now you know my skeletons, and I know yours. I want to survive this and get home. I trust you want the same?"

With a nod, James said, "I do. The sooner, the better."

"Good. We have the same goal in mind. So, there's no reason not to trust one another now, is there?" Okeny held out a hand.

"Agreed," James said, grasping Okeny's hand tightly. He had to admit he might *actually* like Okeny. He was open and honest. From James's experience, those were traits not often found in Crownsmen.

Okeny nodded over to Ryan. "What about him? What's his story?"

"Ryan?" James looked to where he was attempting to engage Richard in a conversation, but the soldier did his best to ignore him. "We've been mates for as long as I can remember. Grew up together in the resistance."

"It's good to have a friend like that," Okeny said. Smiling sadly, he excused himself and returned to the bow.

The French coast faded beyond the horizon as the day progressed, and Reginald came up from below with a chess set around noon.

"Anyone fancy a go?" he asked the men gathered on deck.

Reginald looked nervous when James said, "I'll give it a shot." It'd been years since he'd last played, but James saw it as an opportunity to learn more about the engineer.

Laying the board out on a barrel, Reginald was careful with the pieces, ensuring each one was correctly placed. He was a few years older than James. And an academic. James noted his eyes never left the board. This was a man who'd never experienced the fear of a hidden sniper or faced an overwhelming force.

"You never got out of London much, did you?" James asked after Reginald placed the last piece.

Reginald gave him a curious look from behind his wire-framed glasses. "What a strange question to ask. I've been all over the country. Lots to rebuild, you know." He then waved his hand at the board. He'd given James the white pieces, and therefore, the first move was his.

Picking up a pawn, James said, "During the war, I mean." He rolled the smooth wooden figure between his fingers.

"Oh, well, no. I was apprenticing, you see." Reginald tapped a callused finger on the barrel, looking back down at the board.

"I thought all able-bodied men were required to serve." James placed the pawn one square forward.

Reginald slid a black pawn and said, "Yes, all able-bodied. My heart, you see, it has a murmur."

James moved another pawn, which got a hint of emotion from Reginald—a half-smile he tried to hide with a cough. "And, with your condition, you thought it was a good idea to volunteer for this?"

Reginald moved a second pawn before he answered. "Yes, well, we all have our reasons, don't we?"

Crossing his arms, James said, "I didn't have much of a choice."

Reginald swallowed nervously and didn't take his eyes off the board. "Pardon, but I do believe it's your move."

The game continued in silence.

Reginald was good. Very good. He was able to hide his strategy and went on the offensive rather quickly. James wanted to beat the engineer. But soon, it was clear that was impossible. He shook Reginald's hand, noting the roughness of his skin and a slight tremor.

Stretching his back after the game, James and everyone else on deck were surprised by the signal horn's sudden blare. So focused on the match, James had missed the fact they were headed straight for the Blockade. Elizabeth passed by him as he stared at the oncoming ships. He hurried after her.

"What's going on?"

"It's time to go through. I have to give the password," Elizabeth said. She held a flag in each hand. At the bow, she moved the flags in quick, deliberate movements. Across the water, a man on a large schooner signaled back at her with his own. After a bit of flag-waving, the schooner's horns sounded twice. This was followed by two more from somewhere deeper in the blockade.

The thick chains locking the ships together began to creak and slowly dip into the water as they grew slack. With a strange sense of awe, James asked, "How long has it been since these ships last moved?"

"You know the answer to that. We all do," Elizabeth said, watching as the ships slowly separated. Like the doors of a massive gate, the large vessels parted, opening the way for *The Ophelia* to pass through. It was breathtaking.

"What was the password?" James asked suddenly.

Her attention still on the Blockade, Elizabeth said, "They asked, 'How many ravens remain?' I answered, 'Six and all is well.'"

The Ophelia lurched forward when there was enough room. James looked up at the looming ships as they passed, their hulls caked with years of algae, barnacles, and bird shit. The horn above the wheelhouse gave three long blasts when they arrived on the other side. Already, the Blockade was closing behind them, the chains tightening as the ships were drawn back together again.

"Just in case something happens, what's the password to get back in?" James asked.

Turning back to the wheelhouse, Elizabeth said, "There isn't one."

"Wait. What do you mean there isn't one?" James followed after her.

Elizabeth spun around, and he nearly ran her over. "It means exactly what I said. We were never given one. As far as I know, there's only one way home. You have to succeed in your mission."

James pointed at the Blockade. "How're they going to know? Do we just show up with a boat full of coal and cattle one day and say, 'Hello, chaps, look what we found?'"

"Our contract said we are to bring an expedition to America, and they will take care of the rest. Now, I don't plan on spending this entire voyage answering questions. So why don't you find someone else to bother?"

Elizabeth hurried on but called over her shoulder, "It would be best that you inform Mr. Lloyd about our situation as well. Even if he were able to take control of the ship, he'd have no reason at this point." She walked off, leaving James behind, his mouth hanging open.

There're too many blind spots in the room, a saying he'd picked up from his father. Shaking his head, James hated that he hadn't been told everything up front. Something new was being sprung on him every time he turned around. And, of course, these people didn't trust him. The Crown gave them good reason not to. But that would have to change. They were stuck together, whether they liked it or not. He turned to look out at the choppy water that stretched to the horizon. Suddenly, England felt so very small.

***

Soon after they were through the Blockade, the crew dropped the sails. The heavy fabric whipped loosely until the ship caught the headwinds. James breathed in the fresh salt air and finally under-stood what his grandfather had lost half a century ago. From where he stood on the deck, he had a good view of the wheelhouse, and he could see Elizabeth with a smile on her face. Beside her, Peter was wiping his eyes with a rag. He thought it was about time to meet the captain and made his way up the stairs.

Elizabeth, the smile gone, opened the door after James gave it a knock. "Yes, Mr. Barlow?"

"I'm not quite sure at the protocol for this. Permission to speak to the captain?" he asked.

"Captain?"

"Yes, yes. Liz, let the man in. Stop all this foolishness," Peter said. His glistening eyes were still transfixed on the sea.

Elizabeth stepped aside and let James enter.

"Thanks, *Liz*," he said with a playful grin.

That earned him a withering look as he ducked through the door-way and glanced around the wheelhouse. It was narrow, with barely enough room for two people to pass each other without touching shoulders. An angled table with maps pinned to the surface and a couple of chairs were to his left. By the wheel was a console board lined with switches and levers.

"Port wheel felt a bit sluggish. Why don't you head down and look at it, Liz?" Peter said.

"Are you sure? I can send up one of the others to help out here."
James could hear the worry in her voice.

"Oh, I'm sure we'll be fine. Now, off with you." Without looking, Peter gave a dismissive wave.

The door slammed shut behind Elizabeth, and both men listened as her feet pounded angrily down the stairs. Peter flinched with each step. "I'll be having a lecture for that," he said.

"She's a spirited woman," James said, moving to stand with the captain. It was hard to see out the window unless he hunched over, which did.

"That she is. Takes after her father," Peter mumbled beside him.

"She knows a lot about how the ship works. Did she get that from you?"

Peter chuckled with a nod. "When she was younger, that girl was always full of questions. And what I couldn't explain, she found in her books. She's a better mechanic than anyone on this ship, and most aren't ashamed to admit it."

James remembered the book on electricity she'd been reading. It wasn't a topic he knew much about, nor had any interest in, but good for her. The two men quietly watched the ocean rise and fall as the wind carried *The Ophelia* along for a few moments. Occasionally, one of the seagulls circling the ship would land and look around curiously before taking off again.

After several minutes of silence, James asked, "So, captain, where are we headed?"

"I guess the prince's words didn't sink in. We're going to America," Peter said, giving him a sidelong look.

James closed his eyes and gently rubbed the bridge of his nose. "America is a big place. I meant where, in America, are we headed?" He turned from the window to the wrinkled and yellowed map of the eastern coast of the United States laid out on top of the table. As a boy, he'd enjoyed studying maps, and he and Ryan often had made-up stories about the places they'd never get to visit. Or thought they'd never see.

"I've only ever been there a couple of times, but I believe the best place would be Delaware Bay."

James went over and sat in one of the chairs. He looked closely at the map, tracing his finger down the coast until he found the broad bay that split the states of New Jersey and Delaware. Further inland, a river fed into the inlet from the north along the border of Pennsylvania. "Why there?"

"See that city named Philadelphia? That was a capital of industry back in the day. Also, there are many coal mines and coal fields in the surrounding states, along with farmland. Everything on the king's list is right there.

James shook his head. "You make it sound like all of it will still be sitting there, just waiting for us to turn civilization back on again with the flip of a switch."

James swiveled in the chair when Peter struck the ship's wheel with the palm of his hand.

"Look where I am, lad. After more than half my lifetime, I'm on my ship again, sailing the sea, like my father and grandfather before me. This ship had sat in the Blockade all this time, and she's still as good as the day I had to give her up. I thought I would die without ever feeling the ocean beneath me again. As far as I'm concerned, anything is possible."

Peter's optimism tried to rub off on him, but years of caution were hard to break. James said, "That's good. But try to stay alive long enough to get us back to land again. Agreed?"

Peter said, "I can't see the future, but I'll live long enough to see you there." He looked back at James and gave him a wink.

"You're a lot livelier than you were at breakfast. Salt air agrees with you, eh?" James smiled and leaned back in the chair.

Peter turned back to the ocean and grunted, "I didn't want to say anything to make them take her away again." He brushed his hand tenderly over the instruments next to him. "I said something once and lost her."

"I know it might sound odd coming from me, but you did save many lives. You couldn't know what the Queen would do."

Peter nodded, quietly staring out to sea.

"My grandfather's ship is still trapped in the Blockade," James said.

"Oh?" Peter asked, turning partway to look back at James. The wrinkles of his forehead deepened as he raised an eyebrow.

James nodded. "He'd been forced to give up his boat, like every other captain. Were you in the riots?"

Peter shook his head. "I kept away. After word came down, I couldn't look the others in the eye."

"I never met my grandfather, but my father said he was at the Lamb and Flag Riot. He'd only gone down there for a pint but got swept up in all the shouting and impassioned speeches. Someone set a wagon on fire, and it was like a signal beacon—windows were smashed, shops looted. The bobbies couldn't do a damned thing about it, so the military was called in, and they started shooting. Good old grandpa got away, and when the resistance started to organize, he was right there, ready to fight. It's been a family tradition ever since," James finished with a sad smile.

He noticed the sag in Peter's shoulders and got up to stand next to the old man. Placing a gentle hand on Peter's thin arm, James said, "People were angry. I don't think they understood what was going on. You can't blame yourself for the entire war."

Peter nodded and half-heartedly patted James's hand. "You're a good lad. The others will come about, eventually."

Filling the wheelhouse with the last light of the day, the sun had crept low on the horizon. Peter said, "Might want to get down below deck. It'll be dark soon, and I don't want you falling over the ship's side."

"Thanks, captain," James said. He was headed for the door when he turned back. "Oh, one more question."

"Eh?"

"Elizabeth said she didn't know how we were getting back through the blockade. Do you?"

Stroking the white whiskers of his chin, Peter said, "I haven't the foggiest. The men who went over the details with me said they'd been working on some contraption or something. If anyone knows, it might be that Reginald fellow."

"You're probably right," James said and headed out the door.

Elizabeth had been waiting at the bottom of the steps outside, and she squeezed by without a word on his way down. "Goodnight, Elizabeth."

A mumbled response was all he got before she disappeared into the wheelhouse.

As the days passed, a routine was established on the ship, with James helping where he could. Mostly, he mopped and scrubbed. By doing so, he learned that the crew was made up of men who had worked on the Blockade, maintaining the ships.

True to his word, Nathaniel had taken up residence in the hold. With a sleeping roll and a chamber pot, he only had to come out for meals. The others spent time playing chess or fishing. When he wasn't at the wheel, Peter enjoyed telling stories of his life and places many had only ever read about. The old man had once even visited Paris. He did his best to describe the architecture and beautiful parks of the city while James, Ryan, and more than a few of the crew sat and listened in the galley.

Okeny believed Reginald would need the most training of all the expedition members, so he spent most of his time with the engineer. James sat in on a few survival lessons, such as basic first aid and how to find clean water. Subjects James was already familiar with. Also, given how Reginald would become distracted whenever he was around, James decided it was best to stop attending. He'd have to find another way to get the engineer to open up to him.

That opportunity presented itself on their second week at sea.

One night, a slurred voice came from the galley as James passed. Curious, he stuck his head in and found Reginald was sitting at a table and a half-empty bottle of something dark in front of him. The engineer's hair stuck out at odd angles, and he gestured wildly as he said, "Got ta shee it through. You built it. You . . . you do it."

There was no one else in the galley with Reginald. He was talking to himself.

James took a step into the room, listening to the engineer. Aside from a few added swears, Reginald kept repeating himself. Not wanting to frighten the drunk man, James said, "Ho there."

Reginald jerked around to look at James and knocked the bottle over. Swearing louder, he only managed to spill more as he tried to get a hold of the rolling bottle. Then it slipped off the edge and smashed on the deck. He frowned deeply at the broken pieces of wet glass. "Paid a lot for that," Reginald sighed. His eyes swam up to meet James's. "What do you want? Come for another go at chessh?"

Having moved closer to the table, James could smell that whatever was in that bottle had been very strong.

"Sorry about that." James nodded at the glass and dark puddle that slid back and forth with the motion of the ship. "I was just passing by and heard someone talking. I didn't know anyone was still awake down here."

Reginald nodded, lips flapping as he let out a breath, and some drool dropped onto his pants. The man's glasses were at the very tip of his nose. James feared they'd soon come to the same fate as the bottle.

"Hard ta shleep without some help these days."

"I'm doing quite all right. Though this is the first bed I've had in years." James chuckled.

Reginald laughed bitterly. "That'sh cause you're a damned criminal."

"I know you've been drinking, Reginald," James said, bending down so the engineer could clearly see his face. "But you should mind your words."

"Of course, I'm drunk. How the rest of you aren't is perples... perplassen... perplexing." Reginald's eyes wandered around the room.

James found a chair a few feet away, sat, and took in the engineer. By the tremor in Reginald's hands and the nervous bouncing of his foot, it was clear why he'd be drinking. *He's scared. Of me?* "You build things, right?"

Reginald's gaze drifted back to the puddle on the floor, and he licked his lips. "I'm an engineer."

"I've been asking around, and no one knows what we're going to do after doing what the Crown has asked. But the captain had mentioned a device or something, and if I were a betting man, I'd say you know what that's about."

"Built it myself." Lifting his chin, Reginald pushed his glasses up with a shaking hand. "And this is my congratulations." The words sounded resentful.

"Built what?" James sat forward in the chair. He flashed back to the small box with wires protruding from it and how quick Reginald was in hiding it from him.

"Telegraph machine," Reginald said. His head drooped again.

That's it? Just a telegraph machine? James had been convinced of a big secret the others had been trying to keep from him. "Oh," was all he could muster.

"Isn't it exciting? I wanted to test it myshelf. So, here I am," Reginald said, his head hanging heavy. "Can't trust anyone else to do it. Built it with my own two hands. A shpecial telegraph machine…"

A snore, far louder than what his thin frame should have been able to emit, erupted from deep within the engineer.

"Special? How is it special?" James tried shaking Reginald's shoulder to wake him, but it was no use. Frustrated, he left Reginald in the galley and returned to his cabin. He thought about going to the engineer's room to look for the box but realized any trust he'd built up would be lost if he were caught.

The next day, Reginald didn't leave his cabin. James told Ryan about the previous night's conversation while they sat in the galley. A couple more crewmen were in the room, eating their midday meal at another table.

"What's so special about a telegraph?" Ryan asked, his mouth full of fish. Specks of flakey meat were stuck in the short stubble of his chin.

"Damned if I know," James said as Elizabeth walked in. He watched her prepare two plates and then leave.

The wheels began turning in his head. James knew the telegraph machine wasn't going to change the world, but it was still a mystery. And mysteries had a way of burrowing into his thoughts and become a distraction. *If Reginald is too afraid to talk to me, maybe she can get more out of him?*

Ryan said something unintelligible as he shoved half a loaf of bread in his mouth.

James cracked a smile. "Don't choke on that."

Ryan chewed loudly in response.

After he finished, James went and swabbed the deck right below the wheelhouse, waiting. By the time Elizabeth came down with the two empty plates, the wood was a different shade than the rest of the deck. She gave him a nod, inspecting his work. Casually leaning on the mop handle, James said, "I talked with Reginald last night."

She stopped on her way to the door below deck. "Oh?"

He said, "I did what you recommended and asked around. Reginald's got some kind of telegraph machine with him. He said he built it himself. I think that's how we're supposed to send word back to England."

"A telegraph machine?" she said too quickly, and her eyes widened a bit.

He knew he had her interest. "It sounded all very fascinating but a bit above my understanding," he said. Picking up the mop again, he looked back down at the deck. "Just thought I'd let you know I solved that mystery."

"So, it would appear," she said. When he looked up again, she'd already disappeared through the door.

The deck never looked cleaner by the time James made his way back to his cabin. He passed by Reginald's door and heard excited chatter coming from within. He wanted to stop and put his ear to the door, but crewmen were coming and going. Hopefully, Elizabeth will let him know what makes the engineer's device special.

Later that night, he was sitting on his bunk, preparing for bed, when there was a soft knock at his door. Upon opening, he was surprised to find Peter. "Captain?" James said.

"Fah," Peter said, waving off the title. "Peter will do."

"Something I can do for you, Peter?" James asked.

He looked tired as he peered up at James, but Peter didn't say anything.

James stepped back into his cabin, clearing room for the captain to enter. "Care to sit? You're looking a bit spent. The last thing we need is for you to fall and break something," James said with a crooked grin, unsure what Peter wanted.

The old man nodded and grumbled as he made his way over to the bunk and eased himself down with a groan. He looked around the small cabin while James pulled a chair over and sat in front of his guest.

Wistfully, Peter said, "She's still a good ship, isn't she?"

"Only as good as her captain. That's the saying, isn't it?" The chair creaked under James's weight as he shifted, trying to get comfortable.

"Aye." Peter nodded and finally turned to look at James. "I've got a lot of memories attached to her. Good and bad. You said your grandfather had a ship?"

"He was a fisherman."

Peter smiled weakly and nodded. "When I'd heard the Barlow name, I thought it was just a coincidence."

James's heart caught in his chest. "Coincidence?"

"You're Andrew Barlow's grandson, aren't you?"

James nodded, his palms sweating. He dried them against his coarse pants.

Peter nodded again, his lips moving into a smile.

James swallowed hard. Finding his voice again, he asked, "You . . . knew him?"

The old man eased himself further back on the bed until he was against the bulkhead. "We weren't friends, but, aye, I knew him. Back when I was still apprenticing with my father, we'd frequent the Lamb and Flag. Everyone knew when he'd landed with a big haul because you could hear him halfway down the block. He was a big, boisterous man. And, if I'm to be honest, a bit of a braggart. But he was also a good man. He'd buy rounds for anyone who couldn't scrape two shillings together. One time, these Frenchmen were making a fuss . . ."

They sat together the whole night as Peter told him stories about his grandfather. Here, sitting on his bed, was a connection to a stolen past. And Peter didn't ask for anything in return. He simply wanted to talk. It had been so long since anyone had treated James like anything other than a criminal. He was surprised to admit he'd missed feeling like a normal human being.

When the morning light came through the porthole, James helped Peter to his room. Thankfully, the old man didn't have to be at the wheel until that night. Tired but in good spirits, James was heading back to his cabin to get a few hours of rest when Elizabeth came up from the deck below.

She took one look at him and frowned. "You look like hell. Couldn't sleep?"

James rubbed a hand over his face. "Don't worry. It's just the years of prison showing. I've been told I used to be handsome."

He thought he caught a brief smile crack her otherwise icy expression. "Regardless, you should get some more rest."

James nodded and yawned as he reached for his door.

"Oh, I spoke with Reginald about that telegraph machine," she said, and his hand stopped turning the knob.

"And?" He looked back at her.

"You were right," she said, continuing past him.

He said, watching her go, "About what?"

"That it's how you're to make contact with England again." Looking back over her shoulder, she smirked and added, "And that it's well above your understanding."

James chuckled and went into his cabin and fell onto the bunk. Even with his feet hanging off the end, he couldn't help but feel relaxed. A great weight was off his shoulders. He'd been worried the Crown would get impatient and start executing the rebels if they took too long getting back. With the telegraph, at least they could send word once they reached land. As his eyes grew heavy, a thought crossed his mind, which blossomed into a new mystery and kept him awake for the rest of the day. Do the telegraph lines still work?

THE FLOTILLA

The next night, James was exhausted. He'd just managed to close his eyes when he was thrown from the bed. Sliding across the small room, he struck the wall hard. Dazed, it took him a few seconds to realize the ringing in his ears was the ship's warning siren. Pulling himself up by the door handle, he swung it open to men running in one direction and returning with lanterns a moment later. He grabbed an arm and realized it was Eugene from the engine room. The crewman's shirt was still streaked with coal.

"What the hell's going on?" James asked.

Breathing heavily, the far shorter man said, "Somethings in the water, and we almost crashed right into it."

James let him go. "What is it?"

Already running for the stairs, Eugene called back, "Not sure. But it's big."

Moving quickly through the ship was hard for a tall man, and James came up the stairs with a few new bruises and a curse on his tongue. It was pitch black on the deck. Clouds had rolled in during the late afternoon, leaving only a few stars above them. The only light came from where the crewmen held lanterns on the port side. The sails flapped in the wind just above them, their bottom ropes cut.

Before he could take another step, James flinched as two loud horn blasts echoed into the night. Everyone on deck stood still, but the only answer was the sound of waves brushing against the ship and loose sails. Two more blasts rang out with the same result. James hurried to the rail where the men were frantically pointing their lanterns. It was hard to make out anything in the moving pools of light, but he was sure he was looking at a wooden hull.

"Is that a boat?" he asked. It was no more than ten feet from *The Ophelia*.

"Yeah. We almost hit her square on, too. Lucky for us, Marcus was on watch. Boy's got the eyes of a cat, I tell you," Eugene said.

Nearby, a young man was getting hearty slaps on the back. Marcus looked sheepishly up at James. Just barely out of his teens, and he'll never have to buy himself a drink ever again, not with this story following him home. *Good on you,* James thought and gave him a clap on the shoulder.

Then a near-panicked voice shouted, "What in the bloody hell's going on?"

James watched Nathaniel, a fresh welt on his forehead, lead the others of the expedition out onto the deck. They all looked a little haggard and bruised.

James said, "We almost rammed into a ship. Everyone all right?"

Yawning loudly, Ryan said, "I was having a perfectly nice dream, yeah? Liz was there."

Okeny gave a scolding click of the tongue and said, "Be respectful, mate. She could have the chains back on you."

"Anyway," James sighed, "I'll go and find out more. You lot just stay here but keep your eyes open." He then went up to the wheelhouse and into a heated conversation between a captain and his first mate.

"You could have capsized us!" Elizabeth berated her grandfather.

"It was either spin her hard or crash. Which would you have preferred?" Peter said, attempting to remain calm.

"I don't mean to interrupt a private family moment, but could someone please explain what's going on?" James asked when he could get a word in.

Crossing her arms, Elizabeth nodded to Peter. "The captain was dozing at the wheel and almost rammed a ship. For our sakes, someone spotted it in time and was able to wake him before we hit it."

"I wasn't asleep. How was I supposed to see that ship? It's pitch black out there," Peter said. "And my eyesight isn't what it used to be."

Rubbing the bridge of his nose, James said, "Who was sleeping and who wasn't isn't important. I'm more concerned about the ship."

"Ships," Peter said.

"What?" James lowered his hand from his face with a confused look.

"I said ships. Look down there." Peter stuck a thumb over his shoulder to the crew spreading out along the rail.

Elizabeth pushed by James to lean out the door and shouted down to the crew, "What have you there, Benjamin?"

A skinny, tattooed man shouted back, "Looks like a fishing boat, Miss."

"Did we get turned around somehow? Are we back at the Blockade?" James asked.

"No, we're still on course." Peter rapped his knuckle on the binnacle to his right. They were still headed relatively west.

"Excuse me, Miss." Richard appeared in the doorway.

Sounding tired and irritated, Elizabeth said, "Yes, what now?"

"Some of the expeditionary group are curious about what's happening," Richard said.

"You mean Nathaniel," James said.

"You see," Richard coughed, then quietly added, "he doesn't like being kept in the dark."

"Tell him I'll be down in a few minutes, and I'll *report* to him personally." James was annoyed, and he knew he shouldn't take it out on Richard, but the brothers looked so much alike that he couldn't help himself.

Richard's back went straight. He nodded, lifting his hand, and for a moment, James thought he was going to salute, but the soldier caught himself. He turned on his heels and returned to the deck.

"At some point, you'll have to remind them you're in charge," Peter said. He was looking down and poking at some instruments.

"I know," James sighed. "But they're Crownsmen, and my blood isn't blue enough for them."

"I won't have that kind of talk while you're on this ship," Elizabeth snapped. "That last thing we need is for the old war to break out on deck."

"Noted." Surprisingly, James agreed with her. To hold up his end of the bargain, he'd have to keep the peace, and if that meant suffering Nathaniel's insults, then so be it. At least, until all of this was over, then he'd have a long conversation with Private Kitts.

"What now?" he asked Peter.

"We aren't going anywhere tonight. No way of knowing what's out there," Peter said. "We'll have to use the engine to keep us from drifting into the other ships. Come morning, we'll have a better understanding.

James nodded. "How about we double the watch? I'd feel better with more eyes out there. Just in the case."

Peter said, staring at the mysterious ships, "I don't think we've much to worry about. Those're ghost ships. But you do what you think is best."

"Aye, aye, Captain," James said. He was out the door with a purpose, leaving Peter to scold an empty doorway.

After explaining the situation, only Nathaniel and Reginald disagreed with doubling the watch. The engineer was quick to mention his poor eyesight. His finger kept missing his face when he tried to point at his glasses. It was also hard to ignore the liquor on his breath. And when James dismissed him, he was relieved to see him make it down the stairs to his cabin without falling.

On the other hand, Nathaniel merely informed James that he'd be in the hold, inspecting their equipment for any damage. Rubbing the bridge of his nose, he waved Nathaniel off and spent the remainder of the night holding his tongue each time he passed Richard, even though the other twin looked just as irritated with his brother's behavior as James was.

Several hours later, dawn came, bringing with it clearer skies. Half-asleep on his feet, James had been leaning against the foremast when a shout pulled him from a daze and saw what had spurned the cry of alarm. More ships appeared as the sun's rays skimmed over the ocean waves. Much like the bones of a beached whale, exposure had stripped the wood clean, leaving them bare and pockmarked from storms and harsh weather. More than a few ships had capsized some time ago, leaving only barnacle-encrusted hulls above the surface.

Like the Blockade, the ships were tied together by ropes and chains. With better lighting, James saw the boat they almost crashed into was a large schooner. It was a good ten feet above their deck even as it listed heavily to its side with its mainmast dipping into the water.

"It'd only take a light breeze to topple her over," Okeny said. He was already at the rail, with the others of the crew, when James came over.

"Did some of the Blockade break off?" Ryan asked from further down the rail.

Grimly, James shook his head. "These aren't English ships."

"How do you know?" Ryan asked.

"Use your eyes," Okeny said. He pointed at the boat next to their ship. It was at a precarious angle with its stern barely below the waterline while the bow stuck up in the air.

Ryan looked to where Okeny pointed, then, as if confronted by some dangerous animal, he stepped back slowly. Attached to a small mast were the tattered shreds of something he'd only seen in drawings—the American flag.

***

After the initial shock had worn off, the deck was buzzing with conversation. Most of it was trying to guess how long the ships had been out at sea. Some were in better shape than others, but none appeared even remotely seaworthy anymore.

"You ever seen this before?" James had gone back to the wheelhouse. He was hunched over, watching the derelict ships.

Peter, sitting at the chart table, had his arms crossed. "No. Can't say I have."

"What do you make of it?"

"My best guess? They were trying to escape," Peter said. "Probably thought they could stay ahead of the plague or wait it out on their ships."

Scratching at his chin in thought, James said, "It might be worth our time to search the ships. There might be something useful out there." James turned his back to the large window. Seated beside her grandfather, Elizabeth had her arms crossed just like him, and James finally saw the family resemblance.

"And what would you consider useful?" Elizabeth asked, an eyebrow arched.

"To start with, coal." Before she could even get a word out, he held a hand up to cut her off. "I know everyone thinks there'll be an abundance in America, but that's not how I see things. What if we lose the wind? I've read stories of crews stuck at sea for months because of that." *Who's the cautious one now, Tai?* James rubbed his cheeks to hide his smile.

"I agree," Peter said, noticeably not looking at Elizabeth.

James quickly continued, "And more importantly, information. Even if these ships have been out here for half a century, they might have better accounts of what was going on back home and could fill us in on what to expect. The captains had to have been keeping logs."

Before anyone could cut her off again, Elizabeth said, "I agree too."

James had been expecting to have to argue the point and was caught off guard. "Good. Well, I suppose we've some planning to do then."

Groaning as he got to his feet, Peter shuffled slowly to the wheel. "I'll edge us closer to that fishing boat. You should start there, seeing as she's the easiest to get to."

Tracing a path from the fishing boat to several coal-powered ships, James saw the captain was right. Some of the vessels were tightly packed, making it easy to jump from one to another. They'd have to climb along the heavy ropes to reach the ones further apart.

"The only thing left is to figure out how to get Nathaniel out of the hold."

Turning the ship to bring it closer, Peter said, "Good luck." And James took his leave of the wheelhouse.

He'd only taken a few steps when *The Ophelia* lurched, and he was flung against the wall beside the staircase. A cacophony of shrieking metal followed, and the ship began to list hard to port. The grinding suddenly stopped, and everything was silent; even the rumble of the engine had died. The door above James burst open, and Elizabeth scrambled through, swearing and clutching the handrail as she half-crawled by him.

"What happened?" he shouted after her as he tried to regain his footing.

She didn't answer.

When she reached the deck, she grabbed onto the wall and disappeared out of sight. James hurried after her and found the crew clinging to the portside rail. He carefully slid his way down the steeply angled deck to where Elizabeth leaned out dangerously next to the paddlewheel with her feet nearly off the deck. While she seemed focused and determined, everyone else was dazed.

Still swearing, Elizabeth pushed herself back off the rail when James got to her. He leaned over to see what had upset her and let out a trail of curses of his own. A knot of chains and ropes had wrapped around the paddlewheel. Even worse, the tangled mess had dragged up a sunken ship, the weight of which was pulling *The Ophelia* onto her side.

"We can fix this," Elizabeth said quietly, then began barking orders. "Eugene, Marcus, get the boat hooks. Benjamin—damn it, pay attention!—Get all the knives and the welding torch."

"Is there anything I can do to help?" James asked her after the crew staggered away.

"Just," she sighed, "just stay out of the way. Go and search the ships. It'll take time to cut us free." She motioned to the trapped wheel.

James knew she was right. He was far too big for this job. He made his way over to Okeny and Ryan, who looked a little green and clutched his stomach. "Everything all right?" James asked him.

Ryan burped.

"He hit the rail rather hard," Okeny said. His back to the water, he watched the crew start the preparations to free their ship.

"No breakfast then?" James asked.

Ryan burped again, then heaved the contents of his stomach into the ocean.

James afforded Okeny a slight grin when he saw the Black man giving him a sidelong look. Okeny's lips parted into a broad smile, then he laughed, slapping his thigh.

James patted Ryan on the back as he spit over the side. "Where's Richard?" he asked Okeny.

"Down below, I believe. He wanted to check in on his brother."

"I'll go find them, and Reginald too, while I'm at it. Get some gear together. I'd like to look at some of those ships before we set off again," James said.

Okeny nodded.

James gave one last pat on Ryan's back. "And make sure he drinks some water."

It was a dizzying journey below deck. Having to walk along the lower edge of the wall did strange things to his stomach, and if he wasn't careful, he'd be at the rail alongside Ryan. In the hold, James found Nathaniel alone, rubbing his lower back. The welt on his forehead had changed into a deep yellow and brown bruise.

"Where's Richard?" James asked, getting the soldier's attention.

Nathaniel jerked, and there was a flash of fear on his face for a moment. But the soldier was quick to put up his mask again. Eyes narrowing, Nathaniel's jaw tightened, and he said, "I sent him to look in on Reginald."

"Good. I'll go and tell them to get ready. We're taking a walk," James said.

"A walk?" The mask faltered, and Nate swallowed hard. "On those ships?"

"I'd like to do some information gathering. Reconnaissance, if you'd prefer. We should learn about what we're getting ourselves into."

Nathaniel nodded. "Brilliant," he said, "Be sure to tell me how it goes."

James wanted to laugh but held it in. "Oh, you're coming along too."

Nathaniel shook his head, and the mask fell entirely. "No. I-I'm needed here."

James took a couple of steps toward him. "And what, exactly, are you doing here?"

Nathaniel gripped the rifle to his chest, and James spread his arms to show he meant no harm. Regaining some of his bravado, Nathaniel said, "Protecting our supplies and equipment."

"Nathaniel, look, I know what you're doing. We all do. You don't trust me. But where am I going to go? How would Ryan and I even get back to England at this point? We've agreed to this. All of this is for my brother. I'm sure you understand what that means. Also, I don't want to die out here any more than you do. So, at some point, we'll have to work together."

Footsteps in the hallway approached, and James looked over his shoulder as Richard entered the hold. Reginald, a bit shaky in his boots, kept to the doorway.

With a nod of greeting, Richard said, "Everyone appears to be in good shape down here."

"Great. You two head up. I'm just trying to convince your brother to lend a hand," James said, thumbing back at Nathaniel.

With a sharp edge, Richard said, "Come off it, Nate, stop pretending and get on with it." Then he spun briskly on his heels and left the hold with Reginald keeping close behind him.

"Pretending?" James turned back to Nathaniel.

"I don't know what he's getting on about." Nathaniel glowered at the empty doorway. He closed his eyes and sighed.

"Look," he said, opening them again. "I think someone should stay here to guard the ship." The soldier held up a hand before James could say anything. "What if there *are* people on the ships out there? Just lying in wait for anyone foolish enough to come aboard. Someone should be here to protect the crew. This is, after all, our only means of transportation."

James rubbed the bridge of his nose. The argument was sound, though he hated to agree with Nathaniel. "All right. But," he stuck a finger in the air, "this is the *last* time. No more excuses going forward. And remember, you signed up for this."

Relief showed on his face, and Nathaniel nodded. "Yes. Yes, I did." Tightening his jaw again, he stood straighter.

James left the soldier behind and returned to see how the preparations were going. Okeny was just tying off a rope to the rail. Beside him, Richard was tying a backpack closed and fixing a lantern on another at his feet. His rifle was gone, but he still had a pistol holstered at his belt. Looking a little less green around the gills, Ryan took small sips from a canteen.

Reginald was conversing with Elizabeth a few feet away by the trapped paddlewheel. A cutting torch, burning brighter than the sun, left white spots in James's eyes. He approached the rail and peered down to the fishing boat below. The deck's wood was in rough shape, like the other ships around them, with rust covering anything made of iron.

"Will it hold us?" James asked Okeny.

"It looks solid."

"I'm not going down first," Ryan muttered.

Having excused herself from Reginald, Elizabeth said, "If the weight of the water trapped inside her hasn't cracked the hull in half, then it should be fairly safe to walk on."

"Good to know," James said, looking back down again. A thick rope led from the bow of the fishing boat to a multi-deck ship. The ship's mast, tangled in its rigging, had snapped in half and hung over the side. "I've never seen a ship like that before. What is it?"

"That's a luxury yacht," Elizabeth said. "People used to sail for fun. It used to be quite fashionable."

The yacht didn't have an engine, but several beyond it did. They'd have to cross over from the fishing boat to the yacht and then jump to one of the stout ships with a smokestack from there. He looked to Elizabeth tapping her chin as she studied the myriad of ships. "You wouldn't want to come with us, would you?"

The look she gave him was as if she had just eaten something bitter. "What? Why would I want to do that?"

"You clearly know more about these ships than any of us." *And I can tell you want to.*

She shook her head. "I can't. I need to oversee the repairs."

"Oh, I think I can handle that," Reginald said, having made his way over. His eyes were watery, and by the way he shuffled from one foot to the other, he was obviously still feeling the effects of his late-night drinking habit.

"No, I can't ask you to," Elizabeth said, patting the engineer on the arm. James wasn't sure if she noticed Reginald's condition or if she was just being polite.

"No, no," Reginald said, gently pushing her hand away. "You go on. I know how to cut some rope. Besides, your boys are doing most of the work." He pulled on the straps of his backpack and smiled. "And I've already got all my tools with me."

"But I . . ." she tried to argue.

James leaned in close, speaking softly so the engineer wouldn't hear him over the sounds of the crew. "Let him stay. He won't be much use to us out there, and we truly need your help."

She frowned, looking from the repairs to the flotilla of ships, and rubbed her neck. Finally, she sighed and said, "All right. I'll let the captain know."

"Of course," James said. She left for the wheelhouse, and Reginald gave James an appreciative nod. *Hopefully, now he'll realize I'm not a monster.*

"Are you sure this is wise?" Richard said.

"What?" James asked, turning to the soldier.

Looking over at the crew, Richard said in a hushed whisper, "She's a woman."

For the first time since his arrest, James laughed himself to tears.

With bright red cheeks, Richard looked away. The Crown still had the archaic belief that women were somehow inferior to men. The women of the resistance would beg to differ. *Like Tai...*

When Elizabeth returned a few minutes later, she handed James a sheathed six-inch-long knife with a wooden handle. He raised an eyebrow at her, and she said, "It's a knife."

"Clearly. But why are you giving it to me?" James asked.

As if speaking to a small child, she said, "In case you have to cut something."

Ryan held his hand out expectingly. But when he got only a stare in return, he said, "I don't get one?"

Ignoring the question, she asked, "Are we ready?"

"I believe so," James said. He made a show of slipping the knife into the waist of his pants, grinning at Ryan, who looked dejected.

Reginald was already ordering the crew to tie support ropes to the masts, afraid the weight would bend the paddlewheel spoke. As far as James could tell, the engineer did seem very capable.

Richard was the first one down the rope, with James going last. The wood beneath his feet groaned as he let go and put his weight on it, and for a moment, he began to second guess Elizabeth. But he didn't fall through the deck, even after a few steps, so he mentally apologized to her.

Aside from some bird droppings, the deck was bare. A wheel was at one end, and a sail-less mast sat in the middle of the boat. As James made his way to the others, the deck rocked beneath him. They'd agreed to stand clear of the boat's stern, which barely broke the water's surface.

"It's strange there isn't anything to, you know, actually *fish* with here, yeah?" Ryan said.

Elizabeth looked at the empty deck and shrugged. "Maybe it was swept away in a storm?"

James eyed the next ship, the yacht with the dangling mast. The sails, of which, had long since been taken by the currents. The bow of the fishing boat dipped beneath James's feet as he crossed over to get a better look. He stood still for a moment, waiting, and when the ship didn't drop any further, he continued.

At the tip of the bow, he found he could easily hoist himself up onto the next ship. He climbed up onto the rust-lined railing only to have it fall apart beneath his feet. He'd have fallen into the water if Okeny and Ryan hadn't grabbed onto him. Steadying his breathing and fighting to keep his heart in his chest, James gave them a nod of appreciation and raised himself over the yacht's rail.

Jagged wood and metal were strewn all over the deck. He turned and reached down to help the others up. Elizabeth ignored his hand. Instead, she used the rope that tied the two vessels together. With determination on his face, Richard came up the same way, and James had to fight back another giggle fit.

Once they were all together again, James said, "Let's see if there's anything inside." And pointed across the deck. Two sets of stairs went up to a smaller deck above them with the ship's wheel. Between those stairs was a wooden door.

Ryan asked just as he reached the door. "We're positive no one's here, yeah?"

Elizabeth was the one who answered, however. "I doubt it. These ships have been out here too long."

Even with that assurance, James watched Richard's hand drift toward his pistol.

"We'll take it slow. I don't want to miss anything important," James nodded to Richard, "And let's not go shooting at any shadows while we're down there."

Richard, looking a bit embarrassed, dropped his hand.

"Keep an eye out for anything useful. Like logbooks." James then opened the door.

Dusty stairs led down into the dark interior. James had to duck to climb down them. Guided by the light from the open door, he came to a hallway at the bottom of the steps. He estimated the ship was about the same size as *The Ophelia* with another deck below this one.

Before he even turned to ask for one, Okeny had lit a lantern and held it out for him to take. Thanking him as he took it, James moved further inside. Cabins lined either side of the narrow hallway. A threadbare red and green runner stretched the length of the floor, and smashed crockery crunched beneath his feet as he went. Curiously, heaps of clothing were piled up outside one of the rooms further on.

A faint, strangely familiar smell wafted toward him from the first door on his left. It was acrid yet sweet at the same time. He tried to knob and found it was locked tight, and he felt foolish after catching himself about to knock. Leaning his shoulder against the door, James thrust hard and heard a crack.

"You sure that's wise?" Ryan asked. He'd followed Okeny down as the others followed behind him.

"Like I said, I don't want to miss anything," James grunted as he slammed into the door again. This time it gave way, splitting down the middle, and he stumbled into the cabin.

Inside was a small bedroom, complete with a dresser, closet, and storage chest. Paintings laid in various states of ruin on the floor, mixed with the remnants of a shattered washbasin. The only thing left undamaged was a wall-length mirror bolted in place.

Wiping the thick layer of dust from its surface, James was surprised to see his father's face looking back at him. Ten years had passed since he'd seen his reflection. The prisoners didn't need mirrors in Newgate, and it never once occurred to him to find one on *The Ophelia.* And now, he saw his father's pale blue eyes studying his face. James was only six years younger than his father had been when he'd died. Even if it was just a ghost of his father, it was too much for him, and he watched those eyes swell with tears.

George Barlow had been a natural leader, a man with vision and pride. When James took over the squad, he'd felt like a pale imitation. *I miss you. But even more, you'd have told me if I made the right choice by going through with this.* He rubbed at his eyes until they cleared.

With a sigh, he decided to see past his father and look at what the years had done. They'd kept their heads shaved at the prison to keep disease from spreading, but his mother's dark brown hair was coming through on his scarred scalp. The prison barber didn't have the softest touch and was usually four deep in the barrel before he started shaving the prisoners.

After years of darkness, James had spent too much time in the sun, and his skin was now red, his forehead peeling and tender to the touch. He looked down at the clothes he still wore from prison. A dirty shirt that used to be white and torn gray trousers. The Crown had supplied clothes for Ryan and himself, but someone must have underestimated his size, and none of it fit him. Luckily, a crewman with the same size feet had lent him a pair of boots.

Ryan gave off a whistle as he appeared in the mirror beside him. "Don't we look ready to hit the town?" Playfully, he elbowed James and grinned.

James pulled at the skin around the eyes and then rubbed his face. "How did we get so old?"

"Who're you calling old, mate? I'm just hitting my prime, yeah?" Ryan pampered his short red hair in the mirror.

A crash followed by a gasp had both men turn from their reflections. Richard stood by the open closet with a pile of sticks bound in the scraps of a stained floral dress having tumbled out.

Not sticks. Bones, James realized.

Elizabeth, a hand covering her mouth, quickly left the room.

James knelt as he examined the remains. A cloud of dust, made from the papery skin that had flaked off after it fell, wafted around the room. The acrid smell was more pungent now. *The smell of death.* He was all too familiar with it and had hoped to have gone a little longer before coming across it again.

Okeny squatted across from him. "It was a peaceful death. Skull's intact, no broken bones." Okeny looked from the pile back to the small compartment it had been hiding in.

The awfulness that comes with a decaying body coated the inside of the closet. Shining his lantern around inside, something glinted on the floor, drawing James's attention. He picked it up and rubbed away the decades of putrescence. Then he showed everyone a grimy key.

"I think she locked herself in here," James said.

With a hand still on the closet door's handle, Richard asked, "Was she hiding?"

Still out in the hallway, Elizabeth said, "Come have a look."

James put the key back where he'd found it and went out to join her.

Elizabeth appeared pale in his lantern's light while she pointed her own up at a small, elongated hole in the ceiling. "Wouldn't a bullet do that?" she asked.

He nodded and said, "It had to have been shot from down the hall." And he pointed his lantern in that direction, half expecting the gunman to still be standing there. It was empty, of course, so they moved on.

James opened doors into more scenes of a broken past. Some rooms were filled with fallen statues, torn paintings, and even bundles of banknotes. When he discovered a nursery with children's toys spilled all over the floor, a crib in one corner and a small bed in another, the hair stood up on the back of his neck, and he had a sinking feeling in his stomach. He kept his thoughts to himself and closed the door again.

The last cabin in the hallway was a study. A great oak desk with a leather-backed chair was fastened to the floor. There was a bookcase along one wall, the contents of which were secured by a rope running across each shelf.

"This is more like it," James said and made his way to the desk.

The top of the desk was bare, so he sat and began rifling through the drawers. Almost immediately, Liz made her way to the bookshelves. She ran a finger along each spine as she examined them. Across the room, Ryan flopped down on a leather couch. Richard peaked in occasionally from the hallway. If James had known him better, he'd say the soldier looked unnerved after finding the body. Okeny made his way over and sat beside Ryan with a groan and rubbed at one of his knees.

As he searched the drawers, James found some papers signed *'Charles Vaulkner.'* Looking them over, it seemed the documents had something to do with money.

"Liz, can you make anything of these?"

Holding a small stack of books, she turned and placed them on the desk. Seeing James's bemused expression, she said, "I doubt anyone will miss them."

Then, looking at the papers, she said, "These are standard bank forms. See here?" She pointed at a line. "This indicates an account was closed in June of 1862."

He gave her a playful grin and said, "And here I thought you only knew about fixing boats."

Liz lifted her chin and raised an eyebrow. "My father always said it is best to know a little about a lot than a lot about a little."

"Wise man," James said.

Then a snore rattled the room.

Across the cabin, Ryan, his head resting on Okeny's shoulder and with one eye open, snored again. Okeny shrugged him off, and Ryan let out a forced yawn. "Oh, pardon me. Did I miss anything exciting?"

"Don't worry, mate. You'll be the first to know when the shooting starts," James said. He rapped his knuckles against the desk and then fired a finger gun at his friend.

He opened another drawer with a smile and looked down at a small girl's doll in a blue dress. Moving it aside, he found several drawings made by children. They were mostly depictions of life at sea and ships. One stood out to him, however. It was of two figures holding hands. Below their feet was written in carefully drawn lines, 'Father' and 'Mother.' Next to them was the petite figure of a girl and an even tinier one beside her. The girl was 'me,' and the other was 'baby Gavin.' The uneasy feeling from before grew stronger.

James shut the drawer. "We should check the crew quarters and then move on." He made for the door, and Richard fell in step behind him.

The stairs led down to a sparsely furnished deck of the ship that lacked the same finery as the one above them. One room at the end was marked *galley*. The doors leading off into the crew's cabins were unlocked. Inside, they were bare, with no sign of use, including the room that should have been the captain's quarters. James opened all the cabinets and the closet, finding nothing.

"Not even a scrap of paper," James growled, slamming the closet door.

Richard called out from where he stood at the door to the galley, a grim expression on his face. "What is it?" James asked.

"Best you see it for yourself," he answered. When Elizabeth went over, he moved to keep her out, shaking his head at her.

In the galley, James discovered a dreadful scene. Slumped at the end of a wide counter were the remains of a body dressed in a stained white shirt. A revolver, still gripped in a skeletal hand, lay beside him. Okeny and Ryan joined him as he circled the counter.

"Shot himself," Okeny said, pointing at the hole in the side of the skull. Dark stains had soaked into the wood, radiating outward from the dead man. A large cleaver was embedded in the counter not too far from where he'd ended his life.

James rubbed at his face. A cold sweat trickled down his back. "This must be Charles. I'm guessing the woman upstairs was his wife."

"Think she was hiding from him?" Ryan asked, scratching the back of his head.

"Have you seen any other guns on board?" James said as he eyed a large pot latched to the stove.

"Maybe someone on one of the other ships attacked them?" Ryan suggested.

Steeling himself, James went to the stove and lifted the lid. He took a deep breath before looking inside. Gagging, he quickly turned away and threw up.

Okeny rushed to his side. "What is it, man?"

James could only gesture at the stove as he spit bile on the floor. The dark-skinned man peered into the pot and nearly fell over the body at the counter as he reeled back from what he saw.

"What is it?" Elizabeth asked from the doorway. She'd managed to worm her way past Richard, but she couldn't pry her eyes from the corpse to look over at James.

Acid still burning his throat, James wiped his lower lip and hoarsely said, "Stay out there."

Ryan appeared dumbfounded, looking from James to Okeny and then to the pot. He started to walk over, but Okeny placed a hand on his chest. "What's gotten into you two?" Ryan asked.

James reached over and slowly placed the lid back on the pot. His hand lingered there for a moment, and then he turned for the door. "We're leaving. Everyone back to *The Ophelia*. There's nothing here for us."

Liz sounded both confused and frustrated. "But we've only searched this one ship."

"I said there's nothing here," James barked.

He sighed and closed his eyes. Rubbing the bridge of his nose, he calmly said, "These people hadn't been prepared to live out here. They had no crew with them. Hell, think about the fishing boat. Without the gear, what food were they going to haul up?"

Liz shook her head. "No, but...maybe..."

"Elizabeth, these people left with what they thought was important. Charles left with his money and his…family." James's voice broke on the last word. "They didn't wait for their crew. And I can guarantee it's the same story on the other ships, or what happened here…" James trailed off.

"What are you going on about?" Liz asked. Her eyes kept drifting back to the stove. When he didn't answer right away, she gripped his arm and quietly whispered, "Tell me."

Swallowing down the rising bile, James asked her, "How many people were in that drawing, Liz?"

Elizabeth gasped and covered her mouth. Stumbling out of the galley, she'd have collapsed if Richard hadn't been there to catch her. "That…that's inhuman."

"Too many ghosts on this ship," Okeny said.

James nodded. He said, "Let's go."

No one looked back until they were out in the sun again.

On *The Ophelia*, the crew had worked diligently to free the ship. A cutting torch burned bright on the paddlewheel, and several men watched from the deck. They waved to James and the others.

James said, "Keep what happened here between us." Then added, "At least we learned something from all this."

"What's that?" Ryan asked.

James faked a smile and waved back to the crew. "This nightmare was preferable to what they'd left behind."

After climbing down from the yacht to the fishing boat, James got a better look at what the crew had accomplished. A single chain remained, and young Marcus was crouched over it with the cutting torch. Reginald was behind him, putting some tools back into his pack. James was unsure how the engineer was able to keep his footing in the condition he'd been in.

Maybe I was too quick to dismiss him.

As the others climbed down behind him, James said, "We should be off soon."

Elizabeth dropped onto the deck and looked over at *The Ophelia*. Eyes wide, she pushed past James to the stern of the half-sunk fishing boat. Instantly, ocean water poured around her feet. Waving her arms, she frantically screamed, "Stop!"

James could feel the ship sinking faster beneath his feet. "Get out of here," he commanded the others and pointed to the rope hanging from *The Ophelia*. Then he rushed over and pulled Liz from the rising water. Still screaming for them to stop, she struggled in his arms as he trudged back through the cold, knee-deep saltwater.

Above them, one of the crew had heard Liz and was waving down at Reginald. When the engineer looked up, the crewman pointed at Liz. Somehow, the engineer was oblivious to Liz's cries. He waved to her just as the last chain snapped and whipped around Reginald's ankle, dragging him off the paddlewheel.

Liz shrieked.

Lifting the welder's mask off his head, Marcus looked stunned at the churning water.

Without thinking, James dropped Elizabeth and dove headfirst off the side of the boat.

It was cold. Too cold. As he swam further from the surface, the icy shock forced the air from his lungs. His eyes stung as he searched, but he ignored the pain. A blurry shape was below him, flailing at the chain, still attached to a sunken ship that pulled the engineer further down into the depths.

You can't let him die here! Swim, goddamn you. But even as James tried to reach him, Reginald's movements became weaker. Then, with a body-wracking spasm, he stopped moving altogether. The engineer slid quietly into the inky, cold blackness.

James's chest was on fire as he struggled with what to do next. He had to keep going. There was still a chance he could save Reginald. But could they both reach the surface in time?

In the end, he had to turn back.

Darkness crept into his vision as he fought the instinct to take a breath. He could see sunlight just above him. He screamed as he breached the surface. He ached to the very bone. The frigid water cut through all of his extremities. James coughed as he took a breath and floated on his back, exhausted.

He wasn't quite sure how he got aboard *The Ophelia*, only that the next thing he remembered was a blanket being wrapped around his shivering body. Eventually, his mind cleared, and he became aware of Ryan, soaked and dripping on the deck, with others gathered around him. James was confused by the concern on their faces.

I'm not the one who just died.

Shakily, and with Ryan's help, he got to his feet. With tears on her cheeks, Elizabeth stood beside Okeny and Richard. The two men looked grim.

Through numb lips, James said to Elizabeth, "I... I tried to save him."

Wiping her tears away, she blinked and nodded. "So did I," she said.

Ryan helped him below deck, where it was warmer, and put him in bed. Wrapped in more blankets, James closed his eyes. Images of Reginald, struggling and helpless, ran through his head.

To die so far away from home in a fluke accident.

It's the Crown's fault he was even here.

They're to blame for this.

I couldn't save him.

James barely registered as the engine thrummed around him, and *The Ophelia* set off again.

A NEW WORLD

The crew began looking at James differently the next day. He'd expected disappointment or even hatred for letting Reginald die. What he hadn't been prepared for was admiration.

"I don't understand," James said to Peter. The two men stood at the rear of the ship, watching the waves break in their wake. Thankfully, the midday sun had gone behind the clouds, giving them some respite from the growing heat.

"I think you do," Peter said. The old man rested his arms against the rail with his hands clasped together.

James shook his head, his back aching and stiff. The numbness in his arms and legs had faded while he slept.

The dreams, however, remained.

He saw his brother drifting away, just barely out of reach. And no matter how hard James swam, he couldn't get to him in time.

"Think back to the war. I'm sure you've seen it before," Peter said.

"The war?" James asked, turning to look at the old man.

Still watching the waves, Peter said, "It should make sense. You put your life on the line to save someone. If that doesn't garner you some respect, I don't know what will."

James knew the captain was right. He'd seen it plenty of times. And even felt it a few times after being pulled out of danger himself. "But I didn't save him," James said.

"You can't save everyone. All you can do is try," Peter said.

James nodded.

"Liz told me there wasn't anything on those ships," Peter said, pushing himself away from the rail.

"No," James said. "Nothing of use, anyway."

"That's a shame."

The guilt swelled again. "Reginald died for nothing."

"Perhaps he did. But I never thought he was right for this expedition, anyways."

"That's a bit cold, isn't it?"

Peter's old brown eyes peered up at him. "It is. That bastard wasn't here to help. He was here to serve his own hubris." Peter crossed his arms. "The only reason he was on that paddlewheel was because he wanted to be the one to free the ship, and he almost took young Marcus down with him. From my experience, you can't have someone on your crew like that."

"Selfish reasons?" James raised an eyebrow. Then, he realized the meaning of his dream—Reginald had taken his pack to his watery grave. The pack that had the telegraph machine in it. "God damn it," James groaned.

"What?"

James closed his eyes and gripped the rail. "The telegraph. He kept it in the pack with his tools. I saw him put it in there when we first came aboard."

Peter chuckled and lightly swatted at James's arm with the back of his hand. "That thing? Elizabeth has it."

James quickly opened his eyes. And it was his turn to ask, "What?"

Peter nodded up at the wheelhouse where Elizabeth stood. "The thing about pride is, it needs an audience. Reginald knew Elizabeth would appreciate his work, so he let her study it. It's still in her cabin."

Relieved, James rubbed at his face and smiled. "That's good. That's good."

Before heading back up to the wheel, Peter stopped and said, "Oh, do us a favor and promise me you won't tell Liz I called Reginald a bastard, will you?"

***

Weeks later, a crewman shouted, "Land ho!"

The call went throughout the ship, and soon everyone was on deck to see a rather unimpressive speck just on the horizon. James felt uneasy as he stood at the bow with Ryan and watched it grow into a coastline.

Ryan looked up at him and sighed. "What now?" he asked.

James licked his dry lips and said, "It's that feeling again. I don't like this." The feeling was a tenseness under his skin and a scratching at the back of his skull. It had saved them from several ambushes and traps in the past.

"We don't have much of a choice now, do we? Not like we can just turn around, yeah?" Ryan said, pointing in the general direction he thought England to be.

"Keep your eyes and ears open. We've got to be smart about this. We can't afford any mistakes. And that goes for all of you."

James turned to the three men gathered behind him. Okeny and Richard appeared calm, but Nathaniel's eyes shifted back and forth as if looking for a place to hide.

"Any issues you have with my past have to be left back in England. I won't lie and say it will be easy for me either. Those uniforms don't mean the same thing to me as they do to you." He eyed the brothers. "But for this to work, we have to put that war to rest. I don't plan on dying here, and I don't plan on letting any more of you die either. Can we agree on that?"

"Sir," Richard said.

"I... agree that I don't want to die here." Nathaniel nodded.

"Absolutely," Okeny said, looking past James to the dark continent.

While James had been giving his speech, Elizabeth had crossed the deck to join them. "As long as you keep *The Ophelia* safe, she'll keep you safe."

James nodded. "That's the plan. How long until we arrive?"

"We have to sail along the coast before reaching the bay." Elizabeth took a piece of paper from her pocket, unfolded it, and showed them a map. "I believe we're about here." She pointed off the coast of New Jersey. "And the Bay of Delaware is here."

James grunted his approval. "And, once we've found a cozy little spot for the king to plant his flag, we'll need to find an intact telegraph line to send the message back to England."

"Reginald's notes were pretty specific that he had to send the message from at least as far south as the country's old capital, Washington," Elizabeth said.

James had asked Elizabeth to teach him how to use the telegraph device. He understood the basic premise of how a telegraph worked, and he knew Morse code, but he had a hard time putting it all together. It also didn't help that Reginald's notes were utterly indecipherable to him. He hoped one of the others had a better head for these things.

"And he expected the lines to still work? After all these years?" James asked doubtfully.

"We could spend the rest of our lives trying to find a broken cable," Nathaniel said.

Elizabeth sighed. "The notes said the Crown had communication experts look into it and their readings show that the failure was close to Washington. I think that's why they specifically chose that location."

James crossed his arms and said, "Anything else I should know about?"

Elizabeth shrugged. "I don't know why you think I have all the answers. Our contract stated only that we were to bring you here and wait. I don't know the first thing about what to expect out there."

America loomed ahead of them, mysterious and quiet. A dead continent, or so the Crown believed. James breathed in the rich salt air, trying to relax, but the feeling persisted under his skin.

As they were sailing south along the shore, Nathaniel had spotted numerous chunks of driftwood in the water. Okeny told him to look closer, and it became apparent they were looking at the wreckage of wooden ships. It was then that Liz decided to return to the wheelhouse to help her grandfather navigate around the debris while James and Ryan scanned the coastline with binoculars. If whatever had destroyed those ships was still out there, they'd have to be ready.

"You see those black stumps there? There was a big fire, yeah?" Ryan said.

"It burned through the buildings too," James said. He could make out charred foundations and cracked bricks, left where they'd fallen. It reminded him of the many shelled-out villages from back home. It didn't give him much hope, but at least bits of green had started to grow among the ruins.

"Kind of reminds me of that village we saw across the Channel," Ryan said.

"Yes, but I don't see hanging bodies, do you?"

"Maybe it's not so bad here after all, yeah?" Ryan asked.

Dryly, James said, "We've only just arrived. Give it time."

The nervousness of the crew was palpable. Most tried to hide it by keeping busy, but it was evident in the way they kept conversations short or found excuses to return below deck. James couldn't blame them for being scared. Wild stories had spread in the early days of the plague, with some of the religious types claiming it was a punishment by God. And many feared the disease was still out there, waiting for them like some monstrous creature stalking its prey in the night. James had to admit he felt the same as the crew. Even in the resistance, they'd feared the plague and the idea of stepping foot on the land where it had all started made him rethink his decisions.

Later that day, James found himself up in the wheelhouse with Peter. "Is it like you remember?" James asked as they watched the land go by out the windows.

Peter shook his head. "No. It's nothing like the last time I saw it."

"How was it back then?"

Peter coughed, clearing his throat, and said, "There'd been a war going on."

"My father told me about that. Something about slavery, right?"

The old man nodded. "The northern states against the southern states. It'd only been going on for a year when newspapers started reporting about a sickness some of the injured soldiers had.

"My father had just given me *The Ophelia*. He bought her after my apprenticeship was over. And back then, ships used to go back and forth across the Atlantic. So much so, we often had to wait several days before we could unload."

James looked back at the map spread out on the table behind him, imagining tiny ships sailing across the faded paper as Peter continued.

"So, there I was, a young man, captain of my own ship, a crew of seventy men under me." Peter sounded happy and looked lost in the memory. "We made a few voyages to Europe. Then I got contracted to haul cargo to America. It was dangerous. They'd been fighting on the sea, but the money was too good to pass up.

"Stories about the disease started coming over right before I left, but I had a contract and a cargo hold full of furniture, so off we went. Six weeks. That's all it took to change everything. When we'd almost reached New York City—you can see it there on the map—a ship steered in front of *The Ophelia*, about a hundred yards off our bow and waving British colors. I blared my horn, but she refused to move. I tried going around, but she was smaller and faster and kept getting in our way.

"I was angry, let me tell you, and I thought about ramming that ship, but a man had come out on their deck, waving his flags at me. There'd been something off about him. He looked weak, pale, and could barely stand, but that bastard held those flags high."

Peter was silent for a moment, and his shoulders slumped. But when he spoke next, the old man stood straight.

"That captain told me the disease was widespread and not to land. I had my first mate signal over if they needed help, but he signaled back it was too late for them. He said to turn around and run. After that, he collapsed, and we did just what he said to do.

"Most people said I was a hero when I got home, but I wasn't. It'd been him, that captain, and his warning. If he hadn't taken what time he had left to stop me from landing, England would have fallen too..."

Peter trailed off, again lost in thought.

James knew what toll bad memories could have on a man.

The gentle rocking of *The Ophelia* brought the old man back, and he continued. "By the time I'd reached home, nothing was coming out of America over the telegraph. I thought it was my duty to tell the harbor master what I'd seen. Next thing I knew, I was standing before Her Majesty, telling her the same story.

"It's funny," Peter mused. "Almost like it'd been planned, a messenger had come into the meeting room with a communique from Europe. She'd asked him to read it aloud, and he said the disease had reached continental Europe. I was there the moment she declared martial law. It happened so fast. She abolished the parliament and closed the harbors. I don't blame her, though. We were scared. And, even after all these years, I don't think we've stopped being scared."

James couldn't disagree. From that night in the galley, Reginald's words came back to him—the engineer couldn't understand how anyone could sleep without a bit of aid. But *sleep isn't always a respite from our fears.*

As Elizabeth had said, they'd reached the Bay of Delaware by late afternoon. According to the map, to their south was the state the bay was named after. Peter kept the ship close to the New Jersey side as they rounded the shoreline.

James scanned the shore ahead of them from the deck. A small, rocky outcropping jutted out into the bay, with the remains of a stone building on it. Its foundation was still intact, and the walls lay scattered around it in a rough circle. Most likely a lighthouse, it had been caught up in the fire from up north. And much like what they've seen so far, fresh grass grew between the large, blackened rocks around the foundation.

"Smell that?" Okeny said, coming up behind him.

James sniffed. "Smells like something's burning. Maybe this fire is still going?"

"This fire? No. This one has long since passed. See those trees growing over there? They grew after it stopped burning."

"What then?" James looked back at him.

Okeny breathed deeply and nodded in the direction they were headed. "We'll find out when we get there."

"More mysteries," James sighed.

"Life is full of mysteries. Isn't that why we started exploring in the first place?" Okeny said as he walked away.

A herd of deer was the first sign of life they saw. Ryan excitedly pointed them out, and the animals drew others on deck. Like Marcus, many of the younger crew had never seen a living one before. Strange birds also flitted about in the trees and overhead—a welcome sight from the ever-present seagulls that had harassed them each day since they'd left England. Okeny had caught one on the third week at sea and tried to serve it to the crew. It did not go over well. Most believed it was bad luck. With the appearance of the deer, the bleak remnants of the fire ebbed away, and larger trees grew along the shore. There were also buildings among the trees, ruined by time and neglect rather than flames.

That evening, as darkness began to settle, James went back up to the wheelhouse. "I think we should drop anchor for the night."

Peter grunted, "Makes sense." He called through the speaking tube to lower the sails and drop anchor.

"We shouldn't light the lanterns tonight. It might draw unwanted attention," James said on his way back out of the wheelhouse.

James eyed the shore as the crew prepared the ship for the night. They'd weighed anchor some two hundred yards from the rocky coastline. It was surreal. Like he was looking at a painting.

All those trees.

During the war, England's woods had been stripped of fuel. So, aside from a few sickly trees, he'd never seen real forest. *Too many places for someone to hide,* he thought. The bad feeling only grew as he stared at the silent trees. And when they were swallowed by darkness, James went below deck.

In the galley, James laid out a map of the region—that he'd acquired from Peter's collection—as the others looked on. Elizabeth pointed out where they were most likely spending the night. A place called False Egg Island Point.

The next order of business was to set a watch rotation for the night. James would take the first shift and the last while the others filled in the rest.

"And tomorrow? What should we expect then?" Nathaniel asked.

Sliding her finger across the bay, Elizabeth said, "We should be able to reach Wilmington or maybe even one of the major cities if the wind stays in our favor."

Nathaniel studied the map and then asked, "What makes them so special?"

That was a mistake, and James knew to get out of there as soon as Elizabeth began her lecture on American industry. He excused himself to no one in particular and left for his first shift.

Water lapped against *The Ophelia* in the eerie quiet of the night. Occasionally, something fluttered overhead to break up the monotony. It wasn't a full moon, but it was bright enough to make his way across the deck without a lantern. James had been staring off in the direction of the shore when he heard tapping from up at the wheelhouse. In the dim, silvery light, someone waved to get his attention. After entering the small room, he found Eugene standing at the wheel.

"Got stuck with the night watch?" James asked.

The stocky man muttered, "Drew the short straw." He rapped a knuckle on the glass in the direction of the opposite shore. "What do you make of that?"

James bent down to look through the gloom toward the Delaware side of the bay, and his eyes settled on a single pinpoint of light.

"Not sure. A campfire?" James scratched his chin. "How long's it been there?"

"Showed up at nightfall. But that's not what worries me. You see, it was further up shore. Now it's a lot closer."

James grabbed the binoculars from the pouch at his waist and focused them on the light. It flickered like fire, but it was too small to be a campfire. Maybe a torch?

"Keep an eye on that. I'll watch the other shore. Let me know if anything changes." Eugene nodded, and James returned to the deck.

Inky blackness, that's all there was. But as the next hour went by, he couldn't shake the feeling he was being watched. Out on the open water, their ship was easy to spot. He looked up at the moon, wishing it'd been an overcast night.

Richard soon relieved him, and James let him know what Eugene had spotted. He instructed the soldier to report to him if it moved again. Returning to his cabin, he tried to get some sleep but only managed to spend the hours wide awake.

In the middle of the night, a knock came at the door.

"Come in," James said. Both exhausted and on edge, he sat up.

Okeny stuck his head in and said, "Might want to come up on deck."

Bolting to his feet, James caught himself at the last second and managed not to bash his head against the ceiling. "What is it?".

"Just come up." Okeny left James to struggle into his boots.

The moon was low in the sky, making it darker on the deck. James followed an Okeny-shaped figure and stood with him at the rail. He asked, "Is Eugene still up at the wheelhouse?"

"No, Benjamin took over. That light he'd noticed went away about three hours ago," Okeny said. "But that's not important right now. Listen." He pointed a finger at his scarred ear before nodding at the shore.

At first, James only heard the water and the pounding of his own heart, but then a far-off screech penetrated the silence. "A bird?" James asked.

"Shh," Okeny hissed.

Another screech cried out from the shore directly across from the ship. As if in response, the first screech echoed again from further away.

"Owls?" James asked, shaking his head in confusion.

Okeny leaned close to James and, in a low voice, said, "Those aren't birds."

His throat clenching, James whispered back, "What then?"

"Someone's out there, watching us and telling others what they see. Both bird calls are shit too."

A third screech came from the direction they'd come from yesterday.

"Damn it," James swore and ran to Ryan's cabin below deck. He woke him with a rough shake.

"What? My turn?" Ryan mumbled, slow to get to his feet.

His voice commanding, like in the old days, James barked, "No, we could be in for an ambush. At least three, maybe more. We need weapons."

Immediately awake, Ryan nodded.

The two went for the hold where Nathaniel still kept his cot. The soldier was rolling over when the two rebels came running in. Nathaniel sat up, alarmed, and struggled to get his legs untangled from the blanket wrapped around them.

Shrilly, he asked, "What's happening?"

Then he saw James and Ryan going for the weapons crate, and he doubled his efforts to free himself. James had the box open before Nathaniel could get to his feet and was already handing Ryan a pistol and a sword as he rushed over. "What do you think you're doing? What's going on?"

"What should have been done as soon as we spotted land," James said, picking up the axe. He gave it an approving grunt as he tested the weapon's weight. A click of a pistol's hammer pulling back made him whirl around.

Nathaniel's hand shook as he pointed the gun at James, his eyes wide with fear. "You don't need those. Not yet." The soldier sounded as if he was pleading.

James reached over and gently pushed the pistol away. "I'm afraid we do. Now, it's time to show some of that Crownsman backbone and get your ass on deck. There could be trouble."

Nathaniel released the hammer on the pistol, and his shoulders sagged. Slowly, he nodded but under his breath, he mumbled, "We've only just arrived."

James and Ryan quickly made their way back up to the deck, and soon after, Nathaniel and his brother arrived, carrying rifles. Richard nodded at James and Okeny. There was a quiver in Nathaniel's lip, but he managed to keep the tremor from his hands and held his gun firmly at the ready. Okeny explained the situation once they'd all gathered. James told them to be prepared for anything. There was no way to know what they were up against.

The door to below deck opened as he finished, and Elizabeth emerged with a pistol in her hand, checking to see it was loaded, then placed it back in its holster.

"What are you doing?" he said in a harsh whisper.

"Protecting my family's ship," she said.

"I can't ask you to do that," he said to her quietly.

She reached up, poking him hard in the chest, and said, "You're right. *You* can't ask me. This is what *I* am doing."

In the dark, he could have sworn she was Tai. "Do you know how to use a gun?"

If she'd really been Tai, he'd have expected a bullet to graze his arm. But, of course, Elizabeth wasn't her.

She said, "I do. Grandfather didn't get to have any grandsons, so I told him my sex shouldn't keep him from teaching me what he would have taught them. Now, isn't there something more important to be worried about?"

James let the briefest grin part his lips before he welcomed her to join the group.

They spread out along the ship, watching and listening. Their ears strained for the sound of any movement. The rest of the night was spent in silence. But to their relief, no more sounds came from the shore.

As the sun rose, Nathaniel said from the other side of the deck, "The next time you hear something spooky in the night, let me sleep."

Tired and still unnerved, James turned to say something, but before he could, Richard shouted, "That's enough, Nate. Man up, or swim back to England."

The others exchanged uncomfortable looks, unsure of how to take the mostly reserved brother's outburst.

Nathaniel looked away as his face grew red.

A few awkward moments passed then Peter came up for his shift at the wheel.

"Who's shouting up here?" he asked crankily. "Are you trying to tell the whole bloody continent we're here?" Shaking his head, the old man climbed the stairs to the wheelhouse.

Not able to help himself, James snickered as he went up after him.

Inside, Peter had already given the order to get underway, and the crew had moved out onto the deck, raising the anchors and sails.

"Heard about what happened?" James asked.

Peter nodded. "Can't be helped. Someone was bound to notice us sooner or later."

"They're organized, whoever they are. They've got a system in place. We can only hope they were simply curious and left," James said. He could hear the doubt in his own words.

Peter shooed James out of the wheelhouse when the sails caught the wind.

Everyone on deck looked just as tired as James, but sleep was going to have to wait. He leaned heavily against the mast at the ship's bow and watched the shore slip by. As soon as they rounded the point, the trees gave way to the charred stone and twisted metal of a small village. Broken wooden poles stuck out of the water, the only indication that there'd once been a dock here. A collapsed warehouse with rusted girders had toppled over onto several stone houses, stained by soot. Ash blew around the village in the morning breeze, making the air hazy.

Ryan pointed across the bay to a similarly destroyed village.

"Did the fire jump across the water?" James asked Okeny.

"Could be. A spark, carried by the wind," Okeny said with a shrug. "That air you're smelling? There's something more to it. Stinks of coal and something else…"

James sniffed. It was faint, but he smelled it. "Maybe a mine caught fire?"

"Maybe," Okeny said, his nose pointed in the air. "But it's not from these villages."

The scorched landscape continued as *The Ophelia* sailed on into the afternoon, and it was near evening when they finally saw some green again. Eventually, the bay started to narrow, a sign they were approaching the river that fed into it.

From where she was keeping watch at the bow, Elizabeth pointed ahead and made a sound to get his attention. Following her direction, he saw something on the riverbank ahead of them. Through his binoculars, he saw six huts built from scrap. They were a mishmash of walls and windows. One even had portholes on one side. A small fire, recently put out, still smoked next to one of the odd one-story houses. Nearby, a field had been cleared, and someone had tilled rows into the earth.

James thought he saw a hand move from a sheer curtain in one of the huts with comically large windows as they sailed closer. A flash of a young woman's face peered out at them before quickly disappearing again. James asked Elizabeth to lower the sails. There were people still alive in America, just as he thought.

It took some time to ready the life raft and lower it into the water, but soon Ryan was rowing them ashore from where they'd anchored, a hundred yards past the village. James had brought weapons, but he also wanted them out of sight, so they were stashed at the bottom of the boat.

"I don't want to look like raiders," he said before they left *The Ophelia*. "Let's make it easier for them to trust us."

There wasn't a dock for them to tie on to, so James had to hop out and pull the rowboat out of the water.

On dry land, Ryan rubbed his shoulder and groaned, "Someone else gets to row next."

"Don't go too far from the boat. If I'm reading this wrong, we'll have to secure our escape. I'm going to try that house over there." James indicated the one with the big windows. "If they let me in, I'll signal the all-clear in ten minutes. If I don't, do what you can, but if it's a lost cause, then make for the ship. Understood?"

They all nodded.

"Keep your eyes and ears open. I'll be back."

It was only a short distance to the house, which he studied more closely as he drew near. It appeared to be made from the parts of at least three other homes. Everything from the wood to the colors was mismatched and cobbled together. However, the exterior was clean, and the little porch leading up to the front was freshly swept.

The short steps he climbed might have been, at one point, painted green, and he knocked on the door and listened. Water splashed on the shore behind him, feet crunched the sandy dirt, and distant birds sang, but there were no sounds inside the house. He tried again, saying, "Begging your pardon, but I saw someone in the window as we passed, and I'd like to talk if that's quite all right."

From the other side of the door came the shuffling of feet, then the scraping of metal as someone turned the lock, but it remained closed. Trying the latch, he found it had been unlocked rather than the opposite.

Well, that's a good start.

Slowly, he opened the door and had to bend down to look inside. A man in his forties stood in the center of a short hallway with sandy brown hair and a trim beard. He embraced a frightened young woman with blonde hair and pointed a bent poker in James's general direction. Both were dressed in rough homespun clothes. He wore a simple wool shirt and trousers, and she, a green dress.

"Again, you have my pardons. I'm sorry if I've startled you, but my colleagues and I are new to this area, you see, and we would appreciate a bit of help finding our way," James said in a quiet, soothing voice with his hands spread out to show he wasn't carrying a weapon. He'd dealt with more than a few frightened people in his time, and knew the best way to ease their fears, at least in England, was to be overly polite.

The couple first looked at each other, then back to James, their expressions showing confusion, and the man kept the poker raised.

James tried again. "My name is James. James Barlow. May I ask for your names, at least?"

The result was more of the same.

With a sigh, James muttered, "Bloody hell. The first people I find, and they don't bloody understand me."

The man cleared his throat, then said, "I understand you just fine. It's the way you talk that's confusing." His voice was gruff with an odd accent that sounded like he was hoarding his vowels.

James smiled.

"I could say the same of you. Would you mind putting that down?" He pointed at the poker. "We're not here to hurt anyone."

Keeping his arm around the young woman's shoulders, the man lowered the poker but kept his shoulders square and back straight. "What *are* you here for? And where're you from?"

"I'm from a country called England," James said. He saw the exchange of looks again and continued, "It's a land many thousands of miles from here across the ocean."

The man pointed the poker to the wall just inside the doorway. An old, faded map of the world was in a cracked wooden frame. "I know what England is, son. Just because I live in a shack doesn't mean I'm an idiot."

SILHOUETTES AND FLAMES

The man's name was Brian Johnson, the area's 'Cutter,' which, after an explanation, meant he was the local doctor. The young woman was Jessica O'Bannon, from another village across the bay. She was here as his apprentice and stood in for a nurse when needed. After introductions were made and James waved to the others by the boat, Brian asked, "What're you doing so far from home?"

"A bit of exploring. Our country was spared from the plague, and now we're curious to see what's happened to the rest of the world," James lied. He couldn't tell them the real reason or the Crown's plans for this land. At least, not without first learning the way of things here.

"The Burn's what happened. Wiped out a whole mess of people," Brian said and spat on the floor.

"The Burn?" James cocked his head.

"The damned disease that killed everyone. What'd you call it in England?"

"It was always just the plague. We never saw it firsthand. Word had gotten back to us before it spread that far, and our government blocked all entry in and out of the country." The words tasted bitter, but James kept them from sounding as such. *Maybe I should have been an actor instead?*

The two men were sitting in a small living room. Old anatomy charts and a painting of a city decorated the walls. The rigid chairs they sat in felt as if they'd been made by someone who didn't quite know what they were doing, and James's wobbled every time he moved.

Carrying a pot of tea and a tray of cups, Jessica returned. She served them both on the low table between the men, then said, "I'll go and bring some out to your friends, seeing as no one else will. They're afraid of their own shadows, I tell you. But you can't blame them none, though." She left and headed outside.

"What does that mean?" James asked, picking up the cup.

"Got Talons about. Makes people real nervous," Brian said, staring into his tea.

"Talons?"

"I'm not one for superstitions, but it's supposed to be bad luck to talk about them. Brings them to your door, or so they say." Brian took a sip before setting the cup back down.

"If the people on my ship are in any danger, I'd like to know. The last thing I want to do is go somewhere we shouldn't," James said, raising his cup and tasting what it contained. It wasn't perfect, but it was hot and wet, so he took another sip.

Brian looked briefly to the door, then scooted to the edge of his chair. In a hushed voice, he asked, "You believe in dragons?"

James choked mid-sip and spat it back out into the cup. "I-I'm sorry," he stammered. "Did you say dragons?"

"Yes, I did. Dragons. You know, big teeth, scales, wings, breathes fire. They still have storybooks in England, don't they?"

"Yes..." James said, drawing out the word for several seconds as he tried to understand where the conversation was going. He eyed the doorway, ensuring he had a clear exit, then looked back to Brian.

"Don't look at me like I'm crazy. I don't believe in them. But some folks do. And those people," Brian pointed in the direction *The Ophelia* was headed, "are up that way."

"What are you going on about?" James said, his brows knit together.

"I'm thinking I'd better start over," Brian said. He leaned back in his chair, looking out the window behind James. "My grandfather had been a doctor in Philadelphia when the chaos started." He pointed at the painting of the city on the wall. "And barely got out with my father to the countryside. The Burn had turned neighbors and friends against each other. They burned the whole damned city to the ground, thinking it'd kill the sickness. I came along about ten years after that."

"What exactly was the Burn?" James interrupted.

"It was long gone by the time I was born, so I can only tell you what my father remembered from that time. People had started coming to my grandfather's house with high fevers and aches. The fever's what killed them all," Brian said. "And it spread like wildfire. That's why we call it the Burn. By my father's guess, it only lasted a little more than a year because, by the end of it all, you were either dead or hiding from everyone else, which actually helped to keep it from spreading."

"How did he come by that estimate?"

"It's called an educated guess," Brian said. "He'd taken up the family trade and became a doctor, trained by his father. Never got to meet him. He died before I was born, but I learned what I could from my father before he passed from some damn wasting disease that'd spread from the camps. Took a quarter of us."

Brian shook his head slowly with a pained expression. "Was a damn shame too. I wasn't anywhere near ready. I'm only good at stitching things up and setting bones. Most of the time, I end up cutting off the parts I can't save. But my father instilled in me the Cratic Oath. Got to help anyone who needs it, no matter what. Which means anyone who comes to my door," Brian took a sip of his tea, "That sometimes means Talons."

He winced slightly and gave an embarrassed smile. "Guess I'm taking the long route tonight. Don't get many strangers to talk to these days."

"It's all right. The Talons?" James said.

Brian nodded, putting his tea back down. "They'd show up at night with broken bones or deep gashes. Never told me how they got them, but if I were a betting man, I'd say they did it to themselves. There haven't been any wars in these parts since I was a boy."

Brian leaned in and spoke softly again. "Most are afraid to even talk to a Talon, but I've had more than a few words with them. Let me tell you, they get real talkative when you're pushing a bone back into the meat of a leg. There's a whole mess of them in some old cities up north along the rivers, and they got outposts well beyond their capital and down to Split State.

"From how they tell it, there's thousands of them. I don't know where they all came from, but they've been around since before I was born, you see."

"You still haven't explained what they are," James said.

"A cult of religious fanatics. They got this crazy belief that a dragon destroyed the world. I'm sure you saw what was left after the city burners died out as you sailed on up here."

James nodded.

"They think that was their dragon's doing."

"Wouldn't others know the wildfires caused the damage?"

"No one in their right mind would try and explain that to a Talon. Maybe if the fire hadn't spread as far as it did and destroyed so much more than the city. Makes it hard to believe that anything other than a monster could do that."

"These fanatics, are they bad people?"

A slight tremor appeared in the corner of Brian's eye, and he swallowed dryly before he answered, "Yes."

Brian nodded.

The tightness under his skin returned, and James felt his entire body tense. "Have they hurt you before?"

"No, not me. But I provide a service. Everyone needs to be useful. If you aren't, they'll find ways to remedy that. Entire villages have disappeared in the night. One day they're there, then the next, only ashes remain."

"I think we passed by one of them earlier today."

Brian let out a prolonged sigh. "Must have been Fortsku. Everyone there went missing about four years back. Good people. Kept mostly to themselves. Though there was this one woman…"

Smiling warmly, the Cutter looked lost in thought for a moment.

"Margie," he continued. "She'd come by every now and then with her pa to trade. They'd camp at the water's edge, and we'd talk. I still miss that. It's a damn shame."

James sat back in his chair while managing to keep his balance. "I'm sorry to drag up the past like this, but I want to thank you for letting me know we were headed in the wrong direction."

"It's all right. I'm sorry we hid. But you have to understand, the only ships that pass by here are the Talons'. I was damned glad to see you were too clean when you got off that boat of yours. And you're right. You need to turn around. One of their camps is about ten miles upriver from here. They've got a ship there, covered in iron, just bristling with cannons."

"You mean an ironclad?"

"A relic from the old war between the states, you see. There was a factory somewhere along the river where they were made, and the cult got their hands on one. But that's not what matters. No one's allowed to just travel around without their permission, especially on the water. Weren't you curious why you haven't seen anyone else sailing?"

"We weren't sure anyone else was still alive, to be honest."

"We're a tough people here. The Burn took its toll, sure. The old governments are gone, but people always find a way to survive."

Indeed, they do.

"Which way should we go, then? What's to the south?" James asked.

"I've never been much further south than where you're sitting, so I wouldn't have a clue. A trader once said something about the Free States, but that's all I know."

"Free States?" James repeated, tasting the words in his mouth.

"You're welcome to head that way, but you should do it now. It'll be full dark soon, and the Talons'll be about. Don't take offense, but it'd be bad if they found you here. Not just for you, but everyone in the village."

James nodded and stood. He was reaching out to shake hands with the Cutter when a young boy with barely eight summers on him came running into the room.

"Harry? What's this? Where's Jacob?" Brian asked, worry in his voice.

Bent over and breathing hard, the boy managed to get out, "Jacob ran to the dark men. He didn't want us disappeared."

Brian moved and knelt in front of Harry. Grasping the boy's shoulders, he looked him straight in the eye. "How long ago?" He gave James a concerned glance.

"When the big boat stopped. He told me to promise to stay hidden, but Jessica was laughing with those strangers, so they aren't bad..." The boy trailed off as he finally noticed James and craned his neck to look up at him, his mouth gaping open.

Brian shouted at James while getting quickly to his feet, "You've got to leave. They're coming!"

At the same time, Jessica rushed in with Okeny right behind her. All the color was drained from her face. "It's too late. They're already in the woods."

Okeny said, "It's the same screeches from last night. Ms. O'Bannon went ghost white when we heard the first one. I've counted twenty more since then. They're coming, and fast."

Brian stared at Okeny for a moment, seemingly at a loss for words, then his brow knitted in thought. "That's impossible. How could Jacob have reached them so soon?" he asked. Then he turned sharply to James. "Wait, you heard them last night? They already know you're here!"

"Get everyone to the boat. Now!" James ordered Okeny, then turned to Brian. "You're welcome to come with us."

Brian gave a quick look around the small living room, then nodded. "Jessica, Harry, follow me." He gripped Harry by the shoulder again, but the boy shook his head and pulled away.

"I can't leave Jacob to the dragon!" he shouted as he ran from the house. James and Okeny darted out the door, but Harry had run into the woods, and neither could see which way he went.

From the river's edge, Ryan called to them as he pushed the rowboat back into the water.

James, torn between helping and going after the boy, had the decision made for him when *The Ophelia's* signal horn blared five times, and he heard Liz's frantic shouts. James could do nothing for the boy, so he rushed to the shore.

Screeches echoed within the forest behind him as he made it to the rowboat. Looking back, he saw something dark move in the twilight between two houses. Dread took over, and he practically heaved Brian and Jessica aboard the tiny craft. With a surge of adrenaline, he shoved the boat into the river and jumped in as Okeny rowed with all his might back to *The Ophelia*.

Pointing upriver, Liz gasped, "What is that?"

Past their ship, something bright was flickering out on the water. Above it, a plume of black smoke was pouring into the sky.

Richard pulled a pair of binoculars from his bag and swore under his breath before handing them over to James. Peering through it, he saw a ship covered in dark figures brandishing torches. The ship's hull bristled with metal spikes and cannons. The vessel carried enough firepower to blow a hole through the Great Blockade.

Watching the figures move about on it, James was reminded of ants swarming a beetle. Even over the sound of Okeny's pained grunts as he strained against the oars, James could hear the mechanical chugging of the oncoming ship.

The ladder waited for them when they came alongside *The Ophelia*. The anchor was already out of the water, and the engine belched to life as they began climbing aboard. James was the last one up, and the ship had set off even before he'd reached the deck.

Having stayed behind to guard the ship, Nathaniel stood in the middle of the deck and stared upriver with wide eyes. The knuckles of his hands were white as he held his rifle. *The Ophelia* steered in an agonizingly slow arc as Peter changed their heading. Eventually, they'd turned around and headed downriver.

Flames engulfed the houses of Brian's village.

Jessica gave a startled cry while Brian stood behind her, hands resting on her shoulders. Through the flames, shadowy forms appeared, and an army of torches moved away from the village and into the forest.

"They're still gaining on us!" Liz shouted from the wheelhouse.

As twilight finally faded and the night swallowed the land, their world was guided by fire and the need to escape it. A small island sat in the middle of the bay ahead of *The Ophelia*, and Peter steered to the right of it, taking them closer to the Delaware side of the river. The metal monstrosity burned on the water behind them as it gave chase.

"Can't this bloody thing go faster?" Nathaniel shouted up to her.

"That's not helping, Nate," James growled and went to the rear of *The Ophelia*. As he watched, a red streak shot skyward from the ironclad, and seconds later, a bright flare burst above them.

"What was that for?" Liz said.

"I don't know. But I'm sure we won't like it," he said too quietly for her to hear.

James felt useless. He clamped his eyes shut he willed them to go faster. And when he opened them again, they were, somehow, outpacing the ironclad. He looked up at Liz, still standing on the landing outside the wheelhouse, and gave her a brief smile just as an explosion rocked their ship.

Thrown into the rail and almost going over, James had the wind knocked out of him. Shouts broke out all over the deck, but louder was a shriek above him. Gasping for breath, James whirled around as Liz clung to the hand railing. By the time he made it to the bottom step, she'd already managed to pull herself to safety.

People were getting to their feet on the deck, and he stumbled over to help. Twisted, searing metal from the port side paddlewheel littered the ground among the scattered crew. Brian moved quickly among them, checking for injuries.

James had run to see what caused the explosion when another red flare burst above them. A second ironclad had been waiting in ambush on the other side of the island, smoke still wafting from one of its cannons. With *The Ophelia* crippled, he knew it'd be impossible to get away. But something strange was going on here. *They're close enough to tear us apart, but they only fired once?*

Quickly, he grabbed Okeny. "How close do you need to be to make it to shore?"

Okeny eyed him curiously. "Five hundred yards, give or take."

"And if four people were going with you?"

"Depends on if they're strong swimmers or not."

101

James nodded and turned to Jessica. "Is there someplace safe nearby?"

Jessica stammered, "M-my village is…a bit aways from here…"

"Can you and Brian swim?"

"I-I'm pretty good, but I've never seen him in the water."

"Good," James called over, "How about you, Richard? Can you swim?"

Squatted down next to his brother, Richard had concern on his face. Nathaniel was sitting on the deck and had a cut across his brow and swatted at Richard's hand every time he tried to touch it. Without looking up from Nate, Richard said, "Quite well. Why?"

As plainly as could be, James said, "We're going to surrender." Then he had to shout over the group to say the rest. "But not all of us. Someone has to get away and let England know it isn't safe here."

"And you get to decide who stays and who goes?" Nathaniel asked, struggling to get to his feet. His brother took his hand and helped him up.

James said, "We need to send the people with the best chances of making it out there. Or the Crown will kill everyone I've ever known and cared about."

"At the expense of us," Nathaniel said, brushing his brother's hands aside and stepping up to James.

Ryan worked himself between James and the soldier, but James gently moved him away.

Shaking his head, James smiled sadly. "You know, Reginald thought you were the only one that understood, but I believe he was wrong."

Nathaniel sniffed and took a step back. "Understood what?"

James looked at all the faces around him before landing on Elizabeth, her eyes narrowed, and arms crossed as she came across the deck. "We're expendable," he said. "Why do you think they sent a rebel with a barely provisioned cargo ship and not one of their frigates and a regiment of Crownies? If we fail, what have they lost?"

Nathaniel wiped blood from his forehead and clenched his jaw, clearly mulling the questions over. Then he shook his head and thumped his chest. "They did send red coats."

"It makes sense, don't it?" Ryan said. "Who'd give a fuck about us?"

"What about Reginald?" Elizabeth said. "He was a brilliant engineer."

"Who didn't want anyone else to take the credit for his invention," James said. "That's why he drank. He knew this was a suicide mission. I'll be honest, I had a hunch that's what this was, but now it's pretty clear I'm here because I was first on a list of names."

Elizabeth bit her lip as she watched the ironclads approach. *The Ophelia* was a wounded animal, simply limping along, and the predators knew they could take their time. "Why can't we all take our chances on land?"

James closed his eyes and rubbed the bridge of his nose, pushing back the frustration that bubbled beneath the surface. "There's little chance we'd all get away. None of us know this area. And these people—these Talons—are looking for a crewed ship, and if they don't find that crew, they'll come looking for us all over again. Those staying behind are just buying time for the others to get away. They *need* to send a message back to England."

Nathaniel snorted. "Fah. I knew it. You care more about those locked up traitors than our lives."

Elizabeth's jaw tightened and held him in an icy stare. "That's why, isn't it?"

"What?" he asked.

"Why you wanted to know how to use Reginald's invention. You expected something like this was going to happen. You had this all figured out already, didn't you?"

James tried to get a word in, but she continued over him. "You used me. You had me teach you how it worked so that you could slip away while the rest of us are killed. Nathaniel's right. You only care about yourself. In fact, if I had to guess, you weren't trying to save Reginald at all. You were worried he had the telegraph with him."

"That's not—" James started, his face turning red.

Elizabeth wasn't done. "What was the plan for after the Crown arrived? Steal one of their ships and sail back to England? Oh, and I'm sure Ryan was in on it too."

"I'm staying here!" James bellowed.

Stunned by the ferocity behind his words, Elizabeth blinked and stepped back.

Frightened faces looked at him, except for Ryan, who merely sighed.

Again, rubbing the bridge of his nose, James tried to calm himself before explaining, "I'm staying behind to surrender. Elizabeth, you know more about that machine than I do, so you're leaving. So is Okeny, along with Richard to back him up. Jessica and Brian, there's no reason for you to be here. This was our fault."

Brian, who had been helping an injured crewman, stood and brushed his hands on his pants. "I'm staying."

Brian cut James off before he could protest.

"I don't know any of you, but I have to try to help. You see, they know me. I'm useful to them. It's possible I can get them to let you go." The doubt on the Cutter's face told James he didn't believe he could do it.

"And if that doesn't work, what're the rest of us supposed to do, yeah?" Ryan asked. "Wait for these pricks to flay us alive?"

Placing a hand on his friend's shoulder, James let his gaze travel from Ryan to others gathered around him. He had to give them hope, even for a brief moment.

"Brian, you said you have to be useful, or they'll make you useful, yes?"

Brian nodded.

James took a step back and paced slowly in a circle. "Look how they've behaved so far," he said. "Fear is their weapon. They frighten people by making noises in the night and chased after us with a nightmarishly decorated ship. I think if they only wanted to kill, they'd do it with far less theatrics."

James put on a confident smile as he saw the others nod slowly. "They're bloody slavers, is all. I wouldn't be surprised if their numbers aren't as great as the stories say."

"So, what then?" Elizabeth asked. "You're just going to let yourself and my crew be enslaved?"

"I might be able to talk some sense into them," Brian added again as if trying to reassure himself. "They know my worth, you see. I'm sure they'll listen…"

James shook his head. "No, I don't think they will, but I don't see any other way out of this. Once I figure out where they've taken us, I'll be able to figure out what to do next. Until then, we'll have to endure." He looked back to the ironclad that had hamstrung *The Ophelia* and saw it finally moving in. "This is it. As soon as we get close enough to shore, you're leaving. Brian, it isn't too late for you to change your mind."

The Cutter set his shoulders back and shook his head. "No, I'm staying."

Jessica began crying and pulling on Brian's sleeve, and he embraced the distraught woman, hushing her while stroking the back of her head.

"And what are we supposed to do if we manage to get a message to England?" Elizabeth asked.

With the two locals distracted, James motioned the others closer and said quietly, "Tell them to send their ships to Washington, then find somewhere safe to wait. If we escape, we'll make our way south. But you have to get that message out to England. Let them know we held up our end of the bargain. Please," James said, his eyes locked on hers.

She swallowed and gave a slight nod.

"But first, Okeny, get Jessica home. She doesn't deserve to be punished because of us," James said.

Okeny nodded. "I promise."

Bluntly, Nathaniel said, "This is a shit plan."

"They usually are," Ryan sighed. "But he finds a way to make them work, yeah?"

"I'll go to tell Peter to make for the shore. Gather what things you'll need."

Before he left, James shook hands with Okeny and Richard. When he went to Elizabeth, he handed back the knife she'd given him. Her fingers trembled as she took it. Jessica was still crying against Brian's shoulder, so James let them be.

Inside the wheelhouse, he explained the situation to the captain.

The old man spun the wheel, directing *The Ophelia* to shore. Once the course was set, he said, "All of you should go. Just leave me with my ship."

"If these bastards only find you, they'll figure out what happened, and then no one gets away." He watched Okeny wrap supplies in waterproof leather bags on the deck below.

Eyes searching the darkness beyond his ship, the captain said, "I'm old, James. I don't think I'll fit into your plan, so don't let me be the reason you can't escape. Promise me. If it comes to that, you'll leave me behind."

James shook his head. "I can't promise that. You're one of us. Besides, Liz would skin me alive if I showed up without her grandfather."

Peter laughed softly. "Aye, that she would. She might be strong-willed and stubborn, but she'd come to understand why it had to be done."

James remained quiet for several minutes before patting the old man's shoulder. "I think we're close enough."

On the deck, Okeny had tied a rope to the railing on the starboard side. After giving a nod to his brother, Richard was the first to go. With a grim expression, Nathaniel sat down and stared at the rope. Jessica was next, and she hugged Brian before going over the rail. James felt guilty.

I should have left their village alone.

When it was Elizabeth's turn, she looked across the deck and then up at the wheelhouse and gave her grandfather a small wave. A noticeable tremor in his hand, Peter waved back. Finally, Okeny saluted James quickly and then disappeared into the abyss, along with the others.

"Cut the engine," James said. "Time to give them what they want." And headed out of the wheelhouse.

Those who remained had gathered on deck, and emotions ranged from anger to despair. As the first ironclad drew closer, young Marcus threw up. James shouted for them to get on their knees and remain still, then he laid out all their weapons on the deck. When he reached for his axe, he realized he'd left it back on the rowboat.

Ryan asked, "Lost it, didn't you?" from where he knelt.

Sheepishly, James nodded.

"Some things never change, yeah?"

Peter soon came down from the wheelhouse, and James helped the old man get to his knees before joining everyone else.

"Hands behind your heads. Don't say anything until spoken to first, and keep the answers simple," James said.

There was sniffling and sobs from down the line—the familiar sounds of men who thought they'd soon be executed.

The uneven cacophony of the ironclads suddenly fell silent as they came alongside *The Ophelia*. In their absence, a deep and incoherent chant filled the air. Torches rose and fell with a rhythmic pounding of metal. A voice rose above the others, and the chanting slowed to a menacing pace. As he felt his skin tighten, grappling hooks flew over the rail and dug into *The Ophelia*.

Movement caught his attention, and James glanced down the line to find Eugene was struggling to keep Marcus on his knees. While fighting to get loose of the stocky man's grasp, Marcus pointed to the shore where the others had escaped. Ryan got to his feet first and struck the boy on the back of the head, knocking him out. Kneeling again quickly, he stared at the wooden deck, his face red with anger.

Gently, Eugene laid the boy down.

A dark silhouette rose above the rail, backlit by the torches. The first heavy boot hit the deck, followed by more as they clambered aboard. Spreading out in front of the kneeling crew, James counted forty. Torches were passed up from below, and in the dancing glow, James was finally able to see who'd been hunting them.

James was relieved to see they were just men—albeit men dressed in stitched-up overalls and jackets—and not the monstrous creatures that had briefly run through his imagination. To a man, every inch of exposed skin was smeared with black soot, and they smelled of fire and sweat. Brian's words came back to James at that moment when he said he'd been "too clean" to be a Talon, and James now understood what he meant.

Torches in hand, the men continued to beat out the rhythm against the deck, matching it with stomping feet. When the last man came over the rail, the others stepped aside to let him pass through to the front. He barked, and the chanting stopped. *Like some kind of choir leader,* James thought. This leader was just as filthy as the rest, with a tangled beard down to his chest and his scalp completely shaved.

The Choir Leader passed an appraising look around the deck, noting first the weapons and then the crew. His gaze paused on the body of Marcus, sprawled as it was, but then he continued down the line, stopping again on Brian. Turning, he quietly said something to one of the men holding a torch, pointing at Brian, and the other nodded. Then he stepped closer to the crew and leaned down to stare into their faces. Minutes ticked by before ending with James, who stared back into the dark, bloodshot eyes without blinking.

The Choir Leader straightened and turned his back on the crew. "He's in charge," he said hoarsely and stuck a thumb over his shoulder at James.

James said, "I don't know what you want, but we've surrendered unconditionally."

The Choir Leader tilted his head slightly. "Ever hear a sound like that?" he said to one of the grime-coated men.

The man shrugged and said, "No, Foreman."

"Where's the Souther?" the leader asked, turning back and crossing his arms. His eyes searched the crew again before returning to James.

James looked from the crew to their captors, then back to the Choir Leader. "Who?"

The back of the man's hand cracked across James's face as he shouted, "The Souther!" James was used to swallowing his blood and had become quite good at ignoring pain. Then the Choir Leader yelled, "Bring him up!"

A squirming man bound in chains was pulled up from the ironclad, and a gasp came from where Brian knelt when the torchlight revealed his face.

"Found this cherub roaming where he shouldn't've." The Choir Leader snorted as he laughed. "Tell him what you saw, Jacob." His eyes never leaving James, the man smiled with broken, rotting teeth and waited.

Parts of Jacob's scalp had been cut away, and what little hair remained was stiff with dried blood. His swollen lips parted as he murmured something. The Choir Leader punched him in the kidney and shouted, "Louder."

Jacob gasped in pain, then squealed, "There was a Souther!"

The men holding him up let go, and he crashed to the deck in a groaning heap.

The leader, smiling viciously, took a few steps toward James. "You heard him. Now, where's the Souther?"

"I want you to listen to me," James said, making sure the man focused on him and him alone, "You can understand me, yes?"

The Choir Leader nodded manically, lifting a hand to his ear. "I have no bloody idea what you're going on about."

It was a struggle to keep his food down when the Choir Leader pressed his face close to James's. His rancid breath smelled fouler than any latrine James had ever cleaned out. But even as his stomach sloshed, James could help but notice a mark on the man's forehead, obscured as it was by the filth. After a quick look at the other Talons, he noted a similar mark on all of them.

The Choir Leader took a step back from James and shrugged. "We'll let the boss sort 'em out."

"Wait," Brian said, holding his hands out beggingly.

"Eh?" the Choir Leader said and looked to the Cutter.

"Brian, don't," James said. He fought the urge to get up and put a hand over Brian's mouth.

Brian pleaded, "Please, they don't know who you are or your ways. Let them go. They only made a mistake."

The leader slowly went over to Brian and crouched. The Cutter flinched when a greasy hand was placed on his shoulder. "You're the one that stitched up Hamish." It wasn't a question, but Brian nodded. With an approving nod, the leader took one of Brian's hands into his own. "You have your use." James watched as the leader's grip tightened on Cutter's hand and shoulder. Through gritted teeth, the Choir Leader said, "But, that don't give you a right to tell me what to do."

Brian gasped in pain, trying to pull free from the firm grip.

"Stop!" James shouted.

When The Choir Leader let go, Brian fell backward to the deck, then he barked, "Enough of this shit. Get 'em on the boat."

The Talons swept forward, and James could do nothing as they held him down and tied his hands and feet with rope while the rest of the crew shouted curses and struggled. A foul-smelling hood was forced over his head, and to his surprise, it felt oddly like home.

Lifted from the deck, he was passed along until there was a brief moment of weightlessness before landing hard on his back, and the wind was knocked out of him.

He choked as bodies fell around him, their cursing louder, fueled by pain. Then the chanting started again, and he was dragged across the rough ironclad deck, his unprotected skin riddled with metal splinters. Something heavy slammed shut, and the chanting grew muffled and replaced by quiet sobbing. Then an engine roared to life.

He felt more than heard the concussive barrage. It was a feeling he was all too familiar with, and he knew the other ship had unloaded its cannons on *The Ophelia*. As Peter's ship sank, the sense of freedom James had found slipped beneath the surface with her.

INTO THE MOUTH

They'd been in darkness for days, hours, or perhaps only a few minutes.

Time was lost in the suffocating heat and thrumming of the engine. The hood over his head was drenched in sweat and stink, and every breath made him wretch. At some point, Marcus regained consciousness and called for help. Heavy steps went across the metal floor, and the young man cried in pain before falling silent again. James tried pleading to whoever would listen to leave the boy alone. A swift kick to the gut made him curl over in pain.

Expecting the beating to continue, it took him a few minutes to realize none was coming, and he pulled himself back up to a sitting position with his back against a wall. He tested his restraints and found his hands were tied to his feet, making it impossible for him to stand or even remove the hood.

A loud clang came from somewhere across from him, followed by the sound of rushing water and a much-welcomed breeze. In unison, three men's voices said, "Foreman."

"Get 'em trussed up. Gonna be in Dragon's Rest soon," said the Choir Leader's voice. "The boss'll size 'em up. Then I expect the Head'll want to judge 'em."

Together, the four said, "May she know the will of The Great Dragon, protect us from Its wrath, and provide us with the eternal bounty of Its flame."

Peter said, "Who's in charge here? Your boss or this Head?" He was right next to James, and the rebel was ready to throw himself on top of Peter if the Talons came to beat the old man.

Ominous laughter filled the room instead.

The Foreman said, "You'll all soon find out." And then his steps walked away. The door slammed shut again, taking the cool air with it.

Hands were on him, roughly looping a chain around his throat, and he heard the all too familiar *click* of a lock. There was a tug at his neck as he heard them working on Peter beside him. James sat back when they'd moved on to the next crewman, but felt the chain tighten on his neck. Peter began to cough and wheeze suddenly, and James leaned over to try and find the old man and instantly felt the chain grow slack, and Peter breathed normally again.

The hood was pulled from his head abruptly, leaving James blinded until his eyes adjusted and found they were in a small room with rust-lined walls—the same orange color as the dust on his clothes from when they dragged him inside. A lantern swung in the middle of the room above a table where a Talon sat drinking from a small flask while watching the two other Talons wrapping chains around the necks of *The Ophelia's* crew.

The godawful stink coming from them made James miss the hood.

They were paired off, the same length of chain looping around both necks before being locked in the middle. If either one tried to run, they'd both be strangled. James followed his chain and realized he was attached to Peter. That explained the choking, he thought. Across the room, Ryan was chained to Nathaniel. His friend glowered at the floor between his legs while the soldier stared wide-eyed at the wall above James's head.

When the Talons were finished, the one at the table stood and pulled a large knife from his boot. Beginning at one end of the line, he cut the ropes from the crew's legs and then retied their hands in front. Marcus flinched as he approached him with the knife, and their captors laughed. But when Marcus started to cry, he got backhanded, leaving a greasy black streak on his cheek, before moving on to finish with James and Peter.

A horn, louder than the engine, sounded.

The Talons grinned excitedly as a second muffled horn answered. A steady rhythm pounded against the ship's hull, vibrating the wall and floor beneath James. The three Talons picked up the beat, stomping their feet as their voices joined together in a chant.

"Booom-raaaa-haaa! Kooo-chaaa-kaaa! Booom-raaaa-haaa!"

James found himself tapping his foot. The beat was rather catchy. Peter pulled on their chain and shot him a reprimanding look. He stopped, embarrassed.

The engine cut, and James could feel the ship slowing, but there was no respite. Somehow, the chanting and stomping seemed louder than what he thought was possible.

James's senses were hammered by a deafening roar of voices when the hatch swung open. Fiery light danced across the wall near the door, and the stench of smoke and burning coal was overpowering. Going around the room, the Talons pulled the crew to their feet. James stretched the kinks from his muscles, and the chain tightened between him and the old captain. *Bollocks*. He'd have to stoop from here on.

Eugene and Marcus were shoved to the doorway. Marcus looked out and silently screamed, his eyes wide and mouth open. As James watched, the boy pissed himself. Eugene glanced once at James and shook his head before the two were forced out of the small room. The chanting briefly became a roaring cheer.

Ryan and Nathaniel were next.

To Nathaniel's credit, the soldier didn't try to run as James expected. He stood with his back straight and marched out with all the confidence of a Crownsman, even though James could see the way the muscles were spasming around his eyes and the trembling of his hands. Before he left, Ryan mouthed to James, "Shit."

The chanting voices cheered again.

This continued until, finally, it was James's turn.

A scene from hell was waiting for him.

It was suffocating, chaotic, and primal. Flames burned in every direction, carried by thousands of soot-covered Talons. Voices surrounded him, pummeling him with their chanting. The air itself burned and shimmered from the heat. He could make out a small dock that the ship had been moored to, the only spot clear of the press of bodies. Torches danced while men screamed as he stumbled forward, losing his balance as he tried to keep low. Peter caught his arm and helped him down off the ship, his eyes staring straight ahead as if none of this was happening.

The dark figures nearest the dock parted, revealing a street lined on either side with the horde. The rest of the crew were pushed along the road, and the Talons kept them at a brisk pace. Brick buildings, some four stories tall and stained black with ash, scaled above the masses. Men practically dangled from the windows while they chanted down at the prisoners. Even the roofs were just as packed as the streets, and torches grazed against the roiling black smoke that blocked the sky.

A shove helped James refocus, and he looked back to see the three Talons that had chained the crew and come off the ship. Others from the crowd were shaking their hands and pounding them on the back, giving them a hero's welcome. He was shoved and pulled simultaneously, and it was as if James had lost control of his body. After clearing the docks and reaching the road, he made out a strange shape painted on the surface of every building. It depicted a dragon swallowing its tail. It was the same symbol branded on every Talon's forehead.

Like great monoliths, smokestacks belched black smoke into the air just beyond the buildings they passed, adorned in dragon banners that waved in the searing wind. James had seen enough to piece together that they'd been brought to some factory town, but where? There were little clues left other than the names of companies painted on the buildings, but most had weathered away or left caked in filth. Not that these names meant anything to him.

A stirring in the crowd just ahead of him caught James's attention. Marcus was at the next corner in the street, pulling on his chains and recoiling in horror, while Eugene tried to keep the boy from strangling him. James could do nothing to help them as he was pushed past the two and around the corner where a dragon awaited them.

It was horrifying with its mouth open wide and teeth bared. Flames burned from the beast's eyes as smoke billowed from its nostrils. While it was terrifying, it was only just a sculpture. The massive three-story dragon's head was made of iron and had been built on the front of the largest building. Two Talons came from behind James, dragging Marcus and Eugene towards the mouth, which was actually the building's entrance.

James began to hear a new sound from the crowd as he continued. More than once, a Talon leaned close and whistled at him shrilly, like a bird. Confused as he was already, James was stunned when something struck his chest, and he looked down to see a dead pigeon at his feet. His brain hurt by the time it was finally his turn to step into the dragon's mouth.

They came through to a vast warehouse packed with Talons. Their stomping feet and chanting were even more overwhelming than they had been outside. The expansive space was crisscrossed with rusty catwalks above them, overflowing to the brink of collapse. Men pressed against the handrails, some having to be held to keep from falling. Dragon banners hung from the rafters. Their cloth might have once been white, but years had turned them brown.

From behind, a press of bodies caught James off guard and threw him into Peter, and he tripped over the old man. They landed on the somehow both wet *and* dusty cement floor. Thick, calloused hands picked him and Peter up, and the two were carried by the crowd forward. James was dumped on the ground, and Peter landed next to him. A gash had opened on the old man's forehead, a distant look in his eyes. James tried to get up to help Peter, but the Talons beat him to it and forced the captain up to his knees, taking little care for his age. Angry, James could do nothing as they did the same to him and the rest of the crew before a set of metal stairs.

James could see Ryan to his right. His jaw was clenched, and James knew he was furious. As for Nathaniel, whatever courage he had tapped into was gone. The soldier's eyes didn't blink as he stared at the ground as his body trembled as if he were freezing. To his left, Eugene was doing his best to comfort Marcus. He had his mouth close to the boy's ear and said something to him that James couldn't make out. Marcus's hands were pressed together, and it looked like he was praying.

Two Talons stood at the top of the stairs, with long metal poles, on either side of a glass door. The glass had probably been frosty white and had turned into the mottled gray it was now. Strange, esoteric symbols had been painted on its surface in black ink. The chanting stopped before he could get a good look at the markings.

From where he knelt, he saw Talons staring up at the door, eager and hopeful expressions on all their dirty faces. Hands forced him to bow his head, but he strained against them and could still see most of the staircase. In the wake of the chanting, only heavy breathing remained, and everything else was eerily silent.

Then a door opened, and time seemed to slow down.

Powerful, heavy footsteps echoed within the warehouse as thick boots walked down the stairs. Legs, like tree trunks, were barely contained in black trousers. A broad chest stretched a shirt and vest, also black. The vest had animal ribs, plated in shiny metal, sewn onto it, which glinted in the torch light. A solid length of rebar lay across a set of wide shoulders, with well-muscled, grimy arms draped casually over it. A black cloth covered the lower half of the face with an impressively tangled, dark beard growing out from beneath it. And finally, a bowler hat rested atop the head, tilted forward, keeping the brute's eyes hidden in shadows.

Another set of feet appeared on the steps past the man's shoulders. Much smaller in size and covered in dark cloth wrappings, leading up to a long ebony dress just above the ankles. Slender, pale arms were painted in similar symbols as the door, and a thin hand carried a wooden staff that tapped against the stairs as the feet descended. A belt of vertebrae hung from the hips of a narrow waist. And then the face of a young woman came into view. Her throat and lower jaw were painted black, but the rest of her skin was porcelain white. Striking green eyes peered out from deep sockets. The skull of a hornless stag rested on her head with the red dragon symbol painted in its center. The top of the staff was the last to appear. It had some animal's jaws and sharp teeth lashed tightly to it.

Momentarily distracted by the woman, James almost missed the shouting next to him. Pulling his eyes away from her, James saw

Marcus, clearly panicked, grabbing at the hands holding him down, looking for a way to free himself. Eugene begged him to stop and pointed at the chain that bound them together. The large brute moved faster than James would have thought possible. The length of rebar swung into Marcus's knee with a sickening crack, and the young man cried out and dropped to his knees again.

The brute raised the rebar above his head before slamming it across Marcus's shoulders, driving the boy face-first to the ground. Eugene attempted to speak, but as soon as he made a sound, he was backhanded into silence before the brute returned to Marcus and whacked the boy's back.

James felt the hands holding him in place ease up as the crowd cheered on the beating, whooping each time the rebar fell. The sheer insanity of it all and the fact they were cheering were too much for him. He had to do something, but before James could get up, a gentle hand grabbed his arm, and he looked into Peter's old, painfilled eyes. He'd lost his ship, his granddaughter, and now, his freedom. The old man shook his head and said, "You can't save everyone."

Holding onto James's arm for support, Peter Stillman got to his feet and reached out to the brute, tapping the big man on the back.

There was a collective gasp.

Peter said, "Leave that boy alo—"

The giant turned with a tearing sound, and Peter began to choke. Jagged blades, strapped like gauntlets to the brute's forearm, had ripped open the captain's throat. Then, with a vicious swing of the rebar, the old man dropped, twitched once, then never moved again.

Cheers erupted from filthy mouths, and rage overwhelmed James. The war, the betrayal, and the imprisonment had all left their mark on him, but he'd managed to bottle up the anger to survive Newgate. But this wasn't Newgate. He gave in to his emotions as he crawled over to Peter's body, tears burning in his eyes. Clutching the dead man's hand in his own, James heard the brute laughing as he loomed above him. James grabbed the chain that still connected him to his dead friend and hammered his fists against the ground before surging to his feet.

The two men stared at each other, eye to eye. One's filled with fury, the other in shock and pain after James slammed his forehead into the brute's nose with a satisfyingly wet *thud*.

The cheering crowd grew silent while a dark stain spread from beneath the cloth hiding the brute's face. Blood snorted down from under the mask, spraying the ground. Then the brute started to laugh again and turned to look at the crowd for a brief second before whirling around with the rebar ready to strike James. But James was ready and had been about to kick the brute in the stomach when a shout stopped them both, "Enough!" It was a voice that demanded attention.

All eyes turned to the otherworldly beauty on the stairs, her lips pressed thin and eyes cold with anger. As one, the mob of Talons dropped to their knees, and heads bent in reverence. Only the brute and James remained standing. Slowly, she stepped down the stairs and came toward where they remained frozen, the echo of the staff clicking within the factory. First, she gazed at James, then over at the brute. There was power here, James recognized. The same power that held sway over the Crownsmen back home.

This was another queen.

Stepping between the two giants, she placed a hand on James's chest. It felt warm through his sweat-drenched shirt. Looking up at him, the anger dissipated from her emerald eyes and was replaced by curiosity. She gave him a gentle push, and he took a step back. Satisfied, she looked to the brute and, with little emotion, said, "You are no executioner."

Blood still dripping from the mask, the brute nodded silently. The rebar gripped tightly in his massive hand; the anger never left his blood-shot green eyes.

The woman turned back to James, looking inquisitively again into his eyes. "Who are you?" she said after a few moments.

James stared back, wanting to be defiant, but he felt his rage slowly slip away and replaced with an overwhelming sense of loss. His chest felt tight, but he answered, "James."

"James," she said, trying out the word, and then she turned to the rest of the imprisoned crew. She stood before Eugene, who was holding the battered Marcus in his arms. "And you are?"

The stocky man didn't bother to look up. Without a word, he spat on the ground. The Talons shouted in anger and were getting to their feet when she raised a hand, and the men stopped. James worried that Eugene had signed his death sentence, but only a few seconds passed before she continued down the line until she reached Brian.

"You are known to us. Foreman Jasper vouches for you." She motioned to the Choir Leader from the ironclad, kneeling at the front of the mob, a smirk on his face. Brian didn't hide his relief. "We know your use," she said and pointed to Marcus. "Please, see to the boy."

Brian scrambled to his feet, almost choking himself and the crewman he was chained to. Together, they rushed to Marcus's side. Ignoring the rest, she went back to the stairs and climbed halfway. Turning back, her emerald eyes were once again on James. "Who gave you permission to sail our waters?"

James, his voice cold, said, "We didn't know it was *your* water."

"And what of the Souther seen amongst you? Where did it go?"

James sighed, rubbing the bridge of his nose. "Listen, lady. I don't know what that is."

"Ignorance does not excuse a crime," she said sternly. Giving the kneeling prisoners a final glance, she sniffed and said, "Trespassing on our sacred lands is forbidden. Let the Dragon decide your fate. Canary them all."

The Talons all shouted, "Yes, Mistress!"

She nodded to her large companion. The brute gave James a searing glare before making his way over. The woman leaned down and whispered into the brute's ear at the stairs before pointing the staff at Peter's body. The man gave it only a cursory glance and nodded before they went up the stairs.

Once they'd disappeared through the door and it was shut, chaos erupted again. Shouts and chanting threatened to deafen James as he rushed to get a hold of Peter's body before it was dragged away into the crowd, but Talons held him back, and he lost sight of the old man. Tears poured from his eyes as the dam burst. *You were a good man, Peter. You deserved better than this.* His eyes burned as the Talons pushed him to a side door. *Everyone will know what you did, what you sacrificed, today. And maybe, someday, Elizabeth will forgive me.*

They were marched to a small brick building outside the factory with crude drawings of birds painted on a sign above the door. The press of bodies was missing from the side street, but the air wasn't any less suffocating.

"Big fucker, ain't you?" a Talon said, eying him.

"Least as big as the boss. You see them glaring at each other?" said another Talon.

"Can't believe the old fella touched him. Then this fucker made him bleed," said the first. "Don't know why they ain't crippling him. Maybe the Mistress's in a good mood?"

"Surprised they didn't waste him," another Talon added.

"Probably thinks he'll be useful. Big as he is, he's Canary stock, for sure. See how he was crying? A big ol' softy. Boss would've ripped him apart." The Talon laughed.

James let the tears dry on his cheeks, doing his best to ignore them.

A fourth Talon said, "Might be too big for the mines."

All four shrugged, and one said, "Not our problem."

Inside the one-room building, Marcus lay on the ground, his eyes closed, and Brian felt along his leg. The boy's knee had doubled in size, and he moaned every time the Cutter touched it. *At least he's alive*, James thought. Ryan was gripping Nathaniel's shoulder, who looked on the brink of pissing himself and muttering under his breath. James's friend was doing his best to calm him down, but there was little left to reassure him with. The crew had lost hope. Some openly wept.

Talons packed inside with them, filling up what little space was left. Their stink was overpowering. A heavily scratched wooden desk furnished the room. Behind it was an older man with wild gray hair and a pair of cracked glasses that sat slightly askew on his nose. By comparison, he looked to have had a bath in the last decade, though his clothes were stained. "That everyone?" he asked, leaning back in his chair.

"Yes, Inspector. Mistress said to canary them," said a Talon closest to the desk.

"Hmmm, yes," the man looked over the crew and frowned at Marcus. "He able to walk?"

A Talon next to Brian gave the Cutter a shove with his boot and pointed to the desk. "Walk?" Brian said, shaking his head. "No. That beast broke his leg, you see, not to mention what he did to his head and back."

Murmurs broke out around the room, but the Inspector raised his voice over them. "Now, gentlemen, refrain from acting on your very violent instincts. At least until they're out of my office." Then to Brian, he said, "It's best you don't insult The Claw." The Inspector pushed the glasses back up his nose. "Doesn't work out well. Never has."

Brian swallowed, glanced at the leering Talons, and nodded. "M-my apologies."

"Infirmary him." Inspector snapped his fingers. A Talon unlocked the chain from Marcus's neck and grabbed him by the leg, dragging him back outside. Eugene tried to follow but was held in place. Brian watched the boy go, a look of defeat on his face.

Looking at the Cutter, guilt wormed its way through James's grief. If only they hadn't stopped at his village, Brian and the rest of the villagers would have been left alone, their lives going on as usual. James would have to right this wrong, somehow.

"Now, the rest of you," Inspector said and unrolled a scroll of papers. James caught sight of the Dragon symbol branded on the back of his hand as he did. The documents were maps marked up with weird symbols. "Need some canaries up at Eck..." The Inspector divided the men up.

Luckily, Ryan ended up in James's group, though Nathaniel was separated into another with Eugene. The Inspector rolled the papers back up and placed them in a drawer when he was done. He looked around the room and raised an eyebrow. "Anything else?"

The crew was shoved back out into the street.

Empty carts waited for them down a cracked avenue between the warehouses. Mounted on thin horses, Talons watched them approach. Wagon drivers called out destinations, and the crew was unchained and separated.

Rubbing at his neck, James was glad to be free of the chains. However, that happiness faded quickly when he climbed into the back of a wagon and saw the manacles bolted to the floor. A Talon roughly locked his ankles into place, pinching skin as he did. There were scratch marks surrounding the bolts by his feet, the kind left by someone trying to pry them loose with their bare hands. Dark stains had soaked into the wood, probably left by whoever had been trying to free themselves.

Ryan had a grim expression beside him. "How does the dragon judge us?" he asked a Talon on horseback. The response was a laugh followed by a whistled bird call. Ryan muttered to James, "Bloody loons, yeah?"

"I don't think they're as daft as they're putting on." A *whoop* interrupted him, and the wagons rolled down the street. "There's an organization to all this, and what did my father always say about organization?"

It took Ryan a moment to think, then he grinned. "Organizations lead to routines. Routines lead to patterns, and…"

"Patterns can be broken," James finished.

PATIENCE

James needed to sleep. He was physically and emotionally exhausted. But it didn't help that the wagon rocked violently as they drove over rocks, fallen branches, and large holes along the road. After a while, he believed the wagon driver was doing it intentionally. In the distance, the sky gradually shifted color from charcoal black to a hazy red, and as they continued, he realized they'd still been under the smog from the Cult's smokestacks.

"Something happened awful happened to these people. I almost feel sorry for them," James heard himself say out loud and then glanced around to make sure his captors hadn't overheard.

Ryan whispered, "Noticed there's no women. Well, except for that mistress of theirs, yeah?"

"That would be the first thing you'd notice," James sighed, then smiled. He'd always been able to rely on his friend to get him through the challenging times. Ryan acted like an idiot, but he knew what he was doing.

Ryan grinned. "If they're dirty like these blokes, I'll have nothing to do with them."

They held their breath to keep from laughing aloud, an oft-practiced habit from the war. Eventually, Ryan asked, "Seriously, though, where're they taking us?"

A wooden club, dented and well-used, slammed down between them. "Enough talking," a Talon riding next to their wagon said.

As they came out from underneath the oily clouds and into the ochre-colored light, the roads didn't improve. It was easier to breathe, though the air still smelled of fire and chemicals. The sun, a dull orb halfway up in the sky, was a welcoming sight. Strangely, the Talons averted their gaze from it, looking anywhere else but up in the sky.

After an hour, a fork appeared in the road, and one of the wagons went off to the left while they continued right. The only indicator of destination was a wooden sign. Whatever it said before had been scraped off and replaced with painted pictures and arrows. One direction pointed to wavey lines, and the other was a bunch of small circles in a pyramid-like pile. James's wagon was headed for the pile.

James bumped Ryan's arm and nodded at the sign.

Ryan raised an eyebrow and shrugged.

Careful not to be overheard, James whispered, "No words. Didn't see any on the map either."

Ryan shrugged again. "So?"

"Odd?"

Ryan shrugged a third time, and James gave up.

As the day progressed, they traveled through abandoned villages and towns. Most were overgrown, but a few had been burned. Occasionally, they'd roll by a populated town, but much like at Brian's, the villagers kept out of sight. They passed by a couple of Talon camps along the road, belching thick smoke. Bird calls and mocking laughter greeted them.

James found Nathaniel staring at him from the wagon ahead late in the afternoon. He didn't blink, just stared at him. And then James realized what Richard had meant when he'd told Nate to stop pretending. Nate was scared, but more than that, he'd been scared since the very beginning. That was why he'd spent most of his time below deck on *The Ophelia*. He feared the outside world. Even with all his brave talk, he'd been terrified of leaving England. And somehow, James had missed it and suddenly felt pity for the bastard. Nate's wagon veered away at the next fork, and James gave him a reassuring nod but got nothing back from the soldier in return.

At night, lights dotted the hillsides, and the world seemed more alive in the darkness than during the day. The mood of the Talons improved when the sun went down. They laughed and talked more openly. Here and there, James caught bits and pieces of stories, mostly about chasing people. The word "prophet" was mentioned a few times, which he found interesting.

With his chin tucked against his chest and snoring loudly, Ryan had managed to fall asleep sitting up. It reminded James of the time Crown troops had been searching for them in the next building over, and Ryan had found the only bed in a bombed-out hotel that hadn't been damaged. He'd slept like a baby while James and the rest of the squad waited hours for the soldiers to lose interest.

For several days, they traveled, mostly at night. Occasionally, the prisoners were fed stale bread, but it wasn't enough to keep their stomachs from growling. Going to the bathroom was an ordeal in and of itself, a careful balancing act of sticking your ass off the side of the cart while the man across from you held your hands to keep you from losing your footing.

The journey ended when the wagon rounded a hill and entered a camp of large bonfires. James prodded Ryan, who woke with a start from a sound sleep. "Where are we?" he shouted.

"Your cage, little canary," replied a Talon guard with a smirk.

"What's all this about canaries?" James asked.

"Orintator's work." The Talon spat before riding ahead.

The bright flames revealed slanted buildings, covered in rust and holes, jutting out from the hills that surrounded the camp. Broken-down conveyor belts, left to rot, dangled from a few openings in the old buildings. The wagon rocked on damaged and neglected train tracks that crisscrossed the ground. All of this was centered around a wide-cut hole at the base of the hill—a dark, cavernous mouth that echoed pickaxes striking rocks. Close to the opening was a shack made of corrugated metal sheets, a crude bird cage painted above the single door.

The wagon stopped by the cage building, and the Talons freed the prisoners and commanded them to get inside. After the last of them was in, a Talon stuck a head through the doorway and grunted, "Orintator, new canaries."

"Yes, yes, I can see that. I'm not blind," a gruff voice yelled from the back.

The Talon grumbled, "Welcome to Eck, birdies." And slammed the door shut.

Chains scraped against the outside of the door, sealing them inside, and after a solid shake to test it, James felt more like the prisoner he'd been before.

Looking around his new cage, James was glad that it was at least more spacious than the one he'd left back in England. Several oil lamps let him see that at least a hundred men could have been housed here, but he counted only a couple dozen. They were filthy but hearty. *At least we'll be fed*, he thought. Standing in small groups or laying on rags, they gawked at James. He was used to that reaction, especially after his growth spurt at thirteen.

"All you come back here," called the gruff voice.

James shrugged, and together they shuffled toward the voice. It was darker on the far side of the room, but something sparked as another lamp was lit, and an aged hand placed it on a small table next to a wheeled chair. The first thing he noticed about the Orintator was that he was close to Peter's age. The old man had given up on shaving, and a dirty white beard flowed down his chest. He was bald, and it was hard to tell which were liver spots and which were dirt. The second thing that stood out was his missing legs, just past the knees. But like the Talons outside, the Orintator had the dragon symbol branded onto his forehead.

The Orintator saw him staring at the brand, and his craggy hand went up and rubbed his forehead. "Guessing that's still there," he said. He winked at James and cackled. "Tall son of a bitch, aren't you?" He wiggled his stumps. "Got a couple of feet on me at least." Showing his chipped yellow teeth, the old man cackled again.

Another loon. James sighed and asked, "You're the Orintator, I assume?"

"What's that? Speak up," The old man turned his head and held a hand up to an ear.

"Are you the Orintator?" James shouted.

Eyes wide, the legless man said, "My God, ain't heard an accent like that in years. Sound just like him."

"Like whom?" James shouted the question.

"Enough with that racket. I hear just fine. Was seeing if you could listen, is all," the Orintator said with a wrinkled grin. "And you sound like Jeremiah." He waved his hands around in the air. "The fella that started all this. Take it you're from England?"

James nodded, his curiosity piqued. "Is he still around?"

"Dead about forty years now. His son sounded a bit like you too, not his grandkids, though," the Orintator shook his head, "But you ain't here for stories. Got to tell you what's expected."

Coming to stand beside James, his arms crossed, Ryan said, "They keep calling us canaries, yeah? What's that mean?"

"Ever heard of a canary in the coal mine, son?"

Ryan shook his head.

"I have," said one of the crewmen. "Miners would bring birds down with them to see if they could breathe. If the bird died, they knew they had to leave."

The old man nodded. "You're called canaries because you're the lucky ones that get to see if the new holes they blast open are safe."

"That's it? We're mine inspectors?" James asked.

"Yep, that's it. But while you're all waiting your turn, you get to sort the crap they dig up." The old man strained to pick up a sack next to his chair. "You boys know what coal looks like?"

"Sure. We've coal in England," Ryan said. "Well, at least we did…"

The old man let the sack drop to the ground, sending a small surge of black dust into the air. "Good. Less work for me. Swear that bag gets heavier every season." He raised a dirty cloth and mopped his brow, leaving muddy streaks behind.

James arched an eyebrow. "So menial labor with the chance of death, that sum it up?"

"Sounds about right."

"And everyone else in here are canaries too?" James asked, sticking a thumb over his shoulder.

"That they are. Sentenced here by some high-up muckety-muck. You all got to test a certain number of tunnels before you get to go free. And that depends on your crime. What'd you all do?"

James said while looking at the crew and shrugging, "Sailed without permission, I guess."

Most shrugged back.

"Hmm. Punishments keep changing every year." Orintator picked up a worn leather book from the table and opened it, his face close to the pages as he turned them. Eventually, he found what he was looking for and nodded to himself. "Trespassing. Four tunnels each. That ain't so bad. Most of you will probably make it." The old man put the book on his lap, and James saw similar drawings to the ones on the signs along the road.

"A woman, all in black and covered in weird symbols, said something about the dragon deciding our fate. What's that about?" James asked. Voices murmured behind him, but the other canaries looked elsewhere when he turned.

The old man closed the book and said, "Ahh. So, you've met our Royal Highness, eh? A real believer, that one. The gases that seep up from below are the Dragon's Breath, and if It decides you're worthy, It spares your life."

"You one of them? A believer?" Ryan asked, tapping the middle of his forehead.

The old man rubbed the brand again. "No. It's only a childhood fantasy turned reality, but I knew which way the winds were blowing."

Ryan let out a frustrated growl. "Everyone we've met since coming here has acted like we know what they bloody mean. You do realize we're new here, yeah? I don't have the foggiest idea what you are going on about. You lot have stalked and chased us, destroyed our ship, killed the captain, and sentenced us to possible death. And even if we do survive, I'm sure there'll be something awful waiting for us!"

James put a hand on Ryan's shoulder, squeezing it to quiet his friend.

"Bollocks to this," Ryan growled and brushed the hand off.

"Oh, I'm sorry, did you want me to speak to someone in charge for you? Wake up, son. Ain't nothing right in this world anymore since The Burn came." The Orintator's brow furrowed as his lips tightened into a sneer.

James held his hands up, trying to calm the situation. "I'm sorry. Ryan gets a bit hot-headed."

The Orintator mopped his brow again, shaking his head. "Around here, running his mouth like that ain't a good idea. Take it from me. I'd know." He thumped one of his legs.

"Wait. Are you saying this was done to you? By your people?"

"My people? Them assholes ain't been my people for fifteen some-odd years. Been in this tin box since they crippled me and stuck me with this shit job. Everyone's got to be useful. That's their first law." The old man spat on the ground.

'Don't know why they ain't crippling him,' the Talon had said after the sentencing. This could have been James's fate.

The old man was as much a prisoner as he was. "I just got out of a cell after ten years. Same goes for Ryan. So, as you can imagine, we're a bit at odds with our current situation."

The Orintator narrowed one eye and looked up at James, cocking his head. "What'd you all do?"

"Attempted to overthrow the monarchy."

The old man stared for a good ten seconds before asking, "Do what now?"

"It's a long story. But what I need to know right now is what the hell is going on here?"

Orintator scratched his chin through the beard, eyeing them briefly, then nodded. "It's a long story. You might want to get some rest."

"I'm fine." James held out a hand. "I'm James, by the way. James Barlow."

They shook, and the old man said, "Orintator's what they call me. Real name's Patrick Flanagan. Friends used to call me Paddy."

James introduced the rest, and Ryan apologized for his outburst while shaking the man's hand. With no other chairs in the room, they sat on the dusty floor.

Paddy smiled thoughtfully. "Funny, this is sort of like what started it all. A man telling a story to a scared bunch of kids," he said. "Well, anyway, I had a job down in Phoenixville at the iron works. The floor boss was Jeremiah Hollow. He was a good man. But he hadn't always been a *good* man if you gather my meaning. Looking back on everything, I'd reckon he was trying to make up for something he'd done." The old man paused a moment, and his gaze went distant.

James coughed, and Paddy shook his head as if waking himself up.

"Anyhow," he continued. "I was fifteen when The Burn started raging through the cities and towns. It came from somewhere down south. Blame was being slung on the Rebs and the Union, and neither seemed to really know. But I think, with all that looting and killing, we stirred up something we should've left alone because at the beginning of sixty-two, there was a world, and at the end, there weren't.

"I didn't have anywhere else to go, and neither did most of the children working at the ironworks. When everyone else had fled, Jeremiah had stayed behind with his boy Dustin. He'd lost his wife sometime before. Since I was the oldest, by at least five years, I was in charge of helping him watch after the kids."

When one of the crewmen yawned, the old man snapped, "I ain't boring you, am I?"

"No, no," the crewman said, sitting up straight.

"Good," Paddy said, giving the man side-eye as he continued, "Jeremiah did his best to look out for us. Whenever someone came snooping around the factory, he'd scare them off. He was big and strong, and it didn't take more than a look at him before you were running for the hills." He laughed and dabbed at his eye with the dirty cloth.

"Even with him, I'll admit, we were all scared. And by all, I mean the twenty-seven kids and myself. But if you want to know how all *this* started," Paddy said and touched his forehead. "It began when one of the girls saw the fires spreading from Philadelphia. Jeremiah had sat us all down and figured the best way to keep the younglings distracted was to tell them a story. So, he spun a yarn about dragons and how they'd all been driven out of England by St. George. He'd said those dragons had to go somewhere, and one came here, to America."

"Wait," interrupted Ryan, "Wasn't George the one that killed all the dragons? Are you thinking about St. Patrick and the snakes? That's Ireland, mate."

With an exasperated sigh, Paddy said, "It's not my story, son. I'm only telling you what he said."

Ryan grumbled a response and looked down at his hands.

"As I was saying, we all sat around listening, and Jeremiah said how the war had woken up the dragon. The plague came from its anger, and the cities were burning from its fiery breath. The kids ate it up, even as it scared them to tears. Jeremiah said we were safe inside the iron works. All the metal and coal made us smell like dragons. You look like bright lads. I probably don't have to tell you that's why the Talons cover themselves in soot and grease, do I? He encouraged me to play along. Said it would make the kids happy. So, I did.

"As time went on, and we'd go out hunting, we'd come across other survivors. Jeremiah only invited the ones who had children back to the factory. He'd said that if they were protecting kids, they had to be good people."

After a heavy pause, Paddy said, "They didn't all end up being good people, but Jeremiah always made sure the children were safe. *Always*." The old man blinked and shook his head before continuing. "And he'd keep telling the same story to the children. They grew up believing the dragon was out there and needed to be feared.

"You ever hear something for long enough that you start to believe it?" Paddy didn't wait for anyone to answer. "After eight years of this, most of the parents began to think it was real too. Not many of them could read. Most were laborers or farmhands. And for all they knew, maybe it had been a dragon that killed the world.

"But we weren't sad about it. We'd built our own little world right at the ironworks. We had a few hundred people living there, and we all worked together. Everyone had a job. That was the most important thing. If you didn't, you weren't thinking of protecting the children. Even if they weren't really children anymore, they'd grown up. But there were always more coming along."

"People were surviving out in the woods after so many years?" one crewman asked.

Paddy stared at the sailor for a few seconds, then asked, "Do I need to explain how kids are made, son?"

"No," the crewman answered sheepishly, his face turning red.

"Now stop with the interruptions. I'd like to get this done before morning," the old man grumbled. "Yes, we were plugging away at regrowing the population. Even had a son of my own, once." Paddy grew quiet again for a moment, then shook his head. "But Jeremiah still managed to find lost children or useful survivors whenever he went out. So, I guess you were right. I'm sorry I snapped at you. Just tired is all." He nodded to the crewman.

"While he was away, Dustin would take his turn at telling the story, but he added his spin to it. The way he told it, it was like the dragon had chosen us to survive, that we were special. I remember the old saying that the meek would inherit the earth, but Dustin twisted it to 'the hard workers would rule the earth.'

"'The Dragon gave the land to Its true people,' he'd say. He'd been a quiet boy, but his tongue was as slick as any man selling snake oil by the time he was sixteen. He'd shout stories of the Dragon from the catwalks as the people worked in the factory. It inspired, and they'd work harder. Dustin had us decorate the place with dragon sculptures. It was hard work, but we were stronger for it. And every time Jeremiah came back with more survivors, there'd be more children for Dustin to charm.

"Some of the people he'd found had been Schuylkill Rangers. That was a gang from the old days. Jeremiah knew them and trusted them, so he'd told them about what he had going back at the ironworks. We were lucky, I think. If anyone other than Jeremiah had been in charge, the gang would've taken over Dragon's Rest. That's what we'd started calling the place.

"These Rangers were still having it out with the Plug Uglies holed up in the old city. Jeremiah got them to make peace, leave the squalor and ruin they'd created, and join us back at the ironworks. It wasn't a perfect fit, some died, but Jeremiah got them to work together in the end. It felt like we'd have a chance to build something wonderful, but it all changed when Dustin began the branding." The old man rubbed his forehead. "Jeremiah wanted to put an end to the dragon malarky, but Dustin wouldn't listen.

"At eighteen, he was just as big as his pa, and their shouting matches were heard all over the factory. Until one night, we found Jeremiah's body crumpled—" he stopped for a moment, letting out a slow breath, "crumpled in a heap on the factory floor." Paddy's eyes teared over, and he wiped at them with the handkerchief. He coughed and continued in a steadier voice. "Likely, it was he fell from the catwalk. No one said anything. 'We don't kill if they're here to work,' was what Jeremiah had always said. But we all knew what really happened.

"After putting Jeremiah in the ground, Dustin declared himself the 'Second Head of the Dragon.' He'd said his father had been the first. These days they just call Jeremiah the Prophet." The old man frowned and sadly shook his head.

"So, if Dustin's in charge, who was that woman then?" Ryan asked.

The old man's voice had grown tired. "No, Dustin died about five years back. That woman is the Third Head of the Dragon, Sarah Hollow, his daughter. Did she have a big guy with her?"

His lips tightening, James said, "Yes."

"That's her twin brother. The Claw of the Dragon, Render Hollow. General of the Talons."

"Twin? Thought twins were supposed to look alike, yeah?" Ryan said. "Like Nate and Richard? He's a mountain compared to her." He was met with blank expressions.

"Talons, Claw, Head. This is all insane." James closed his eyes, rubbing the bridge of his nose.

"You wanted to know what happened here," Paddy reminded him. "Can't blame me if you don't like the answer."

"How long do we have to wait around before running the tunnels?" Ryan asked.

"You're going to have to be patient. Sometimes days, maybe even weeks, can go by before they open new shafts," Paddy said with a yawn.

Patient. James opened his eyes and stared off into space. He envisioned the Claw killing Peter, and the rage boiled inside him again. Letting out a slow breath, he regained control. If there's one thing these Dragon cultists would learn, James could be a very patient man.

THE HUNTERS IN THE WOODS

In the darkness of the shore, hidden among the trees, Liz watched *The Ophelia* sink beneath the surface. Cold and wet from the tiring swim, tears trickled down her cheeks. All of her grandfather's dreams were destroyed before her eyes, and she was helpless to do anything to stop it. Not long after the cannons faded, one of the two ironclads turned upriver, leaving the other behind. Someone pulled gently at her shoulder.

Okeny had returned.

Looking back, she saw Richard hefting his pack and readjusting his rifle. Jessica sat on the ground close by, looking at the remaining ship in wide-eyed horror. A wave of fear crashed over Liz as she thought of her grandfather, and her hands began to shake. *Please, James, be right.*

The ironclad's engine chugged to life and moved toward the shore.

Far less gently this time, Okeny pulled Jessica to her feet. He said, "They won't be able to dock here. The shore's too rocky. I spotted an old boat launch half a mile down river. We need to stay ahead of them. Leave nothing behind."

Liz wiped the tears from her face, steeling herself, and picked up her pack. When Okeny handed her a pistol belt, she stared at the gun—tied into its holster with a string—for several seconds before taking it. Its weight made the situation more real for her and more dangerous.

"Don't use it unless there's no other choice. There's no telling who'd hear it and be drawn to the sound," Okeny said and hurried out of the trees.

Not wanting to say goodbye to *The Ophelia*, she didn't look back and followed the others. She had a promise to keep. *Maybe the Crown will get here in time to save grandfather.*

Ahead of her, the shape of Richard bobbed above the tall grass in the clearing past the trees. Then, off to their left came chanting—the same as what they'd heard come from *The Ophelia*. Her first instinct was to run in the opposite direction. And she almost did if Richard hadn't stopped short in front of her.

"What is it?" she whispered.

A shush was her only answer before she was pulled into the grass. She hadn't even heard Okeny come up beside her, but now he was on top of her, his finger to her lips. Richard dropped to a knee, bringing Jessica down with him. The young woman had been so quiet since they'd reached the shore that Elizabeth wasn't sure if she knew what was going on.

From the direction Liz had almost run toward, she heard faint shouts, growing louder until they were nearly on top of them.

"What's it now?" said a loud voice, close to where the group was hiding.

"Dunno. Something's got the river camp hunting," shouted a reply that was further away.

"Heard cannon fire," said a third voice.

"We sure they ain't just drunk again?" the first said.

"It ain't an Initiation Day. What'd they be celebrating?"

A long, spine-chilling screech called out in the night, and the men stopped talking. A shrilling response came from the direction of the chanting. One of the men responded with a shorter screech, and another grunted.

"Bah. Let's go, boys."

Liz could hear their running feet. They sounded so close.

"Let's be quick. I can smell rain on the wind. Didn't bring my leathers."

Somehow, the huddled group went undiscovered. Liz remained where she lay, with Okeny's hand on her mouth for what felt like an eternity before he let her go. He motioned to stay low, and they continued through the field on their hands and knees. Every time Liz's hand snapped a twig, she expected the night to come crashing in on her.

Before long, they were back in the trees, moving downhill. The chanting was louder, almost parallel to the direction they were headed. Liz couldn't see anything moving in the woods, but that did little to reassure her. Again, she was that frightened child, scared of the battles raging in the streets, hiding in the basement each night. Fear made her angry. She'd worked so hard not to be afraid anymore, to be able to sleep a whole night without waking up screaming. She fought the urge to curl up in a ball and cry and followed Okeny.

It was dark in the woods, with only shafts of silvery moonlight to show them the way. They continued until they came across a well-worn path, clear of trees. Okeny knelt and ran his hands along the ground, then stood and looked in both directions. He motioned for the others to sprint across and back into the woods.

Liz whispered, "Wouldn't it be safer to stay on the path?"

"Man made this. Animals avoid it. We use it, we'll be caught. We go through the woods, and it might look like a large animal passing through," he whispered back.

This was a different Okeny from the one she'd met in England. There'd been a sadness about him, almost like he was lost and without direction, but when he smiled, it lit up the room. And his laugh was contagious. But now, he seemed surer of himself. Elizabeth could see why the Crown had sent him on this journey. *James is wrong. This isn't a suicide mission. It can't be.* She crossed the path and waited with the others as Okeny used a branch to cover their tracks. Curiously, he walked up the path for a bit before hopping off and making his way back to them so they could continue.

Right before dawn, it began to drizzle. The chanting faded as the drizzle turned into a steady rain. Liz felt relief from both the quiet and the shower, but Okeny wouldn't stop just because the chanting did. "They'd been giving away their position with all that racket. Now there's no way of knowing where they are."

Jessica still had the look of a woman on the verge of shrieking, but she followed Okeny's orders, so at least she was aware of what was going on. *We need to get her home. Quickly,* Liz thought. *More for our safety than hers.*

Crouched down behind the cover of a large fallen tree, Liz asked, "Do you know where we are? Are we headed in the right direction?"

Jessica stared at Liz for a few seconds, then croaked, "I live in Lums." And something woke up in Jessica, and she looked around. Then, tilting her head back, she felt the rain on her face, and a smile crept across her lips.

"Do you know how to get there from here?" Okeny asked.

Jessica nodded and pointed to the northwest, the fear evaporating from her voice, "It's not far from here. We will have to cross the canal, but they don't toll that bridge."

Okeny placed a reassuring hand on her shoulder. "We'll get you safe. I gave my word."

Jessica patted the hand. "I believe you, Mr. Okeny."

Richard, who had been keeping watch, crawled over. "Still no sign, but we should most likely proceed."

"Ain't got to worry," Jessica said. "They don't like the rain much."

"Why?" Liz asked.

Jessica stood and splashed her foot in a small puddle. "They're not fond of washing."

Even with her reassurances, Okeny urged them to keep quiet while he scouted ahead. He came back periodically, showing them the path to take with the most cover. They arrived at the canal just as the rain ended and the sky cleared. The sun was still low, drawing long shadows between the trees. Morning mist swirled up from the crumbling stone and patches of lush moss that grew along the man-made waterway. A few yards away was a wooden bridge made from split logs.

"Needed to build a new bridge two years ago. You see, the old one got destroyed, and we lost three good men from an accident during its construction." Bitterly, Jessica added, "All because we didn't get our tithe ready on time."

"Tithe?" Okeny asked.

"Lumber. Everyone has to be useful, and everyone needs to pay," she spat.

Scratching at a bleeding bug bite on his cheek, Richard said, "And what is it you're paying for?"

"Protection. They say they keep the area safe, and it's—oh, how do they put it?" She thought a moment, then said, "'Through our work, the Dragon is appeased.' Nothing but a bunch of thugs, if you ask me."

"Dragon?" Liz asked, missing a step and tripping on the bridge. She caught herself before she fell.

"They believe a dragon destroyed everything or some such nonsense," Jessica said. She worked her arm through Liz's, and together they made their way across the bridge.

"They? You mean the ones chasing us?" Okeny said.

"You see any other crazies running around?"

Okeny gave a polite shake of his head.

"They got all sorts of weird ideas. At least some of it makes a little sense, but I draw the line at the dragon business."

"Had you ever believed?" Liz asked.

"No. Never did." Jessica frowned. "One of them comes by every couple of years. Makes all the children sit down around him and tells a story about the dragon. The ones that believe it go with him. We never see them again."

"Not that I believe it either, but why didn't you?"

Jessica shrugged. "Didn't make much sense. My grandda had told me about what had happened during The Burn and never once mentioned a dragon."

There was an old rusty sign on the other side of the canal. Most of the words had faded, except for one: *Lums*. "This way," Jessica said and took a path into the woods.

Liz looked back across the bridge to dark shadows within the tall, dense trees. Whoever those men were, they were still out there. Why were they chasing them? What do they want? Okeny had the same questions on his face, looking at the same trees, so Liz asked them aloud.

He shook his head and said, "I really can't say. What troubles me most is how they knew we left the ship." And followed Jessica and Richard on the path to Lums.

As the sun rose higher in the sky, the previous night's terrors faded to a general unease. The weather was chilly, with a light breeze. Birds chirped merrily in the branches. From somewhere up ahead, they heard the sound of axes cutting into trees. It grew louder until they found four men taking turns swinging their broad axes, beating out a steady rhythm. They were so wrapped up in their work they gave no notice of the passing group.

Further on, they came to a large clearing with several low buildings spread out along the forest's edge and a glistening pond just through the trees on the opposite side. The buildings had started as old storage sheds, but they'd been worked on and expanded over the years. Porches had been built, extensive gardens added, and one had a sign of a frothy mug hanging by the door. Women were working the gardens with the help of a few older men. It should have been a lovely, peaceful moment, but the way the villagers stopped and stared made Liz uncomfortable.

"Most'll be out in the forest cutting wood, like Francis and his boys back there," Jessica said with a smile.

"They'll be glad to know you're here, I'm sure. Now, is there someone here who could give us directions to Washington?" Okeny asked.

Jessica frowned. "You're thinking about leaving already?" she asked.

"If any of these dragon people find us... You saw what they did to Brian's village...," Liz said.

Jessica waved the words off. "You've nothing to fear during the day."

Liz shook her head, fighting off the guilt she'd been holding onto. "I'm afraid we can't stay. We've got to send word back home."

"I heard you all talking about that. What'd James mean about a deal?" Jessica asked.

Neither of Liz's companions seemed to know how to respond, so she gave it a shot, "I-it's not important. He's worried about his payment. Honestly, we'd just like to let them know we're safe."

"How're you supposed to do that?" Jessica asked. "England looked awfully far away on the map. Hell, I couldn't even find Lums on it when I'd look."

Liz looked to Okeny for help, but the Black man shrugged. So, she said, "Do you know what a telegraph is?" Seeing the confusion on Jessica's face, Liz explained how the old world had a way to send messages over long distances through wires and electric pulses.

After the explanation, Jessica seemed intrigued. "And you expect them wires to still be connected all the way back to England?"

Liz couldn't see the harm in telling Jessica the truth. "We know they aren't. But a… friend discovered how to send messages without a need for the wires to be connected. We only need one long enough to act as something called an antenna, to send the message to another wire across the ocean."

Richard coughed and whispered, "That's not what you told James."

Quietly, Liz said, "I know what I told him, but do you really think he'd believe me if I said we were magically sending the message through the air?"

"Point taken. Are you sure it works?" Stubble had left a faint shadow on his cheeks, and he scratched at the bug bite again.

"Reginald had worked on the problem for five years and assured me it would work. I've read his notes, and it makes sense to me." She dropped the pack she'd been carrying and pulled out a heavy wooden box. Inside the case was a small device with a knob and metal plate. On one side of the box was a hole. "That's where I put this," she held up a metal crank, "Turning it will generate current. But the most important part will be the wire for the antenna. It has to be long enough to send the signal. That's why he'd planned on taking the expedition down to Washington in the first place."

"Hey, Jessica!" A man came running over from across the clearing.

"Uncle Roger!" Jessica squealed when she was engulfed in a hug and swung around.

"What're you doing home, darling? Weren't expecting you back for at least another season." He had the arms of a man who swung an axe all day. Dressed simply in trousers and a wool shirt, he kept his brown hair tied back from his face.

After being put down by her uncle, Jessica said, "Something happened over at Cutter's Shore. These folks came by boat, and, well, they were spotted."

The man's smile turned into a frown. "Spotted, eh? Cutter make it out?" He turned to Liz and her companions, eyes lingering on Okeny.

Liz said, "I'm afraid not. He was taken with the rest of our crew."

Roger raised an eyebrow. "Never heard anyone talk like that. Where're you all from?"

"England."

Roger scratched the back of his head, looking confused. "Huh? Where's that?"

"Uncle, they've important business to get to and need to keep moving." Jessica placed a hand on his arm, imploring him.

Roger shook his head slowly. "Shame about the Cutter. Met him a couple of times when they'd let us cross over for surveying. Where're you trying to go? Washington? That around here?"

Jessica sighed. "Marble. They're talking about Marble, that old capital. Grand-da talked about it, don't you remember?"

Roger prodded the ground with the heel of his boot, looking down. "Sorry, darling. You know I'm not so good with the past, not when there's work to be done in the here and now. Why don't you introduce them to Fieldstone? I'm sure he'd know. Then after that, make sure you check in on your ma and sister. They'll be happy to know you're back."

"I will, Uncle." She gave his hand a parting squeeze before leading the way over to the building marked with the mug.

The hinges squeaked loudly when they entered the empty tavern. A short middle-aged man in a dirty apron over a stained shirt was cleaning a table with a rag on the room's far end. Sleeves rolled up and teeth clenched; he scrubbed hard on a particularly stubborn spot while wisps of blond hair dangled from his balding head.

Richard let the door slam behind him, and he threw the rag angrily at the table. "Shouldn't you all be out working?" Looking up, he said, "Jessica? Jessica O'Bannon? Shoot, what're you doing here?" He took in everyone else, and just like Jessica's uncle, his eyes lingered strangely on Okeny.

Before Jessica could answer, Liz stepped past her. "Are you Mr. Fieldstone?"

"That's a weird accent," he began.

With her hands on her hips, Liz said, "I could say the same. Do you know how to get to Washington?"

"Washington? Sure, but what's going on?" The man placed his hands inside the pocket of his apron.

"We've business down there, and we'd like to see it concluded as quickly as possible. Can you help us?" She asked, keeping her hand away from the pistol at her waist.

Jessica gave him a reassuring nod, which relaxed him, and he took his hands from the pocket. "Most people call it Marble these days on account of what's left. When I was a kid, my pa took me there once when I was a kid, back when you could move around a bit more freely."

"Would you be able to draw us a map? Or show us where we are on ours?" Liz walked over to him and spread out the map she'd brought from *The Ophelia* in one of the waterproof pouches.

The tavern owner leaned over and examined the paper while drumming a finger against the table. Eventually, he straightened and said, "Sure, but not with this. Size's all wrong." He then hurried behind the bar and pulled out a sheet of parchment and a stick of lead. He returned to the table and started drawing.

At the top of the page, he wrote the name "Lums" and drew lines leading south from there. He chuckled and, with a sly smile, said, "Don't tell the Cult I remembered how to write."

"Why can't you write?" Liz asked while she watched him work.

"It's against their scripture or something. Probably because none of them can read," Fieldstone said. "Now, let me alone while I do this."

Liz looked at Jessica, "They can't read?" The very idea shocked her more than she'd thought possible.

"That's what we think. Granted, no one's ever really asked a Talon if he could or not. But books aren't allowed here. Any village found with one gets disappeared."

"That's enough of that. I don't need you bringing them to my doorstep," Fieldstone huffed.

After apologizing, they left him alone.

Seated at another table, they relaxed and drank water from a pitcher Jessica had brought over. Liz didn't realize how tired she was until after she'd sat down and struggled to stay awake. Clearly, she'd lost the battle, as the next thing she knew, Fieldstone was laying the map down on their table.

"There. That ought to get you down to Marble. Keep in mind, it's been thirty years since I've set a foot out of Lums," Fieldstone said, looking at the map. "Probably take you a week, if I had to guess."

Liz stretched the sleep from her muscles and then studied the drawing. They'd have to head west and then veer in a south-westerly direction if it was accurate. Several rivers needed to be crossed as well.

From over her shoulder, Okeny was examining it along with her. He said, "If we can manage to avoid their patrols, it looks possible. Do you know how wide this river is?"

Without looking at Okeny, Fieldstone said, "I-it's been thirty years. I remember my pa and I using a raft to get across. Wasn't too wide, though."

Liz folded the map, placed it in the pocket with her own, and stood. "Thank you for your help and hospitality. We'll be getting out of your hair now."

Fieldstone smiled. "Well, Jessica likes you, so you can't be bad people. You all be careful out there. Not everyone's as welcoming as us folks here."

The sun was high in the sky when they left the tavern. Men had come back from their work out in the forest. Dirty and sweaty, they eyed Liz and her companions. More than one pointed at Okeny.

"We should leave before we cause any more problems," Richard said, his face hardening. Liz was glad she wasn't the only one who noticed how people had behaved around Okeny.

"Don't worry," Jessica said, "They don't mean anything by it. It's just they think Mr. Okeny's a Souther."

"A Souther?" Okeny asked.

As if it were apparent, she said, "People from down south. They're all supposed to look like you."

"Like me? What does that mean?"

Jessica looked a bit embarrassed. "Um, well, you got the same color skin as them. At least that's what I've heard." Too quickly, she added, "But I never met a Souther before yesterday. Not that you're a Souther. Seeing as you're from England and all."

Okeny sighed. "That would explain how they knew we'd left the ship. Someone must have spotted me on the deck when we arrived in the bay. This is my fault."

Liz frowned. "How come it has to be your fault, Stuart? Couldn't they very well be looking for the only woman aboard?"

Okeny rubbed his chin and nodded slowly. "Perhaps. But I suppose this isn't the time nor place for that debate. Our top priority is reaching Washington." He turned to Liz. "Do you require more rest? Should we stay the night?"

"If you're going to leave, you should do it now. There's still plenty of daylight left," Jessica said. Liz could tell Jessica didn't want them to go by the way she shuffled her feet and bit the side of her lip.

As tired as Liz was, her memory of the horrific chanting and night of terror prompted her decision. "I agree. We should put as much distance between us and… those people as possible."

Jessica asked everyone to stay a moment and went back into the tavern. While they waited, Okeny had them check their packs to make sure nothing had been lost or come loose. "The last thing we need is for a pan to fall out while we're trying to hide."

Richard kept an eye on the men from the forest as he went through his belongings. Assuming he was watching for danger, Liz said, "They seem harmless, but I think staring at them like that makes them uncomfortable." Richard's face went from pale to beat red within seconds, and he made of show of repacking his things.

Before Liz could ask what was wrong, Jessica came running back and handed her a sack. "Fieldstone wanted to give you this as thanks for getting me home safe," Jessica said, her smile genuine and kind. "Though, you'd never get him to admit it." She laughed.

Liz looked over at the tavern and caught a glimpse of the older man in the doorway before he quickly ducked back inside. Opening the bag, Liz saw a good helping of dried meat and crusty bread. "You'll have to give him our thanks."

Jessica smiled. Only a few hours ago, fear had taken this kind woman's voice away. However, that fear was now gone. But Liz remembered the flames of the last village she'd visited. "Are you sure everything will be fine after we leave?" Liz asked.

"I'm sure. Our tithe is paid on time. Honestly, I'm more worried about you," she said, her smile turning sad. "And your friends, of course. I hope James is right."

"So do I. Take care, Jessica." Liz clasped hands with the woman. "And try not to worry too much about us." Jessica nodded and headed over to a house near the tavern. She waved from the doorway before walking inside.

WANDERING

With no more good-byes left to be made, the three left Lums and followed a path down toward the pond, where they passed several young women washing clothes. Skirts hiked up to their knees and ankle-deep in the water; they scrubbed shirts against washboards. They looked up at the sound of someone approaching and froze.

Okeny elbowed Richard in the ribs and tried to point to the half-dressed women discretely. Walking behind him, Liz saw everything.

As they walked by, Okeny gave a wave and greeted them. "Ladies."

"Get a good enough look, or should we head back for another round?" Liz asked once they'd continued by them.

"Oh, uh…" Okeny began before he fell silent.

Men, she thought. But not all, Liz realized. Strangely enough, Richard had given the group barely a glance. Perhaps he believed they wouldn't pose much of a threat like the men back in the village. Or maybe it was something else…

Eventually, they exited the forest and entered a stretch of fields. It was in these grasslands that Liz's senses were overwhelmed. A small herd of deer at the top of a low hill, the skittering of squirrels through the grass, and the ever-present buzzing insects that flitted about stunned her. *The Crown was right,* she thought. She'd never seen so many animals in one place. Aside from the copious amounts of rats, there were hardly any left in England. Even what little fishing there was had dwindled.

After a good rain and the increasing heat, the air was growing humid. Above them, the sun, as if shining through brown colored glass, beat down on them with no shade in sight. The sky was a strange shade of sickly yellow, and the hot breeze carried smoke with it—a constant reminder of their danger.

It was an odd sensation of serenity and threat.

They were in an unfamiliar place with no idea what lay over the next rise. Okeny, his head constantly moving as he looked from the hills to the field ahead, she why he was here. Bringing up the rear, Richard watched their flank. James was right in sending them on this task, but why was she here? Because she knew how to splice together some wires? He had put a lot of faith in someone he barely knew. If she somehow messed up and couldn't send a report back, would the Crown go through with the executions? And if they do, would it be her fault?

This isn't what she'd signed up for.

When the Crown representatives first came to her and her grandfather and offered them five-hundred thousand pounds each to sail to America, she'd been quick to take the offer. Now, she wished she hadn't. *Grandfather didn't even care about the money, but when they said he'd get his ship back... Oh, did his eyes light up!* With a sigh, she thought of *The Ophelia*. To finally be sailing her had felt like a dream, but now she'd been sunk and left to rot. *Maybe she could be salvaged, just maybe...*

Liz was dragged from her thoughts when she felt someone grip her arm, stopping her. Blinking, she saw they'd come to a small bubbling creek. She didn't even remember hearing it until just now. *Dangerous,* she thought. *You can't keep making mistakes like this.* Okeny let her go with a disapproving look. She mumbled an apology.

Richard was already down in the small ravine, and the two scrambled down to join him as the path continued along the other side of the shallow water. Suddenly, Okeny pointed to a plume of black smoke at the top of a hill in the distance. Together, they dropped down below the rise.

Whispering, Okeny said, "We'll head north. Follow the creek for a while. No way to tell if that's a hunting party or another village. Can't chance it."

By the time Okeny raised a hand for them to stop, Liz's back was throbbing from being hunched over for so long. Working his way up the ravine, Okeny laid on his chest and slowly stuck his head up to get a better view. He stood, nodding back to them.

Stretching, Liz sighed with relief before climbing out of the creek. The black column had dwindled to just a speck on the horizon, but not taking any chances, they headed quickly across the open field and into a gathering of trees.

Deciding it was best to stay off possibly patrolled roads, Okeny found animal trails that led them in generally the right direction. They rested for a quick meal in the shelter of a large overhanging rock balanced on the edge of an outcropping. The meat gifted to them was salted and rubbed in some spice Liz had never tasted before. It was, in fact, divine. Taking her time, she chewed each piece until it was tender before swallowing.

As they ate, Richard continued to keep watch in the direction they'd come from. There was a nervousness to him, and she thought it was the strangeness of this place, the unease. At least, that's what had been bothering her the most.

Reminiscent of the old feudal system that had ruled Europe for centuries, the local population was sedentary and kept ignorant. Rumors and tall tales were accepted as truth. And Liz was beginning to believe it was that way by design, which meant someone had to be in charge. She'd have to add that in her report to England. Then she remembered a line from one of her books. "*A people without central leadership are far easier to conquer.*"

What would that mean for Jessica and her village?

Do I even tell the Crown about this...this cult?

Do they have the numbers to fight against our military?

James had thought there weren't as many of them as the locals believed, and she hoped he was right. But they'd already underestimated the Cult before...

The sun began to set as they continued through the forest. Bird calls turned into the twittering of bats flying overhead. Several strange animals—fur-covered round bodies with almost mask-like faces—walked across the path and chortled at them before running back into the shadows. Liz was as startled as the creatures until Okeny calmed her fears, telling her they were a native species to America called raccoons and harmless to humans.

She laughed as a cool breeze blew through the trees. It was a relief from the sweltering heat of early June. The weather was so different than back home, as was the odor. She'd grown up around the stink of garbage and human waste. At least on the blockade, she could get away from it for a while.

When she was young, and the war was still raging, she hadn't been allowed to leave her home, not even for school. Most children were homeschooled back then. The only time she'd ever socialized with other children was at church on Sundays. Her mother insisted they go. She'd been devoted to her faith and had believed God saw their bravery in chancing the journey from their home to the church. Of course, that ended after the church had been razed. No one knew which side had been responsible. And to those just trying to survive, it didn't really matter.

Liz stopped, and Richard walked into her. Angry at herself again for letting her mind wander, she hit her thigh. Richard politely apologized, even though he sounded more than a little annoyed. She responded with a terse nod before continuing up the path.

Okeny came to a halt just outside the remnants of another small village crowded among the trees. Thick ivy had wormed its way up every wall, the added weight making them buckle with time while a carpet of moss ate the paving stones. In the fading twilight, they carefully made their way off the path and moved among the old structures. Rusted pickaxes and shovels were stacked to one side of a large building, and Liz figured there'd been a mine nearby.

"Could be safe to spend the night here," Okeny said.

Having spent a whole day on the move, she couldn't help but agree. Not waiting for Okeny to pick a spot, she went over to the first house, climbed over a fallen door, and went in.

It was musty inside, and the ground was littered with small bones and scat. A patch of moss grew just beneath a hole in the roof, letting in a bit of light from the moon. She'd have preferred not to stay here, but it would be safer.

After scraping away a clean spot with her boot, she put down her pack and slid down the wall to sit. A warped desk rotted in one corner of the room, and in another sat a small, rusted heating stove by a filthy pile of hay and torn cloth. What was left of a table and chairs were scattered in the center. The others had come inside after her, but she could barely keep her eyes open by then.

She awoke abruptly with a start. Okeny was crouched in front of her, his face shadowed by the moonlight behind him. His hand was pressed against her mouth while he placed a finger to his lips, then pointed at his scarred ear. Heart pounding, she struggled to hear anything other than the thunder in her chest.

Closing her eyes, she focused.

Sticks cracked outside, and then footsteps.

Many footsteps.

Okeny leaned closer, placing his mouth to her ear. Breath hot against her skin, he said, "Don't move. Heard them earlier. Covered our approach."

Liz couldn't move her head, not with his hand still on her mouth, but she was able to look over at the doorway. The door had been replaced, convincingly hung from one hinge. Richard was there, back to the wall, gripping his rifle, ready for anyone who came through.

"Dragon?" Liz whispered through his fingers.

Okeny shrugged and removed his hand. "Too dark. No chanting."

Anxiously, they listened as whoever was outside stomped through the village and were getting closer. Liz closed her eyes and balled her fists until her knuckles ached. Something brushed up against the wall behind her. Next came a knock and then silence.

Minutes went by as everyone held their breath, then the footsteps moved away. Okeny waited a long time before he stood and quietly went over to Richard, patting him on the arm. The soldier relaxed, but only slightly. Slowly, Okeny leaned to look through a gap in the crooked doorway. Seconds passed before he whispered, "All clear."

Memories flooded back, sparked by a mixture of fear and relief. Liz tried to fight it, but it was too late. She remembered the explosions and gunfire that came at night the most. When it was too close to their house, her father would take her and her mother into the cellar to hide. He'd said they'd be safe. But then came the night they'd heard the front door crash in. People ran through their home, shouting and smashing furniture. Her father had told them to keep quiet while he crept up the stairs.

The last time she ever saw him, he'd looked back just before opening the cellar door. Hands reached through and dragged him away. Yelling and gunshots. Her mother screamed as she ran after him, only to be gunned down by a wave of bullets at the bottom of the stairs. Liz had sat, peeking out from the cabinet she'd been hiding in, staring at her mother's lifeless body for two days before her grandfather had found her. He carried her out of the cellar while keeping her face pressed into his shoulder. He wouldn't let her go until they were out on the street. She never learned which side had killed her parents.

Liz opened her eyes to Richard holding her hands. He had them in a firm grip, but it didn't hurt. "You're shaking," he said, sounding worried for her.

She swallowed, fighting back the tears and grateful for any human contact. After a moment, she let out a calming breath and gently pulled her hands from Richard's. "I... Thank you," she said quietly.

The soldier stood and took a step back, giving her room to get up. Slowly, she picked up her backpack and breathed a heavy sigh before rubbing her face. Her hand came back wet, either from tears or from sweat. She couldn't tell. She smiled to assure Richard that everything was all right and said, "Sounded like they came from where we're headed."

Okeny, still peering out at the empty village, said, "Seems so. Ten of them, at least. I don't think they're looking for us. They'd have searched these buildings, otherwise."

"Either way, we should quickly head in the opposite direction," Richard said and shouldered his rifle.

Okeny moved the door aside and listened for a few seconds before going out and holding it for the others. Quietly, he closed it and moved along the wall with Liz and Richard in tow. Stopping about where Liz had heard the knock, he knelt and rubbed a hand over the ground. Standing again, he said, "Whoever they are, they've a lot of gear. They left behind some deep footprints."

They passed through the outskirts of the village and continued west.

DEADLY MISTAKES

Liz began to sense a pattern: night was for the woods, and day was for the fields. Or at least that's what it felt like as they left the forest just as the sun began to rise. In front of them was another stretch of open land, occasionally interrupted by a hill or thicket.

Even with the map and a compass, Liz had no way of telling where they were but believed they'd hit a river at some point if they continued west. Fieldstone's directions said to follow the river northwest and cross at its narrowest.

Along with the sun came the heat. Insect buzzing grew louder as the heat increased, and by late morning everyone had shed at least one layer of clothing. She found it odd to see Richard without his red coat on. Even with little chance of coming across a commanding officer, he made sure to keep it tidy and clean. With the coat now stashed in his pack, he tugged at the sweat-soaked undershirt that clung to his chest.

In the midafternoon, they came across a long wooden fence. Gray with age, sections of it had warped and cracked, leaving wide gaps for anyone to pass through. A small distance from where they'd crossed the fence, they discovered a fort made from logs lashed together with rope. Parts of the outside wall had caved in, making it clear that no one had been here in a long time. Even so, they cautiously made their way over to two heavy-looking doors, still barred from the inside. A carved sign above it read: *No Diseased, Rebs, or Negros.*

"I've not studied American history all that much, but would that make this a Union fort?" Richard asked.

"I believe so," Liz said, nodding.

Richard looked puzzled.

Okeny peered up at the sign with disgust on his face and then spat on the ground.

Seeing his reaction, Liz said, "To misquote an Italian philosopher, 'Fear makes enemies of us all.'"

She went over to a collapsed wall and was greeted by the sight of two skeletons gripping rusted rifles in flesh-stripped fingers. Quickly, she backed away and grasped at her chest.

"What? What is it?" Okeny asked when the two men rushed to her side.

Liz rubbed her face with shaking hands until she had gained back some of her composure. "I'm sorry. I-I just wasn't expecting... For some reason, I had this foolish hope that we wouldn't see any of the dead."

"Ms. Stillman," Richard said. "I believe there will be quite a few more bodies before we've finished this journey."

Okeny agreed. "It's best to try not to see them as people." He sighed, and with a touch of sadness in his voice, he added, "That's how I was trained."

"I'll try," Liz let out a deep breath. "I can't imagine what it took to get through that awful war and still be sane."

Okeny nodded, eyes growing distant, and his hand went to his disfigured ear.

"I was too young to serve," Richard said. "However, veterans I've met rarely wanted to talk about what they'd done. They were just glad it was over."

Feeling as if she was intruding, Liz continued around the fortification. Around the side, her foot kicked something metal beneath the tall grass. Pushing it aside, she picked up a rusted can. Searching around, she found more as she continued until she was back at the entrance. Some distance away, Okeny called her over and pointed out old firepits dotting the field. Amongst them were scattered piles of rusty sabers and axes.

"Was there a siege?" Liz asked. The evidence pointed in that direction.

"I believe so," Richard said, crouched over the depression of a firepit while looking up at the fort. "The question is—who was on the outside?"

Okeny pointed at the sign. "My guess, one of them."

Just over the next rise was a gully littered with gray bones. Okeny surmised this was the dumping ground for the assaulting force. Amongst the half-buried bones were scarps of threadbare cloth. Long faded, some were still adorned with buttons. Richard pulled a few free and looked them over. Shrugging, he showed them to Liz.

One button was decorated with an eagle, its wings spread. The other only had three letters engraved on it. She took that one, rubbed some dirt off, and read aloud, "C.S.A."

"What is that?" Richard asked.

"'The enemy of my enemy is my friend,'" she quoted again.

"More from your Italian philosopher?" Richard asked.

She nodded.

He took the button from her before placing both with the scattered dead.

Liz felt uneasy after they left the fort. Over time, she realized what bothered her was the lack of other people. *This is what we'd been hoping for when we left England.* The Crown wanted a vast, empty continent, ready to be exploited. But Liz couldn't help but feel stifling loneliness. She'd been born and raised in London. People had packed the city out of fear of the rebels. The sounds and smells of city life could be deafening at times. But not here.

Here there was only stillness, only occasionally punctuated with fear and panic.

On the ocean, she had still been with her crew. But now, in these quiet rolling fields, she started to get homesick. On a whim, she asked, "If we were back home, what would you be doing?"

Richard took no time to answer. "Have either of you been to Simpson?"

"Simpson's Tavern? Can't say I have or are they finally letting women in?" Liz asked. Smiling, she was glad not to be the only one thinking of home.

"No, no, Simpson-in-the-Strand. My friends and I would drink there every Wednesday," Richard said. Frowning, he asked, "What day is it?"

Liz blinked. She had no idea.

"Thursday," Okeny said, ahead of them both. "And I've eaten there a few times. They served a good rabbit stew. Not sure what they really put in it, but it was good enough."

"I bet they've gotten themselves banned by now. They're a bit of a rowdy bunch, and if left on their own…" Richard quietly laughed, shaking his head.

"I was always fond of Newman's until their prices reached the point of ridiculousness. They had such wonderful pies."

Richard told them about the shops and theatres he'd frequent. "All Crown approved, of course," he added.

Liz was just content to listen.

Liz wasn't allowed to leave home during her early years, so most of her memories were of what she'd read about in the books her grandfather brought home. "He called it his granddaughter tax." She smiled while fighting back the tears. "He promised me he'd take me to see the places I'd read about, like France." She sighed. "The closest I ever got was the Blockade."

Okeny, spreading his arms to the empty grassland, said, "We all know you've read quite a bit about America. So, in my eyes, he kept that promise."

Liz only nodded, knowing her voice would break if she said anything, and she wouldn't be able to hold back the tears.

Lucky for her, Okeny began to tell them about his great-grandfather and great-grandmother. About how they'd fled slavers in Africa, found passage to Europe, and eventually settled in England. "They weren't the only refugees from Africa, of course, but it was such a strange place to them. At least they managed to find work and start a family." The Black man frowned a moment, then continued. "Only myself, my sister, and her daughter are left. I haven't seen her in years. She blamed the military for the war and disagreed with my decision to join the army." Okeny pulled up a few blades of grass and grew quiet.

Richard filled in the uncomfortable silence. "My father signed up Nate and I once we were of age, four years ago now. Even with the war being over, we had much to live up to. He was a local hero, after all. Have you ever heard of Hippolyte Kitts?"

When Liz and Okeny only shrugged, Richard seemed content. "We both excelled in our training. He'd accept nothing less from his sons. And he was very adamant that I had to come out tougher than when I went in." Richard's words were bitter.

"What about Nate? I'm sure he demanded the same of him," Liz said.

Richard shook his head. "Not Nate. Nate never let him down."

"What'd you do to let him down?" Okeny asked.

Richard sighed. "It isn't a matter of what I did, but rather what I am."

"And what's that?"

"Something he'd never want. Or be able to forgive," Richard said in a hushed voice, barely audible.

As evening fell, they finally spotted a river. Liz checked the map and could only guess this to be the river they had to cross while wishing Mr. Fieldstone had given them a few more landmarks to work with. The river was about half a mile across, and Liz was already tired from the day's march, so she eagerly agreed when Okeny suggested they rest before attempting to cross.

Scouting ahead, Okeny returned and shortly took them to the river's edge, where he'd found large boulders to hide behind. The companions sat with their backs to the hard stone with a good view of the river. But anyone on the other side would easily be able to see them. It wasn't ideal, but Okeny assured her it was safe enough.

With night settling in, Liz tried to calm her nerves by listening to the breeze and the leisurely flowing river. Next to her, Richard leaned his head against the rock with his eyes closed. Volunteering for the first watch, Okeny was crouched behind a smaller boulder, watching the field behind them. Liz tried to sleep, but out in the open like this, she just felt too exposed. The first few hours were spent staring at the twinkling stars. She even tried counting them but to no avail.

Before it was her turn to take watch, Okeny gave a soft hiss. Sitting up straight, Liz turned to his silhouette. He was nodding toward Richard. Liz reached over and shook the soldier's arm gently to wake him. He was immediately awake and alert, picking up his rifle, but remained silent.

Footsteps approached the boulders from where they'd been walking. As the sound drew closer, she could hear hoarse voices attempting to whisper.

"Can't be far now. Spotter got them crossing that field."

"Could've gone across the river."

"Nah. We'd still be hearing their screams if any of Theron's got a hold of them."

Knowing chuckles sent a shiver down Liz's spine.

One of them came closer to the boulder where Liz hid. After a moment, the sound of hissing against the rock followed a deep sigh and a warm liquid began to pool around her hand. The smell was horrid, and it took everything she had to keep from retching. A few seconds later, it stopped.

"You three head back into the field while the rest of us finish looking before the crossing."

There were grunts of agreement, and the footsteps split up.

Once enough time passed, Okeny signaled that it was clear. Liz had waited while her hand sat in a mixture of mud and piss. She could feel it under her nails, burning in the cracks of her dry skin. Liz felt the bile boiling in her throat and scrambled to the shore, not wanting to vomit on her friends. But would her retching give them away? She's never witnessed anyone throw up quietly.

Liz fought for control of her stomach, breathing in and out slowly. She used the coarse dirt of the riverbed to scrub her hand clean. The smell, however, would stay with her for a long time. Okeny came over, his expression hard to make out in the darkness, and stared at the river.

"They'll be looking for us over there too," Liz said, swallowing the last of the bile.

"Yes." The disgust in his voice made Liz forget her hand. "I didn't even see the one that spotted us. I'm sorry."

"It isn't your fault. You couldn't have known." She turned to him only to have him look away.

"Mistakes here could be a matter of life or death." He sighed.

"You've kept us alive this long. And you've got nothing to prove, Stuart. I don't want to hear any more sulking. Now, what is the plan?" She stood, put her hands on her hips, and looked down at him.

Shaking his head, he said, "I don't know. They're headed the way we need to go, and they have people across the river and more back the way we came."

"There'll be more at the crossing," Richard added, listening in as he watched the road.

Okeny's shoulders slumped as he nodded and sat down with his arms resting across his knees.

"But is that the only crossing?" Liz asked. "We're still relatively near the coast, and if this river was used for transportation, there could be a dock or something along the way to the ocean."

"Like a custom's house…" Okeny said quietly.

"Shouldn't we be worried about whoever this Theron is?" Richard asked.

"One thing at a time. Besides, at least downriver, we know there's only three we'll have to slip past. I like those odds better than what we'll find the other way," Liz said, extending a hand down to Okeny. "So, Stuart Okeny, are you with us?"

Okeny nodded, reaching for her hand, but pulled back at the last second. Liz realized what she'd done and offered him her other hand, which he grasped firmly and said, "Yes, Ma'am."

Setting off again down the river, Okeny crept on unnaturally silent feet. With the river on their right, they used trees and gullies. Like before, Okeny would scout ahead and return to direct them to the next hiding place. It was slow going, but they had to side with caution, especially now. Eventually, Okeny brought them along the side of a hill, dense with trees, and motioned them to follow him.

As they delved into the woods, the glow of fire appeared just ahead. At the edge of a clearing, three men sat around a cooking fire with their backs to the trees. They were slathered in black filth from head to toe, even on their clothes. And the stench. It made her already unsettled stomach churn.

Passing a bottle between them, the three men hummed a tune. Each time one lost pace with the others, he'd take a swig. A drinking game, Liz deduced, and all three had been playing poorly. Beyond the fire, she could see the river. From here, anyone passing along the riverbank could be spotted easily.

Okeny pulled a long knife from his boot and motioned the others to do the same. Liz shook her head. Face illuminated by the dancing flames, Okeny's eyes narrowed, and he nodded. First, he pointed at the Talons, slid a finger across his throat, then pointed at her and made the same gesture.

It's either them or us, she thought.

Next to her, Richard pulled his sword slowly out of its sheath. Hand trembling, she drew her grandfather's knife. Looking at the blade now, it seemed so inadequate. On Okeny's signal, they crept behind the preoccupied men.

Okeny held up three fingers and began counting down.

Liz's hand shook so badly that she had to grab the handle with the other to keep from dropping it. When Okeny lowered the last finger, his arm whipped out and wrapped around the head in front of him, pulling it back as he slid the knife into the exposed throat. A spray of blood shot into the fire, sizzling on the hot rocks. Richard stabbed his sword through the other's neck. Choking and gagging on his blood, the man slumped to the ground. Liz watched and was unable to blink. Suddenly feeling lightheaded, she fell to her knees.

In front of her, the dark figure stood up, swaying on his feet. "What'sh happening?" he slurred.

Liz panicked, slashing her knife through the back of the man's ankle, and he dropped face-first into the flames. Screaming, and with his beard on fire, he rolled off. Liz couldn't take the painful wails and just wanted him to stop. She scrabbled onto the thrashing man's chest and drove her knife into the flames, stabbing up under his chin.

The man's body twitched beneath her even as his eyes glazed over, his skin sizzling and smoking. Falling back between the man's legs, Liz stared at her hands. The hair on her arms was singed.

Blood, cooked in the heat, painted her fingers. Woozy, she looked from her hands to the knife—still buried in the man's head. The world became fuzzy, and her vision blurred. Unrecognizable words barely registered in her awareness. When a hand touched her shoulder, she jumped. And her senses realigned.

The bodies were gone, moved out of sight. Richard stood above her, holding something out to her. He said, "I'd like to tell you it gets easier, but it won't."

It was her knife.

She took it, hand still trembling. The blade had been cleaned, but the charred handle would always remind her of what she'd done. Bile rising once more, Liz got on her hands and knees and finally let go.

When she was sure her stomach was empty, she looked around with watery eyes. Okeny was kicking dirt on the fire, smothering it. "We need to move," he said. His voice had a hard edge she hadn't heard before. "I don't know if anyone heard him scream, but we can't take the chance. You need to get up. Now."

As if observing from somewhere outside her own body, she saw herself stand on shaky legs and slide the knife back into the sheath on her belt. She watched as she placed one foot after the other, following them back down to the river. Liz was drawn a little closer with each step until she finally felt the ground beneath her feet again.

Dawn was approaching as she blinked. They'd been walking for a long time, she realized. Okeny said something next to her she didn't quite catch. She shook the last of the cobwebs from her thoughts, apologized, and asked Okeny to repeat himself.

Softer sounding than she'd last heard him, he said, "There are a few cabins about a mile up ahead near an island halfway across the river. We'll use it as cover when we cross over, but we should wait until nightfall before we do."

Liz nodded, feeling weary and sore. They continued until Liz saw three squat cabins with green grass sprouting from their roofs. Fishing cabins, long since abandoned. Liz didn't care if they'd belonged to the King himself, only that she found the door unlocked. She let herself fall to the dirt floor and welcomed the bliss of unconsciousness.

A knot in her stomach woke Liz at dusk. Ravenous, she pulled out a large chunk of dried meat from her pack and tore into it like an animal. She was already working on a second piece when Okeny entered the cabin and said, "Just making sure you're still alive."

Liz nodded, chewing. "I felt like I could have slept forever. Sorry."

"It was a tough night," Okeny said.

"What now?" Liz asked after swallowing.

"It's been quiet all day. It rained some, so hopefully, it's true about this cult's distaste for drab weather. Richard is on watch. And it's almost time to head out again."

"Let me clean up, and I'll be ready." When Okeny said there was no need to hurry, she said, "I've rested enough." A spike of anger made its way into her words. "I was utterly useless last night. I've always earned my keep, and it's high time I started doing just that."

"We'll be ready when you are." He closed the door behind him. She went to the bathroom in the corner of the cabin and cleaned herself up as best she could. After gathering her belongings, she went out into the dimming light and stood at the river's shore. In her exhaustion that morning, she'd somehow missed the wooded island nearby.

Next to one cabin, Okeny flipped over an old rowboat. Luckily for them, the oars had been safely stored beneath it. Okeny smiled at her and picked them up. "A good sign." After the two dragged the boat to the water, Richard joined them and gave them the all-clear.

Okeny rowed slowly while the others kept an eye on where they were headed. It didn't take long to cross over. They pulled the boat onto the island's rocky beach as Okeny went into the dense trees. If it's safe, they would carry the boat across to the other side. While they waited for Okeny to return in the fading twilight, Liz saw a collapsed bridge further downriver. The bridge's supports stuck out of the water while the rest had been dragged away by the river's current.

Okeny returned and said, "It's dark but passable." He grabbed the front of the rowboat, and Richard picked up the rear. The two hoisted it with a grunt, and Okeny led them off the beach.

Okeny wasn't exaggerating. It *was* dark. The canopy blocked the starlight and made it impossible to see where they were headed. Liz had to walk with one hand on the boat while she felt for trees. She slapped at the insects buzzing around her ear. There was a sound of rustling leaves, and for a moment, she thought someone was out there.

Then a twig snapped.

The three stopped.

A screech cut through the darkness, and Liz would have run if Okeny hadn't whispered, "Just a bird. An owl, I believe."

A wet huffing sounded nearby. Liz's heart raced, unsure if the heavy breathing that followed was hers or whatever was out there.

Okeny whispered again, "Move slowly. Don't make—"

A thunderous roar cut him off before he could finish.

Liz screamed as something crashed into the boat, sending it tumbling on top of her. A paddle struck her head, leaving her dazed.

Muffled chaos broke out. Something struck the boat and hammered it repeatedly. That terrible roar came again and drowned out her friends' faint yelling. Her heart skipped a beat when she heard a gunshot. An inhuman cry of pain preceded another roar, and then the boat shifted as something slammed against it.

The rowboat wouldn't budge when she tried to move it. Panicked, she pounded against the wooden hull, screaming. Then, it was gone, and her screams grew louder. A wet hand covered her mouth as she tried to get away.

"Liz!" Okeny whispered sharply.

"She's scared half to death," Richard whispered.

Both were panting.

The familiar voices calmed Liz. She stopped struggling. The hand moved from her mouth, and her lips felt sticky.

"That gunshot will draw them right to us," Okeny said. He grunted in pain as he moved away from where Liz lay.

Still holding her tightly, Richard said, "We need to move. Can you do that?"

Swallowing, Liz said, "W-what was it?" She licked her lips, tasting bitter copper.

"Bear," Okeny said. "Let's go."

Richard released her, and she got to her knees. Feeling shaky, she reached out to find something to help her up and touched coarse hair. She recoiled, but Richard caught her and helped her to her feet. The rising moon's light filtered through the trees. It showed Okeny attempting to drag the boat by himself. Beside her, a large dark mound lay on the forest floor.

"Can you walk on your own?" Richard asked.

When she nodded, he went and helped Okeny with the boat.

Liz picked up the oar that had struck her and prodded at the dead bear.

"Liz!" Okeny called back to her in a harsh whisper. The men were moving quickly, leaving her behind. She hurried to catch up.

They'd slid the boat back in the water on the other side of the island but waited several moments. Okeny wanted to make sure no one was waiting for them on the shore. Liz saw dark stains on Richard's pants and coat in the moonlight. Okeny was rummaging through his pack and pulled out some bandages.

"Are you all right?" she asked Richard.

"Me?" He looked himself over. Saw the stains. And said, "That's not my blood."

She turned back to Okeny, who was wrapping a bandage around his right forearm. "You're hurt," Liz said and went to help him.

Okeny waved her off. "I can do it. A bloody claw snagged me. It was my fault. Shooting it only seemed to make it angrier," he nodded to Richard while tying off the bandage, "Though, I did make a good distraction for Richard. He stabbed it right in the heart before it managed to take a bigger chunk out of me."

Liz still couldn't believe what had just happened. "Could there be more of them?" she asked.

"Probably, yes," Okeny said. He had closed his pack and was getting to his feet. "This is their country," he held up his bandaged arm, "this was a good reminder that it's not just the humans we should be mindful of."

With no movement on the other side of the river, Okeny deemed it safe to cross. Once there, Okeny cast the boat back out to the river, letting the current take it downstream. Because of how Fieldstone drew his map, they'd need to reorientate themselves by getting close enough to the crossing to follow the remaining landmarks. It wasn't the best plan, but it was all they had, Liz thought. Okeny took them back into the woods.

Liz was tired of trees.

THE WIRE AND WHERE IT LEADS

It was a quiet night, to everyone's relief, and by dawn, they'd found shelter in a narrow cave. It was a tight squeeze, but the cave's protection was much more important than comfort. At least it was cool. When dusk settled in again, they crawled out and stretched the kinks from their muscles.

The trio continued along the river, falling back into their routine. Okeny scouted ahead, and the rest followed. Night had fallen when Okeny came back and said there was a patrol along the river, headed in the same direction they were. "We should keep our distance but follow them for a bit. It might mean we're near the crossing."

Keeping to the shadows cast by the clouds enveloping the moon, they moved on. Voices and marching feet came to them from out in the darkness. What sense did it make for them to be so loud? Liz thought if she'd been searching for someone, it'd make sense to stay quiet and let her prey make a mistake. These were very strange men, indeed.

Eventually, the light from the crossing glowed along the river. Okeny went on ahead while Liz and Richard hid in a deep ravine between two hills. He returned shortly and said, "There's a lot of them. Lucky for us, we went the way we did."

Lucky? Liz could still smell burning hair and flesh and hear the Talon's scream.

At least they had their landmark and were back on Fieldstone's map. Headed away from the river, Liz felt turned around without it being on her right and pulled out her compass. Its phosphorus-coated needle glowed faintly in the dark. A little guilty for not trusting Okeny to keep them on course, she slid it away before he'd see.

The few paths they found were all headed in the wrong direction. "We'll have to make our own then," Okeny said.

The forest floor was thick with thorny plants and roots that grabbed at their feet, tripping them with silent curses. Each tumble cemented Liz's hatred for trees. *Please, God, I'd rather be in a dingy, at sea, and with a storm on the horizon.* She almost made her thoughts known when the distinct sound of horses being driven hard came from nearby. Okeny swore and motioned them to stop. Sitting in the brambles, they waited until the noise faded.

For two days, they trekked through the underbrush. They'd rest when the sun rose, then move again at night. Okeny decided to follow the same pattern as the Cult. They'd have the cover of night and be able to hear the Talons long before coming across them. On the third morning after they'd heard the horses, Liz realized they'd gone the whole night with neither sight nor sound of their hunters. She didn't let herself believe they'd finally evaded them, but it was a welcoming thought.

Looking for a place to rest for the day, they entered the ruins of a large town. Sunlight beamed through the broken windows of a row of buildings lined up along a wide road thick with weeds. Faded signs hung crookedly outside businesses, advertising barbers, smithies, and a general store. Liz saw an old post office sign tangled up in the weeds on the ground. She brushed some of it away, giving the past a name—Towson, Maryland.

Liz marveled at how preserved it was as they made their way down the road. Of course, there were some collapsed roofs and shattered glass, but the rest simply looked neglected, not abandoned. Passing a schoolhouse, Liz imagined laughter coming from inside and a teacher scolding the children for not focusing on their lessons. Growing up, she'd always been jealous of the children in books. For the life of her, she couldn't understand why most of the characters hated going to school. The idea of attending one seemed like the epitome of safety and comfort in Liz's eyes. After the war, the Crown had made sure to reopen the primary schools and the universities, but enrollment was still sparse.

The tall weeds stirred in the breeze blowing between the buildings. It was a soothing sound, and Liz sighed with contentment. Okeny chose a small brick building to rest in with bent, rusty tables outside. Thick ivy had worked through some of the windows, making the floor a bed of twisted green vines and leaves. Okeny hacked away at some until he freed a table and chairs. Liz noted a small shelf of books on one wall but found them moldy and warped from a leak in the roof. She returned to join the men at the table and took out her map and Fieldstone's. On hers, she found Towson, which placed them just outside of Baltimore.

"This is turning out to be more than a week's journey." Liz sighed, guessing it'd be at least another week before they reached Washington.

"I'm sure Mr. Fieldstone wasn't traipsing through the forest at night with his father," Richard said while chewing on some dry bread.

Liz nodded and put away the maps. She leaned back in the chair and looked out the green-smudged window, somehow miraculously unbroken. She sighed, feeling the distance between her grandfather and crew growing. With her constant fear, she hadn't had time to think about what could be happening to them. James said he'd do everything he could to keep them safe. That Cutter, Brian, said people just disappeared when they were taken, never to be heard from again. *Could these cultists be headhunters? Are they so primitive as to have given up all sense of civility?* Despair swelled within her, and she whimpered quietly.

"What is it?" Okeny stood, looking out the window.

Liz shook her head, tears forming in her eyes. "I'm just worried about the others, especially my grandfather. Not knowing what's happened to them, I'm left to imagine just the worst scenarios."

Richard put a hand over hers, he didn't look her in the eye, but she could see he was doing his best to hide his pain. They both shared the same loss. She smiled sadly at him before brushing her tears away.

Sitting back down, Okeny looked at the bandages on his arm and flexed his hand. "Should we find a place to bunk for the day?" he asked.

Liz cleared her throat. "I could go a little while longer. It's a nice day, and maybe some sun would lighten the mood?"

They followed the road south. Houses and businesses grew denser as they headed into the center of town. Liz came up short at a cross-roads and stared down a side street.

Okeny tensed.

With a smile forming, she pointed, and Okeny turned. It took him several seconds to realize what she wanted him to see. Down the street, held up by two wooden poles, was a telegraph line. Liz took off in that direction, and the others ran to follow.

To her relief, she saw the contiguous line running parallel to the street in both directions. "This is it!" she said excitedly and slapped the pole. "This should take us to Washington."

"Are you certain?" Richard asked, sounding doubtful. "There could be more than one telegraph line."

"The more, the merrier," Liz said.

Both men looked confused.

Her smile not breaking, Liz said, "With more lines, that's more wire to make up our antenna. And we only need to follow the line that heads south."

With renewed energy, Liz set a brisk pace. By midday, the trees hid the rust-covered metal frames with moss and ivy growing along brick walls. Towson had been left behind, and they'd found them-selves walking among discarded factories. With all the decay she'd seen since coming here, what were the chances the fragile cables were still intact? If she believed in such things, she would have thought it to be a miracle. Then they came to the outskirts of Balti-more, and all thought of miracles stopped.

"Do we chance it?" she asked.

Okeny said, "We don't know what's in there. For all we know, it could be a stronghold for this cult. I say we go around."

Richard agreed.

"We might lose the bloody line if we do," Liz said. She looked up at the wire and then the direction they were headed. "Well, there's no telling how the line faired in the city. We could at least try and test it now."

Opening her pack, Liz slid some tools into her pocket while Okeny took the portable telegraph out. She took the two leads from the device and stuck them between her teeth. Borrowing Richard's belt to help climb, she worked her way up the fifteen-foot pole to the line above. It took some time, but she was able to splice the leads with the heavier cable.

Liz wiped the sweat from her forehead when she was finished and climbed back down. She handed Richard his belt back. He had been awkwardly holding his trousers up with one hand. Kneeling by the device, she inserted the handle and cranked it to get power. When she figured she'd generated enough, Liz tapped out a message in Morse code, "I-N A-M-E-R-I-C-A."

So focused on what Liz was doing, they were all caught off guard by a cough behind them.

Liz turned quickly. Okeny and Richard already had their guns drawn and aimed at six dark-skinned men just a few yards away at the edge of the trees. Liz fumbled for her pistol when she realized these men weren't covered in black filth. They *were* Black. Dressed in well-used clothing, each carried a rifle, which, to Liz's relief, wasn't pointed at them. Also, none seemed bothered that Richard and Okeny had their guns aimed at them.

One stepped forward, smiling at Okeny. "Afternoon."

Okeny nodded back, not lowering his gun.

"Heard someone's gone and stirred up the hornet's nest up north. Came to see for ourselves. Reckon that's y'all?" Words were like syrup rolling off his tongue.

Liz stood slowly. "And if it were?"

His head cocked, the man said, "Well, you got about five minutes before a whole mess of them dirt boys come down that road. Theron's real keen on finding someone. Even got them out in the day-light."

Liz glanced back up the empty road. "And how do you know that?"

"Some of our boys been tracking y'all that night you was in that old mining village. You almost got caught if they hadn't pulled the dirt boys off your trail," he said and paused momentarily. Then continued. "You're welcome, by the way." He nodded back at the road. "Now, we have four minutes. We can keep talking if you like, or we can high-tail it out of here and finish this conversation someplace more proper. Up to y'all."

Maybe it was her mind playing tricks on her, but Liz swore she heard horses somewhere in the distance and someone shouting. Then she was sure she heard it and felt the hooves rumbling the ground. Thinking of the telegraph, she quickly turned to look down at it.

Richard said, "There's no time." Saying out loud what she already knew to be true. There was no way she could get up the pole and remove the wires in time.

The black men had already stepped off the road and made their way among the trees toward the factories, except the one that'd been talking. "Why should we trust you?" she asked.

Walking backward, with a smile, he asked, "Ma'am, what other choice you got?" There was no menace in his voice. And that smile was genuinely warm.

Liz gave the wooden box one last look before she fled with the others into the cover of brick and wood. It felt like she was abandoning Reginald's legacy, but there was no other choice. As she hurried around the corner of a factory, faint clicking followed behind her, which was lost to the thunder of approaching horses.

For several miles, they traveled in silence, sticking to long-abandoned paths among the dead shells of industry. Broken carts and crumbled masonry were everywhere in this new forest. The Black men marched with the speed of someone who knew where they were going. So, much faster than Liz had been accustomed to. And did it somehow get hotter? Like a river, sweat poured down her back.

They lost all sense of direction as they moved through old buildings and upheaved roads. Passing through one treacherously unstable factory where holes had formed in the rotten wood flooring, Liz saw a mass of bones piled below them. She slowed and stared. *There must be over a hundred people down there.* The Black man behind her patted her shoulder, shook his head, and motioned to keep going.

After hours of trekking through the maze-like forest, they arrived at a building no different than all the others except for the dark-skinned man standing by an iron door, waving as they approached. The leader, as Liz thought of him, waved back and went over to exchange a few words as the others entered the building. The man, a guard by the looks of him, smiled at Okeny as he passed. Liz and Richard, however, got a curious look and a nod of greeting.

Inside, it was anything but an abandoned factory. The old machinery had been crammed into the back, leaving room for several rows of beds. A fire pit was carved into the cement floor. A kettle hung above it, brewing something with a rich smell that Liz couldn't place. Around the fire, men sat and chatted while drinking from steaming cups. Others stood around a table by a stack of caged pigeons.

Leaning his rifle against the wall with the other guns, the leader came in and said, "It's safe here. Y'all can rest for a while. Coffee?" He smiled, nodding to the fire pit.

Liz knew what coffee was but never tasted it before, seeing as England had run out of it long before she'd been born. Curious to try the almost mythological drink, she nodded, and he went and fetched her a cup. When he handed it to her, she said, "Thank you, Mister...?"

"Favre. Thomas Favre," he said and extended his hand in greeting. She took it and introduced herself and her friends.

Thomas shook Richard's hand as he had Liz's, but when it was Okeny's turn, he held on a bit longer, looking him over. He pointed at Okeny's bandaged forearm. "You hurt?"

Okeny shook his head. "Just a scratch."

Thomas let go of his hand and said to Liz, "Reckon this might be a bit confusing to y'all. Us showing up out of the blue and all. Why don't we sit and chat for a spell?" He directed them toward the fire. The men already seated there grumbled and made their way to the beds.

They sat with Thomas settling himself across from them. He was probably about her age, early twenties, with close-cropped hair and a round face with small creases around his eyes. He was not a big man, but he had a firm grip. Admittedly, she thought him relatively handsome, then scolded herself.

Time and place, Liz. Time and place.

She took a sip of coffee, found it shockingly bitter, and began coughing. Sheepishly, she said, "First time." And lowered the cup to her lap. "Why did you help us?"

As if it were all the answer needed, he nodded at Okeny. When it was clear she didn't understand, Thomas added, "We're sworn to help brothers and sisters make their way to the homeland. Honestly, though, been a real long time since any've come down this way."

With a look as baffled as Liz felt, Okeny said, "Pardon, but I think you have me confused with someone else."

"What's to be confused about? You're Black, ain't you? That ain't dirt on you, is it?" Thomas asked, chuckling.

"Yes, sir, I am," Okeny said, still puzzled.

"Then you've a place in the Great Southern Free States," he said with a proud smile. "A bit long, I know. Us locals just call her the Free States for short."

Liz remembered Jessica had called Okeny a strange name back in Lums and said it out loud. "Souther…"

Thomas nodded. "Yes, ma'am. That's what they call us up north. But," he added quietly, "that's not a word we like to use. So, if you wouldn't mind, it'd be best if you called us Black. Hell, even Staters, if y'all want."

"Oh, I beg your pardon. I meant no offense," Liz said quickly, putting a hand to her chest.

Thomas took a sip of coffee and waved a hand. "None taken. Y'all just don't know any better."

Uncomfortable, Liz sought to change the subject. "How did you know where to find us?"

"I told you already, that big hubbub up north. Reports got sent back of a Black man heading our way with two white people," he said with a shrug. "Mamma June's got us out here just for these situations."

"Mamma June?" she asked.

"Governor of Turner," Thomas said. Met with more confused faces, he sighed, shaking his head. "Y'all really don't know what I'm talking about? You northerners need some better schooling. It's just west of Split State."

Curtly, Liz said, "We are not northerners. We're British."

It was Thomas's turn to apologize, then he said, "That explains the accents." He shouted back to one of his men on the beds, "You owe me, Collins. They ain't from *New* England." Collins swore and made a rude gesture at Thomas. Both men laughed. Turning back to Liz, Thomas asked, "So England? How's she faring?"

Liz didn't know how much she should share, if anything, about the war, so she chose the official propaganda. "Exceedingly well since we were spared from the plague. Queen Victoria the Great had rallied her people to keep it from coming ashore. And our current ruler, King Edward VII, has kept us safe since she passed."

Thomas rubbed the back of his neck and gave a low whistle, then asked, "So what're y'all doing here?"

Liz stared blankly at him for several seconds. Then, she lied. "We've come to investigate what is left of America and initiate diplomatic communication if we find a reestablished government."

"Guess that's why y'all were sending a message back there. Just letting people at home know y'all made it."

Liz couldn't hide her surprise in time.

"I know what a telegraph is," Thomas said. "We still got them in the Free States. Our skin might be darker than yours, but that doesn't mean we're a bunch of savages." Grinning, he reached over and slapped Okeny on the knee.

Okeny only stared, wide-eyed, back at him.

Face turning red, Richard said, "Now, sir, we never thought—" But Thomas cut him off with a wave of the hand.

"Don't worry none. If the first people I came across were dirt boys, I'd think everyone else here was just as backward," Thomas said. "And a bunch of lunatics, too."

Liz took another sip of coffee, and it went down a little smoother. "To answer your question, we were only testing to see if the lines were still in working order."

"Well, sorry we interrupted your test, then," Thomas said.

"You saved our lives, it seems. There's nothing to be sorry about," Liz said, even though she still felt the pang of guilt for leaving Reginald's device behind.

Thomas stood and brushed the dirt off the back of his pants. "Y'all should rest up. If you want to have some *diplomatic talks*, we got to get you to Mamma June. She's the one you're gonna want to talk to."

Panic setting in, Liz stammered, "C-ouldn't we go back for our telegraph first?"

Thomas shook his head. "Reckon dirt boys'll be crawling all over the area by now. Ain't safe for no one. Besides, as I mentioned before, we got telegraphs back home. You're welcome to run all the tests you like there."

Richard placed his untouched mug down on the ground and stood. "What about Washington? Surely there must be some national government remaining?"

"Washington? Ain't no one there. Just a bunch of old broken buildings and busted canals. It's turned into a real swamp," Thomas said.

"Could we talk privately?" Richard asked.

Thomas said, "Sure, sure. Do as you like." He took a few steps back, giving them some room.

Richard sat back down and whispered, "We did our part. We sent a message. What did James say to do after that?"

Liz bit her lower lip. "Find someplace safe."

Okeny appeared distracted. He remained quiet as he watched the others gathered around the camp.

Richard said, "If what Thomas said is the truth, I think the Free States would qualify as a safe place."

Almost hissing, Liz whispered, "What about my grandfather? Your brother? The crew and James?"

Okeny leaned in, apparently having listened to the conversation after all. "They were able to find us out there. If the others escape, I'm sure the *Staters* will find them as well."

With her heart beating fast and suffocated by panic, Liz knew Okeny was right. She let out a slow breath and released the death grip she had on the mug in her lap. She looked over at the man that had rescued them. He sipped his coffee while staring up at the trees through a hole in the ceiling. She asked him, "How long will it take to reach Mamma June?"

Thomas grinned, giving him a boyish look. "Charleston's just a few weeks away. Ain't been home for months, now." Lifting his mug in salute, he added, "Y'all are our ticket back to civilization." And laughed.

INITIATION

Sorting coal was not as easy as it sounded. After weeks in the mine—lifting heavy rocks and moving minecarts—the muscle he'd lost during his years of incarceration had returned. Often, he thought of his brother and the other rebels, forced to work for the Crown, while he sat all day in his cell and felt guilty.

Also, panic and frustration.

He hoped Elizabeth managed to send word back to England but had no way to know. And that only made him more agitated. *Only focus on what's in front of you. Everything else will come in time,* his father's voice said in his head.

He'd already finished half his sentence, having completed two tunnel runs. Surprisingly, he found the Cult had developed an elaborate system around the punishment. The runner had a long rope tied around their waist with a knot set every five feet. A Talon would be on the other end, letting the rope slide through his hands while the runner went down the newly blasted tunnel, and at each knot, he'd tug at it, and the runner had to tug back. If they failed to do so, the Talon would pull them back out, and if the runner was still alive, his sentence was doubled, and they'd get a beating.

The Talons bet on whether a Canary lived, how far they'd get before reaching the tunnel's end, or if a cave-in would kill them. Basically, they'd bet on anything they could think of. What exactly they gambled with, James had no idea. He never saw any money exchanged.

The Canaries had to remove the rocks Miners dug out of the hill between runs, just as Paddy said. Just another way for the Cult to exploit people for labor, James realized. The prisoners spent more time sweating over rocks than working off their sentences.

Only one of *The Ophelia*'s crew had died so far from a shoddily supported tunnel. The rope had grazed a poorly placed beam, and tons of rock crashed on top of him. Miners had cleared the tunnel again, not to retrieve the body but to get the coal. James and the crew were given what was left to bury.

A large dirt field marked by stones lay at the edge of the camp, the Canary graveyard. Under the watch of the Talons, they buried the crewman with nothing but their hands to dig with. The Talons joked among themselves while they worked, and James could feel the fire in his blood but had no way of venting his anger. The second they placed the stone at the head of the grave, they were dragged back to the Canary House.

The day after the burial, a Talon had knocked a basket of rocks out of Ryan's arms before telling him to pick them back up. Being the hotheaded loudmouth that he was, Ryan told the Talon what he could do with the rocks and earned himself a beating. They were careful not to break any of Ryan's bones or hit his head too hard. He was left sore but still able to work.

At least the food was better than what he got in Newgate. The thick gruel was hearty and filled the stomach, which helped Ryan's body to heal. After recovering, Ryan had been eager to find that Talon again, but Paddy convinced him to keep his head down through his sentence. "It'll be easier for you in the end."

A couple of weeks after that, James and Ryan were sorting rocks in an alcove when a deep blaring of a horn echoed through the tunnels. Miners, Canaries, and Talons all came running by toward the mine's entrance. James grabbed one Canary by the arm and asked, "What's going on?"

The Canary looked over his shoulder anxiously and said, "Inspection." He pulled his arm free and ran off.

To Ryan, James muttered. "What new hell is this?"

"Who bloody knows?" Ryan said with a shrug. "Suppose we should go, yeah?"

"Seems so," James sighed.

The Canary House was emptying as everyone gathered in the central clearing between the two hills. Acrid smoke filled the air from the bonfires that lit the camp. James wasn't sure if it was good that he'd grown used to the smell, but at least he wasn't choking on it now.

The horn came again from the other side of the hill, and one of the Talons stepped forward, lifting a dinged-up trumpet and blared a note of his own. A party of twenty or so Talons came around the hill, riding along the dirt road leading into camp. At the head of the riders, James immediately recognized the brute that had killed Peter. Referred to as The Claw, he appeared much the same as before. The face was covered except for his eyes, though the tilt of the hat he wore prevented others from seeing them. The metal ribs on his vest glinted in the firelight. Lashed tightly to his massive forearms were the jagged metal bracers that had taken Peter's life.

Fists clenched and teeth grinding, James wanted revenge. Ryan gave him a nod, recognizing the look on his face. Slowly, James let out a calming breath and relaxed his fingers. He had a promise to keep and couldn't do that by blindly running into a fight he didn't understand.

The riders spread out before the gathered men of Eck. As one, they dismounted, and The Claw, his thumbs hooked into his belt, sauntered over. This was a man who knew his power and feared nothing. As he passed the different groups, each man fell to a knee. First the Talons, then Miners, and finally, Canaries. Instinct told James to keep standing, to defy this bastard, but what would that mean for everyone else?

Half-kneeling, James tried to catch The Claw's eye but couldn't find them in the shadows. Expecting The Claw to recognize him, James was disappointed when he turned away without noticing him.

The Talon general kept inspecting the other Canaries before his voice boomed, "Barkus!"

A skinny Talon sprinted over and knelt before The Claw. Breathing in short gasps, he stammered, "V-v-v-arkus, my lord."

The Claw loomed over the kneeling man. "Barkus suits you better." His deep voice rumbled. "Like a dog, you always come when your master calls."

Every Talon that accompanied him laughed, as did the others in the camp.

Varkus nodded and chuckled nervously, all the while keeping his eyes averted. "Your joke never gets old, my lord."

The Claw waved a muscled arm at the Canaries. "Seems you've been having good luck with the tunnels lately. Got quite a flock here."

"Yes, my lord. We've only lost three Canaries in the last two Moons. At the moment, The Dragon is in a state of Inhale. It lets us spread further below and produce more yield. The Dragon's Breath will return, my lord. As it always does. The Dragon's Will is unpredictable."

"Is that so? Or could it be your Miners aren't digging deep enough? Perhaps you're not working them as hard as you should be?" The Claw said. The threat was far from veiled in his words.

Voice trembling, Varkus said, "N-no, m-my lord, we work them night and day. I-Inspector should have the quota records."

"Yes, I've been told the records," the brute said absent-mindedly as he looked to the mine. He plucked Varkus off the ground, making him stand. "And I think you could do more."

The skinny man winced as The Claw placed a heavy hand on Varkus's shoulder and led him to the gaping hole in the side of the hill. The Talons, Miners, and Canaries stood when the two disappeared inside.

The only one who hadn't been kneeling was Paddy, who had been wheeled out by a Talon and left near the Canaries. The old man looked troubled, and Ryan asked, "What now?"

The old man ran his fingers through his beard and grumbled, "Something's not sitting right. We've a steady yield. There's no good reason for Render Hollow to come all the way up here." James

could see something more was troubling him. The old man looked at
the mine with something close to regret.

Before James could ask him what he thought was really going on,
a Talon began banging his cudgel against a cook pot, demanding attention. Once all eyes were on him, the Talon shouted, "By order of
The Head of the Dragon, we're to have us a Test of the Talon." A
vicious grin smeared across his face as he looked right at James.

Ryan whispered, "What's all this then?"

Quietly, Paddy said, "You beat one of them in a fight; you get to
stop being one of the common folk. Might even get to be a Talon if
you're strong enough for it."

James sighed. He'd heard the first rebels had been boat crews and
street gangs with odd rituals that new members had to perform.
James remembered from Paddy's story that the Cult had mixed with
nearby gangs in its early days and knew what was coming.

Initiation by beating.

A large circle of Talons formed in the middle of the camp, and the
man with the pot walked along the perimeter. "You want to leave
this wretched life behind? You want to stop digging in dirt," he
waved the club at the Miners, "or be free from your sentence?" he
pointed to the Canaries. "You can eat what you want. Fuck who you
want. And break anyone who looks at you the wrong way. All you
gotta do is beat just one of us." He slapped a Talon's back in the circle.

Miners and Canaries murmured among themselves before a few
stepped forward with hands raised. *The Ophelia's* crew looked at
James. When he shrugged, two of them lifted their hands slowly.
James had to hold Ryan back. "It's their choice," he said.

Ryan sputtered some colorful curses and spat at the crewmen.

It played out just as James thought it would. One initiate and one
with a Talon would fight while the others cheered on. It was usually
over quickly, with a Talon standing over a bloody, moaning body.
When someone managed to win, they were escorted to the horses.

One of the crewmates had won his fight. He looked back as he
limped his way into the Cult's ranks with a bloodied grin. Three of
his teeth were missing, and one eye was swollen shut. The other
from *The Ophelia* didn't fare as well. After a few punches to the

head, he crumpled to the ground. The Talon, most likely expecting a better fight, began stomping on the crewman.

Too quick this time, Ryan slipped past James and burst through the watching Talons. He tackled the Talon stomping the crewman from behind and hammered a fist down on the side of his head. James swore and ran in when another Talon left the circle and headed for Ryan.

The Talon was about to strike the back of Ryan's head when James grabbed his wrist and smashed a hand against the Cultist's elbow. The joint snapped, and the Talon screamed. Still holding onto the wrist, James spun him around and kicked him in the back, sending the Talon into the circle. Flailing, the screaming Talon knocked over two Cultists before he landed and writhed in pain.

The circle stared at James as Ryan continued his assault. James patted him on the back, and Ryan looked up at him, then over at the Talons with death in their eyes. Slowly, he got up from the unconscious body.

It may have been ten years since he'd been in a fight, but James's muscles hadn't forgotten how to hurt someone. Heart beating faster, he was looking forward to it. They stood back-to-back in the center of the circle. Around them, clubs were drawn by madmen with eager grins on their soot-smeared faces.

James quickly searched the ground for a weapon, but as he did, the first Talon came at him from the right. James let him get close enough before sidestepping out of the way and tripping the Talon. The momentum sent the Cultist sliding face-first along the ground. Another Talon jumped over the other's body, club swinging. James pushed the arm out of the way and slammed an elbow underneath the Talon's chin. Falling backward, The Talon landed hard on the back of his head. From the corner of his eye, James saw Ryan got his hands on a club from a fallen Talon at his feet.

"Two and two," James shouted.

Ryan grunted as he drove back another Talon. "Didn't know the count started yet."

James narrowly managed to step back in time before getting a club in the face. He took the blow on the tip of his nose and fought off the sudden urge to sneeze while the Talon bent forward, off-balance. Annoyed, James punched at the back of the man's neck, slamming him to the ground. Crushing the Talon's wrist with his boot, James pried the club free and looked up in time to see two more circling him.

James watched them closely. When the one in front of James looked past his shoulder, he knew the other was making a move. Swinging the cudgel behind him, James felt a satisfying crack and the sound of someone hitting the ground. The one in front charged, but before he reached James, a club was thrown at the Talon's legs, tripping him to his knees, and James kicked the side of his head. Ryan snatched up the club he tossed with a grin and gave James a quick salute. Warmed up, James waved for the next Talon to come at him.

An angry shout froze the Talons in place.

Emerging from the dark mine, The Claw stalked toward the circle with Varkus in tow, his legs pumping to keep up. "What do you ass-holes think you're doing?" The Claw's voice rippled across the camp.

A Talon stepped forward. "Lord Claw, these men broke the rules of the Test. We were simply reinforcing the sacred rites—" The Claw cut him off with a punch to the face, sending him sprawling.

"Let me start again," The Claw said, loud enough for all to hear, "What do you assholes think you're doing by starting without me?" He bellowed in laughter, and after a few seconds, the rest of the Cultists laughed along.

Cracking his knuckles, The Claw entered the circle and spread his arms wide. Talons unstrapped the bladed gauntlets before he took off his bowler and handed it to another Talon, who took it with bowing reverence.

From across the circle, James stared daggers at The Claw.

Render Hollow said, "Drop the club and call off your dog. You want some revenge for that old man? We do it our way." Shrugging off the vest, he held it out for a Talon to take. Muscles bulged and stretched at the woolen shirt The Claw wore beneath the vest. "And this time, The Head isn't here to stop us."

James let go of the club and signaled Ryan to keep his distance. "Let's see how this plays out," he said. That meant to watch his back while James took the lead.

The circle was cleared of injured Talons as the two giants glared at one another. The Claw's fingers flickered against his palms, a nervous tick, James noted. When everything was ready, a Talon called the fight to begin, and The Claw charged.

James braced himself, but The Claw stopped halfway across the circle, laughing. Around him, the Talons laughed along with their leader, and James knew he'd made some mistake. Embarrassed, James met the man at the center. He looked down into The Claw's eyes and froze, confused. While James was distracted, The Claw landed an uppercut to his stomach, doubling him over and knocking the wind out of him. The Claw smashed his face with a good hook and drove James to his knees.

Dazed and tasting blood, James couldn't keep The Claw from grabbing his collar and pulling him in to whisper, "You brought this on yourself." And punched James in the mouth. James hit the ground hard when The Claw let him go.

The world throbbed, and sounds were muffled as if behind thick wool. He heard Ryan shouting for him to get up and then grunt in pain. Anger brought the world back into focus, and he slowly got back to his feet.

The Claw was working the crowd when James was able to see clearly again. Spitting blood, James felt a loose molar. "There a bloke named Dentist around here?" he said.

The Claw turned and barreled straight at him again. This time, James was ready and met him at the center, swinging a foot up into the brute's groin. The Claw bent over, and James grabbed the back of his head as he slammed a knee into Render's face. When the Cult leader stumbled back, James hammered both his fists into his chest, sending him flat on his back.

Surprisingly, The Claw managed to kick one of James's legs out from underneath him. James hopped out of the way, fighting for balance, which gave The Claw enough time to get back up. The Claw pulled the black cloth from his face and spat a tooth from his bashed and bloody lips.

James pointed to the tooth. "So, no Dentist then?"

The Claw charged at him with arms stretched out to tackle James. Simply stepping aside, James kicked a leg out from under The Claw and sent him back to the ground. Growling like a caged animal, the brute got up and ran for the circle of Talons and grabbed a cudgel from one of the onlookers. A cold stare quieted the resulting whispers before The Claw turned and pointed the club at James.

Crossing his arms, James raised an eyebrow and asked, "What about your sacred rites?"

"This isn't a test. This is personal," The Claw said and charged at James, swinging the club sideways. James stepped into the swing and caught the arm and the club with both hands. Using the brute's own force, James spun and flipped him to the ground and stomped the club in half.

The Claw grabbed James by the foot and pulled him off balance, sending James down to the ground with him. The Claw was on his chest before James could react, fists pounding at his ribs. James knew they'd soon break if he couldn't get free, but his legs couldn't find purchase as he struggled beneath The Claw's weight. Groping mindlessly at the dirt, his fingers brushed against a broken piece of the club. He grasped the jagged wood and swung it at The Claw, driving it home between the brute's ribs straight into his heart. Several seconds passed before the body realized it was dead. With a look of shock, The Claw stared down at James before collapsing onto his side, blood pooling in the ashy dirt.

There was no relief in killing him. It felt like all the others. A dazed memory tried to fight its way forward, but the pain in his chest kept his thoughts muddled. Gasps echoed around him as James stood slowly. Blood dripped from his mouth, and he clutched at his ribs, certain a few were broken.

Dirty faces eyed him hesitantly, unsure of what to do until an overweight Talon with a top hat adorned with black feathers and a pair of welder's goggles smiled with sickly yellow teeth. He pointed at the body in the circle and said, "Thinking you bested the boss? We'll see." He turned to the rest of the Talons. "Looks like we got us a waster here. Wrap him up, boys. And that loudmouth dog of his too," he ordered.

The Talons shouted, "Yes, Foreman!" And the circle rushed James. In no shape to fight back, he was pulled to the ground, and ropes bound his arms against his chest tightly, pushing them against his ribs. They dragged him to a horse and threw him across its rear. Ribs digging into the meat of his chest, he cried out. Before he passed out from the pain, he heard Ryan's colorful take on what the Talons could do with their rope, and then everything went black.

***

Render's back ached. Stooped down as he was to peer through the spyhole to look out to The Den, he wished he'd waited until after he stopped growing to carve it. He welcomed the pain, though. It fueled the rage he felt as he watched his sister. She was dressed in the purple and torn robes of mourning, with woven purple ribbons through the mouth and empty eye sockets of her skull crown. Rivulets of black ran down her cheeks from her tears, smearing the dark paint around her eyes. Those who looked on saw what she wanted them to—a distraught woman after losing her brother and closest ally.

Oh, how he hated her.

"Stay inside for a few days, and then we'll reveal your resurrection. They will love us and fear you all the more," she had told him when word of Grayson's death had come back to Dragon's Rest. Few knew about Render's body double; luckily, one of them had ridden out with Grayson to Eck. He'd been quick to report back, which allowed time to create this farce of a funeral.

With nails biting into the wall, Render watched with his veiny, red eye as she descended the stairs to the shrouded body. Quietly, she waited as a Foremen lowered the cloth to reveal Grayson's face. For most of his adult life, Render had worn a black cloth on his face, people found it intimidating, and he reveled in that fear. The only people who remembered what he looked like were his sister and the dead man on the wagon.

Sarah raised her arms above her head and let out a shrill wail. The gathered Foremen chanted the funeral dirge of The Dragon's Chosen as Sarah Hollow turned to the stairs, looking straight at the spyhole, and a smile parted her lips.

Damn the Trespasser, and damn you too, Sarah. One day, I'll rip the faces from both your skulls.

His rage seethed.

INTO THE PIT

Ash-covered ground passed beneath him. The same ash he breathed in, kicked up by the horses. It made him cough, and the pain in his ribs drove him back into oblivion. The final time he came to, he was pulled down from the horse and tossed into a cage on the back of a wagon.

Through the bars, he could see cracked and charred brick walls. Wherever they were, the smoke was much thicker here than in Eck. Ryan was with him in the cage, his arms and legs tied and a bruised left eye. His friend said, "We have to stop meeting like this, yeah?" And attempted a shrug.

James gritted through the pain and managed to work his way into a seated position. "Any idea where we are?" he grunted.

"Far as I can tell, we came south for a few days. But as usual, no one would tell me anything." Ryan winked his left eye and winced. "Wasn't for lack of trying though, yeah?" He chuckled.

James could feel the bridge of his nose itch, wished his hands were free to rub at it, and sighed. The wagon was by a Talon camp in the ruin of an old, partially collapsed building. Thick metal beams with pointed ends had been used to shore up the hole in the wall. As he'd grown accustomed to seeing, a large bonfire burned at the center of the camp, surrounded by grimy tents. It was hard to make out through the haze, but when the wind pushed the smoke around, he saw more ruins beyond the camp. Far more than he'd seen since arriving on *The Ophelia*.

"Where are we?" he asked a Talon outside the cage.

"What's it matter to you, Waster?" He rapped the bars with his cudgel. "Only place that matters is where you're going."

"And where's that?"

"Fighting Pen. All Wasters go to the Fighting Pen," he said.

A whip cracked, and the cart creaked slowly through the charred streets. Twisted metal frames and sooty rubble had been piled on both sides of the cleared road, mostly obscured by the heavy layer of smoke that clung to the ground, reminding James of the fog in London. Aside from the occasional warped stump of a tree, there was little in the way of life in the ruins. James remembered Cutter Brian's story about how people burned the infected areas of the city, killing anything caught up in the flames.

They crossed a dirt field and passed by a dry fountain with a wide river beyond it. Ryan shifted next to him and gave off a low whistle. James followed his gaze to a massive stone wall that rose above the destruction just as the wagon turned a corner and headed in that direction. A portion of the wall had collapsed, leaving a ten-foot gap near an archway flanked by stone towers. It had an all too familiar look. "Prison," he said out loud.

"Yeah," Ryan bitterly agreed.

"We always end up back here," James sighed.

Men and women then appeared on the road, their faces covered to protect them from the smoke. They held up baubles to the Talons on horseback. Some had baskets of scrawny vegetables and skewers of meat. *Whatever this place is, it's important for these people to live here.*

The original gates of the prison were long gone, leaving the entrance wide open. He could make out long, one- and two-story buildings in different states of disrepair through the archway. Several had caved in entirely, but a few were still serviceable in sections. The wagon crossed the small dirt yard to a low building and stopped by a door. Talons went over to the fallen section of the wall as James watched. They caressed the broken stone before bowing their heads.

The door opened, and two men came out, one in his mid-twenties and the other a few years older than James and had bushy eyebrows. Both were dressed like Talons, their clothing dark and filthy, but their skin was cleaner. The older one spoke to the Talon at the head of the wagon while staring at the back. Grinning, he shook the wagon driver's hand, and James saw the Dragon brand on his wrist. The younger man followed him as he made his way to the back of the wagon. He peered closely through the bars at the two prisoners. His thick eyebrows furrowed, and he asked, "Injuries?"

"Ribs," James said.

Ryan shook his head.

"My Cutter here'll look you over." He nodded to the other man. "Know why you're here?"

"Killed a bloke for trying to beat my chest in."

"Correct. You're a Waster," he said and told a Talon to open the cage. The Talon limped over to unlock it, his arm in a sling. "You two do that?"

"Damn right we did," Ryan said, taking pride in his work.

The older man's eyes gleamed, and he said to the Cutter, "Get the word out. Finally got us some bonafide fighters." Then to James, he asked, "You know who it was you wasted?"

James nodded.

The man leaned in and whispered, "You might be surprised." He cackled as he turned away from the cage. The bars were opened and James, once again confused, was dragged out and separated from Ryan.

The Cutter didn't take long to determine that James's ribs weren't broken, just terribly bruised. James sat on a rusty table in a hot, wet, moldy room. Once, the room had probably been lined with white tiles, but now the walls were cracked and stained, some of which was blood. The older man, who was called Warden, looked relieved after the diagnosis. He was practically drooling when he asked the Cutter when James would be able to fight. "Week. Week and a half at most," the Cutter said, still poking James, causing him to groan.

He was kept in a cell like the one back in Newgate, except windowless. Three times a day, a chunk of hard bread and meat was slid beneath the door with a cup of water. By week's end, the pain of his ribs had diminished to a dull ache. On the eighth night, Warden had James hauled back to the Cutter and was given a clean bill of health.

Clapping with excitement, James was taken to a new cell in a different wing. When he crossed through a rundown section, he got a brief look at what he later learned was called the Pit—a large hole in the ground at the center of the prison. Like the spoke of a wheel, buildings radiated from the Pit. James could only imagine they'd once been connected at some point before the hole was dug. Not dug. It was more like ripped from the ground as if a hand had come out of the heavens and scooped up the earth, taking buildings and all with it. Tiles, wood, iron beams, and broken furniture still lay from where it spilled out. Around the Pit, a small wall was built with metal posts along the top, angled down to keep anything from climbing out.

James already knew what he was looking at and why this place was called Fighting Pen. It was a gladiatorial arena, built by someone who had heard a story from someone else who had heard about the fights in ancient Rome. It even had a small stage built beside it.

Leaving the dreadful scene behind, he could hear other prisoners. He ducked through a doorway and into a two-story prison wing. Men rattled their bars and shouted at one another until they noticed James, and it grew eerily quiet as they gawked at him. A few wore eager grins, just like Warden's. The prisoners spat at him as he was paraded through the block, and even a few threw shit from above.

The guards brought him up to the second floor, where he passed a Black man with a wiry build and hair as thick as rope tied behind his head. He gave James a silent nod. James was ordered into the next cell. It was a bit smaller than his previous one, but there was a cot and a small window near the ceiling. The cell door was closed behind him with a definitive clank of the lock.

James had looked for Ryan as he came through but didn't see him. He asked his neighbor if he had seen a man fitting Ryan's description.

"That new fella? Dragged through here about a week ago? Got a mouth on him, let me tell you." Whoever this was, he didn't sound like a local. If Cutter Brian had been hoarding his vowels, this man was giving them away while whittling down the rough edges.

"He never knows when to shut up." James smiled, relieved someone had seen Ryan. "I'm James, by the way."

"Connor," said the Black man. "Mighty strange accent you got there, James."

"Well, mate, I hate to break it to you, but you've got an odd one too."

Connor snickered. "Where you from?"

"England."

"Shoot, you're awfully far from home."

"Long story. What about you?" James asked.

"A bit south of here." Connor laughed as if he told a joke that James somehow missed.

"Do you know what this place is? I have an awful feeling I already know, but I'd rather be certain," James said, resting his arms on the cross bars of his cell door and pressing the side of his head against it to see Connor's hands sticking out as well.

"Ain't it obvious? This here place is where the Cult sends their most unwanted. Everyone here's killed someone, and they don't let that shit go. Don't matter if they deserved it or not. So, here we are, bein' useful by beatin' and killin' each other for their amusement." A wad of spit flew from Connor's cell to the floor.

James asked, "I take it that's why you're here as well?"

"Yeah. Killed a Talon for tryin' to rape my sister." Connor's voice hardened. "Me and her didn't even know we crossed their border. Damn dirt boy said it was the toll for trespassin'. Now, I wasn't about to let that happen and bashed his head in with a rock. Almost made it back across before they found us and hauled me up here. It's been three months, and I... I don't know where they took my sister."

"I know that feeling all too well. I haven't seen my sister in nearly ten years."

Connor was quiet, but his hands were rubbing together.

James knew when to change the subject. "Are the fights here always to the death?" *There's a cheery topic, lad.*

Connor coughed, clearing his throat. "Nah, it depends on who you killed. The rest get by with broken bones and cracked skulls but live to fight another day. If you don't mind me askin', who'd you, you know...?"

"The Claw."

Connor clasped his hands together as if praying and said, "Damn, James, They'll Main Event you right quick. You're gonna mean freedom for someone in here if you ain't careful."

"Freedom? How so?"

"I guess I left that part out," Connor said. "Makin' it out of a Main Event gets you your freedom." In a quieter voice, he added, "Hey, you ever notice how they don't got executions here? I reckon there's somethin' in that batty religion they got that makes them have to give you a fightin' chance."

Like running tunnels in a mine. People have to be useful, and how useful could they be if everyone was dead?

"It'd be almost noble if they weren't a bunch of slavers," Connor growled.

From the other side of Connor's cell came a shout, "We don't slave anyone!"

"You pay your workers, dirt boy?" Connor shouted back.

A snort and the rattle of a cell door were what he got for a response.

"That's Heimlan. Used to be a Talon 'til he *mistakenly* killed his Foreman. You hear his side of it, the rest of his crew was supposed to help, but they let him take the fall," Connor said, then whispered, "He's still a believer, and an asshole, but not as much of an asshole as the rest of the Cult. But don't tell him I said that."

James sighed. Prisoners around the cellblock were shouting at each other again. "When are the fights?" James asked.

"Every two days. Main Events are held once a week. Got a few more days before the next one."

"What do we do in the meantime?"

"Well, Englishman, we train."

***

The training yard was at the back of the prison—a dirt field with six-foot wooden posts lined up in rows. Each prisoner was given a length of rebar and instructed to strike the post while moving around it. Initially confident in his abilities, James soon discovered the task was a lot harder than he'd thought. The thick, smokey air of the city made breathing a chore in and of itself, though the other prisoners appeared unhampered by it.

As he trained, James kept an eye out for Ryan until he spotted him several rows over, gasping for breath while heaving the rebar around. The two locked eyes and James made to go over to him, but a club tapped his arm, and a Talon grunted, "Pairs is later. Keep working."

James exchanged a look with Ryan before returning to swing at the post. He found the rebar was about the same weight as his old axe and easy to wield one or two-handed, but the balance was quite different. Connor had followed James to the training yard and taken a spot behind him, sweat glistening on his naked back. James moved around his post until he could see the Black man and asked him, "Are these the only weapons we can use?"

Connor shook his head, wiping the perspiration from his brow. "Nah, these're just to add muscle. What weapon you get depends on what kind of match. Regular ones are clubs like Talons got. Main Event gets you blades."

James glanced back at the Talons watching them and commented, "They *only* use clubs? Not just the guards?"

"Broken bones heal, which means you can get back to work. It's harder to hit your quota if you're missin' an arm or got your head blown off."

A Talon glared at the two and took a step in their direction. James picked up the rebar and swung at the wooden post again. The Talon grunted and settled back to watch.

The Talons didn't seem to mind if they talked, just that they kept training as they did. So, they continued their conversation between swings and moving around in circles. Connor was surprised to learn that another *civilized* nation like England had managed to survive after all this time. Interest piqued, James asked him what he meant.

"I mean, look around you. Ain't none of this the height of civility now, is it?"

"What's it like 'a bit south of here'?" James grunted as he struck the post.

Connor snorted a laugh. "Can't even compare the two. The Great Southern Free States ain't like here at all."

Free States. Brian had mentioned them when they'd first met. James wanted to know more, especially since he'd told Elizabeth to head south.

Connor told him he'd originally been from Tubman but had moved to Turner for work. Turner was the northernmost state, putting it right on the border with the Cult.

"How many states are there?"

"There's five. Aside from the Tubman and Turner, there's Lincoln, Coffin, and Douglas."

The names meant nothing to James, but he recognized Lincoln from somewhere. "Would it be easy to get to from here?"

Connor stopped and leaned against the pole, looking at James as if he'd grown two extra heads. "You think I'd be in this shit hole if it were?"

"Point taken," James muttered.

The two danced around awhile in silence, but then Connor asked, "You familiar with an American map?"

Muscles aching and mouth dry, James swung the rebar and said, "Quite a bit, yes."

"Turner's closest, but the dirt boys got that border sealed up tight. Tubman's west of there, used to be called Kentucky before things went to shit. But we'd be trekkin' through Dragon Territory if we head that way, same if we tried goin' south through Split State to Lincoln. No, sir, it ain't easy," Connor snapped, angrily striking at his target.

"I take it you've thought about this quite a bit."

Connor nodded. "Got plenty of time to think in here."

James asked, "Who controls Washington? You or the Cult?"

"Not us, I can tell you. No one really has claim on it as far as I know. Why?" said Connor.

"Some friends of mine are headed that way," James said. Then he realized they should have made it there by now. He could only hope they'd been able to send a message back home for his brother's sake.

The conversation was cut short when a Talon said, "Break."

Pale-skinned men came out onto the training yard, carrying buckets that sloshed water with each step. A pile of tin cups was dumped from a burlap sack when the pale men put the buckets down. None of the men would meet his eye as James followed the other prisoners. They only looked at the ground, their hands folded in front of their loose-fitting, mud-colored clothes. Each was scarred on the side of the neck with the Dragon symbol.

The prisoners dipped the cups in the buckets and gulped down the water. James sniffed at it first, but it was hard to smell anything other than smoke. He sipped the water, and it tasted all right, so he downed the rest and went for more.

He emptied a second cup to find Ryan, breathing heavily and with soot streaked across his forehead, standing in front of him. "Thought they'd done you in, yeah?" He grinned.

James clapped a blistered hand on his friend's shoulder. "Had some mending to do. But nothing was broken."

Ryan gave him a playful poke in the ribs. "Good to see the old Barlow Luck still works."

James winced, more from the memory of it than from actual pain. "I wish some of that luck would find us a way out of here..." he grumbled.

After he introduced Ryan to Connor, James took in the old prison. Stone guard towers were built into the corner of each wall, and The Cult had erected additional wooden ones around the interior. Tall barricades kept prisoners from sneaking out of the training yard, leaving only one way in or out. Craning his neck, he could just make out the prison entrance across the Pit and the fallen section of the wall. He asked Connor about that.

"Dirt boys call it Prophet's Gate. It's holy to them or some such nonsense. At least, that's what Heimlan told me. Whoever founded the Cult blew that hole durin' a battle here."

"Pairs," said a Talon, kicking over the buckets. What water remained soaked into the ash that dusted the ground.

The prisoners were led to a second fenced-in yard without posts. A table was set up by the gated entrance, laden with clubs wrapped in thick cloth. Each prisoner picked one up as they passed. Inside, rows of circles had been carved into the ground, wide enough for two men to move around in.

Ryan and Connor looked at James, then back to each other. "I know I can't take him. Why not give it a shot, yeah?" Ryan said to Connor. He then tapped another prisoner.

Connor shrugged and gestured to a circle. "Seein' all that huffin' and puffin' you was doin', not sure you'll be much of a challenge. But, just in case, remember, Englishman, this is practice. Save the real fightin' for the Pit."

James nodded as a clang reverberated across the yard. Distracted by trying to figure out what the noise meant, James missed it when Connor moved in and whacked him hard on the leg. James stepped back, more surprised than hurt. Positioned like a sword fighter, but with the club in his back hand, Connor gave him a quick nod.

James raised his club and held it out defensively but soon grunted after Connor snatched it out of the way and hit him on the other leg with one fluid, circular motion. Yanking his club out of Connor's hand, James used his longer legs to his advantage by shuffling back and kicking out simultaneously, widening the gap between them. Connor was quicker than he'd anticipated, and after spinning out of the kick's range, he darted in to strike at James's leg again.

But this time, James had been ready. Parrying upward and using his height to overextend Connor's arm, James brought his club back around and struck him on the side with a hefty smack. Connor grunted and moved around, rubbing where he'd been hit.

It was James's turn to go on the offensive.

He darted in at Connor with a flurry of strikes from different angles. Connor deftly blocked each one while backing away. With the last swing, Connor ducked low to avoid it but didn't see James twist at the last second and took a knee to his chest. James shoved him back, and Connor hit the ground.

James held out a hand to help him up. Connor, catching his breath, smiled and grabbed it firmly. "Guessin' you've done this before?" Connor asked.

James returned Connor's smile. "I'm still a little rusty. You should have seen me in my prime."

Eagerly, Connor said, "We'll get you there. That's one for you. Let's go again."

James won fifteen out of the twenty-three sparing matches by the end of the day's training. Both went back to their cells, bruised and sweating. James had hoped for another rest period to find out where Ryan was being held, but it never came. *I'll have to pair with him tomorrow. Even if he tries to squirm his way out of it.*

Laying on his cot, with feet dangling off the end, he went over the layout of the prison he'd made in his head. The only possible exit was out the front entrance, but he'd have to go through the processing area and get across the open yard with no cover. James grew frustrated and unable to come up with a plan that didn't end up with him leaving Ryan behind. Abandoning his friend was out of the question.

Tossing and turning on the hard cot, what little sleep he managed to find was marred with nightmares. *His mother, a noose around her throat, cried out to him when the floor dropped out beneath her. Looking down, he saw his hand on the lever.*

James clawed his way out of the dream, waking in a cold sweat.

The last bits of evening sun filtered in from the small window above his cot. He panicked, not recognizing his cell, but then remembered he wasn't in Newgate. James closed his eyes and rubbed the bridge of his nose, hoping to calm his nerves. When his heartbeat settled, he stood and stretched his sore muscles. He felt the bruises from the previous day's session on his arms, legs, and especially a particularly deep one on his back where Connor had hit him with the handle of his own club. The pain felt strangely satisfying, even comforting.

Then, like nails on a chalkboard, a high-pitched squeal came from outside in the cellblock. James hobbled over to the bars and saw one of the strange pale men was moving along the row of cells on the other side with a rusty wheelbarrow, the wheel of which was in desperate need of oil. The other prisoners were at their cell doors, holding out metal bowls. When the wheelbarrow passed, prisoners dipped their bowls, scooping up something that resembled yellow porridge.

The sound of the first wheelbarrow masked the approach of the second one until James saw it roll in front of Connor's cell. James searched for a bowl and found it thrown under his cot. He made it back just in time and scooped a bowlful of whatever it was they were being served. He sniffed and found it wasn't that unpleasant. It had a sweet flavor he couldn't place, so he asked Connor what they were eating.

"Corn mash. Dirt boys must be cookin' up some moonshine 'round here."

James ate some more, then asked, "What's with these blokes pushing the wheelbarrows?"

"From what I hear, they're the guys that couldn't live up to the Talon standard. They tried, which puts them above your everyday slave, but they still slaves."

An audible grunt came from the other side of Connor's cell.

"Shut it, Heimlan, or I'll tan you somethin' fierce in pairs."

Heimlan grew quiet, so Connor continued, "Like I was sayin', they might have won their fight to be a Talon, but it ain't all sun-shine and rainbows after that. They fail their trainin', then they get to be Workers and do the Cult's biddin', no questions asked."

James was amazed at how this Cult functioned and how all too familiar it was. This society was based on industrial exploitation but as a religion. The parallels between them and the Crown were far too similar for his liking. *If a resistance had grown under the Crown, there must also be one here.* Dropping his voice to a whisper, he asked, "Has anyone challenged the Cult? Tried to overthrow them?"

Connor chopped a hand in the air and clicked his tongue. "You don't want to be caught talkin' like that." He slipped away from the cell door, ending the conversation.

James sat on his cot and finished eating breakfast. It was strange to think of it as breakfast just as night began to fall, but that's how things worked around here. Thinking back on Connor's warning, he wondered what else they could do to him that'd be worse than fighting to the death for their entertainment?

***

After his 'funeral,' Render had been forced to stay cooped up in his rooms for two weeks. Not able to take it any longer, he barged into his sister's office where his sister sat, back rigid, behind their father's desk and wearing that ridiculous deer skull crown she made after taking over as The Head of the Dragon. Strangely, she was watching the clock above the door.

"You made it far longer than we'd anticipated," she said, nodding slowly, with one eyebrow arched.

Render sniffed. "I'm done waiting, sister. Do whatever it is you've got planned and resurrect me."

Sarah's eyebrow lowered, and a smile worked its way across her lips. "Of course. We wouldn't want the Body to think we would leave them unprotected. What good are Talons without the Claw to guide them?" Rising to her feet, she picked up her staff from where it leaned against the desk and weaved her way through the assortment of tables weighed down by all manner of books. She paid extra careful attention so as not to knock over the stacks piled on the floor until she came to stand before him.

Render, eager to get out and breathe the air of Dragon's Rest again, stepped aside to let his sister by. Staff clicking against the floorboards, she walked far too slowly down the hallway. Following, he could see the orange fires that burned nonstop in the Den through the milky, painted glass. His freedom was so close, and it was all he could think about.

Then came the touch at his chest, and he paused. His sister looked into his eyes, and he felt the excitement brushed away with a shake of her head.

"It will take a few days, dear brother. The Body must first learn what our intentions are. Then, with our guidance, they must pray to The Dragon. They shall fast. They shall go without sleep. And in the end, when you emerge—alive and whole—their devotion will be stronger than ever."

Fists clenched, Render looked to the door at the end of the empty hallway and then to his sister. *There's no one here. I could just snap your neck and walk out. Your death would be my rebirth.* She walked away from him as he thought how good it would feel to finally be rid of her. He imagined the crowds gathering for him, and him alone, while she opened the door to the Den and left him standing all by himself.

It happened just as she said it would. On the third night, Sarah beckoned him into the Den. His arrival was met with a roaring crowd. Render spread his arms to show the masses he was fit and whole again, then pounded his chest. Their screams intensified. The Talons in the crowd took up the holy chant. Render gave into the rhythm, the power it contained. He stomped against the stair to the rhythm, and soon the chant drowned out the rest of the Body. It was beautiful.

But it all ended when Sarah raised her staff. The crowd that took up the entire Den and overflowed to the streets dropped to their knees before The Head of the Dragon. Render read it as a reminder of who was truly in control here. And in this moment of triumph and return, he fumed.

THE MAIN EVENT

In the oppressive summer heat, the training continued. It was worse back in their cells during the day when they tried to sleep. The air was humid and stank of waste. At least James had managed to spend more time with Ryan, but they couldn't devise a plan to escape. For now, they would have to continue playing the Cult's game.

James had also trained with a few other prisoners and discovered that the territory under the Cult's control was far more extensive than he'd thought. One man with a thick accent came from the far north, near the walled city of Quebec. He had come down to trade and mistook a Talon for a bandit trying to rob him, so he killed him.

Another prisoner had been captured somewhere to the west in his village of Ashtable. He described a large body of water that went all the way to the horizon, called the Eerie. James tried talking with the pale men, but they'd only stare at him and remain silent. If Talons were near, they'd back away with their eyes to the ground.

He managed to corner one of the bucket carriers at the back of the training yard before they were broken up into pairs. Quietly, he asked where he'd come from, if he had family, and if he missed home.

A blank expression was his only answer.

Frustrated, James kicked the bucket by his feet.

Finally, this got a response. In an angry whisper, the pale man hissed, "You need to learn your place, prisoner." With strangely dull eyes, he looked at James as he picked up the bucket and hit himself in the head with it

James tried to stop him, but the man hit himself harder than the first time. Blood flowed from a ragged cut on his forehead, staining his unnaturally white skin. Dropping to the ground, the pale man cried out in pain, which drew the attention of nearby Talons.

In shock, James hardly noticed when he was surrounded. He could only stand there and look on as the man rolled back and forth in the ashy dirt. Blood splashed from the wound and onto the boots of one of the Talons as the pale man fingered James.

A Talon with a scar running down the middle of his shaved scalp stepped up to James with murder in his eyes and splattering saliva on James's chest as he yelled, "Waster!" The Talon barked up at the watchtower by the training yard. A rapid bell rang out and was picked up by the other towers.

Two Talons held James as Warden came strolling across the yard, appearing as if he'd been awakened from a deep sleep. He blinked at the light cast by the various fires in the prison yard and yawned. "What's going on here?"

The scarred Talon said, "Tall one here bashed the Worker with a bucket."

Warden rubbed the sleep from his eyes and said to James, "Can't have you wasting Workers." He turned to the scarred Talon. "Get him in the next round of fights. We'll see what The Dragon has in store for him." Without even looking at the pale man, Warden walked away.

James started to protest, but a Talon clubbed him in the gut, and he was dragged away to a different cell block with solid hatch doors. Thrown into a dark cell, James ducked to keep from striking his head against the ceiling as the door slammed shut. There was no window this time. The only light he had now came from the small slot at the base of the door.

A Talon shouted from the other side, "Get ready, Waster. You're in the Pit tomorrow."

Crouching in the darkness, James could only stare at the tiny sliver of light and feared that if he stayed here much longer, the insanity that infected these people would soon spread to him.

Where's the pattern?

An image of his father appeared in the black emptiness as he sat in the darkness. George Barlow towered over him, just as he had when James was a boy, with his brown hair swept back, neatly trimmed mustache, and blue, piercing eyes that stared down at his son.

You said there'd always be a pattern.

There is, his father's voice whispered from inside James's head. *You're just not looking hard enough.*

I'm so tired. Why couldn't I have lived a normal life? James asked.

Because, son, you're a Barlow. We fight. That's what we do.

James covered his face with his hands.

***

No meals came through the slot, only silence. He might have slept, but there was no way to really tell. Then the deathly silence ended with the sound of marching feet and chanting voices that grew louder until it was right outside his cell. A bright light blinded him when the door opened, and he had to shield his eyes with his hands. He tensed as the chanting continued, but no one came in to drag him away. As his eyes adjusted, he looked through the open cell door to the Talons, standing in two rows, staring back at him.

Still disoriented, James slowly stood and went to the doorway, and as soon as one foot left the cell, they grabbed and pulled him into the hall. He stumbled but managed to keep his feet underneath him. The Talons closed in from behind and herded him toward the end of the hall, where they passed another group of Talons chanting outside a cell down the row. But before James could see who emerged, he was shoved outside and greeted with cheers.

A crowd gathered around the Pit, made up of the haggard men and women from outside the prison, with Talons and Workers mixed among them. The Talons picked up the chant and stomped their feet in time with James's escort.

A dirt ramp sloped down to a gate leading into the Pit. Like in the training yard, a table had been set up with a few weapons and a weathered breastplate. A Worker behind the table picked up the armor and held it out to James with a sneer. James could feel how weak and brittle it was with rust flaking off it. He tried to hand it back, but one of the Talons grabbed the breastplate and shoved it into his chest, then another tied the straps tight on his back. There were a few swords and a club to choose from. The swords' edges were nicked and bent, so he opted for the club. As soon as he picked it up, the Talons pushed him through the gate.

It was intimidating, to say the least, as he looked up at the cacophony of screaming voices and stomping feet. The crowd leered down at him, faces lit by firelight, through the twisted rods that circled the Pit's rim. Among them, the pale Workers were silent, but their glares told him all he needed to know. They didn't need liberating. This was what they wanted.

"Fucking hell," James muttered and went about circling the Pit to get a feel for it.

Maybe forty feet or so across, its floor was dirt, and the walls were shorn up with slabs of cement that barely fit properly. James stuck a finger in the cracks and felt the loose soil behind it. Turning away from the wall, he saw another man standing at the gate, a man he didn't recognize from the practice yard. He had long brown hair and a braided beard. Black knotted lines were tattooed on his toned arms and shoulders. His chest was bare except for a breastplate. He brandished a sword in far better shape than the ones James had been offered. Eyes filled with fury stared at James from across the Pit.

Silence fell over the crowd when a voice called for order on the stage above the Pit. Warden wore a proper suit that might have been in fashion half a century ago and mended to the point where it no longer fit properly. One sleeve was longer than the other, and there was a different colored lapel than the rest of the jacket. His salt-and-pepper hair was combed to the side, and he'd shaved for the occasion.

Raising his arms, Warden shouted, "People of the Dragon, welcome to this week's Main Event!"

The crowd applauded and whistled. Warden waited for them to stop. "I bring you the guilty. Wasters of the Dragon's Chosen."

The people booed.

"They have committed the most heinous of crimes against The Dragon."

They hissed.

"And now, they will fight for their right to return as a productive member of our society. In the words of our Prophet, death leads to more death." Then, looking down into the Pit, Warden said softly, "Let the fight begin."

There was no fanfare or signal bell. James was still looking at Warden when he heard his opponent close in. Lifting his club, he managed to fend off an arcing swing of the sword, the blade biting deep into the wood. James jerked his club to the side, throwing the prisoner off balance. The prisoner had a strong grip on his sword and fell to the ground but was also able to pull his weapon free at the same time.

James was ready when the tattooed man got back up, spinning to face him. With determination in his eyes, he came at James, who tried to block again. At the last second, the prisoner adjusted his grip and thrust the sword instead.

James turned, and the blade tip grazed against his breastplate with a chilling metal squeal. He almost lost his nose when the sword swept up his chest and over his head. Before James could react, the prisoner brought the sword around to cut into James's unprotected back. James tried to duck below the blade, but the sword sliced into his shoulder. Gritting his teeth, he let out a groan of pain met with cheers from the audience.

Moving away, James needed to get some distance between himself and his opponent. His back was wet with blood seeping from the wound. It stung when he tested the shoulder, but it still worked. James grunted, watching the other man's eyes dance around, looking for an opening.

Speed was his opponent's advantage, and James knew he couldn't wait for the man to tire himself out. He'd have to try a different tactic if he was going to survive, so he moved closer. The prisoner swung at his stomach, but James hit the sword from above, forcing the tip into the ground. Then he stepped on the flat of the blade, making the man bend forward, and hammered his club against a tattooed shoulder with a solid *crack*. The prisoner let go of the sword, his arm dangling at his side, and backed off with a pained sneer.

The crowd booed.

He must be the favored bet.

Foot still on the blade, James eyed the prisoner who was clutching his arm close to his stomach. The fury James had seen in the prisoner before had cooled and replaced with bitter acceptance. He wouldn't fight an unarmed man. Especially not for the entertainment of another. "Everyone deserves a fighting chance. Even here," he said and kicked the sword over to his opponent.

The prisoner snatched it up with his left hand and moved the sword around in a series of flashy maneuvers, showing he was just as deft with his left as he'd been with his right. James offered a salute with the club, and the two ran at each other. The wiry prisoner swung high, and James brought the club up to block, but then the man dropped to a crouch, and the blade slid across James's thigh. Cold pain shot throughout his leg. James kicked with his good leg, sending his opponent onto his back, and clubbed the man's breastplate hard enough to dent it and force the wind out of him.

Gasping for breath, the prisoner clutched at his chest as James closed in. But it had been another trick, and the man lashed out and cut into his calf. James hobbled back with blood dripping from multiple wounds. He knew he had to end this.

Hair covered most of the prisoner's face as he got up on one knee, coughing. Limping in, James deflected the blow he knew would be coming and kicked the prisoner's knee. The man toppled back to the ground and only just managed to roll out of the way as James slammed his club mere inches from his shoulder.

James planted a foot on the man's arm in mid-roll and popped his shoulder from its socket. The tattooed man gasped in agony, his eyes rolling back in their sockets. Stepping back, James felt sick. This wasn't what he'd imagined. This wasn't a duel. It was torture. The prisoner's face was a mask of pain as he looked up at him in defeat.

That was when James heard the crowd shouting, demanding death. He looked at the grinning, excited faces floating up there. Returning to the tattooed man, he saw tears trickling down the prisoner's cheek. He didn't want to die any more than James did. There was a moment between them when they locked eyes. Then the prisoner closed his.

James, after so long, finally found the pattern. And how to break it.

Dropping the club, he walked away.

Silence followed.

He went to the gate leading out of the Pit, and the crowd began to murmur. He waved at a Talon to unlock it. The Talon seemed unable to comprehend what James was asking.

"Only in death do you win your freedom," Warden called out.

Not turning around, James shook his head. In a clear voice, he said, "No."

The murmuring became whispers and then grew into angry shouts.

Warden called for calm and then addressed James again, "What do you mean *no*?"

James shouted, "I'm not killing for you bastards!" And turned from the gate.

Warden ran his fingers through his hair, messing it up and making it stick out at odd angles. Confused and almost pleadingly, Warden said, "But you have to. It's the law."

Defiantly, James said, "I won't."

Warden looked worried then, glancing at the Talons around the stage. They did not look pleased. One went up the short steps and approached the older man. Warden shrunk back when the Talon leaned in close and whispered something in his ear. Warden's face changed from fearful to relief, and he nodded enthusiastically. He said with a vicious grin, "Then you'll just have to keep fighting until you do."

The gate clanged open behind James, and Talons dragged him, once again, to the ground. The tattooed man, still on his back, stared at James with gratitude while the crowd hollered and threw whatever they could down at them. James was silent and didn't fight back as they carried him to the cell, but a smile crossed his lips when the door slammed shut.

VALLEY OF DEATH

It was a long journey for the troop of twenty and their three guests. Far longer than Elizabeth had anticipated.

First, they had to pass through Virginia, which was heavily fortified along the border with the Free State of Turner. Virginia was rich with the materials the Cult coveted the most and protected it at all costs. "Only thing is," Thomas said, "the Free States got no intentions or want for their land. Dirt boys is just extremely paranoid by nature."

Ever curious, Liz had questions. She always did. Her grandfather had given her all those books mostly to keep his sanity. She asked about the men hunting them, and Thomas seemed perfectly happy to chat with her when he could.

So, she learned that Theron, the only name she'd heard so far, was the leader of the Southern Dragon Forces, a massive army amassed near the border. That was why the Free States had many garrisons along the edges of Turner and Lincoln to counter any assault that might come.

"Rumor has it he wanted to be The Claw but got shunned by The Head of the Dragon after some incident years back. Got himself exiled and had to settle with overseeing their border," Thomas explained. "A real whipper too," he added. They were passing through an old farm deep in the Appalachian Mountains' foothills, with fields grown thick with weeds and a pile of rotting timber that used to be a barn. "He drives them Miners day and night. Trying to be more productive than the Northern mines. Personally, I reckon he just wants that queen of theirs to take notice."

Strolling alongside Thomas, Liz asked, "How is it you know so much about them?"

Thomas scratched the back of his head. "We trade some and hear things. But mostly, we got people inside their territory letting us know if they planning on starting something again. They tried a few decades back, and it didn't go so well for either side."

"What did they do?"

"Before I was even a thought, they tried to take Turner. It was back before we'd been fully organized, mind you. Heard it was a pretty lousy war, but they managed to drive the dirt boys back. Lots died, though, on both sides. But back then, they were led by The Second Head of the Dragon, and from what I hear, almost reasonable compared to who's running things now.

"Anyway, he got to talking with our first governor, and they hatched out a peace treaty that put the border right down the middle of old Virginia."

"Split State," Elizabeth whispered, finally understanding why it was called that.

Thomas said, "Exactly." And smiled. "If I was a betting man, though, I'd say they pushed that border further west than we wanted, but we just weren't in a good enough place to do anything about it. So, we end up sending them food, and they trade back tools for our farms."

"And people spy for you?"

"Yeah, some decent folk are sympathetic to our cause. Now, if you hadn't noticed, us Staters can't just waltz on up there. Don't got the right skin tone, is what I'm saying," Thomas chuckled. "Oh sure, we got our outposts, like the one you saw outside Baltimore. But it isn't easy going back and forth, so for the most part, we just skulk around and communicate with carrier pigeons. Funny little guys, them."

As the foothills grew steeper, it slowed down their progress. Each time they passed by a dilapidated wooden wall or a weathered stone building, it bothered Liz. These places had once been someone's hopes and dreams, left to rot with no name. All the rest gave the ruins no mind. Liz tried to do the same but found it challenging.

Camped in another old village, Liz had already lost count of how many she'd seen. Many buildings were simply gone except for the foundations where they once stood. Only a church, with a broken bell tower blocking the entrance, remained.

Thomas came and sat beside her while she and her companions ate from the deer Collins had brought back. "How's the cooking?" Thomas said as he settled down.

Liz hoped her smile appeared genuine and said, "Delicious. Thank you."

"Good, good. We lucky Collins didn't shoot this one. He usually don't pick the buckshot out of the meat," Thomas said. He picked at the meat on his plate, turning it over and holding it closer to the light as if just to be sure. The Staters knew better than to use guns while crossing through Dragon Territory, which meant any game had to be caught by traps.

Liz forced another smile.

"Something not right?" Thomas asked. "Ain't enough spices? Don't know where Collins learned to cook, but it sure weren't from anyone back home."

"No." Liz shook her head. "The food is delicious. Really. It's just where we are. I can't help to think about the people who lived here."

"Oh," he said and pointed over to the outline of the old church in the twilight. "Looks like God-fearing folk." Then shrugged.

"That's all?" She gestured with her fork at the chipped foundation at the edge of the campfire's light. "Maybe that could have been a bakery." She pointed to another. "And that a school. This must have been a lovely town before, with good people. They had a story."

Thomas nodded. "Probably right. But all's left is that church. And, just like most things, folks are only gonna remember what's been left behind."

Liz looked at him sharply, angered by his dismissive behavior. "You don't care what happened to them?"

"Liz," Okeny said quietly, lowering his plate.

Thomas waved a hand to Okeny. "It's all right." Then to Liz, he said, "It ain't that I don't care. It's because I know who they were."

Liz's brow furrowed, her food forgotten.

Thomas continued, "Well, not exactly who they were. Just what they represented. Remember, everything around here had gone to shit well before the plague came, what with the war and all. And these people? They might have left because of some battle brewing somewhere nearby." Voice taking on a bitter tone, he said, "But that don't change which side they was on."

Liz covered a gasp with her hand. "Oh, oh, Thomas, I'm sorry. I completely forgot where we... I wasn't trying to imply..."

Thomas sighed. "I ain't angry, so nothing to apologize for. This just proves my point, don't it?" He pointed at the church again. "You only saw what got left behind. You don't know any better without *context.* Sure, they had a story, but it wasn't a good one for people like me." He stood and nodded to Okeny and Richard. "Have yourself a good night, Miss Stillman." And left to join the troop at the other campfire.

Liz watched him go, feeling like she'd somehow disappointed him.

In the third week of slogging through the mountains, the haze in the air grew thicker, as did the smoldering, acrid smell. As they crept up along a ridge, Thomas said they were close to the border now, but they'd have to travel close to a mining operation. Below them, the valley was filled with black smoke and fire.

Liz was reaching for a pair of binoculars a trooper had lent her, but Okeny put his hand on them first. "Careful with those," he said. "It'd give us away if you catch the light wrong."

Liz felt embarrassed. *I'm useless out here. Without anyone watching me, they'd have caught us long before now.* They headed along the ridge toward a path leading into the forest that circled the valley. There were two large encampments down there, and the only safe way was to go between them.

"This is about the only place left we can cross over," Thomas explained earlier. "Theron's been patching up all the old holes along the border, and I reckon we'll lose this one soon too."

It was harder to breathe as they descended into the valley, and Liz began to cough every couple of feet. "It gets worse from here," Thomas said when they came to a small brook. He handed Liz and her each a handkerchief. Even before Thomas started to explain, Liz soaked the cloth in the shallow water and tied it around her nose and mouth. The damp cloth made it easier to breathe, but the day's heat soon made the mask humid and uncomfortable.

Near the brook, Liz found a soiled banner on the ground. Picking it up, she shook off a layer of ash to reveal a depiction of a dragon eating its tail. Thomas looked over her shoulder and told her it was the Cult's emblem. "They brand themselves with it too."

"How barbaric," she muttered as Thomas continued on with the others. She ran a finger over the embroidered beast, feeling the raised scales and wings. Whoever made the banner had put a lot of effort and care into it. Then she thought of the same symbol being burned into her skin and shuddered and dropped it back where she'd found it.

"I hope you don't mind me asking so many questions," she said after catching up with Thomas, though he continued walking ahead of her.

He didn't say anything for a moment, which worried her, then looked over his shoulder with an encouraging smile, and she felt some of her misgivings slide away. "I admit, some find my curiosity off-putting. If I should stop, please tell me," she said.

Slowing to walk beside her, he said, "No, no. You go on and ask away."

She was glad the cloth on her face hid her red cheeks.

A scout whistled from up ahead, ending the conversation. In their time together, Liz had picked up a few things and knew this meant to find cover and quickly joined the troop as they left the path and melted into the trees, staying low.

Minutes passed before five Talons jogged up the path with three men trailing behind, just as filthy and carrying pickaxes, much like the kind miners would use. Hidden beneath a shrub, Liz felt cold fear shooting through her veins. Thomas had taken this path because it was old and not well-traveled. Clearly, something had changed.

Liz held her breath as the Cultists passed, only letting it out again when they didn't spot her. She smiled at Okeny, who had his back against a tree a few feet away. The smile immediately faded when the Talons stopped a few yards up the path. One man put his pick down, crouched beside it, and felt along the ground. Liz's heart skipped a beat when he pointed in her direction.

Drawing a heavy club from his belt, a Talon nodded and used it to push the miners together while the other Talons fanned out. The same Talon then stepped off the path and banged the club against the side of a tree, its sound filling the once quiet forest. "Who's out there?" he shouted in a hoarse voice.

When no response came, he moved further into the trees with the other Talons following. He growled, "We saw your tracks. Toby comes from old hunter stock and knows they're fresh."

While the Talon spoke, Liz watched another draw close to the tree where Collins hid. Knife at the ready, Collins waited until he passed, then quickly kicked out the Talon's knee before driving the blade into his jugular.

The Talons turned at the noise, and the forest came alive. The troop pounced, and before Liz could even get out from beneath the bush, all five Talons were dead. The miners dropped their pickaxes on the path and sprinted back where they'd come from. Richard and Thomas moved to intercept, but one still managed to slip by. Collins gave chase, following him out of sight, while the remaining two miners struggled.

Liz finally crawled out from the bush and stepped around the dead Talons and into a debate. Some troops wanted to leave the miners tied up, but a few chose just to kill them. Thomas, as always, had the last word.

"They ain't dirt boys, which means they ain't got no say in what they do. Grab the rope and leave them for another patrol to find. Reckon once these fellas don't check-in, someone'll get sent out here. Maybe."

The miners looked just as relieved as Liz. Afraid she might have to witness an execution and unsure how she'd handle it. What the Staters had done to the Talons was terrible enough, but she could rationalize it after what she'd learned about the Cult and what they did to people.

Forced to the ground, the miners swore as they were tied to a tree. Collins ran back up the path as the last knot was tied. His report came in gasps as he fought to catch his breath. Liz only saw that he'd lost the other miner in the woods.

"Toby knows these woods better than anyone," said a miner. "You damn monkeys ain't gonna fi—"

Thomas kicked him in the face, cutting off whatever else he was going to say, and then barked, "We got to move. Now!" Heading back into the woods, the troop fell in quickly behind him. After a while, a bell began to ring somewhere far off and was answered by another to the south, then a third from the north. But it was the faint screeching from multiple directions that quickened their step.

Minutes passed, and they were running along the slope of a hill when the screeching stopped. Suddenly, something crashed into the ground behind them, leaving a flaming wood pile in a small crater. Then there was another explosion to their left. Looking up just in time, Liz saw a smoking barrel arcing in the sky to their right.

"Are… are they using catapults?" she asked softly. Then reality set in, and she cried out a warning.

"Run!" Thomas shouted without even having to.

The woods burst into flames.

Terror drove her muscles pumping as Liz ran up the hill. All the times she had run from bombings in London, the mortar shelling, and not knowing if her home would even be there, it all came flooding back.

As they climbed, a barrel crashed between Thomas and Collins. Thomas was furthest and managed to roll just in time, but whatever had been in the barrel splashed all over Collins, engulfing him in flames, and he screamed wildly. Liz ran to help, but Thomas grabbed her by the arm, holding her back. A jagged piece of wood shrapnel was buried in his shoulder as he looked at her with anguish. Fighting back tears, Thomas shook his head and pointed up the hill. There was no time, Liz knew. And nothing could be done to save Collins. She left him on the hillside, covering her ears to block the screams.

It was a mad scramble, with more screaming. Too afraid to see who it was, Liz kept running, chasing after those ahead of her. Dense smoke burned her lungs, even with the mask. Bleary-eyed, she lost her sense of direction, then something crashed into her back, throwing her several feet. Rolling to a stop, she found Richard on top of her, panting. Dragging her back to her feet, he held her hand as they ran. There was a crater where she'd been just seconds before.

Those who had already reached the top were shouting to guide the others. When she finally reached them, the explosions sounded distant enough for her to catch her breath. The forest had become an inferno. Trees cracked and splintered, toppling in the heat that swirled up the hill, making her take a few steps back.

Only nine Staters had made it, and her heart sank. Thomas, moving among them, no longer hid the pain he was feeling. Some continued to call down the hill, hoping their friends were still out there.

Thomas shouted, "Stop!" When his soldiers turned to him, he said, "We got to keep going. Their sacrifices gonna mean nothing if we don't get these people to Turner. Now, we got to make the dirt boys think they got all of us already. We ain't gonna let them find us, so that means we got to stay ahead of them. So, run, *mon sòt*." He pushed a couple to get them going. Some gave one last look at the burning forest, then they turned and jogged away. Liz had no idea what '*mon sòt*' meant, but now was not the time to ask.

Thomas pulled the piece of shrapnel from his shoulder as he ran. Blood flowed freely from the wound, and his face began to turn gray. Okeny noticed it before Liz and said, "Let me take care of that."

Thomas shook his head. "No time. Got to keep moving."

"Lose enough blood, and you won't be able to."

Liz hoped Thomas would see reason, but he kept running.

With the explosions gone, the only ringing in Liz's ears was the alarm bells. She had no idea where they were and feared they'd stumble into one of the Dragon camps. Their pace was slowed by a wall of dark smoke rising from the wildfire below. Trees would seemingly appear out of nowhere in the murky woods.

They followed the ridge of the hill until the smoke thinned out, and Thomas ordered them back down the slope. He urged them to keep going even as his own pace slowed. Okeny tried a different tactic and pointed out the trail of blood Thomas was leaving behind. "You're making us easy to track."

Gruffly, Thomas said, "Ain't nothing for it."

"At least let me give it a quick dressing," Okeny said. "One minute, that's all I'll need."

He was quiet for a few seconds, and then Thomas nodded. "Make it fast."

Okeny took bandages from his pack and wrapped the wounded shoulder.

Liz saw more than pain in Thomas's face, even before Okeny applied pressure to his wound. "I'm… I'm sorry about your men," Liz said.

He nodded, not looking at her, and said, "Ain't the first time I've lost men, but that don't make it any easier."

"How are we going to get out of this valley?" asked Richard, watching the rest of the troop getting further away.

Thomas said, "We'll make a sprint for the border. Hopefully, they'll be so focused here, what with looking for survivors, that we'll pass right on through. Just a few more hours, I reckon, and we'll be in Turner." There was a glimmer of hope in his voice.

Again, Liz was reminded of the times she'd fled through the streets, knowing everything would be all right if she could only make it to her grandfather's house. And it was, but the journey was filled with panic.

Liz was sure her feelings had been showing because Thomas gave her a reassuring smile and said, "You'll be safe soon. You just wait and see."

Okeny gave the bandages one last tug and patted Thomas on his good shoulder, "Good to go."

Thomas gave his work a quick appraisal and nodded appreciatively at Okeny. "Much obliged. Now, get."

The fire spread behind them as they ran down the hill. Liz couldn't help but think of the damage these mad men had caused. *Why would they do this? What do they want? To kill us, or do they have some other desire?* So few of the troops were left, and Collins's screams still haunted her. A sudden realization sent ice through her veins—James had been wrong all along. The Cultists do kill. Grief for her grandfather and crew swelled, and all she wanted to do was turn and run back north, but she knew she wouldn't make it on her own. So, she cried, knowing the others wouldn't be able to tell the difference between tears from the smoke or sadness.

They followed a row of low hills that led to the giant mountains that made up the valley walls. The alarm bells were muffled momentarily, to Liz's relief. But that was short-lived as she heard chanting behind them. Okeny, without a word, sprinted up the mound to their right. Liz called to him, but he didn't turn back.

When she tried to go after him, Richard grabbed her arm and pulled her along. He said, "Okeny knows what he's doing." Even so, Liz couldn't help but worry for her friend.

They managed to stay ahead of the Cultists for more than an hour, with the horrific chanting driving them on. Liz's body was on the brink of collapse. Only adrenaline and fear kept her standing. Barely able to draw air, her chest was on fire, and her legs felt like they weighed hundreds of pounds.

Occasionally, some men would fall behind, but Thomas would run back to encourage them to keep going. The toll it took on him was apparent. He had lost a lot of blood, and his skin had an ashen hue. Out of every horrible thing she'd witnessed since crossing the ocean, here, at least, was a good man. She wanted to tell him that, but then Okeny re-appeared on the path ahead of them.

Gasping for air and unable to speak, Thomas gave him a questioning look. Okeny pointed back in the direction he'd come from and said, "Nearly a hundred on the other side, combing the woods for survivors. We need to go up that way." He indicated the hills to their left.

Liz looked at the steep slope of dense trees and groaned.

"Lucky for us, they're getting predictable. These are the same tactics they used on the river," Okeny grunted next to Liz as they began the climb.

Thomas, just ahead, looked down at him and croaked, "What's that mean?"

His fingers searching for roots to pull himself up, Okeny said, "Trying to herd us toward an ambush. They want us running scared."

"Doing a fine job of it," Liz said with a cough as she pulled herself over a fallen tree trunk.

Below them, the chanting drew ever nearer. Almost a quarter of the way up, Okeny hissed and ducked behind a tree. Hurrying to find cover, Liz slipped on some loose stones and felt herself sliding back down the hill. Richard grabbed onto her pack in time and pulled her behind another tree. Liz closed her eyes and gripped Richard's arm tightly as the awful chorus and marching feet just below them. Then it receded as the Talons passed by, continuing their search.

Tempted to keep her eyes closed, Liz wanted to sleep, even just for a minute, but Richard shook her shoulder, and she knew they still had a long way to go. With a defeated sigh, she opened her eyes.

It was a grueling climb that left everyone caked in dirt and sweat. Mercifully, when they reached the top, Thomas said to take a few minutes to rest. There wasn't much in the way of comfort. The ground was rocky, with sparse weeds and bushes that pushed through stone cracks. Thomas slumped on a flat boulder, coughing smoke from his lungs, and looked down into the next valley. Liz sat next to him, worried for him.

He pulled the cloth mask from his face and tried to smile at her, but it was too weak to be reassuring. "Don't you fret none, *dam mwen*." He nodded to another line of hills across an expansive forest below them. "Right over yonder is the great State of Turner." A little louder, he said, "Almost home, boys."

The only response was tired grumbling.

Hope was on the horizon, but the sky was just as dark as it had been in the previous valley. Smoke rose from a Dragon camp on the other side of the hill—a camp that stood between them and the world beyond.

Okeny clicked his tongue behind her, and she knew it meant nothing good. Flat on his stomach, Okeny was watching to see if anyone had followed them. Liz slid to the ground and crawled over to see Talons climbing up the hillside, slowly and quietly. Okeny pulled her back from the edge before she was spotted.

Thomas eased himself off the rock, looking as if anything stronger than a breeze would knock him over, and hobbled over. He only looked tired as he backed away from the edge and ordered the men back on their feet. Groaning, they did as they were told. And with Okeny on rear guard, they moved silently away from the Talons.

But then a horrifying bird call froze them all in their tracks.

Turning back, Liz saw a grizzled Talon, a wolfish grin on his filthy face, pointing a gnarled club at them. Over his shoulder, he yelled, "Southers!"

A tumult of screeching responded, and the troop had to run again.

It was a stampede behind them as they made a mad dash and nearly tumbled over the side when they reached a steep slope leading to the next valley. Skidding and sliding on the loose gravel, Liz grunted in pain when something hard grazed her shoulder. She hadn't heard a gunshot, so she looked back and wished she hadn't.

At the head of the pack, Talons swung chains above their head. One released and barely missed Thomas's legs.

"Chains!" Thomas shouted.

Liz put on a burst of speed as the troop swerved between the trees. Halfway down, Richard cried in alarm beside her and tumbled along the ground with his legs wrapped up. Dodging another throw, Okeny and Liz grabbed Richard by the arms and dragged him down the hill between them. However, the added weight slowed them down, and they soon lost sight of the others while the Talons closed in.

"Leave me," Richard yelled.

"No," Liz said. Gritting her teeth, she pulled harder.

Richard didn't make it easy for them as he struggled to free his legs. Like a bola, the chains had iron balls on each end that twisted together around the legs of their prey, making it nearly impossible to remove without help. Liz looked over her shoulder just as more Talons poured over the hilltop and down the slope. Panicked, she missed a step and fell, letting go of Richard and scrapping her palms against the rocks. As she did so, a chain whizzed above her head and struck the tree in front of her.

"Keep pulling!" she shouted. Okeny grasped Richard's other arm and dragged. Liz tried to keep up, scrambling even as rocks and trees crashed behind her.

As she ran, Okeny managed to pull ahead. Sweat poured from his brow as the muscles on his neck bulged. At the base of the hill, Thomas and two of his men waited for them, and when Okeny arrived, they quickly freed Richard from the chains. Okeny spun around, calling for Liz to hurry.

She was only a few yards away when a hand clamped on Liz's shoulder and yanked her to a stop. Pulling her around, she came face to face with the same grizzled Talon with wild, bloodshot eyes, his teeth bared. His stench was awful, but somehow his breath was even more appalling. As if it were in slow motion, Liz watched him raise a club, and she closed her eyes.

A gunshot made her open them again. Bloody meat splattered the tree beside the Talon, coming from the hole in his head. He dropped dead at her feet, and, still shaking, Liz turned to see Richard only a few feet away, raised pistol still smoking. "I suppose, given the situation, guns are back on the table?" he asked.

A wave of rage-filled screeches swelled even louder behind her. Liz trembled and looked back up the hillside at the Talons standing in place, their mouths open, screeching until it turned into shrieks of anger that rolled up the hill as more of them saw the dead man at her feet.

Okeny came around to block her view of the ferocious mob surging toward her. He grabbed her arm and—as if the sound of the forest being torn apart behind him wasn't enough—said, "Run."

Lungs burning, she focused on Okeny's back, knowing she'd be lost if she couldn't keep up. He, in turn, was following Thomas and the two troopers with him. *How is he still standing?* She wondered, remembering how weak Thomas had looked just moments earlier on the top of the hill. Gunfire erupted behind her, and she flinched as Richard shot at their pursuers. The mob would scream louder each time he felled one of their own.

There was no time to reload, not on the run, so when he fired his last bullet, Richard shouted, "I'm out!"

Not looking back, Okeny pulled a pistol from his belt and tossed it over his shoulder, making Liz duck. Richard caught the gun and opened fire again.

The rest of the troop was ahead, spread out and making their way through the trees. Then, from the left, a trumpet cut through the screams. *What new hell is this?* Talons on horseback emerged from a gully. It was enough to sap what little hope she had left. Deep in the forest, Liz didn't know how far they'd already run or how close they were to the border. At some point, she knew, her body would give out, and she'd be at the mercy of the screaming insanity.

Liz watched a Talon run down one of Thomas's men, clubbing him in the head as he rode by. She was filled with hopelessness as the Stater fell. Faces passed through her memory then. First were her parents. Then James, Ryan, and her crew had sacrificed themselves to protect her. These bastards had taken her grandfather from her, and soon Thomas and all his men.

As the Talons trampled over the fallen trooper, something snapped inside Liz. Hopelessness was replaced with anger. Enough was enough. It was her turn to protect someone.

Lip curling to a sneer, she shouted at Okeny, "We need to get those horses!"

He looked at her with surprise, then at the horses, and shook his head. He shouted back, "There's too many of them."

"We can't run forever!" Liz yelled. She untied the string from the holster on her belt. Drawing the pistol she'd been carrying since they'd abandoned *The Ophelia*, she looked at Richard and nodded.

Together, they ran toward the men on horseback.

Liz called out to get the attention of four riders chasing down a couple of Staters. Half of them spun their horses around and came straight for her and Richard. Just like her grandfather had taught her, Liz raised her pistol, breathed out, and pulled the trigger while Richard opened fire. Only one Talon fell. Liz quickly ducked behind a tree to keep from being trampled. Liz thought she missed and meant to shoot the Talon in the back, but then he slumped in his saddle and fell off.

Liz stared at the dead body until Richard shouted her name. Stunned, she came around the tree to find two riders almost on top of her. Richard fired once before she could get a shot off, but both Talons collapsed. Liz blinked, confused by the knife protruding from a Talon's chest. Then Okeny ran by her as he went for the horses.

The Staters they'd saved had mounted up and fired at the approaching Cultists. Liz grabbed the reins of a frightened horse and climbed into the saddle while the others retrieved what they could. With the sheer number of Talons headed their way, Liz knew they wouldn't be able to fight their way out of this. Turner was their only chance.

When they returned with the horses, the gratitude in Thomas's eyes made her smile, though only briefly. In no shape to ride by himself, Thomas climbed behind Liz. She could feel how weak he was getting by the way he could barely hold on to her hips as they raced for Turner.

Liz still couldn't catch her breath. Adrenaline made her hands tremble, and she was afraid she'd drop the horse's reins. She'd killed another person. But, this time, she didn't feel any guilt, only anger at what the Cult was turning her into.

Thomas grunted in her ear, "Hurry."

Behind them, more Talons whipped at their horses as they came for them. The troop was doubled up on each horse, with one spun around in the saddle to fire back with their rifles. Richard and Okeny kept close to Liz as they raced through the forest. A Talon broke away from the others and sped toward Okeny. Richard warned him in time, and Okeny ducked below the Talon's club before it caved in his skull. Sitting back up, Okeny grabbed the Talon's arm and rode for the nearest tree. The Talon struggled to pull free, but Okeny was stronger. He held on until he smashed the Talon's arm against the tree, shattering it. Liz heard Thomas chuckle by her ear.

Thick smoke settled over them again as they rode. Coughing, Liz pulled the cloth back up over her nose as she spotted fires burning along the ground to her left and right. She feared the Talons were bombarding the forest again for a moment, but there were no explosions this time. The smoke stung her eyes, making it even harder to see where she was going. Someone gave off a pained cry to her right, and when she looked, there was only a riderless horse. Behind them, she saw a silhouette of a person flailing in mid-air with their feet kicking wildly. Another shout came from her left. Startled, she turned forward and spotted a rope strung between two trees ahead of her. Instinctively, she let go of the reins and pushed back on the stirrups, knocking Thomas off the horse before falling after him.

Sore and seeing spots, Liz stumbled to her feet before helping Thomas up. "Are you all right?" she asked.

Blood soaked through the bandage on his shoulder, and it took him a few seconds to focus on her, but he managed a nod. Satisfied that he wouldn't die that minute, Liz left him standing on shaky legs as she ran to find the horse.

Somewhere out in the smoke, Okeny and Richard were calling her name. "I'm all right. Be careful! They've strung rope up between the trees," she shouted back.

An ominous thunder grew louder within the burning forest while Liz frantically searched for the frightened horse. But it was no use. The horse must have bolted off. Carefully, she made her way back to Thomas. She called to her friends, hoping they'd still be close by. Maybe they could see where the scared animal had gone. Until then, she and Thomas needed to run.

The ground shook when she found him holding onto a tree for support. "We have to go. Which way?" she asked.

Thomas raised a weak hand just as a rider burst through the smoke next to him. The Talon leaped off his horse and tackled Thomas to the ground, crushing him under his weight. There was little Thomas could do little to protect himself as the Cultist beat him with a club. Liz pointed her gun at the tangle of bodies, but fear of hitting Thomas kept her from pulling the trigger. Instead, she made to grab at the Talon's shirt, which was slick with grease and grit. Readjusting her grip, she pulled at the collar, hoping to choke the bastard, and the Talon got up on his knees. Liz struck the back of his head with the butt of her pistol, which only seemed to irritate him. He swung his club over his shoulder, narrowly missing her face and hitting her arm. The pain forced her to let go.

While the Talon was distracted, Thomas pulled his legs in and kicked up at him. The Talon fell back onto Liz, sending them both to the ground. Face bloodied and one eye swollen shut, Thomas rolled on top of him and punched the Cultist in the throat. Liz scrambled away from him before getting up. The filthy-skinned Talon coughed and gagged but still tried to swing his club at Thomas, only stopping when Liz's heel stomped the side of his head. He ignored the pistol she aimed at his face and looked right into her eyes. Liz was shaken by the anger she saw there and pulled the trigger.

She helped Thomas with numb hands while the very forest shuddered as if the gunshot had summoned an earthquake. "We need to run," Liz said, and Thomas nodded, leaning heavily on her. "I-I can't carry you." Her voice hitched. *And I can't leave him.* Liz grabbed Thomas's arm and put it over her shoulders, and marshaled what strength she had left. *I* won't *leave him.* She had only taken a step when Okeny and Richard came out of the smoke, leading a second horse.

Even as the earth felt like it was about to collapse, he yelled for them to mount up. Moving quickly, Liz climbed into the saddle and then helped Thomas up. There was no strength left in him. She pinned his arms to her waist with one hand, and the other took up the reins as she kicked the horse into a gallop.

The smoke thinned the further they got from the fires. But even more encouraging was that the ground began to climb upward as they entered the hills at the border to Turner. Liz glanced back and immediately regretted it—a mass of dark riders emerged from the haze of smoke and ash she'd just left. Turning around, she prayed her horse was a fast one. Ahead of her, Okeny whipped the reins as Richard yelled for him to hurry. Horses screamed and snorted behind her as Talons thrashed at them. Over it all, she heard the awful chanting.

The stench of them was pervasive. Any second now, she knew Thomas would be ripped away from her. But they were so close. The top of the hill was right there. Thomas had made it sound like all this insanity would end as soon as they made it to the border. And that's all she really wanted. Just a moment to breathe. A moment to rest. Tears in her eyes, she whipped at the horse.

She made it.

And came face to face with a wall of guns.

"Down!"

She quickly hugged the horse's neck, pulling Thomas down with her just as the rifles opened fire.

The chanting and thunder were replaced with screams of pain from both animal and man. She'd lost control of her horse and sped toward the rifles, but a hole opened up to let her through. Liz managed to sit up, pushing Thomas back, and took hold of the reins again, slowing the horse. It was her heart that she couldn't regain control of, and it sped faster as she tried to make sense of what was happening. Over a hundred dark-skinned men and women aimed and fired another volley at the approaching horde on the slope. Fallen Talons were trampled beneath hooves. Then, like a flock of birds, the mass of Cultists split in two and retreated into the smoke-filled forest.

Stunned by it all, Liz gawked at the dark blue jackets the soldiers wore as they jumped from their horses and advanced with rifles raised, firing one last round down the hill.

Okeny edged his horse over to her with Richard behind him, amazement on his face. Liz felt a soft pat on her shoulder. Thomas gave her a weak grin, and his swollen eye made it look like he was winking at her.

In a tired whisper, he said, "Welcome to Turner." Then passed out.

BORN REBELS

The time for ceremony had passed. When they came now, James was dragged from the cell and dumped in the Pit. With each fight, the crowd swelled as word spread of the man who wouldn't kill for his freedom. At first, they ridiculed him, but the longer he endured, the heckling became cheers.

After each win, he was hauled back to the darkness and left to mend his own wounds. His body bled more than it healed, and he could feel fractures in several of his bones. He'd run out of shirt to use for bandages two fights prior and had started working on his pants legs. It was in these brief moments to himself that James tried to figure out how he kept winning. He was in far worse shape than his opponents, yet he'd still get the best of them. The Talons and Warden appeared just as confused, and that only made them angrier.

Sometime after his sixth fight, the floor shook, and if James didn't know any better, he'd swear it had been an explosion. Even with trouble tracking the passage of time, his hunger pangs told him something was going on. Days must have passed before he realized he was long past due for another fight. Perhaps Warden was giving him a break? James knew it couldn't really be that. The master of the Pit relished the spectacle and power of the arena.

He was on his back when he heard shouting and eased himself up until he sat with his back against the wall. Then came the unmistakable sounds of battle out in the hallway as something heavy struck the cell door. It was over in a matter of moments, and then everything was silent once again.

Crawling to the slot at the base of the door, James pressed against the dusty stone floor to peer out. A Talon stared back with dull eyes and blood pouring from a shattered skull. Footsteps approached, and a pair of tattered leather boots stopped right outside. The dead Talon was kicked aside, and James heard metal jingling. He knew the sound of someone fiddling with keys and got ready. Hunched over and sore from head to toe, he stood. Whoever was trying to get in wouldn't take him without a fight.

On squeaky hinges, the door swung open to reveal Ryan, grinning and blood splattered. "Beauty sleep's over, princess. We've got a prison to take over."

James just stared back—his mind unable to interpret the signals being fed to it.

Ryan called down the hall, "Found him. Go and free the lot of them." And he tossed the set of keys to someone nearby.

Connor stuck his head in the door. A gash was on his forehead, but he had a big toothy smile on his face. He gave James a nod and said, "Mornin', Englishman." Then disappeared again.

Finding his voice, James managed to say, "What?"

Ryan stepped into the cell, handing James a Talon's club. "Should probably fill you in, yeah? We've taken the cell blocks. Warden and some Talons are trapped in the old guard room above the entrance. The gates and the breach in the wall are secure."

James shook his head, then stammered, "H-how?"

Ryan pulled on his arm, coaxing him out of the cell. "I'll explain on the way, yeah?"

Still stunned, James followed.

Several dead Talons lay strewn about in the hallway as prisoners, newly freed, looked just as bewildered as James. Connor was there, handing them weapons from the fallen Cultists. The first man James had fought, the one with the tattoos, was standing over a dead Talon with one arm in a sling and brandishing a bloody sword. He greeted

James by raising his sword in a similar salute from the Pit. By reflex, James returned the salute with his club.

Connor came over after he'd finished arming the others. He had a long metal pole dented at one end to form a rough point, like a spear. Ryan clapped the Black man on the back and told the prisoners to follow him outside. The freed men, some still bearing the bruises from their fights with James, looked up from the dead Talons to see him out of his cell. Each one saluted him.

Slowly, James asked, "Could someone please explain what in the bloody hell is going on?"

Already on his way down to the end of the hall, Ryan called back, "I'm sure you'll figure it out. Now, come on!" The prisoners followed him, leaving James to stand alone among the dead Talons. He sighed, rubbing the bridge of his nose, then he went to catch up.

James stepped through the bent, metal frame of the door, newly ripped from its hinges, and was greeted by a round of cheering. Prisoners filled the yard outside. A few were injured, but, like Ryan, many had someone else's blood on them. The guard tower by the Pit lay toppled on its side while the others were left unmanned. And as for the Pit, the fencing and gates surrounding it had been stripped.

James looked down in the hole while Ryan tried to explain. "You did all this." When James looked up sharply, he continued, "You refused to play their games, yeah?" Ryan nodded at the prisoners. "Showed these blokes they didn't have to, either. I got to thinking there's more of us than them. So, Connor and I got the word spreading. Then at training a couple of days ago, we gave the signal and took the padding off." Ryan grinned, showing James his bloody club. "Really, only got themselves to blame, yeah?" he chuckled, "Dumb bastards kept us in shape."

The two walked along the edge of the Pit. "It wasn't easy," Ryan said. "But soon we had the training yard. The tricky bit was the guard towers. They had rifles and picked us off, mostly leg and arm shots. They were still careful about the whole killing thing, even after we'd killed a bunch of them." Ryan shrugged.

James said, "I've given up trying to figure them out. It's less of a headache that way."

"You might be right," Ryan said. "Anyway, Connor got Heimlan to show us where the munitions were kept. They had some dynamite in there too. So, I thought, 'Why not?' and blew up the first tower, yeah? The bastards had to know they were done for after that. Anyone that couldn't get to one of the cell blocks ran with all the Workers out the front gate." Ryan pointed at the other buildings. "Took us a couple of days, but we cleared them and freed more prisoners."

James scanned the yard as he listened. Even with all the prisoners, it somehow looked empty without the looming Talons guarding them. "And Warden is still here?" he asked.

Ryan thumbed over his shoulder and laughed. "The loon thought we could be reasoned with, yeah? Shouting from the window like he still owned the place. A few warning shots got him to shut up."

James nodded and scratched at his chin, impressed with what the prisoners had accomplished. He'd never been one for beards, but he hadn't had time to shave since leaving England.

Sounding less cheerful, Ryan said, "Guess you'll want to see what we're up against." And headed for the front.

James sighed. *I knew it was too early to get my hopes up.*

As they went, James saw Connor talking to a man he'd never seen out in the training yard. Bearing the brand of a Talon, it was strange to see that only his face was covered in soot. The rest of his skin, from his shaved scalp to the neck below his beard, was clean. Well, not *clean*, but less filthy. It was the Dragon brand on his forehead that drew James's attention. It had been mutilated. As if someone had angrily sliced at it with a knife and left a crosshatching of scars.

Ryan said, "That's Heimlan. He's a right bastard, but he doesn't want to end up like the rest of the Cultists here. Though I'm sure he'll make a run for it once we get out, yeah?"

Heimlan gave him a curt nod as James walked by.

They rounded the last cell block and went to the entrance where prisoners manned a barrier built out of the cement blocks and metal grates from the Pit. Most were armed, and a few had their guns aimed at the windows above the stone archway. Rifle barrels pointed back down at them, though neither side fired at the other.

James went over, and prisoners came up, slapping him on the back and shaking his hand. Without thinking, he accepted their accolades, but when he looked at Ryan, his friend said, "You're a bloody hero again, yeah?"

"This was all you and Connor. If you recall, I was in a cell," James said, pointing back to the prison block for emphasis. He did admit he felt a bit disappointed at missing the first battle.

Ryan said with a boyish grin, "We're just born rebels, you and I."

Above them, an all too familiar voice shouted, "And look, here he comes. The great warrior himself!" Warden's head stuck out between two rifles in the window. He looked like shit, James thought. His salt-and-pepper hair was messy, and bruise-colored bags were under his eyes. "Finally come to gloat, have you?"

Eyes narrowing, James loudly said, "This has nothing to do with me. These men freed themselves." He held his arms wide, taking in the other prisoners who cheerfully raised their voices.

"In all the years of the Fighting Pen, no one has ever broken the Prophet's rules before you. Then we suddenly have our first riot a few weeks after? That can't be mere coincidence," Warden said.

"Or maybe these fine men disagreed with their treatment. Perhaps they're tired of being your entertainment," James said to shouts of agreement.

"These men are nothing more than Wasters. You all deserve to be here. Do any of you know how many men you wasted in just the last couple of days?"

"Either murder each other or turn on the real enemy. We chose sanity over madness," James said, surprising himself. He felt his father's words channeling through him. George had been a gifted speaker, and James could only wish for a fraction of his talent. "Now, how long are you planning on staying up there?"

"Oh, not much longer, I think," Warden said. "I'm sure The Claw will be here soon."

James stared at Warden for several moments, cold creeping up his spine.

Warden cackled. "Oh, hadn't you heard? By the will of our Mistress, The Dragon has returned Lord Claw to us. And once he's learned what you've done, he'll be eager to come."

Shaken, James said quietly, "That's…not possible. I watched him die."

He went back to the fight with Render Hollow. The mine, the circle of Talons, the pain in his chest. Then he remembered right before The Claw sucker-punched him, he had been confused. But what about? Like a flash, it came to him. He had to look down to meet the man's eyes—eyes that should have been green. *It wasn't him.* Whoever he'd killed had been shorter than The Claw and had blue eyes.

When you let instinct take control, you'll miss the important bits, his father's voice said from the back of his mind.

James felt like a fool. How could he have let that detail slip by him? His subconscious had known, but he'd been so angry. He only wanted his pound of flesh.

Warden's laughter drew him back to the conversation at hand. "Won't be long. Won't be long," Warden said in a sing-song voice. "He'll be here. He'll. Be. Here."

James could only hope Warden's words were just the ramblings of another mad man, but he already knew better. Ryan looked skeptical beside him, though even with his chin held up in defiance, he looked a bit worried. "I told you some Talons escaped, yeah?" he whispered out the corner of his mouth. "Been trying to figure a way out of here before more show up."

James went to the makeshift barriers to see what his friend was talking about. Out in the cracked walls and crumbled foundations, a couple hundred Talons milled about in a camp. *They're not going anywhere.* None of the locals that usually crowded near the gates were in sight. *Probably cowering somewhere safe in this blighted city.* The Talons out there didn't worry him so much as the cannon they aimed at the barricade.

Taking a step back, James asked, "Is the prison surrounded?"

"No. They're just gathered here," said Ryan.

"There's no way we can hold this position. You know that, right?" James sighed. He turned away from the gate and looked at Ryan.

Ryan's face twisted in frustration. "We don't really have much of a choice now, do we?"

"Once reinforcements get here, they'll break through. So, do we have a way out?"

His frustration turning into defeat, Ryan said, "Not yet."

"We should come up with something then." James clapped him on the shoulder and headed back for the training yard.

"He's lying, right? About The Claw?" Ryan asked. "I saw you kill him."

James shook his head and sighed. "It wasn't him. Just some bloke that looked like him."

"Damn," Ryan muttered.

Passing by the Pit, Connor fell in step beside James as he continued toward the rear wall of the prison. "Got a feel for it now?"

James hated impossible situations, and because of that, his response was bitter. "It's a shooting gallery out there, and if we stay in here, they'll soon have the numbers to swarm the place. That sound about right to you?"

Connor frowned and nodded. "Yes, sir. That's what I reckon."

James sighed and rubbed the bridge of his nose. "Please don't start with that 'sir' shit," he said. "I'm sorry. It feels like I haven't slept in days, and I'm more than a tad sore."

Connor nodded again, still frowning.

To Ryan, James said, "This feels like the Tower. How did we think we were going to hold that position?"

Ryan thought a moment, then said, "Because Uncle was there to help…"

Standing at the base of the rear wall, James looked up at the nearly thirty feet of stone blocks. "Guess we'll have to start thinking like him then. And, as usual, I'm afraid we might not like what he'd come up with."

"Who's Uncle?" Connor asked.

With a faint smile, James said, "One of ours back in England. He had a real passion for science."

Ryan grinned. "Good chap, yeah? Really knew how to make things go boom. Though I couldn't figure out what the hell he was saying most of the time."

"It was his accent," James was quick to add. "Not the science." Then nodding to the wall, he asked, "Is there a way up there?"

Following the wall to one of the stone guard towers, they found a sealed door. It took a bit of muscle to pry through all the rust, but the men soon climbed up the shaky metal stairs that spiraled inside.

At the top, James had hoped to have a better view of what lay around the prison, except a thick layer of brown haze blanketed the city. He could make out a few partially collapsed buildings and rubble-blocked avenues.

After walking the length of the wall, he saw a single building still standing with wagons lined up outside. James pointed to it and asked, "Any thoughts on what that is?"

Connor held a hand over his brow and looked. "Ain't sure, but you see that white smoke comin' outta that pipe on the roof? Looks like steam to me."

James studied the building for a few more seconds before Ryan's stomach growled loudly.

"Pardon," Ryan said, rubbing his belly. "She's a bit empty. Mind if I go and grab something to eat? I'll bring something back for you, yeah?"

James had been doing his best to ignore his own hunger pangs, but now that Ryan had brought it up, he admitted he was famished. Then something clicked in his head. "Corn mash."

Ryan nodded. "Not sure where the pale buggers keep it, but I'll have a look around."

"No, corn mash," James said. When the other two still looked at him blankly, he continued. "Connor, you said the corn mash probably comes from where they're making moonshine, right?"

Connor nodded, raising a questioning eyebrow.

James pointed to the building with the steam pipe. "If I were to guess, I'd say that's it."

"So?" Ryan asked. Then he quickly looked worried. "What are you thinking?"

"Uncle would probably say it's crazy," James said, scratching his chin.

Ryan patted his stomach, then sighed. "All right, let's hear it."

James grinned. "Moonshine means alcohol. Alcohol is flammable. Get enough together, put a light to it, and things go—"

"Boom," Connor finished with a big toothy grin.

"What goes boom? Us, the prison, or the bastards outside?" Ryan said, looking from James to Connor. "Because I don't care to go boom, yeah?"

"Not us," James said with his arms crossed while looking at what he hoped was a distillery. "The bastards. But they won't *be* outside. Not for much longer."

"It's a shit plan," said Ryan when James was done explaining the details. Connor agreed, as did Heimlan and all the rest they'd need for it to work. But, since no one else could think of anything better, it was the only plan they had.

First, they needed rope and a lot of it. They ransacked the store-houses inside the prison until they had collected enough. Then James tasked Ryan with getting things ready on the back wall while he returned to the barrier. Pulling aside a few prisoners, he told them to keep the Talons distracted at the front of the prison.

"But don't get them too riled up. We aren't ready for them to launch their attack yet," James said. They seemed to understand, and he left them to their work.

Back at the rear wall, Ryan had set fire to a wood pile, using the smoke to obscure the view from the Warden's office. The ropes had been tied off, and the strongest prisoners had been gathered.

James joined Connor, Heimlan, and two others at the top. Connor waited by a coiled length of rope that fed into a pulley. The opposite end was in the hands of prisoners down in the training yard. Heimlan stood next to Connor, brooding. Taking a closer look at Heimlan's scarred brand, James could see there would be no going back for him. He'd be unable to hide what he did. *That's why he agreed to help. He has no other choice.*

Everyone within Dragon Territory had bloodshot eyes, irritated by all the smoke in the air. So, it wasn't too shocking when he finally noticed Heimlan's angry, brown eyes staring back at him. "What?" Heimlan asked with only a slight snarl.

James realized he'd been staring at a mark of shame for Heimlan. "Just getting used to having you along."

Heimlan grunted and went back to checking his weapons.

James did the same. He adjusted the rifle on his back and made sure the club was where he left it on his belt. Connor still carried his spear, and Heimlan opted for two clubs and a pistol. James waited until the smoke from their fire had become thick enough, then said, "All right, throw it. And remember, we have to move fast." Connor tossed the rope over the wall and descended, followed by Heimlan. The last one down, James tugged on the rope, and it disappeared back up.

They had plotted the best route beforehand to avoid being spotted by the Talons at the front of the prison and moved from cover to cover. When a gunshot went off across the ruins, James swore. Then a few more went off before falling silent again. No explosion of cannon fire, no battle cries, so the three continued.

It took only ten minutes to reach the small, ash-coated brick building. Back in the prison, Heimlan had told them there wouldn't be any Talons here, only Workers, maybe ten or so. Several empty window frames lined the side near the front, their glass long since shattered and mixed in with the soot and dirt on the ground. Heimlan made his way along the wall to look around back while Connor crouched low and peered through the window. Ducking back down again, he held up five fingers and pointed at his neck, then a balled first and pointed at his forehead. Heimlan was right, no Talons. Connor then edged to the other side of James before standing up. Having disappeared around the corner, the two had to hurry to catch up with Heimlan.

The rear of the building was featureless except for a single door, propped open by a rock. A ratty tarp covered a sizable mound, with muddy ears of corn spilling from beneath it.

He'd been betting the entire plan on the fact that this was a distillery, and moving to the door, he was rewarded with rows of barrels lining the walls. In the center of the room, two Workers tended to an apparatus made of twisted pipes, basins, and fire. Having seen his fair share of them back home, he knew distillation equipment when he saw it. A third pale man counted barrels on one wall, while another shucked corn before handing it off to have its kernels removed by a fifth.

James unslung his rifle, held up three fingers, counted down to zero, and they rushed inside.

"Don't move! Get on the floor!" James barked.

Startled, the Workers looked up from their tasks to a giant waving a rifle at them—and froze.

Connor muttered beside James, "You told them not to move first."

Out of the corner of his mouth, James said, "Still a bit rusty."

Heimlan crossed over to the one that had been counting barrels and pushed the gun barrel under the Worker's trembling chin. Teeth bared and spittle flying, Heimlan growled, "On the ground!"

Connor swung the butt of his spear around, knocked the legs out from underneath the shucker, and then placed the point at the back of his head. The rest of the Workers got the idea and dropped to the floor. James had hoped for someplace to lock up the Workers, but the building consisted of just one room. Then James found some empty barrels and said, "Shove them in these."

Once the lid was pounded tight on the last barrel, James made sure the bungs were removed so the pale men wouldn't suffocate. The three then got to work moving moonshine-filled barrels out the wide front doors where the hitched wagons were waiting.

It was hard work, and as James was hefting the last barrel, he caught a flash of movement out the corner of his eye. Someone ran from the side of the building to across the street.

James swore. Tired and still not having eaten yet, he gave chase.

The figure ducked behind a gutted building, and James lost sight of him, but not before he'd seen telltale pale skin. *Shit.* Hearing someone move on the other side of the wall next to him, James gave chase until he saw, through a crack, that it was only Connor. James hurried along the wall in the same direction, hoping Connor had eyes on the Worker.

Rushing down a cleared path between two foundations, James watched Connor sprint down the street, the fleeing Worker ahead of him, screaming for help and running straight for the Talon camp. James bolted after them. Like all the other Workers and Talons, this one's head was shaved, but something about his clothes seemed different. Less dirty. The man glanced back, and James got a quick glimpse of his face and thought he'd seen it somewhere before. The Worker must have realized how close his two pursuers were because he put on a burst of speed. But he didn't see Heimlan, who tackled him from the side.

The Worker yelled as he struggled while Heimlan attempted to pin him down and cover his mouth simultaneously. As James hurried to help, he finally got a good look at the pale man and paused. With parched lips, he asked, "Nate?"

The soldier froze at his name. His neck was freshly branded with the Dragon ouroboros, and he looked ten years older since the last time James had seen him. Haunted eyes stared back at James for a split second, then redoubled his thrashing.

James grabbed his shoulders to hold him down and whispered sharply, "Nathaniel Kitts, are you daft? It's me. James." They were far too close to the prison now.

"We don't have time for this," Heimlan growled, reaching for a pistol.

Fiercely, James whispered, "No!"

Heimlan sneered in disgust, keeping a hand on the gun.

Connor sighed and struck Nathaniel on the side of the head with the blunt end of his spear, knocking him out. "There. Can we get the fuck back to the wagons, or do you want to let the whole damned city know we're out here?"

Nate lay on the ground, limp, while Heimlan and James got up. James knew Nathaniel had recognized him. *What the hell did they do to you?* He had Heimlan grab Nate's legs while he lifted from underneath his armpits, and together, they carried Nate back to the wagons. "Friend of yours?" Heimlan asked.

"I wouldn't say friend," James said. "But I knew him."

Following along next to them, Connor said, "Sorry about hittin' him."

"Probably better than what this one had planned." James stuck his chin out at Heimlan.

The former Talon grumbled, "Wasn't gonna shoot him. Too loud."

"What do you want to do with him?" asked Connor.

"We'll bring him inside with us. I want to know what the hell he was doing here."

"Working," Heimlan muttered.

They propped Nate up on one of the wagon benches, and James said, climbing up next to him, "Let's do this slowly. And be careful of bumps."

Connor looked at the potholes in the road and said, "It's all bumps."

"Don't hit the big ones then."

The wagons creaked as they rolled out. Connor had been right: it wasn't an easy ride back to the prison. More than once, James had feared a barrel would shake loose and wished he'd done better to secure them. His nerves wouldn't let up, even after they made it back behind the prison. Aside from Nate's sudden appearance, the operation went off without a hitch. *When does it all fall apart?*

Ropes were tossed from the wall, and they got to work tying off barrels. After the moonshine was secured, prisoners down in the yard would pull them up, and the process would repeat. It took longer than James was comfortable with, but they eventually got them all inside. They sent Nate up the wall last before scaling up after him.

Ryan stood over the unconscious Crownsman when James pulled himself over the top. "Bloody hell. Is this Nate?"

Breathing heavily from the climb and really starting to feel the aches and pains from the last few weeks, James coughed and took a sip of water from a canteen another prisoner offered him. Then he nodded and said, "Found him out there."

"The fuck they do to him?" Ryan bent over and grabbed Nate's chin, turning his face from side to side.

"I don't know. But he was trying to get to the Talons." James sat on the edge of the wall, rubbing the soreness out of his legs.

Scratching the back of his neck, Ryan asked, "Eh? Didn't he recognize you?"

"Looked right at me and still tried to get away," James said. "Let's put him in a cell before he comes to. I don't know what's happening, but let's play it safe." He got back up with a groan. "Then get the barrels in place."

EMBERS AND SPARKS

"Why did you run?"

James was on a wooden chair outside the cell. Shortly after being put inside, Nate had regained consciousness but refused to speak. He ignored the food and water James had brought to him, leaving them untouched. For over an hour, James sat, arms crossed, and studied him before asking the question. Nate, on the cell floor with his back against the wall, only stared back at him in anger.

"What happened to you after we separated?"

Nate barely blinked.

"It's my understanding that the Workers tested to become Talons and failed. Is that true?"

Nate's hand went to his neck, slowly scratching at the brand.

James sighed. He leaned forward and rubbed at his sore eyes. Even after two months, they still felt like he had sand in them. Everything felt gritty, and all he really wanted was a clean bath. In fact, he couldn't even remember the last time he'd washed. Not here or in Newgate. *Has it been ten years since I had a bath? That can't be right.* He pulled open his shirt collar and sniffed. Other than the smell of sweat, it wasn't all that bad. James shrugged and looked back at Nate, who had raised an eyebrow.

"I was thinking of the last time I bathed and just checking…" James started to explain, but Nathaniel closed his eyes and shook his head.

"They seem to keep you clean."

When Nate opened his eyes, he looked like a man remembering something he wished he could.

James stood, holding onto the cell's bars, and leaned his forehead against them. "When we get out of here, you'll have two choices: either you can come with us or not. I don't know what the Cult wants with you, but I'd rather you choose the former. If we ever find your brother again, I want to be able to say I didn't abandon you."

Nate's eyes focused, and in a dry, hollow voice, he said, "I have no brother, only The Dragon's Chosen."

James tried and failed for several more hours to get Nate to speak again.

Tired, he eventually gave up and left Nate in the dark. James crawled into the bed in the next cell, knowing Ryan would have everything prepared. All he needed now was a good night's sleep. He'd need his body and mind ready for whatever came next.

***

Render Hollow groaned. The pounding at the door ripped him from a deep slumber. He sat up, his boots hitting the floor with a hefty *thud*, and the bed frame creaked when he stood. He almost forgot his bowler and went back and grabbed it, placing it on his head. Then he paused. Taking it off again, he looked at the hat—the hat that had belonged to his grandfather, The Prophet. With the reverence such a relic deserved, Render carefully put it back on.

After tying the black kerchief over his face, he opened the door and growled, "What?"

"L-L-Lord Claw," stammered a young Talon in the doorway, looking at the ground out of fear.

Barely a hatchling, Render thought, *who doesn't yet know what genuine fear is.*

"I said what." The leader of the Talons glared down at the boy.

"M-m-my apologies for waking you, my lord. Someone's here from the Fighting Pen. H-he says there's an emergency." Sweat trickled through the holy black sacrament on the boy's skin.

"What emergency?"

"A r-riot, Lord Claw."

The kerchief hid Render's excitement. *Finally, relief from this boredom.*

"Bring him to the Den. I'll get the Mistress." Render patted the boy on the shoulder.

Quickly, the young Talon said, "The Head is already waiting for you, my lord. She's the one who sent me."

The Claw pulled the door closed behind him with enough force to shatter its cloudy windows. The Talon fled down the hall, stopped halfway, and turned back with a look of pure terror.

Like a wolf stalking its prey, Render strolled toward him. "My father used to say, 'Discipline is everything.'" The young Talon's trembling grew the closer the giant got to him, with his eyes locked on the blades strapped to Render's thick forearms. "Don't worry, boy, I won't cut you."

The boy had only a moment to look relieved before his face was engulfed in The Claw's hand. Render slammed the back of the Talon's head into the wall, leaving a dent. The boy's muffled cries against his palm gave him a rush of joy.

Lifting him by his head, Render growled into the boy's ear, "Next time there's an emergency, you come to me first. I decide what my sister needs to know." Finally, he let go, and the boy crumpled into a heap.

The door to the Den was open when Render arrived. His sister was at the top of the stairs, looking down at a group of kneeling Talons as one begged her forgiveness.

"Please, Mistress. We couldn't stop them!" the Talon whined.

"Begging is for the weak!" Render bellowed after ducking under the doorframe.

All the other Talons knew better; none flinched and kept their gazes on the ground. The begging man's eyes only grew wider as his words turned to nothing but unintelligible sounds.

Render's words boomed throughout the Den. "*You* are a Talon of the Dragon. You carry *Its* Wrath and remember—" A hand on his chest stopped him short. How he wished to break those fingers. To hide his disgust and hatred, he closed his eyes.

Looking away from him, The Head of the Dragon said, "Now, Talon, you were about to tell us exactly what happened?"

"The prisoners, they… they all turned," the Talon said, eyes averted. "They've gone crazy, Mistress. They've *wasted*," the Talon hissed. "They've taken it all, the whole Fighting Pen. Put up a barrier to keep us out. A-a-and defiled The Prophet's Gate."

Render stiffened. His anger was boiling, as it did inside his sister. He felt her fingers dig into his chest; it took a few moments before she could continue. "And what of Warden?"

"I don't know, Mistress. It was chaos when I left."

"And none of you tried to fight back?" Sarah took her hand from her brother and stood imposingly at the top of the stairs.

Swallowing hard, the Talon said, "There's only a hundred or so of us and a couple Foremen, Mistress. We're gonna need more. There's at least three times that many Wasters."

"How did this happen?" Render asked.

The Talon said, "H-have you not heard, my lord?"

Render crossed his arms. "About the one who won't follow the rules of the Pit. I trusted Warden to take care of that."

"He was, My Lord. He made him fight every Main Event. But it's like he doesn't want to be free. And some of the Body even started cheering him on."

"Who is he?" Sarah asked, a hungry look in her eyes.

She already knows, Render thought.

"The big one, Mistress, w-with the strange voice."

The leather on Render's forearms crackled as his fists clenched. "Trespasser," he growled at Sarah. "I should have crippled him when they first brought him in. He wasted Grayson, and now this!" Grayson, his body double, had been the closest thing he'd had to a friend.

Not looking at him, Sarah asked, "How many do you think we should send?"

"I'll get my men together—" Render started, but Sarah held up a hand, cutting him off.

"We were not addressing you, Lord Claw," she said and gave a dismissive wave. "This Talon knows the Fighting Pen far better than you."

Render seethed while the helpless Talon stared in shock at the floor. "I-I-I'm not sure, Mistress, Lord Claw w-would be better..." The Talon trailed off.

"You may leave, Talon. Give us time to think of a suitable response." She dismissed him, turned, and with her dark skirt sweeping across the grated flooring, retired to their private quarters.

Finally free of her insufferable presence, Render glared at the Talons and slowly descended the stairs, singling out the messenger. After cracking his knuckles, The Claw grabbed the Talon by the collar, hoisting him up to stare at his face. The man's body danced like a fish on the line, trembling in Render's hand.

"How could you have passed the Test?" snarled Render. "All you know is fear." He gripped the collar tighter as red filled his vision.

Like hot iron on ice, Sarah's voice cut into him. "Lord Claw, we would see you in our office," she said from the doorway.

Render threw the fear-stricken man to the ground with a growl, then stormed up the stairs after her.

Finding the office door shut, Render slammed it open and found his sister seated behind the old desk, the skull crown placed to one side. To get across the room, he had to pass through the maze of books stacked on the floor after Sarah ran out of bookshelves and table space. She pointed at one of the two chairs at the front of her desk when he was close enough. "Take a seat, brother."

Render ignored her command and said, "You should have let me waste the trespasser."

Sarah stared at him. "Why should we have done so?"

Pressing down on the desk with both hands, he leaned over her. "He's made us look weak, wasted a loyal servant of the Dragon, and refused to obey the Prophet's laws. Now, the trespasser sparks insurrection. He is wasteful, and"—he shouted—"The Dragon does not abide waste!"

Unphased by his fury, Sarah said, "And how were we to know he would do all of that?"

Render glowered at the multitude of books. "You know the secret texts."

Sarah looked down and rubbed her temples. "Render, we've talked about this many times before. Books can't tell the future. They only contain the knowledge of the past."

Render snarled and heaved over a table, dumping books to the floor.

Shooting to her feet, Sarah yelled harshly, "Render Hollow, you stop right now!"

Glaring at her, he trudged back to the desk, though not before grinding an old book under his boot. Standing across from her again, he bent down to look her in the eyes, and she slapped him. She was preparing to hit him again, but he grabbed her wrist and squeezed until she yelped.

"You also made *me* look weak," he growled.

Locked in his grip, Sarah pulled until he finally let her go. She looked up at her brother and yelled angrily, "*I* am the Head of the Dragon. *You* are simply Its Claw. You cannot treat me this way!"

"You're only the Head because you could read the texts," he sneered.

"The Dragon chose me to read them. Just as It had for father. I *am* Its rightful Head." She slammed a hand on the desk for emphasis.

Render gazed at her a moment longer, then let his shoulders slump—a sadness from deep within quickly replaced his anger. He said in a quiet, somber voice, "I tried, Sarah. I did. The symbols just keep moving around on the page. None of it makes any sense."

Sarah placed a gentle hand over his. "I know, Render, I know. I've seen you in here when you think I'm sleeping. You're still trying to understand them." Slipping a dagger from the sleeve of her dress, she stabbed through the back of his hand, pinning him to the desk.

Render bellowed in rage but was forced to silence once more by another blade placed just beneath his chin. Coldly, his sister said, "You will never be the Head, do you hear me? Only the one who can read the texts can. And that will *never* be you."

Render swallowed hard as fury shook his body. The blade nicked his skin when he spat, "Yes, Mistress."

Eyes locked, she slowly lowered the knife and sat back down. Render pulled the dagger out of his hand and let it clatter to the floor.

"Besides, dear brother, you have your own role to play in all this. You are The Claw of the Dragon. The world trembles beneath your feet." She leaned forward in her chair, green eyes gleaming in the lamp light. "Rally your men and bring me the heads of all those prisoners. We must make an example of those who would do us harm."

The thought of battle brought a rare smile to Render's hidden face. "Yes, Mistress."

Leaving The Den through The Mouth, Render turned to look up at the wall of the great factory that had sheltered and protected his people long ago. The old man's body swung in the breeze beside the young one who had refused to kneel before him and his sister. Render grew eager to see the same wall covered in the heads of his enemies, especially the Trespasser.

* * *

James woke to a voice whispering in the dark. It grew louder until Nathaniel shouted, "It's only a test! It's only a test!" James listened for a moment as the soldier talked to himself, "They're just tools. You must prove yourself. You must be strong. It's only a test. It's only a test."

James climbed out of bed and moved into the torch-lit hallway, and Nate quickly quieted down. "What's only a test?" James asked. The Crownsman was as far as he could be from the pool of light in the back of his cell. "Nate, who are you talking about?"

Nate muttered, "If I answer, I might fail. If I don't, I might fail."

"What are you going on about? This isn't a test, Nate."

Nate scurried over on hands and knees to press his face against the bars. "How do you know it's not?"

"What would it be a test for?"

"Loyalty to The Dragon."

James knelt to look Nate in the eyes. They were red, glassy, and unfocused. He said, "Nate, there's no test here. Don't you understand where you are?"

247

Nathaniel's eyes began to dart back and forth. "This is Hell, James. And the only way to survive in Hell is to join the Devil's legion."

"Is that what you did? Willingly?"

Nate's eyes found their way back to James with some clarity, and he shook his head. He looked down and said quietly, "I... I didn't want to die." Nate shuddered and lifted his head. Tears trickled down his cheeks. "Eugene didn't survive his first run. I had to bury him with just my bare hands." He held them up and stared at the strange pale flesh.

James felt a pang of sadness. He'd liked Eugene and the way he didn't mince words. Reaching through the bars, he grasped Nate's hands. "I'm sorry. He was a good man."

"I couldn't stop—"

An explosion shook the prison.

Ryan ran down the hallway and shouted, "They're here! Blasted cannon blew right through the barricade."

James was up quickly. "Is everything ready?"

"Yes," Ryan said, then looked down at Nate on his knees. "What about him?"

"Decision time, mate. You can either come with us or take your chances with them." James thumbed in the direction of the explosion.

James watched a myriad of emotions cross Nate's face as he struggled to decide. Then quietly, Nate said, "I-I think it's best if I go with you lot..."

Unlocking the cell door, James asked, "Any of that Crownsman fight left in you?"

"I hope so," Nate said as James pulled him to his feet.

"While this is touching and all, we should get out of here, yeah?" Ryan said.

"Right." James nodded, and they went for the exit door. "How many are we looking at?"

"A few hundred, maybe five," Ryan said as he led them toward the ruined barricade. He slowed briefly and looked back at James. "Warden wasn't lying. The big bastard's out there."

James swore. He had hoped Warden had only been trying to get under his skin. Steeling his expression, he said, "Doesn't change anything."

A few prisoners manned the shattered barrier while the rest would be further back in the prison, just as they'd planned. James moved through the twisted wreckage and gazed at the Talons amassed outside the prison, far more than five hundred.

I'm starting to think Ryan doesn't know how to count.

And at the front, with a thick length of rebar in his hands, was The Claw.

That's more like it.

There was no doubt. James knew this wasn't another double. To the Claw's right, Talons were busy reloading the cannon as a second was wheeled out and aimed at the other barricade filling the hole in the prison's wall.

To be heard from across the ruined street, James cupped his hands at his mouth and said, "I guess the rumors are true. Did you get dragged out of your hole because they ran out of people to send in your place?"

James could feel The Claw's eyes burning into him even if he couldn't see them.

"Trespasser!" The Claw bellowed. "You've dug your own hole. Six feet deep!"

The Talons hooted at their leader's joke.

Then Render Hollow began to stomp his foot, the laughter ended, and the chanting started. Primal and ferocious, it made the hairs stand on the back of James's neck. He was fascinated by it and how the Talons obeyed The Claw with absolute loyalty. *What could do this to these men? If we survive, I really need to have a chat with Heimlan.*

While James was mesmerized by the chanting, he missed when Render pointed at the second barrier but saw the spark near the cannon. He shouted, "Get down!" And dove away as the second barrier blew apart.

Head fuzzy, James rolled onto his back with Warden's voice cackling, "Wishing you'd won your freedom now, don't you, prisoner?" Warden looked down from the window above the arched gateway.

"The Dragon has come to wipe away more waste!" Suddenly, the window burst and heavy chunks of stone and gore rained down.

Stunned, James slowly tilted his head and peered through the demolished barricade. The Claw pointed at where the office had once been. The old masonry crumbled and settled, blocking the entrance again. James couldn't fathom why The Claw had obliterated Warden and his remaining guards. That thought filled him with dread because an unpredictable enemy was almost impossible to fight. James got up, wiping dust and blood off his face. Only a couple of prisoners remained where they'd fallen, as the rest stood, looking a little shellshocked.

Over the ringing in his ears, he shouted at Ryan, "I need to keep their attention. Get the rest back to the wall!"

Ryan nodded, hauled prisoners to their feet, then shoved them in the direction they needed to go. Only Nate stood, with a blank expression, seemingly unmoved by the chaos around him. Ryan got his attention with a push, and the soldier went with the others.

James held a hand up when Ryan came to stand with him. "Hate to break it to you, mate, but I think it's me he wants. You go get ready. We need to time this perfectly."

Ryan's lip curled, and he bitterly said, "You never said anything about being bait, yeah?"

"How else do you catch an animal in a trap?" James tried to put on a reassuring smile.

Ryan looked doubtful but still gave James a salute before turning away.

With the main gateway sealed off again, James went to the only opening left in the prison, the so-called Prophet's Gate. He stepped out of cover and stood right in the very center.

Raising his hand, The Claw stopped the chanting.

"That's it? A bit of a sing-along and some fireworks? I've barely pissed my trousers," James called over.

Render Hollow took a single step forward and yelled back, "I'm going to enjoy taking your head."

"Will that be any time soon, or are we waiting to see if your sister will let you first?"

The Claw pointed at him, and the Talons surged forward.

That did it.

James darted back into the prison, chased by the chant. He ran for the Pit, where a line of prisoners waited—a show of force to draw the Talons further inside. James turned to the oncoming horde while the prisoners opened fire, targeting arms and legs as they'd been instructed. James had been afraid they'd retreat if too many were taken out. But seeing how they scrambled over their fallen, James realized that retreat was not what the Cultists had in mind. Pain only seemed to spur them on as they swarmed into the courtyard, pressed tight by the rubble laid down to funnel them into the center of the prison. Knowing they'd soon be overwhelmed, James ordered the riflemen to the rear wall and ran with them.

Ryan shouted from the top, "Ready!"

"Hold!" James yelled, holding his hand up. He had to be sure all of the Talons were inside the prison. The horde was forced to split as they ran around the Pit, a mere fifty feet away. Warden's stage shattered beneath their weight as they tore through the prison.

Twenty feet.

Ten.

There was no time left. James had to get the rest of the prisoners out. He dropped his hand. "Now!"

A *whoosh* and a flash sparked near the front of the prison as the first barrels of moonshine erupted. The next line went up seconds later, followed by the third. James watched as each explosion drew closer. Shouts of surprise were mixed in with the screams of burning men. The Talons caught at the choke point by the Pit didn't know whether to keep going or turn back. However, the choice was made for them when the barrels inside the hole exploded.

Those left alive had death in their eyes and charged at James. Right when he was within their grasp, James and the last of the prisoners grabbed the ropes behind them. On the other side of the wall, the other prisoners heaved, and James flew quickly to the top just as the final barrels shredded the remaining Talons.

From where he stood above the prison, James could see The Claw standing in the courtyard, illuminated by the flaming wreckage. He waved to the brute before he dove off the wall, guided by the rope and pulley, and into the arms of the prisoners who cheered when they put him down.

"Quickly," James shouted, "before they can regroup, we need to head north." He grabbed Heimlan by the shoulder and said, "I'm trusting you to take us around the Dragon camps."

Heimlan nodded.

James felt pride as they ran together. They were only a few hundred men, but each was a trained fighter. In this sea of insanity, he finally had something he could hold on to. Something he understood. After all, Ryan had been right—James was a born rebel.

This time, it'll be different, he promised himself. *This time, we'll win.*

***

Render Hollow screamed with rage among the flames and burned flesh until the intense heat drove him back out of the prison. Nearly every Talon, except his personal guard, had been wasted in the assault. Expressionless, the guard stood, waiting where he'd left them. A wave of fury came over him. He grabbed one and smashed him in the face. The others took a step back while Render beat the Talon into a bloody pulp, stopping short of killing him.

Satiated for the moment, The Claw pointed to the three nearest and growled, "Get on your horses and find out where they're going." The hardest part wouldn't be tracking them but gathering more Talons to bring them down.

Damn Theron!

Somehow, Theron had stirred up the Southers, and The Head had to send reinforcements to the border. Thinking, Render knew the only troops he had at his disposal would have to be pulled from the outer camps. He turned to the rest of his men and divided them up, sending some to the western camps and others east.

Before they left, Render gave them all a message for the camps. "Put away the clubs and chains! Now is the time of blood and rending! Let them see how sharp the Dragon's Talons truly are!"

AND WHAT WAS LEFT BEHIND

Paradise.

The further they rode from Dragon territory, the easier it was to breathe. The plants were greener, and even the sun appeared brighter. To Elizabeth, it was like a dream she hoped would never end. But she also knew many people had died to bring her this dream.

A medic had come to Thomas's aid after the Talons had been driven back and the location secured. He also examined Liz, but except for a few scrapes and deep bruising, she was relatively unharmed. "Someone upstairs been looking out for you, miss," the medic had said.

Only two other members of Thomas's troop had made it across the border, and Liz could not understand why they had sacrificed themselves just to get her and her friends here. *There must be some reason. This couldn't have all been just for us.* A lifetime raised to be suspicious of anyone other than family made it hard for Liz to believe the Staters had no ulterior motives.

It was a long trip from the border to Charleston, the capital city of Turner. While Thomas was carried on a litter, they rode by villages and small towns with children playing in the streets, their parents casually gossiping. Not one building was in ruin, and homes were freshly painted. Even the roads were maintained. People were just going about their lives without a care in the world. Liz had only one complaint: it was a bit warm for her liking.

Thomas's descriptions hadn't prepared Liz for how different the Free States were from where they'd just been. Like most of her countrymen, she had believed the propaganda and thought England was the last bastion of civilization in the entire world. And now, she felt foolish.

As they passed a schoolhouse, one with actual children lined up to go inside, Liz blurted out, "How… How did this happen?"

Riding alongside her, Lieutenant Waltham, the leader of the platoon that had rescued them at the border, answered, "It was a lot of work. But it was work that needed doing."

"Is it true that everyone here is…" Not knowing how to ask the question correctly, Liz trailed off.

"Black?"

Liz's cheeks flushed, embarrassed for asking, and she nodded timidly.

Waltham gave her an appraising look. He was older than her and a hundred pounds heavier. He smiled, putting her at ease. "Don't you fret none, Miss Stillman. Just go ahead and ask your questions. And to answer the question, sure, we got some white folks here. Not many, mind you. Though it ain't just Black and white here, either. There's a whole mess of folks from China down in Douglas. They got some from India too. Us Black folk just make up the majority, that's all. Up north, they got it in people's heads that we're only friendly to our own race. Probably got them thinking we're a bunch of cannibals down here, living in mud huts." Waltham spat.

Liz shook her head and smiled. "Anyone with a set of eyes and a brain to think could see they're wrong. I'd say this place is a wonder."

With the same pride in his voice that Thomas had when he spoke of the Free States, Waltham said, "It sure is, Miss Stillman. It sure is." She could not recall the last time anyone had sounded that way about England. Oh, they would put on a good show, especially if Crownsmen were within earshot, but everyone knew the writing was on the wall.

From the border to Charleston, it took a week of travel. Thomas slept through most of it, occasionally waking for food and water. As they drew closer to the capital, the towns grew denser and the farms less sprawling. When the dirt road turned into a cobbled thorough-fare, Liz realized they'd finally arrived.

It was a shock at first.

Signs hung everywhere, advertising restaurants, stores, law offic-es, and the local newspaper. Uniformed constables patrolled the street, greeting people as they went. Market stalls, selling all manner of food and goods, lined a central square. No one looked over their shoulders or shied away from the constables. Riding through the square, Liz was struck by a longing mixed with sadness, almost as if she had been robbed of something but couldn't quite recall what.

The lieutenant brought them to a hotel just off the square where they would spend the night. In the morning, they were to meet with Mamma June at the governor's office.

The rooms were simple but clean, with a dresser, a desk, a leather-backed chair, and, more importantly, a bed that looked as soft as a cloud. It was almost too sumptuous when Liz slid beneath the blan-ket, and she practically purred with delight. Never wanting the expe-rience to end, she fought hard to stay away, but it was a losing battle. Soon her eyelids became too heavy, and she fell into a dreamless slumber.

A time later, a knock at the door woke her, followed by someone clearing their throat. Stretching, Liz asked, "Yes?"

A woman chirped from the other side of the door, "Miss Stillman? I've come to fetch y'all for breakfast with Governor June."

"Thank you," Liz said. "I'll need to freshen up a bit if you don't mind."

"By all means. But do be quick about it, Mamma June ain't really all that patient."

With great reluctance, Liz left the bed and went about freshening up. After being in the wilds for so long, she had almost forgotten what it meant to be presentable, so for the first time in what felt like ages, she combed her hair and washed her face.

Finally ready, Liz opened the door to a pretty, young Black woman in a plain blue dress out in the hallway with her dark hair in a neat bun.

"Sorry to keep you waiting, Miss...?" Liz asked.

"Jacobs. Cindy Jacobs," she said with a slight curtsey.

"Nice to meet you, Miss Jacobs. Shall we then?" Liz went to close the door.

Cindy coughed to get her attention and then pointed at the pistol and knife on Liz's belt. "You won't be needing them, Miss Stillman."

"Oh, pardon." Liz gave an embarrassed laugh. "I'm just so used to carrying them."

Smiling, Cindy said, "Don't you worry, Miss Stillman. I assure you Charleston is perfectly safe."

Liz felt naked after placing the weapons on the desk. Perhaps the wilds had left more of an impression on her than she had thought.

Cindy led the way out to the street, where a carriage waited. Ducking inside, she found she was the last to arrive as Richard and Okeny were already seated on the wood benches. Both of them looked sleepily outside the window of the carriage door. Liz slid into the empty seat beside Richard, and Cindy sat next to Okeny. When Cindy shut the door, the driver set off.

The four sat silently for a few moments until, longingly, Richard sighed, "The beds were quite wonderful, weren't they?"

This caused a round of chuckles.

Cindy smiled. "I'd reckon a nice bed would seem almost like heaven after what y'all been through."

Matching her smile, Okeny nodded. "That it does, Miss Jacobs."

The city was just waking up as the carriage trotted along. Stalls were being filled, and store entrances were swept. Laughing children raced off to school between loaded wagons from outside the city. The smell of freshly baked bread wafted in, and Liz felt like she would tear up at any moment. To no one in particular, she asked, "Is this how our lives could have been if The Burn had never happened?"

"Oh, we don't call it The Burn down here, Miss Stillman. In the Free States, it's The Blessing."

Taken aback, Liz turned away from the window to look at Cindy. "The Blessing? That makes it sound like a good thing."

"Don't get me wrong, ma'am, I hear the plague times were terrible, but the old folks say it was both a blessing and a curse." The young woman shrugged. "So, we ended up just calling it The Blessing. If it weren't for that, they say we'd all still be slaves because the old masters wouldn't have up and disappeared."

"Disappeared?" Liz asked.

Before Cindy could answer, the carriage rolled to a stop by a small, well-groomed yard with a garden filled with blooming lilies. A flagstone walkway led from the street to the porch of a two-story house painted white with green trim. *This can't be the governor's office,* Liz thought.

As if reading Liz's mind, Cindy said, "Here we are."

There was nothing grand about it in any way. Nothing that made it stand out from all the other houses on the street. It was a stark contrast to the arrogance of the Crown.

Cindy was about to open the carriage but stopped when a man stepped out of the house's screen door. He wore a well-tailored black suit and carried an ebony cane. His hair was thick and ropey, with a hint of gray. After sharing some parting words with someone on the other side of the screen, he waved goodbye. As he turned, Liz watched his warm eyes and smile shift into a disdainful sneer. Cindy quickly closed the curtain on the carriage door before the man passed by the window. They sat in silence as they listened to the sound of the cane striking the stone street.

Once it faded away, Richard asked, "Who was that?"

In a whisper, Cindy said, "Monsieur LeRoux. He's the Vodun ambassador to Turner."

"Vodun?" Liz asked.

Cindy opened the carriage door and peeked her head out. She then stepped down and beckoned them to follow.

As he got out, Okeny asked, "Is he dangerous?"

"No. Well, least not to us," Cindy said but then pointedly looked at Liz and Richard. "He's Vodun, though."

"I'm sorry, but we don't know what that means," Liz said.

From the house, a husky voice scolded, "I said breakfast was at nine o'clock sharp. It's ten past, Little Cindy."

An old woman held the screen door open with a stern look. Like Cindy, she had her wispy white hair in a bun and wore a red dress that went past her ankles with white lace cuffs around her wrists.

"Sorry, Mamma June. They're real good sleepers," Cindy said. She quickly ushered the companions up to the small porch. "But seeing as if we'd arrived on time, Monsieur LeRoux…"

"Wouldn't have wasted the last five minutes of my morning with them accusations." The old woman turned and let the screen door slam shut for emphasis, muttering about young'uns with no respect for other people's time.

Grinning, Okeny chuckled and shook his head. He said, "She reminds me of my grandmother."

Liz asked, "Any advice?"

"Be polite." He held open the door for her to pass through.

They entered a parlor furnished with a plush sofa and comfortable-looking chairs. There were cabinets to one side; each shelf had peculiar carvings of misshapen forms. Liz realized they were meant to be people and other creatures, possibly horses or cows. While she stared at one particularly grotesque abomination, the old woman came in from another doorway and said, "School children make them for Founder's Day as gifts for the governor. Kept every single one since I was elected. My attic's packed to the rafters."

Liz straightened. "They're…uh, beautiful."

"Ain't got no time for lies in this house, young lady," Mamma June chided her. "Children made them, not Michelangelo. Now, all y'all get into the dining room before breakfast gets cold."

A small feast was laid out for them on the table in the next room, piled high on trays, and carefully placed to keep from staining the white tablecloth. It was almost as grand as the meal Prince George had provided before they set off. Trays of food, piled high with biscuits, eggs, bacon, and sausage, smelled so good that Liz's stomach growled. Mamma June stood at the head of the table and welcomed them to sit.

After they settled, the elderly woman personally served her guests. She gave Richard an extra helping of bacon after commenting that he was far too skinny. Cindy came in from another room, presumably the kitchen, with coffee and filled the mugs by their plates. When everyone had a plateful, Mamma June sat, but the food remained untouched. Frowning, she said, "Don't be waiting on me. I didn't make all this just to be stared at. Go on, now."

That's all it took for the guests to dig in. The eggs were buttery soft, the biscuits flakey, and the sausage and bacon had just the right amount of grease. Richard finished his first and went for seconds while their host only picked at her plate, eating sparingly and observing her guests.

Cindy took a sip of coffee and asked, "What was Monsieur LeRoux doing here, Mamma?"

Mamma June scowled. "Just some huffing and puffing about the goings-on at the border." Her wrinkled face eased into a kind smile. "Don't you fret none."

Liz put her fork down. "I apologize if we've caused any trouble, Mrs. June."

Mamma June kept the kind smile as she said, "First of all if I'm anything, it'd be Mrs. Wilson. And secondly, there ain't been a Mr. Wilson for near on ten years. Y'all can just call me June."

"Well, June, once again, I'm sorry."

"Ain't nothing for it. Bad luck is all," Mamma June said dismissively. "Them Cultists were bound to get stirred up about something sooner or later. Besides, once had a chance to calm down, they'll be back begging for food again. The ambassador just wanted to know if we needed help. So, I told him we're doing just fine."

An uncomfortable silence followed while they ate while the old woman watched. It was strange, and Liz gathered the governor was assessing them. Nervously, Liz said, "Charleston is a lovely city."

"She is, ain't she?" Mamma June beamed. "Course, she weren't always like this. You should've seen her when we first settled in. Shoot, she was a ramshackle of a thing back then and far too big for her own good. We tore down what couldn't be saved and used all that to fix up what we could. Patched up the old farmhouses and roads too. Now, we've got the most cobblestone streets in all the Free States."

"When did all this happen?" Richard asked.

"Oh, a few years after The Blessing. Right after we finally got ourselves all organized but before we made the Free States official."

"Were you there? Before The Blessing?" asked Liz.

"This white hair didn't just show up overnight," Mamma June said with a polite laugh. "I was a slave girl down on Quewhiffle Plantation back in North Carolina, what we call Lincoln these days. From slave girl to governor," Mamma June mused. "Ain't that a funny thing."

"Cindy mentioned the landowners disappearing?" Okeny said.

"I wouldn't say they disappeared, but that's about near enough to what happened. You see, most of us Black folk didn't really move around all that much, so all we knew about what was going on came from the house slaves, and we didn't much trust them. Least not at Quewhiffle.

"Anyways, one day me and my mamma went out to the fields, but there weren't no overseers. We kept right on working, though. It'd be bad if we was caught lollygagging. Then here comes old Oscar, the house butler, down from the main house. He says there weren't anyone in the house when he got up that morning. Well, after we took a look to see if he was telling the truth—which he was—we sent him to a neighboring plantation. He came back saying the same thing happened over there.

"We waited for days, but when no overseers or any of the landowners came back, we started working for ourselves. Then we got to holding meetings and such with the other plantations about what we're gonna do. That all led to some loose agreements, but what really got us relying on each other was that spat we had with the Cult."

"Thomas mentioned that before," Liz said.

"Oh, poor, sweet Thomas," Mamma June sighed. "Such a good boy. Gonna be a while before he's up on his feet again."

Wracked with guilt once more, Liz said, "I can't express enough how sorry we are."

"And I said there ain't nothing to be sorry about," the old woman frowned. "Now, I don't like repeating myself. I ain't got enough time left for that."

Liz mumbled an apology.

Mamma June took a sip of coffee and straightened her napkin. "Now, you were asking about the landowners. It ain't that much of a mystery, really. Folks by the harbor said there weren't nothing seaworthy left. That was the case for every port along the coast too. It was pretty obvious what happened. They piled themselves in those ships and sailed off, hoping to outrun the plague. Didn't even give us a second thought, but that weren't nothing new. They was all just a bunch of selfish cowards."

"When we came over, we found a large gathering of empty ships in the middle of the ocean," Okeny said.

"However, at least one of them was from New York. I'm not sure if these were your lost landowners," added Richard.

June scowled. "Lost? You make it sound like we want them found. If you ain't figured it out, we're mighty happy they're gone."

Richard paled and said, "Sorry, ma'am."

"There's an awful lot of sorry happening at this table," Mamma June said with a sigh. "Boils down to the fact we just don't know all that much about each other yet. Ain't nothing but simple misunderstandings."

"I agree," said Liz. "We'd love to learn more about your people and the Free States."

Pouring herself a fresh cup of coffee, Mamma June said, "And I'd love to tell you, Miss Stillman, but first I'd like to know what y'all have planned in coming all this way." She placed the coffee pot down and raised an eyebrow.

Liz blinked, momentarily taken aback, then blurted out, "We're here for diplomatic reasons, I assure you." She could feel sweat forming on her brow and her pulse quicken. These people had sacrificed so many to save them, but what would they do if they learned the real reason behind the Crown's expedition.

The old woman pursed her lips and wiped her mouth with a napkin. "I'm sure you are, dear. But tell me, how's England been getting on since The Blessing?"

Under the governor's piercing gaze, Liz wasn't sure how much longer she could keep from telling her everything. *Why is this my responsibility? I'm no statesman. I should still be on* The Ophelia *with my grandfather and crew. Maybe if I tell the truth, they'll be better prepared to negotiate with the Crown if they send more ships? I should be honest. But what if that puts us in more danger?*

To Liz's relief, Okeny answered for her. "Our county remains un-ravaged by the plague, ma'am," he said. "But, while we were able to keep it out, the strict measures we had to endure were met with some resistance. We've only just recovered from a long civil war of our own."

"Wars can be just as bad as plagues," June said. "Which do you reckon would've been worse for England?"

"I would expect the plague, ma'am," Richard said.

"Plague ain't as destructive as war. Plenty of places were still standing when the bodies got cleared out," Mamma June said, tap-ping a finger thoughtfully against her chin. "And plague don't need nothing but bodies to fuel it. War, on the other hand…"

Liz started to panic and nearly dropped her coffee mug.

She couldn't know why we're here, could she? No, this is all just coincidence. It must be.

Trying to appear calm, she said, "It was a dark time, yes." She thought for a second and added, "But England is still strong as a na-tion." Liz didn't want to betray her country, but she also didn't want to see these people subjugated. If Mamma June is as astute as she appeared, maybe she'll interpret what Liz said as a warning.

The old woman gave Liz a knowing smile. "I'm sure it is, Miss Stillman, I'm sure it is." She sipped coffee while looking at her guests over the rim of the mug. After placing it back on the saucer, she smacked her lips before continuing. "Now, what're your plans for the future?"

"I-I'm not sure," Liz said, thrown off again by the governor's question. "We've lost people up north. I'd hoped you might have had word about them getting away, just like you'd heard about us." Liz sighed. "I can only hope my grandfather is alive and being taken care of."

The old woman reached over and patted Liz's hand gently and said, "I'll send a few pigeons out to some of our spy stations. Can't promise nothing, but it also can't hurt to check."

Liz smiled sadly. "Thank you, Mamma June. I… I just need to know."

The old woman nodded.

Liz swallowed the lump that'd been forming in her throat and said, "I suppose we could stay here until we've learned anything. Then, eventually, we'll just head for the coast and find a ship to take us home."

"Ain't no ships," Cindy said at the other end of the table.

"What?" Liz asked, puzzled.

"She said no ships, dear," June answered. "Like I said, all the ships went with the landowners."

"And you haven't built any of your own? In fifty years?"

"Why would we?" Mamma June asked bitterly. "Ships is what brought my people here in the first place. Why the hell would we want to get on another one? Besides, you know of somewhere better?"

Liz was stunned into silence.

Mamma June brushed back a wisp of hair that had fallen across her forehead. Calmer, she nodded and said, "The fact is, dear, there just ain't no place else to go."

AND WHAT COULD BE

Is this where I'll spend the rest of my life? Liz thought later back in her room.

After the breakfast with Mamma June, they had ridden back to the hotel in silence, each lost in thought. Liz had felt set adrift with no sail. Strangely, Okeny appeared to be in good spirits, with bright eyes that watched the city go by from the carriage. Once back at the hotel, they made loose plans for dinner later, and Liz returned to her room.

Sitting by the window, chin resting on her arms as she leaned on the windowsill, she looked out at the city of Charleston. She studied the red brick buildings and painted signs of the market square and the homes with little gardens she could see on the next block over. Again, she noticed how relaxed and unafraid the people were below her window.

"I supposed it wouldn't be so bad," she sighed. But how could she be happy here if her grandfather was still in danger?

Liz attempted to visit Thomas at the hospital the next day but learned he had never been admitted. Fearing the worst, she was on the verge of scouring the city when she bumped into Lieutenant Waltham near the market, and he told her Thomas was well and recuperating at the base just north of Charleston. Liz thanked the lieutenant and smiled all the way back to the hotel.

A routine was established as the weeks went on. Liz and her companions would meet for breakfast and dinner most days. Each one had found odd jobs to do around the city. Liz spent her free time at the library. Being around the books comforted her and kept her distracted. She often felt regret for the books she'd lost on *The Ophelia* and those still in her apartment back in London, but the Charleston library had a few of her favorites.

While there, Liz would ask the librarians about the Free States. They indulged her curiosity, and when they could no longer handle her barrage of questions, she was handed a copy of a book titled *Of the Free States and Freedom.* From this, she learned that the Free States maintained the same rights as the previous United States but allowed everyone to vote, including women.

Without a president or central leader, the governors became facilitators of the laws that the people voted on, as well as de facto heads of state for each of the five Free States. Like a council, the governors would meet regularly and settle grievances between the states, thus keeping the peace. Militarily, a standing army protected the northern border, and a much smaller one was stationed along the Vodun territory to the south. There wasn't much written about the Vodun people, and the librarians would not go into much detail, though they encouraged her to stay off the streets when Monsieur LeRoux or any of his men were in town. Especially the one that carried a sword and was referred to as a hunter.

On an evening in mid-September, the three sat outside a small restaurant along the main street, which had quickly become their favorite. An older man played a piano, entertaining the restaurant's guests as they chatted and ordered from the menu. Then, someone coughed loud enough to get their attention, only to discover Thomas standing just a few feet away. With a smile that reflected the table's candlelight, he sauntered over and said, "Looks to me like y'all are settling in quite nicely."

"Thomas!" Liz smiled and hopped up, giving him a tight hug.

"*Ay!*" he exclaimed but returned her embrace. "I'm glad for the greeting, but still a bit tender."

"Oh, I'm so sorry," she said, letting him go.

"It's fine," Thomas smiled. "Real glad you folks decided to stay on in Charleston."

Even though he included Okeny and Richard, Liz couldn't help but notice his eyes lingered on her. Feeling nervous and a bit flustered, she chastised herself. *You're being foolish. It's only guilt, that's all. How would he feel about you if he knew you had thought about leaving him behind? You barely know the man, and he knows practically nothing about you. Stop acting like a lovesick schoolgirl.*

Lost in her thoughts, she had missed the rest of what Thomas had said except, "How're you liking our fine city?"

Okeny stood and shook his hand. "You know, one of these days, I'll catch you sneaking up on me." They laughed, and then Okeny said, "Quite a remarkable place you have here."

"Such a lively city," Liz blurted out. She wanted him to look at her again, even for a moment. "Always something to do."

Thomas smiled at her, then said, "How about you, Richard?"

"It's very nice," the soldier said.

"He's been spending most of his time down the street at the grocer's," Okeny said. Turning to Richard, he added with a laugh, "Does the owner have a pretty sister you aren't telling us about?"

Richard looked down, and Liz could see his cheeks turning red.

Thomas stared at the soldier curiously for a moment, then said to Okeny, "Take it you ain't had time to get to know the neighborhood. That store's owned by Bennington. He's one of those, uh, real clean types. Ain't nothing wrong with that, but Richard, I never took you for—"

Nearly shouting, Liz cut Thomas off and asked, "Where've you been all this time?" It had taken her a while, but Liz finally figured she knew what Richard was trying to hide from everyone, including herself. She gave the soldier's arm a gentle squeeze and felt him trembling. Afraid Thomas might press the subject, Liz added, "I went to the hospital and found you'd been taken to a base nearby."

Thomas looked pleased as he smiled at her. "Glad to know you cared. Well, after getting all patched up, I had to write my reports about what happened. Glad to say, that's over." He laughed." But I just got assigned a new batch of soldiers, and we're getting ready to head back out there." The smile on his face faded.

"Just like that? They aren't going to give you more time to rest?" Okeny asked.

Thomas shook his head and shrugged. "Not with all that's going on up north."

Liz said, "Like what? I've read that the Dragons had pulled back from the border." She'd made a habit of checking the local newspaper.

"Further north."

"What do you mean?"

Thomas leaned in close so only they could hear and said, "Guessing someone's finally had enough of the Cult's shit because rumor has it, they got a rebellion brewing. The governors reckon we should go on and see if they'd like some help."

After sharing a brief look with her companions, Liz said, "There's been no mention of that in the paper."

"And there won't be. It ain't right to get people's hopes up in case nothing comes from this. So far, there's been a few labor camps cleared out, but that's it. Gotten a few eyes on them, though, and if you'll believe it, there's a giant with them."

"A giant... James! They're talking about James!" Liz clapped her hands once, caught up in the excitement, disturbing a few patrons who had been doing their best to ignore them. Mind racing, Liz barely registered their annoyed mutters.

Thomas gave them an apologetic nod before asking her, "James? You mean that convict fella?"

Rubbing his scarred ear, Okeny said, "Actually, he was a rebel leader back home. I guess he hasn't quite retired from his old profession."

Richard nodded. "It was James's idea for us to head south. He also said he'd try and escape once he figured out what he was up against." Thoughtfully, he added, "I suppose he's learned enough."

Liz grabbed Thomas's wrist and asked, "Wait, have they seen an old man with them?"

"I ain't got all the details, Liz." He patted her hand. "All I know is they want me to head north to find the rebels. My priority is to offer them aid, or if they want, guide them south just like we did with y'all."

Without so much as a thought, Liz volunteered them all. "We're going with you."

After a few seconds, Richard nodded in agreement. Okeny, however, remained silent.

"I can't just bring you along. Mamma June'd chew me out the second I got back. You ain't seen a temper as bad as Mamma June's, believe you me."

"I don't care. We're going," Liz said, letting go of his arm. "Now, you can either help us, or we'll go by ourselves." Taking a pencil from her pocket, she started drawing a rough map on a napkin. "Where are they?"

Thomas slipped the napkin off the table and smiled politely at the guests listening in from a nearby table. Quietly, he said, "We ain't having this discussion here."

"I'll gladly take it up with Mamma June if you'd like?"

Looking skyward, Thomas mumbled something before he sighed. "I'll meet you there. But for my sake, make sure to tell her this was your idea."

***

"So, y'all got out of the dragon's mouth just to go right back in. What sense does that make?" Mamma June asked, sitting in her parlor while working on a floral needlepoint.

Hands on her hips, Liz said, "I have a duty to my crew."

"*Your* crew? Thought your grandpappy was the captain." Mamma June pulled a green thread through the white cloth, not looking up from her work.

"I'm the first mate, which makes them just as much my crew as his. And he was captured too, as you know." Liz sifted through the mess of emotions coursing through her. Softly, almost begging, she said, "Please, Mamma June, he's the only family I have left."

The old woman sighed and lowered the needlepoint to her lap. She picked at some loose strings before finally lifting her head to study the unexpected guests in her home. "And y'all feel the same?"

Richard said, "Yes, ma'am."

"Looking like it ain't so unanimous," June said.

Confused, Liz turned to see what the governor meant. Okeny, quiet since they had left the restaurant, had a pained expression on his face. "Stuart?" she asked.

Okeny, not meeting her eye, rubbed his hands together. Then, after a sigh, he said, "I've come to a decision, Liz. And I hope you and Richard will forgive me."

Liz took a step closer to him. "What decision?"

Shaking his head, Okeny said, "I don't want to go as I am now."

"I don't understand," Liz said.

Okeny turned to face Mamma June. Clearing his throat, he said, "Back in England, I was thrown out of the military because of who I am." He patted his chest, not hiding the disgust on his face. "I lost my pension, rank, and even the small amount of respect I'd scraped together. Not once did I hear from anyone in my former life until this expedition. The damned Crown could have sent anyone, but they were more than happy to get me off their island."

Fists clenched, Okeny let out a slow breath. "But here," he smiled, "It's different. Here, I feel like I belong. Not because my skin's the same color as yours, but because this place is something special. This could be the beacon the world needs to guide it back from the brink. So, with your permission, ma'am, I beg for asylum and wish to join the Free State Army. That's who I want to be before I go north again."

Mamma June pursed her lips, looking at Thomas at the back of the room before giving him a knowing smile after he nodded. The old woman's smile dropped, and she scolded Okeny. "Don't be a damned fool. You were a citizen of the Free States the second you set foot out of your mamma. You just didn't know it then." Okeny's shocked expression made her laugh, and she continued, "Everyone that wants to be a citizen can be, so long as they're willing to help us build a better future—but joining the army? Well, that's another thing. Thomas, you want to take him under your wing?"

"He's a scrapper and a better tracker than some of the folks we already got, so it's fine by me."

Okeny said, "It's finally time I fought for something *I* believe in, Liz. I hope you understand."

With a tearful smile, Liz nodded. "I understand, Stuart," she said. "And I'm glad we aren't losing you just yet." After all this was over, she knew she'd have to decide where her loyalties lay. Right now, she could only feel happy that Okeny found what he'd been searching for all this time—a home.

Richard said, "England won't know what it has lost today, but the Free States know what they've gained." He clasped Okeny's hand firmly and patted him on the shoulder.

Mamma June appeared to be blinking back a few tears as she had picked up her needlepoint again. She said, "Guess it's settled then, ain't it? Suppose I can't stop y'all from going, so might as well give my blessing." She stuck the needle into the cloth and said, "Now, mind if I get back to my crafts? Evening's usually my private time." Mamma June shooed them out while mumbling about young folk bothering her whenever they felt like.

Out on the street, Thomas told Okeny to report to the barracks first thing in the morning to get everything squared away with the unit. Okeny would also have to talk to the quartermaster about where to send his monthly stipend, which shocked him a bit to learn he'd be paid for his service. During the war, the Crown would hold all pay until after a soldier's term of service was over.

Thomas chuckled. "Everyone gets paid for their work here. We ain't been slaves in generations."

The night wasn't too cold, so the four decided to walk back to the hotel. The streets were empty as most places were closed after sundown. It was quiet and peaceful. Then a heavily accented voice came to them from a dark alley. "I reckoned I smelled some pale fish 'ere." The words were said slowly, almost painfully.

Out of the shadows stepped a man dressed in a black suit, hair cut short and face covered in white powder, which gave him a ghostly appearance. Aside from the powder, what truly stood out was the sword sheathed at his waist. Very few people went around armed in Charleston.

Thomas quickly put himself between Liz and the stranger. "Chasseur Dupeux, these people ain't any of your concern. You go on about your business."

A voracious grin parted the man's lips. "You 'ave a lick of da tongue on you, boy." Then continued in a language Liz did not recognize, but Thomas did, as he answered him in kind.

While Dupeux spoke rapidly while Thomas took longer to respond. Even without understanding, Liz could tell the two were having a heated argument. Dupeux circled them slowly as he spoke, but Thomas adjusted his position to keep Liz behind him. Several times Thomas tensed before relaxing again, and after a few minutes, the conversation ended with Dupeux stepping back into the alley and disappearing into the darkness.

Thomas gently pushed Liz down the street and waved the others to follow while setting the pace at a jog.

"Who was that?" Liz asked.

"*Li nan pwoblèm.*" Thomas grunted and spat, then continued, "Sorry. Meant to say he's trouble. Vodun had a feeling you was in the city, but they got to lay eyes on you before they can do something about it." As he spoke, Thomas kept looking over his shoulder.

Richard, instinctively reaching for a pistol that wasn't there, asked, "What do you mean by 'do something about it?'"

"Vodun ain't never gonna forgive."

"Forgive what?" Liz asked. All she knew about the mysterious people was that they lived along the Gulf coast.

"Being made slaves," Thomas answered. "They got a price on white folk. And that man back there? That was Chasseur Dupeux is Monsieur LeRoux's headhunter."

"Are we in danger?" Okeny asked.

"You?" Thomas shook his head, "It's these two I got to worry about. They're the prize. We got to get your things from the hotel, then hurry y'all to the barracks. Headhunters can't conduct their business on government property."

"And what business is that?" Richard asked.

Thomas said, "Ain't it obvious? Killing white folk."

Soon after they had gathered their belongings from the hotel, they rode inside a carriage to the military base a few miles out of the city.

Thomas appeared more relaxed than he had earlier, so Liz asked him about the strange language the Chasseur and Thomas had used. He told her it's how the Vodun speak, a mix of French and African languages. "How do you know it?" she asked.

Leaning back in his seat, Thomas said, "I was born Vodun, but my parents moved us when I was very young. I'm out of practice, but it comes out now and then." With a playful grin, he asked, "You telling me you ain't never noticed I sound different than folks around here?"

Liz giggled and said, "If you recall, *we're* the ones with the odd accents."

The two of them laughed.

Okeny and Richard, on the other hand, remained uneasy.

"Why did your family leave?" asked Okeny.

"They didn't like how the *houngans* and *manbos* was changing things." Seeing their confused expressions, he explained further, "They kind of like priests. Y'all still got religion and church back home, right?"

"Of course," Richard said.

"Well, I was too young to remember any of this, but my parents told me the old religion preached about peace, but after the Blessing, things got twisted up with revenge."

"What religion?" Liz asked.

"The religion of the slaves in the deep south, *Vodou*. The Vodun come from the French plantations in old Louisiana. Anyway, my parents had enough when the religious folks started with all this headhunter shit. There'd been talk about getting the Vodun to join the Free States, but the *houngans* wanted nothing to do with our laws, so we treat them much like we do the Cult. But at least the Vodun got a bit of civility to them, and we get along just fine for the most part."

"Will there be trouble because they know we're here now?" asked Richard. He'd lifted the curtain on the window slightly to keep an eye on the road.

"No. Monsieur LeRoux ain't gonna want to get on Mamma June's bad side by stirring things up in her own state. Chasseur Dupeux is a

whole other story, though. He's as crazy as a dirt boy. That's why
y'all be better off at the barracks until we head out."

Okeny asked, "Is Chasseur a name or a title?"

"A title. Means 'hunter' in French," Thomas said. "Y'all really
don't know any French? I reckon you would, seeing as they're your
neighbors and all."

Okeny frowned. "The Crown did away with... foreignness."

A question suddenly popped into Liz's head. "After you argued
with this headhunter, why did he just let us go?"

With a shameful expression, Thomas said, "That wasn't an argument. We were negotiating. I told him if he gave us a twenty-minute
head start, he'd be able to do what he came to do. Lucky for us, he
enjoys the hunt more than the catch."

Liz's mouth hung open, and Richard's eyes narrowed as he turned
away from the small window.

Hands held up to calm them, Thomas said, "Hey, I knew what I
was doing, don't worry. We were only ten minutes from the hotel."

***

Before the plague, the barracks had been a mill. Support buildings
had been added on over the years within the compound, including a
mess hall, ammunition depot, stables, and a music hall for the occasional celebration. All of it was secured behind a high brick wall.

Once they arrived, the three were shown to their bunks. Upon sitting on the cot, Liz immediately longed for the soft bed back at the
hotel. Later, they were invited to meet the base commander, Colonel
Scott. A thick man, the colonel stretched the limits of his blue and
grey uniform. He was gruff and not very friendly, but he politely
welcomed them. Then he inspected Okeny closely before giving him
a nod of approval.

Afterward, Thomas showed them his new unit. They all appeared
eager and more than ready to head out. "Remember, this's just a
recon mission. We're only looking to talk with the rebels, that's it,"
he said. "I don't want none of y'all running off to fight the first dirt
boy you see."

Then Thomas introduced the troops to their newest member. Okeny was met with smiles and slaps on the back. Later, he mentioned to Liz that they hadn't been so welcoming the last time he joined the service.

After the meet and greet, Thomas brought them into his office. At his desk, he shuffled some papers aside. He rolled out a map that depicted the northern region of Turner and the entirety of the known Dragon territory with handwritten notes and lines scribbled all over it. To Liz's amazement, the Cult's lands expanded north past New York to the river that fed the Great Lakes and as far west as Ohio. Everything east of New York was blank, which Liz found curious.

"Your friend James's been busy attacking Dragon camps for the last month or so." Thomas pointed out five red *X*s in northeastern Pennsylvania. "The Claw's pulled most of his forces from the west to reinforce the northeast while he tries to hunt them down. He's left that border wide open, so that's how we're getting in."

"Wouldn't it make more sense to have one of the scouts inside their territory contact James? They could guide them safely out of Dragon Territory," Liz said, looking up from the map.

"We ain't about to compromise our scouts' positions. If one were to lead the Talons back to their hideout, then we'd be blind in that region. But I will admit that policy's also why we can't figure out where the rebels are, just where they've been. So, we got to be like the Dragons and go looking for them."

While Thomas went over more of the plan with Richard and Okeny, Liz could see this wasn't the same man who had helped them outside Baltimore. From how he treated his new unit, he was clearly trying to keep them at a distance. The loss of his last soldiers must have hurt far more than he was willing to admit.

Looking back down at the map, she knew further losses were inevitable. Aside from the weeks of peace in Charleston, she has experienced nothing but pain and death that began with the loss of Reginald beneath the waves. Not a day went by that she did not think of him. So how, after everything they had been through together, would she handle the deaths of any of the men here now? What were they hoping to accomplish here, and how would any of this make a difference in the end?

She felt angry. Before she could stop herself, Liz blurted out, "What are we doing here?"

The men looked up from the map, and with a raised eyebrow, Thomas asked, "What're you getting on about?"

Waving a hand over the map, she said, "I mean, what is the goal of all this? So we make contact with the rebels, then what? How many of them are there? How would we travel together without drawing attention to ourselves? And what if he doesn't want to leave?" Thomas tried to get a word in, but Liz kept going. "And what will these Dragons do in response? From what I've experienced, they aren't reasonable people. This is just going to lead to more bloodshed. Unless we end it!" She slammed a fist on the table.

"You see, I…" Thomas started, then closed his mouth.

Richard stared at Liz for a few seconds before looking at Okeny, who was staring down at the map, his head tilted curiously.

Liz sighed in frustration, then pointed along the southern border. "Look, you said Theron's troops have this border sinched up tight, but the west is open." She slid a finger to central Pennsylvania from the west. "So, doesn't that mean a greater force could march in as well as a small platoon?

With all the Talons divided in opposite directions, we'll be able to swoop in behind the northern forces and crush them between ourselves and James's rebels. Then we can move south and end this madness once and for all." Liz stopped to breathe. The more she talked, the more nervous she had become and hoped it remained unnoticed. Most of her knowledge had come from books, which included a few on warfare—a subject she, understandably, had never been fond of—and she hoped what she had just proposed made sense to the ones who were far better trained in this field.

For several minutes, the men remained quiet while looking down at the map before Thomas shook his head slowly. A lump formed in Liz's throat, and she knew she had made a mistake. To them, she was nothing more than a young girl playing at being a soldier. Thomas moved quickly to the door, and Liz was sure he was about to throw her out, but then he shouted, "Get me Colonel Scott!" And he looked back at her with a wide smile.

Colonel Scott was less receptive.

"Lieutenant Favre, you want me to put the safety of every man, woman, and child in the Great Southern Free States in jeopardy, because this woman"—he pointed to Liz standing in the corner of the room—"reckons we can take down the whole damn Dragon army?"

"The plan makes sense, sir. She's right about the forces being divided. The western brigades could be mustered." Thomas put a finger on the map. "There's at least two thousand we got between Marshall and Wetzel, not to mention the soldiers in Tubman. We move on in and let the other states hold the border for a while."

Scott shook his head. "That leaves our own western border undefended."

"From what, sir? Ain't nothing out there, and you know it. Them boys is just twiddling their thumbs," Thomas said. Liz could see the annoyance on Thomas's face. In a way, she found it assuring.

Colonel Scott continued as if he hadn't heard him. "What happens when Theron realizes what's going on and marches into Turner?"

Thomas waved off the questions and said, "We mobilize Morgantown's militia. Reckon that'll put a lot more bodies in old Theron's way. And mind you, that'd be people who know the land a lot better than those dirt boys."

Colonel Scott leaned over the table and grumbled, "We've survived for more than thirty years under the treaty with these Dragons. Why do we need to go and stir up the pot now?"

Moving from the corner, Liz said, "Because you've probably never had a better chance than right now. And ever since we've arrived here in the Free States, not one day has gone by that someone hasn't flaunted how civilized and free this place is compared to the Cult's territory. But how can you justify that when you know people are suffering across the border? Change can be painful. It can be hard. But sometimes, it's the bloody right thing to do."

Colonel Scott turned on her, his lips tight, and said, "Miss Stillman, I appreciate your vigor, but even if I did agree, it's not like I get to make that decision. There's a chain of command here, or don't you got that back in England?"

With her hands on her hips, and lips just as tight, she said, "We do. To be honest, more than some would like. But if you don't decide on this fast enough, we might lose this chance."

The thick man eyed her. Not backing down, Liz returned his gaze with a steely look of her own.

Colonel Scott finally sighed and said, "I'll have to take this to Mamma June. She's the only one that can get General Frasier to muster the troops." The colonel grumbled and left the office.

Thomas moved beside Liz and gave her shoulder a reassuring pat which sent a flutter of butterflies to her stomach. "It's a good plan. Mamma June will see that."

"Let's hope," she mumbled. She truly believed what she'd said to the colonel. The Free States could make a real difference in this land. But really, she knew this was her best chance of getting her grandfather back.

Later that night, Liz's back was sore after an hour of staring at the exposed rafters above her bunk. Sitting up, she tried to rub the soreness from her muscles, but it did little to help. She fought with the blanket wrapped around her ankles, trying to free herself to get up. A walk would do her good, she thought. The metal lattice beneath the mattress squeaked when she slid her feet to the ground. She tried to be quiet, but Richard rolled over to look at her from the next cot.

"Is everything all right?" he whispered. He was alert and barely looked like he'd been asleep just a moment ago.

"I'm fine. I just can't sleep," she whispered back. Almost fifty bunks were in the room they shared with the other soldiers housed there. Most were snoring, but candles still burned in the large room, and she could see someone reading several cots over.

Richard sat up on one elbow and brushed the hair off his forehead. "I wanted to thank you. For earlier," Richard said, somehow sounding even quieter than before.

"What do you mean?" Liz tilted her head quizzically.

Richard quickly glanced at where Okeny slept on the other side of Liz before he said, "Bennington…"

"Oh," Liz said. "I, well, you're welcome."

"I… It's not what you think. If that *is* what you're thinking," the soldier said, clearly flustered.

"Richard," she whispered, "I don't think anyone around here would think less of you if it were."

He looked down and pricked at a loose thread on the mattress. "He has a unique view of the world. The things he talks about, you couldn't get away with that back home. I enjoy listening to him and think he likes me as his audience." In the faint light of the room, Liz could see him blushing.

"After we get back, you should bring him around," Liz said. "I'd love to meet him."

Nodding, Richard slid back down to his pillow. "I think I'd like you to meet him too."

Liz put on her shoes and waited for the soldier to fall asleep before standing, hoping a walk would ease her back and mind. It was a short stroll to the gate that led outside the perimeter wall of the base. A guard let her pass after telling her not to wander too far.

Alone, she looked up at the stars. A cold breeze blew leaves across the road. *Almost October*, she thought. All the horror, pain, loss, and even brief moments of joy played through her head as she watched the stars move slowly across the sky. *It feels so much longer than six months.*

Leaves crunched beneath a foot in the darkness.

Thinking Dupeux had found her, Liz reached for her gun but realized she'd left it inside. When Thomas passed into a splash of moonlight on his way over to her, Liz relaxed. Without a word, he leaned against the wall beside her, and together, they stared at the sky.

After several minutes, Thomas cleared his throat, ending the blissful silence. "Awful dangerous for you to be out here, *dam mwen*. Dupeux's probably angrier than a cat caught in the rain right now."

"My mind is too restless, and I couldn't sleep," she sighed. Shivering, she slid cold hands into her pockets.

"Ain't no use worrying about it until the morning. Mamma June'd throw a fit if someone woke her up for anything other than the Dragons knocking at her front door."

Liz laughed softly. "She's a strong woman. I can see why everyone here respects her."

"So are you, Liz," he said, looking at her. "Richard and Okeny are real fond of you. Heck, they ain't the only ones." Thomas didn't hide his feelings for her as she stared back at him.

Liz loved the way his brown eyes sparkled in the moonlight and wanted more than anything to lean in and let him wrap his arms around her, but instead, she stepped away from the wall. "We experienced a lot of hardships together. Strong bonds tend to form when you could lose everything."

A flash of disappointment crossed Thomas's face, and Liz hated herself for causing it. Clearing his throat with a cough, he turned away from her. "Well, hopefully, we ain't gonna lose everything, not when there's so much to gain." He pushed off the wall and slowly went back toward the gate, waving over his shoulder and wishing her a good night.

"Thomas?"

He paused, looking back.

"You had called me *dam mwen* before. What does it mean?"

Before disappearing out of sight, he said, "'My lady.'"

Liz sighed and hugged herself for warmth as she looked back at the stars. Someday, she promised, life would make sense again, and she'd let herself be happy. Unfortunately, now was not the time.

THE ENGINE

First, James freed some birds.

They attacked Eck at dawn, just as the Talons were preparing to bed down for the day. It was over quickly as the camp only housed around twenty Cultists at any given time. Afterward, he made a show of breaking down the door to the Canary House and found everyone inside huddled together, scared.

Everyone, that is, except for Paddy.

It was like the old man had been waiting on James with the ledger in his lap. Quickly, he thumbed open to a page before reading off, "Insurrection. That'll be fifteen runs."

Smiling, James said, "There won't be any runs, not anymore."

Even though his whiskers did little to hide the grin beneath, Paddy tossed the ledger over his shoulder and crossed his arms in a huff.

"Now," James turned and motioned for the door, "how would the lot of you like to get out of here?"

The miners were the hardest to convince. They were there voluntarily, and most had families nearby. Even so, Ryan and Conner managed to persuade a handful to join. Untrained, they didn't know the first thing about fighting, but their labors had made them strong, and pickaxes made a damn fine weapon. James told the recruits to grab supplies but also made sure they left enough for the miners that hadn't joined.

"Should burn the whole camp to the ground," Heimlan muttered beside James as they gathered to leave.

"We're not conquerors. We should be seen as liberators," James said. "Their way is fear, not ours."

After escaping the Fighting Pen, a small voice in his head told him he should leave to find Elizabeth and the others, but a need for something else drowned it out: revenge. James wanted to kill The Claw for what he did to Peter and for the suffering the Cult inflicted on their people.

But even more, he knew this was his second chance.

Barlow's fight. It's what we do.

At times, when they'd rest, James would sit and watch the escaped prisoners and wonder if he was being selfish for using them to overcome his past mistakes. Then he'd see the fire in their eyes and knew they wanted this even more than he did. He was responsible for giving them hope, so shouldn't he see it to the end...?

Always alert, they never stayed in one place for too long.

After Eck, they freed small work camps as they moved northeast. Only a few weeks had passed since escaping the prison, but their numbers had already swelled to nearly six hundred men. The fresh recruits knew the area well and guided them away from the major roads, which helped avoid detection.

The day after a steady downpour, they were trudging through damp leaves and sticks when the forward scouts reported back that they'd found old railroad tracks ahead. James hadn't thought anything of it, as they'd often come across rusted rails. However, a former miner with only one eye told him if they followed the tracks north, it would take them to a place called Hones.

"Should be ripe with weapons and much-needed supplies. Least, that's what I'd overheard back at camp," The one-eyed miner said.

James had seen his fair share of wounds and battle scars over the years, but there was something about an empty eye socket that always unnerved him. Leaning against a tree and listening to the miner while trying not to stare into the dark, red hole, he jumped when Na-

thaniel grabbed his arm. Embarrassed, James let Nathaniel pull him
aside before he noticed the Crownsman had a desperate look to him.

Nate's eyes narrowed as he whispered, "Hones isn't just an out-
post."

Still a little unsettled, James moved Nate further away. In a quiet
voice, he asked, "What're you going on about?"

"It's a training camp, with a lot more Talons there than we've
faced thus far. We'll take losses if we go there," Nate said. In the last
few weeks, the soldier had become more himself again. He even
helped with strategy and training. But something about Hones clearly frightened him.

James waved over Heimlan.

The former Talon, who James was convinced had been born with
a sour expression, spat then gruffly said, "Yeah?"

"Tell me about Hones."

The merest hint of a smile tugged the corners of Heimlan's mouth.
"For us? Could be good. Could be bad."

James sighed and rubbed the bridge of his nose. He'd grown tired
of how pretentiously cryptic the people on this side of the Atlantic
were. "Explain."

"Hones is where we—I mean *they*—send the passers of the Test.
While there, you either complete the training, or you fail." Heimlan
gave Nate a hard look before turning back to James. "If you're thinking about going up there, you'll probably want the miners to start
digging our graves now."

Paddy was quick to join them, riding over on a horse. They had to
leave the wheeled chair behind, but the old man said he could still
ride. At first, James wasn't sure how he'd even stay on the saddle,
but Paddy had fashioned a harness to keep him in place. Apparently,
he had plenty of time to think about it over the years. "What're you
all going on about Hones for?" Paddy asked. The mare, which he'd
named Old Betsy, gave an irritated snort.

James said, "I'm thinking we might take a good look to see what it
offers."

Paddy scratched at the stubble on his chin. He had shaved off the
long, knotted beard soon after being freed. "Well, now, been a few
years since I'd been up there last. Used to be called Honesdale back

before The Burn, an old train town. I even tried to find work there before heading down to Phoenixville. Anyway, it's become a nasty place with these chemical baths…" He trailed off after looking at Nate. Paddy readjusted the straps holding him on Old Betsy and sat straighter. "I guess it won't hurt to check it out."

"But we'll be outnumbered, at least three to one," Nate said.

Paddy gave him a cold stare. "How many you think are tracking us, boy?" James had noticed Paddy had a hard time trusting Nate. Something put him at odds with having a Worker in their ranks, especially after he'd learned how James found him. All James cared about was that they stayed civil, which for the most part, they did.

Swallowing hard, Nate looked south as if he could see The Claw's men sweeping the land.

"That's right." Paddy nodded. "You want to hedge our bets a bit? We've got to get whatever fresh conscripts they got up there before turning full Talon."

"What makes you think they'd join us?" James said.

"Same reason as these folks." Paddy nodded over his shoulder at the men spread out in the trees, eating what they could while rubbing the soreness from their feet. Here and there, some wrung rainwater from their clothes. "These fellas are tired of the hand they'd been dealt. Here is a chance at something new and all that started with you."

Unconvinced, James said, "I don't understand why. I'm only a failed revolutionary. Hell, I'm not even from here." At the same time, he felt something stirring deep inside. It was the same feeling he had after taking over his squad. He knew what it was and where it could lead, so he tucked it back down where it belonged while remembering his father's words. *Power can corrupt even the best of men. Give them just a taste, and they'll yearn for more.* Power was a trap, and James didn't want to get caught in it.

Patty smacked James upside the head. "You idiot. You're proof the world isn't completely dead. And if it isn't, that means hope for something better, right?"

James nodded, ignoring the fact that Paddy had just hit him. He didn't want power, but these men needed a leader right now. They trusted him, and he had to make the right decisions for their sake.

Pushing back the doubt and uncertainty, he gave a more decisive
nod. Pointing first to Heimlan, then Nate, he said, "Draw up a map
of Hones. I want everything. The layout, terrain, defenses, even
where they keep the bloody privies."

The two went about the task, arguing as they sketched a map in
the dirt. James was glad to see a bit of Nate's smug attitude return as
the two men shouted at each other. Eventually, and begrudgingly,
they agreed they were finished.

James studied what they'd made for a few minutes with Paddy
over his shoulder. "How far is it from here?" he asked the old man.

"My guess would be about a day's march, maybe a day and a
half," Paddy said.

James had Connor get the men ready. He wanted them on the
move in ten minutes.

Ryan was still studying the map after the dark-skinned man left.
James asked, "What do you think?"

"I think we broke out of one prison just to break into another,
yeah?" Ryan pointed at the towers on the edge of the map.

Nathaniel drew a wide circle around the main camp and said, "The
actual town has been left to rot. What they call Hones is nothing
more than a converted train factory. The area immediately surrounding it had been burned and cleared. Not that I was measuring, mind
you, but I'd wager there's a hundred yards or so between the forest
and the compound with no cover."

Heimlan dropped a wide, flat rock on the south side wall of the
camp and said, "Got fucking big gates too."

"We'll figure it out as we go." Feeling his skin tighten at the base
of his skull, James looked over his shoulder to the forest behind
them. He knew to trust his danger sense. "We should get moving.
Now."

Clapping his hands, Ryan yelled, "Double time it, lads!"

Heimlan stayed behind while everyone else left, shaking his head
with his arms crossed.

"What?" James asked.

With only the slightest of sneers, the former Talon said, "Can't
believe I'm going along with this."

"The plan—" James began.

"Not that," Heimlan cut him off. "This." He pointed a finger at James, then thumbed back at himself.

James said, thinking he understood what Heimlan was getting at, "It's hard killing your own countrymen. If you don't want to go on…"

"Killed my people well before this. Remember how we met? Just strange how fate turns out," Heimlan said and stalked off.

James was left scratching his head. He took another moment to memorize the map, then cleared it away with his foot before he felt eyes on him. Looking up, he saw the wild man he'd first fought in the Pit staring at him. Shamus was his name, and that was the only thing James had managed to get out of him. Arm still in a sling from their fight, he watched James, then his eyebrow twitched once, and he walked off.

Connor had a conversation with the wild man once after they escaped the prison, and he said Shamus believed he owed James a life debt. Even so, whenever James tried to talk to the heavily tattooed man, he only got grunts in response. As he watched him leave, James thought he made Heimlan appear cheery.

They spent the rest of the day and into the night on the move, hoping to keep ahead of James's feeling—the sense of foreboding that something was lurking right behind them. It was a cold, damp night, and James wished for nothing more than a warm fire, but even as the rear scouts reported they'd found nothing, he wanted to keep going.

As dawn broke, shafts of orange sunlight illuminated the forest, revealing abandoned buildings hidden among the trees. The set of tracks they'd been following had become a spiderweb of metal trails that flowed in all directions. Nate had said the actual town of Hones had been left to rot, so they had to be close now. James ordered them to halt and told the men to rest.

The men were so tired that only a handful gave appreciative groans before sinking to the ground.

James continued for a few more paces, squinting north along the main tracks. Seated on a fallen log, Ryan asked, "What is it?"

"I want to have a look. See what we're up against with my own eyes before I commit to anything," James said. His feet ached, and he needed to eat, but something told him to keep going.

With a begrudging sigh, Ryan stood. "Guess that was a good enough break as any, yeah?"

James shook his head. "Let the men rest up. I'll go."

"Like hell you are. We're in enemy territory now, yeah? No one goes alone, just like the old days." With a tired grin, Ryan punched James playfully in the arm.

"Fine," James conceded. "But not everyone. Tell the men to move to the buildings over there." As the sun rose higher, it revealed more of the lost town. Trees grew through the roofs and along the tracks. Rusty signposts, half-swallowed by the forest, stained the tree bark orange.

The scouting party grew by two more after Nate and Heimlan volunteered to come along. Guessing it would only take a few hours to go up the tracks and back, the four set out while the rest of the men found what comforts they could find among the trees.

The morning air was still crisp, but the sun was warm when they stepped out of the shade. Alongside the tracks, they found some warped wooden steps and an equally misshapen platform. The remains of a small building had fallen in on itself, its beams gray with age and splintered. James touched the platform as he passed, leaving a trail in the muddy soot weighing heavily on it. Ever so slowly, this once quaint train station was being buried in ash.

In sharp contrast to the decay, birds chirped in the trees, and gray squirrels scampered among the grasses and leaves. It was calm here, and James wished it could remain that way. Shortly after that wish, shouting could be heard from somewhere ahead, and the four receded into the shadows to wait. In time, it stopped. With no indication there was anyone nearby, they relaxed.

James had been leaning against a tree and found the bark had stained his arm with more ash. Thicker than it had been at the station, this ash was utterly black. A sure sign they were close. "Careful, now," he said in a whisper and crept forward.

Nate, a distant look in his eyes, remained frozen in place. James shook his shoulder to get his attention, and the soldier blinked before apologizing.

More ruins appeared along the tracks, increasing the danger of being spotted from some hideout, so they opted to move into the trees.

Old stone foundations and scattered boards made up much of the forest floor. On top of worrying about stepping on rusted nails, James wondered about the lack of patrols. "It's too quiet," he muttered.

Heimlan grumbled, "Don't go and jinx us."

"Got to agree with him there," Ryan added.

"Oh?" James gasped jokingly. "Ryan Lloyd, as I live and breathe, are you worried about having to fight our way out of danger?"

Ryan chuckled, then smacked James hard on the back. "Oi! Life's full of surprises, yeah?"

While the two laughed, a breeze blew in from the north, carrying something other than fire and ash. The air was bitter, almost acidic, and strong enough to make James think his nostril hairs had wilted when he sniffed it. Gagging, James's eyes watered as he brought his shirt collar up to cover his nose. At the same time, Nate collapsed to his knees and vomited. The pale soldier's back heaved as he wretched. Coughing and rubbing his eyes, Ryan leaned against a tree. Heimlan, however, had tied a handkerchief over his face and just stood there with his arms crossed.

The chemical smell lingered even as the breeze faded, and Nate slowly tried to get back to his feet. James went over to help him, and Nate gripped his arm for support. The soldier was trembling. "Everything all right?" James asked.

Not looking up, Nate spat something horrifically yellow between his feet. "I... I shouldn't have come."

Turning him by the shoulders, James made Nate face him. "Explain yourself."

Staring only at James's chest, Nate had that same distant look again. James shook his shoulders gently, and Nate's eyes grew hard for a second. Then he blinked, and they softened. Shaking his head slowly, Nate said, "I'm sorry. I just wasn't ready for..."

"What was that?" Ryan asked, eyes still leaking.

Nate quietly said, "It's what... what..." Then looked down at his pale hands.

Bluntly, Heimlan said, "It's called liquid convincing."

"Liquid what?" James's head turned to the former Talon.

"Convincing." Heimlan shrugged. "It's what they use to get people's heads working right."

"You don't know what it is?" James asked.

Heimlan sniffed and straightened his shoulders. "Course not. Never needed it. I'm Dragon-borned, not some Test-passer."

Nate let out a sigh and James let go of his shoulders. The Crownsman appeared steadier than before, so he asked, "What happened? What did they do to you?"

Nate took a deep, shuddering breath. "They told us whoever passed their test would be free to join them. I think I focused too much on the free bit. But it wasn't really true." Looking down, he rubbed the back of his neck. "They... they tortured us. Remember Paddy said they had strange chemical vats in Hones? That's what that smell is." Bitterly, he added, "Have you ever wondered what it felt like to drown in fire? You'd do anything, agree to anything, just to make it stop." Looking up, he locked eyes with James, and a shiver ran down the tall rebel's spine. "Anything."

James had to look away, stunned by Nate's pain. "I had no idea. I'm sorry, truly. You should have gone with your brother."

Nate coughed uncomfortably, then started to walk away. "Well, we can't change the past now, can we? Let's get on with it."

With a shrug and an odd look of concern, Ryan followed Nate. As if he'd heard it all before, Heimlan appeared unphased while waiting for James to get going before he took up the rear.

Not long after, they came out of the village ruins and discovered Hones. Half a century ago, it had been just another factory, producing trains that ran along the tracks. It was now a stygian fortress that rose above the scorched earth, with black smoke billowing from inside its walls. Massive iron gates rested atop the main track they had followed to get here, and he had to admit, they were intimidating to look at. Guard towers lined the empty landscape between the trees and Hones. Just as Nate and Heimlan had said, there was minimal cover.

Sighing, James moved further back into the trees. "I don't know," he said more to himself than the others.

"Guards look thin," Heimlan said. He nodded at the towers. Less than half were manned. "Not many on the walls either. Probably not expecting an attack."

Rubbing the bridge of his nose, James said, "How much explosives did we get from the last mining camp?"

"Got to be enough to put a dent in that gate, yeah?" Ryan said.

Shaking his head, James muttered, "I just don't know." Then louder, "We should go back. I might have to rethink this."

By midmorning, they'd found their way back. Paddy, with Old Betsy, waited on the tracks to greet them. "How'd it go?" the old man asked from up in his saddle.

James shrugged, then frowned. "Doesn't look good."

"It's the gates, isn't it?" Paddy asked.

James nodded. He walked beside Paddy as he rode slowly into the trees along one of the branching tracks, the others following behind.

"Yep. Figured they'd be a problem."

"Big problem," Ryan said.

James came up short when he heard hammering and chopping deeper in the woods. "What's going on?"

Paddy said, "Found something that might help. That is if we can fix her up quick enough."

Feeling a headache coming on, James asked, "What?"

"A nice surprise." Paddy flicked the reins, and Old Betsy rode on, leaving them all behind.

"Bloody hell," Ryan said after they came across some rebels wielding heavy sledgehammers and pounding at the tracks to straighten a warped bend. Connor was with them, watching them work.

"Care to explain this?" James asked the dark-skinned man.

"Nah." Connor grinned and pointed down the track to a building twice as wide as it was tall. Like everything else around here, it was more rust than metal at this point. The rails ran right up to it, with light coming out of its half-opened doors. Over the years, trees had crushed the smaller sheds around it, but somehow, this big shack had been spared.

James pointed at Connor. "We're going to have a talk when I get back." Then went over to see what the great mystery was about.

Pulling the double doors open wider, James found the light was from oil lamps, which were much needed as the building lacked windows. But what those lamps had lit up made him pause. A steam engine was sitting on the tracks that continued through the shack and out another set of doors on the other side.

James, still holding onto the doors, couldn't think of what to say and stood with his mouth gaped open.

Ryan wormed his way past him and, once more, exclaimed, "Bloody hell!"

Rebels were around the engine, passing tools and parts to men standing on its side, while Paddy barked orders. The old man told them to tighten this or turn that while James, dumbfounded, remained in the doorway.

Connor tapped his arm, getting his attention. The Black man grinned and said, "What'd you want to talk about, Englishman?"

James blinked and turned back to watch the men work. "What are you all doing?"

"Fixin' us a battering ram. What else it look like?" Connor said.

"Somebody better start explaining. Now," James said loud enough to get Paddy's attention.

After coaxing James inside, Connor and the old man explained that one of the rebels had found this work shack with trees blocking the doors, which were rusted shut. More out of boredom than anything else, they decided to look inside and found the engine.

"This was a repair shop," Paddy said. Worktables and tools filled up one side of the shack. The old man had come off his horse and sat on one of the tables with Connor standing behind him.

"How is it in such good shape?" James asked.

"With the doors shut tight as they were, not much could get in to bother it," Paddy said.

"And you are doing what, exactly? Fixing it?"

Brow furrowed, Paddy scolded, "You aren't the only one who can make plans, boy."

James held up his hands. "All right. All right. Just explain it to me." He sat down beside Paddy and crossed his arms.

"Well," Paddy said, looking back at the engine. "Yes, we're fixing her. She's a bit like me. Aside from a few cobwebs and the need for some grease, all the good parts still work."

"And you called it a battering ram?" James asked Connor.

The Black man nodded enthusiastically.

James closed his eyes, rubbing the bridge of his nose again. "Do any of you even know how to do this?"

Paddy said, "Worked in factories since I was a boy. I know how to tighten a bolt or two."

Connor smiled and said, "Back in the Free States, we still got trains runnin' between the capitals. My sister and I's job was reparin' tracks and salvagin' old ones." His voice turned somber as he continued. "That job's what got me stuck here. We were pullin' up some rails near the border and got too far ahead of all the others on the crew. Heck, we didn't even know we'd crossed into Dragon territory. Not like they got a line or nothin' to mark it."

James put a reassuring hand on Connor's shoulder. "When this is over, we'll get you home. I promise."

Connor frowned. "Ain't worried about that. Care more about findin' my sister."

"We'll do that too," James said. "Now"—he nodded at the steam engine—"if this does work, how do we power it?"

Connor cleared his throat and pointed to a trap door in the cement floor across the shack. "Coal's in there, been kept nice and dry. Not much, but I reckon it'll get her there."

"It needs water, right? To make steam?" James asked. He had a rudimentary knowledge of trains, mostly about how to destroy them.

Paddy said, "There's a creek about half a mile from here and some buckets. I'm sure you can figure that one out."

"Is it me, or are you starting to get cranky, old man?" James said.

Paddy huffed. "Bah! Just need to keep an eye on these idiots be-fore they put something on backwards."

"Fine, fine. Have at it," James said and got up from the table. Connor walked with him while he circled the engine. "You think this will work?"

"Don't see why not?" Connor shrugged. "Only thing stoppin' her is some of the tracks need some care. Got men out there poundin' them back in place. Some junctions needed realignin', so we're doing that next."

Worried about all the noise, James looked to the doorway.

Connor moved to stand between him and the exit and said, "They know what they're doin'. You ain't got to be protectin' them all the time. We're all fighters here, ain't we? 'Sides, you seen any patrols out here?"

James nodded with a sigh. "You're right. But"—he pointed at the engine—"there's one flaw to your plan."

Connor frowned. "What?"

"It's facing the wrong direction. The main line is back that way," James said and stuck out a thumb toward the open door at the rear of the engine.

"Oh, ye of little faith," Connor laughed. "I knew you was too tall to see your feet."

Tilting his head, James looked curiously at Connor, then down at the ground. An inch-wide gap split the cement and circled the engine. "It's a turntable," James muttered, embarrassed that he hadn't noticed it before.

Connor smiled. "It sure is."

"How long will all this take?" James asked, quickly changing the subject.

"Paddy figures about another day. Tracks are the bigger problem."

"If we can get them sorted out, we might have a chance at this after all," James said. Standing next to the train, he gave it a good pat. "Now, about those explosives…"

The next day was spent hoisting machinery, hand tightening bolts, and whatever Paddy demanded of them. At the same time, repair teams returned to the camp after doing what they could for the tracks. Surprisingly, one pair managed to make it to the junction right before Hones without any sign of Talons.

As James listened to their reports, an angry shout came from outside the shack. He hurried outside just as a man, surrounded by onlookers, was pushed to the ground. James loudly demanded to know what was going on.

The rebel standing over the fallen one said, "We were out working the junctions, and I caught this bastard a ways out in the woods, making a mark on a tree. It looked like a trail sign to me." He kicked the man in the gut. Grunting in pain, the man scurried back, collided with James's legs, and looked up with only one eye. It was the miner that had told him about Hones.

Motioning for everyone to stay back, James crouched. "Is it true?"

The miner stayed silent, though the fear in his eye told James all he needed to know.

"Who was the mark for?"

The miner's lips trembled, but he still said nothing.

James gripped him by the chin and roughly turned his head left and right, looking for a Dragon brand, but found none. He checked the hands and wrists, but still nothing. Next, James ripped the man's shirt at the collar and revealed a brand on his chest. James's blood turned to ice, but he made sure to keep as calm as he could. "You've been helping them."

Silence.

The rebel who had dragged him back to camp kicked the miner in the face, making him cry out in pain. With an angry look from James, the rebel took a step back. Whispers began to grow louder while some of the other rebels edged closer. Fearful the one-eyed miner would be torn apart before he could get anything useful from him, James looked for Ryan and Connor to help. The two had come out of the shed with him and pushed into the crowd. They did their best to keep the rebels from becoming an angry mob while James interrogated the possible traitor.

James stood and hauled the miner back to his feet. Like a drunk man, the miner could barely stand after the last kick and sank into James's arms. "Tell me the truth."

Through bloody lips, the man groggily mumbled, "My family…"

James took him by the chin again to keep his head up. "What about them?"

"Hurt my family if I don't help 'em," the miner said. Blood from his mouth trickled down James's fingers.

Gripping tighter, James asked, "How long?"

"Since Eck. Was told Lord Claw chose me." The miner tried to sound proud, but it only made him appear more pitiful.

"How could he know we would return to Eck?"

The miner winced as he tried to shrug. James looked from him to the rest of the crowd as his mind raced. How many spies had The Claw planted? A hundred? Ten? Was this a trick just to sow doubt among them? He needed time to think and a place to keep the miner.

"Put him down with the coal for now. I'll figure out what to do with him later." He handed him to one of the rebels. Roughly, the rebel pushed the miner toward the work shack. Soon, the crowd drifted apart, and only James, Ryan, and Connor were left on the tracks.

"How many do you think there are?" James said once they were all alone.

Connor said. "Should start checkin' for brands."

"Couldn't hurt, yeah?" Ryan agreed.

James nodded. "We've had a good go of it thus far, but I've a feeling that's about to change." Growing frustrated, James pinched the bridge of his nose and said, "This is the same bloody one-eyed bastard that got us here. Wouldn't it make more sense to leave?"

"That's up to you, Barlow," Ryan said. The only time he ever used his friend's surname was when James needed a reminder of where he'd come. Barlow's had always been smart fighters.

Leaning on his spear, Connor said, "We're almost done anyway. It'd be a real shame if all that hard work was for nothin'."

James sighed and spun around in a slow circle, taking in the tracks and the ruins. Out in the trees, the rebels had split up into small camps. Word would get out quickly about the betrayal, and then suspicions would start flaring up. When he finally came around to look at the rusted work shack, he had made his decision. They still had the advantage of surprise. The Talons wouldn't be expecting a train to break down their gates.

"We'll be ready by morning. Get the men who were here and check them for brands. Then put them on perimeter duty. Keep the gossip to a minimum," James said. Connor and Ryan nodded and went about following his order.

No more brands were found, but that did little to ease James's mind.

GATE CRASHER

As if on cue, the Cult attacked at dawn.

Luckily, while attempting to creep in the shadows, the Talons were spotted by one of the guards. One shout of alarm led to more, and soon James came running from the shack with a club in hand. At first unsure of what the shouting was about, it soon became apparent when the Talons took up their chant and rushed into the clearing.

Pushing into the battle, James was thrown off balance when his club was unexpectedly caught on the blade of a sword. Another Talon swung an axe wildly at James's hand, but he only managed to split the club in two. The axman pivoted quickly and chopped at his legs. While getting out of the way, James stumbled and fell backwards, landing at the feet of the swordsman. Above him, the leering Talon had his blade raised when a spear thudded into his stomach. For a brief moment, the swordsman looked down at the spear before collapsing.

Connor leapt over James and pulled his spear from the dead Talon. Then swiftly bashed the blunt end into the axman's face. James scrambled to his feet and punched the stunned Talon hard in the chest. Gasping for air, the Cultist dropped the axe, which James snatched up, and chopped into the Talon's midsection. He wrenched it back and pulled out intestines and gore with it. Connor finished off the Talon, who was screaming in agony, by stabbing him in the throat with the tip of his spear.

Recovering from the adrenaline surge coursing through his veins, James found only a handful of Talons were still alive. Nate had one pinned to a tree, his forearm crushing the Talon's throat, while Ryan helped by smashing the Talon's face with a club. A gun went off, and another filth-coated man fell on the tracks. James turned to see who had fired and saw Heimlan a few yards away, pistol still smoking.

Behind Heimlan, Shamus shrugged off his sling and drew the two swords he'd been carrying. He clashed with a Talon, sending the other's sword arm wide, then plunged his second blade up through the ribs and into the Cultist's heart. Finally, the only enemy left had a small man on his back who repeatedly plunged a knife over and over into his chest until he eventually fell face-first to the track with a sickening *crack* as his neck broke.

Hoping it was over, James ordered medics to look after the wounded.

Ryan wiped the grime from his club on the body of a Talon, which only made the weapon dirtier, and then headed over. Spying the woodcutter's axe in James's hands, he grinned and said, "Try holding onto that one, yeah?"

James hefted the axe and looked it over. The balance was off, but it still served its purpose. He slid it into his belt and double-checked the loop was tight enough to keep it from coming loose. "You'd have thought they'd send more."

Connor agreed, using a cloth to clean the tip of his spear. "If you ask me, it's downright insultin'."

Heimlan grunted, "Scouting party. Maybe working on their own. Probably thought one of them'd make Foreman if they took you down."

James wasn't so sure. Not after yesterday's discovery.

Nate, still breathing heavy and with sweat beading on his pale skin, looked less frightened than he had the day before. James thought there's nothing like seeing your monsters die a few dozen times to remind you they're just as human as you are. It may take a few hundred more, but eventually, Nate would shed himself of whatever the Cult had done to him. Or at least, that's what James hoped.

James said, "When more arrive, maybe they'll come to their senses and see it won't be so easy." Adrenaline still pumping, he eyed the scattered bodies. "Leave their dead. I want to know how many we lost. Then get the rest marching for Hones. It's about time we turned the engine around."

The plan was for the rebels to wait in the trees outside of Hones near the main line, and when the train struck the gates, that was their signal to attack.

With the orders given, James returned to the work shack, passing by Shamus sitting on a log and sharpening a sword. "Glad to see your shoulder is better."

After weeks of only grunts and nods, Shamus looked up, blood-smeared hair covering half his face like a veil, and said, "Bah. It'd take a wee bit more than your love taps ta put me under."

James stopped, recognizing that accent. *What's an Irishman doing here?*

Turning slowly to face Shamus, he asked, "Where are you from?"

The heavily tattooed man nodded once to the northeast.

"Here? In America?"

"Aye." Shamus returned to sharpening his sword.

"Are there more… like you here?"

Shamus grunted and got up. He slid the sword back into his belt and stalked off.

Guess that's all he has to say. James thought he'd been getting a handle on this place, but something new was always thrown at him every time he did. He continued to the shack before he got a headache from overthinking this new revelation.

Inside, Paddy was on a workbench while several men finished up on the engine.

"She won't pass any inspections, but she'll get where she needs going," Paddy said before James could ask. "Anything I should be worried about out there?"

"Heimlan said it was a scouting party. We took care of it." James added, showing the axe on his belt, "They've real weapons now. Guess we managed to get their dander up."

"War-time tools," Paddy said, then quieter, "You've done more than make The Claw angry."

Good. James stepped toward the engine and said, "Are we ready to turn this thing around? There might be more on the way."

"Didn't do all this for nothing." The old man nodded at his horse. "Old Betsy'll help." Two heavy bars had been inserted into the short pillars on either end of the turntable. The mare was tied to one. "Gonna need more hands, though."

"Did you know Shamus was Irish?" James asked, not able to shake the revelation.

"Sure," the old man said.

"How did he get here?"

Paddy shrugged. "Never bothered asking."

Rubbing the bridge of his nose, James sighed. "Go get some volunteers."

A couple of dozen rebels, including Shamus, stayed behind. The turntable beneath the train groaned as it moved. It was slow, grueling work, but the tracks finally aligned after an hour.

James climbed down the short ladder into the hole where they were hauling buckets of black coal. He wanted to see their prisoner before setting off. The ceiling was low, and James had to nearly crawl on his hands and knees to make his way over. Tied up and gagged, the miner's single eye pleaded to him.

"We lost five men today." James leaned closer to him. "You did this to protect your family, or so you said. Well, right now, this is *my* family."

Tears smeared through the coal dust on the miner's face.

"I won't kill you. I'm just going to leave you here. If you make it out, remember that people died because of your actions. And, if no one finds you..." He shrugged.

James turned and made his way back to the ladder. Brushing the dust from his pants, he stood, not bothering to look back at the miner. He waited until the last buckets were lifted out and climbed out last. Muffled wails followed him from the darkness below, silenced only after James sealed the hatch.

Typically, an engine would have a coal cart directly behind it. Unfortunately for James, they didn't have one. So, wedged in the back of the machine were two metal barrels filled with coal. This left just enough room for him to operate the controls. Everyone else would stand on either side of the engine.

James quickly went over the plan to ensure they hadn't missed anything. They would head down the track until they were ready to get the train up to full speed. Then get off right before James jammed the throttle and let the engine do the rest of the work. He hoped it would be that simple as the last thing he wanted was to see if luck could get him through a train crash.

James was careful around the black powder they'd strapped to the front of the engine during his last inspection. It was a bit over the top, but James liked a bit of showmanship from time to time. Satisfied that everything was ready, he called out, "You chaps ready?"

The men climbed aboard and grabbed whatever wouldn't take their arm off once the engine got underway.

James nodded. "Shouldn't take too long." He swapped places with the rebel keeping the furnace warm. It was a tight fit with a low overhang that forced him to stand hunched over. With only some chains strung up on either side, he felt exposed. *We couldn't have found a train with a nice, enclosed cab, could we?* Daylight spread on the tracks ahead of them, coming down through the leaves, as he leaned out to make sure the way was clear. There was nothing left to do but ease the throttle open. With a frightful lurch, the heavy engine belched hot steam, filling the shack as it crawled forward.

The men, excited to see the fruits of their labor in action, encouraged her onward by slapping the engine as if it were a mule. On the other hand, Paddy followed close by on Old Betsy, and James could have sworn he saw the old man's eyes tear up right before he lost sight of him in the steam.

For the first time in decades, the clanking of gears would be heard along the rail line. Compared to this racket, the trains back in England sounded like a well-tuned orchestra. Leaves rained down on the locomotive as it emerged from the shack; her chimney swept through the low branches that hadn't been there the last time she'd come this way. The cool morning breeze was lost to James as he opened the furnace's hatch and heat poured out. He began shoveling in coal. After only a few minutes, sweat drenched his shirt.

"Slow and steady," Paddy shouted over the engine's noise. Old Betsy was agitated, but the old man had her under control as he kept pace with James.

James nodded. He wished he didn't always have to volunteer for the most challenging part of every plan. "Delegating has never been one of my strong points," he grumbled.

The tracks that ran through the ruins had been overgrown and had become uneven over the years. Connor had done his best to straighten them with his crew, but the train wobbled one too many times for James's liking. Gripping the shovel tighter, he reminded himself, *Slow and steady*.

James felt the tracks shifting as they came to a curve in the rails right before it would meet up with the main line. Paddy rode up along the left side of the engine, his eyes always on the machinery. He gave James a thumbs up and turned his horse around to check the other side. Frantically, the old man pointed at something behind the train and shouted something that James couldn't make out over the engine. Glancing back, James swore, "Fucking hell." Talons on horseback weaved through the abandoned hulks of repair shops as they raced toward the locomotive.

Hoping Connor's repairs were as good as he said they were, James pushed the throttle to pick up speed and shoveled more coal into the furnace. Paddy wheeled Old Betsy back around, whipping her reins, and disappeared out of view as he rode ahead. James drew his pistol and placed it at the ready on a small shelf next to the controls, where it rattled and jumped around.

With one hand on the throttle and the other shoveling, he looked back and counted a dozen riders. But there could be more flanking them in the trees. Sticking his head out the side, James called out until he got Shamus's attention and quickly pointed at his own eyes and then at the woods. The wild man let him know he understood with a salute.

Just as James ducked back in, a bullet ricocheted right where his head had been barely a second earlier. Letting go of the throttle, he grabbed the pistol from the shelf and fired back. His shot grazed the side of a horse, which reared and threw its rider off. The Talon hit the tracks and narrowly avoided being trampled as the others swerved around him. Faint gunshots came from the train's left, and two more riders fell.

James left the fighting to his men as he turned back to the controls. He had to keep their pace even as he increased the speed. If he pushed her too fast, the train could seize up. However, it was hard to stay focused with gunfire erupting around him. Then the train rocked violently, and only his grip on the throttle saved him from falling over the side. Adrenaline coursing through his veins, James held steady when the train rocked again. Connor had promised him he'd make sure even the most damaged part of the track wouldn't throw the train, and James was glad the bloody bastard had been right.

The train finished rounding the curve, finally putting them on a straight course to Hones. *We won't be able to slow down if those Talons are still chasing us.* Then James remembered the explosives at the front of the engine and what a stray bullet might do.

He chanced another quick look back and saw one of the Talons standing in his stirrups as he got ready to jump aboard. James shot him. Another rider came bearing down on him with a makeshift pike, and before James got off his next shot, something fell from the overhang above his head.

That something turned out to be Shamus, who tackled the pike-wielding Talon right off his horse. The two tumbled back along the rails before rolling to a stop. Recovering quickly, Shamus grabbed the Talon's head and slammed it into the track until it was a bloody mess. As a new wave of riders came around the bend, Shamus leapt up, ran for the dead Talon's horse, and rode back to the train. Blood flowing from a broken nose down into his braided beard only made his smile that much more gruesome as he rode by James.

James stared after him a moment and shook his head. *What a bloody loon. Good thing he's on our side.*

The new batch of Talons opened fire at the engine, hitting one of the rebels. Gritting his teeth, James turned from the controls and tried to get a better shot. The train shook beneath his feet as if it were going to come apart at any moment. Carefully aiming down the sights at the closest one, he pulled the trigger. And missed.

The Talons concentrated their fire on him, forcing James to duck behind the barrels for cover, where he slammed his knees hard against the furnace door. Pinned down and swearing in pain, James could not feed the engine and felt it begin to slow.

However, that was what ultimately saved them.

Like generals on a battlefield astride their horses, Paddy and Shamus led the rebels in a charge. Shamus had materialized a rifle in the few moments since James had seen him last and used it to take down two riders as the rebels sprinted at the approaching Talons.

While the train continued to slow, the men formed a firing line on the tracks. It wasn't long before the riders were on top of them. Even after losing nearly half their numbers, the Talons kept coming. James wondered what drove them to such madness, then recalled what Nate had said. *"Have you ever wondered what it felt like to drown in fire? You'd do anything, agree to anything, just to make it stop."*

Drawing ugly, brutal-looking swords, the Talons closed in and hacked at the former prisoners. Shamus swung his rifle like a club, smashing a Talon across the face and sending him to the tracks. Some rebels died in the first wave, their blood seeping into the ground. But the rest fought with as much abandon as the Talons. They pulled their enemies from their saddles and fought hand-to-hand. However, one rider did get through and headed for the engine.

Teeth bared and wild-eyed, the Talon had his sword pointed at his target. James fired his pistol but realized he was out of bullets. Dropping the gun, he got his axe up just in time to keep the sword from skewering him and the deflected blade slashed along his forearm. The cold, familiar sting didn't distract him, even as blood seeped from the wound, and he braced himself for the next attack.

Off-balance and awkwardly hunched over, James tried steadying his breath to calm himself. He knew fighting would be easier if he got off the train, but he couldn't chance another Talon taking the controls. Baring a shark-like grin, the rider raised his sword to come at James again and froze as a pistol barrel was pushed into the side of his head. The Talon blinked in surprise before Paddy shot him dead.

Bodies, both Talon and rebel, mixed on the tracks. They lost seven when everything was said and done. Seven to just over a dozen Talons. *Again, why so few? None of this makes sense.* Horses were seized, and the wounded were carried back with Shamus leading the way.

Paddy shouted to James, "You all right?" And pointed at his arm.

James flexed it and could see the cut wasn't too deep, but it still stung like hell. "Just a scratch. I'm more concerned about the gunfire. It's given us away."

"This train's louder than that little dust-up." Paddy snapped his fingers and then pointed toward Hones.

James sighed. Almost wishing he could've been hurt enough to hand the shovel to someone else, he fed coal to the hot furnace, and the train slowly got underway again.

It wasn't long until he caught sight of the pile of rocks the scouts had left to indicate they were almost two miles from Hones proper. James slowed the train with Paddy riding beside him. The old man called over, "About that time."

"The others?" James asked.

"Gone ahead."

James shoveled what was left into the engine, hoping it'd be enough to get her the rest of the way on its own. Then he tied the throttle back with a length of rope and moved to the platform's edge. Paddy moved forward in the saddle to give James room on Old Betsy, and the tall man hopped on the horse's back. Old Betsy must not have liked the added weight because she bucked at the last second, and James nearly slid off before he grabbed on to Paddy. The old man grumbled as he struggled to keep his horse under control.

Once the horse had settled, they watched the train speed away from them down the tracks. Sadly, Paddy said, "Mighty shame to see her go. She'll probably be the last train I ever see."

"She's got a job to do. Get moving so we can do ours."

Paddy clicked his tongue, and Old Betsy galloped along the tracks behind the engine. The old man tried to keep up with it for as long as possible. White steam spewed from the furnace as it picked up speed, contrasting sharply with the dark, looming clouds. Before they came to the edge of the trees, Paddy slowed the horse. Ryan and Connor stood up in the woods near the tracks and waved them over. James kept his eyes on the train as he slid down from behind Paddy.

He should have been going for cover, but he wanted an unobstructed view of what was about to come next.

Barely breathing, James watched the engine race toward the iron gates of Hones. A haphazardly built guard tower had one of its supports on the tracks. James's heart skipped a beat, fearing the explosives would detonate, but the train sheered right through it, and the tower collapsed behind it. Then, just as it was nearly there, the train toppled off the tracks and plowed into the dirt, sending it in all directions. Momentum, however, was still on their side.

The old, crippled train—abandoned and alone in the woods for decades—reached her last stop.

James shielded his eyes from the booming explosion, and when he looked again, all that remained of the gates was a smoking gap. Dumbstruck by the turn of events, James could only stare at the destruction. Then Ryan coughed beside him. With both eyebrows raised, Ryan tilted his head toward Hones. It slowly dawned on him, and while still staring at his friend, James called out the order to attack.

Axe in hand, James led them across the ash-dusted field. He reached the tower close to the gate and climbed. Up top, two Talons stared at where the gates had once been and barely looked up before he cleaved through them.

From the walls above them, Talons opened fire on the rebels. James slid back down the ladder, and ignoring his instincts to find cover, James let out a battle cry that the others picked up, and they ran for the gates. The closer he got, however, the more he wanted to gag as the stench of chemicals wafted out to meet him. Powering through it, he spat the bitter taste from his mouth and kept running.

The train had done more than tear through the gates. It had carved a path of flaming destruction; its twisted wreckage had torn through buildings, leaving mangled and burning bodies in its wake. Among the ruin, Talons gathered, drawn by the sound of gunfire. As stunned as they were, once the surviving Talons spotted the rebels, they took up their weapons.

Rebels and Talons stood off, staring each other down until Ryan shouted, "What're you waiting for, mate? Let's go, yeah?" And smashed a Talon across the face with his club.

That's all it took, and the battle began.

The Talons' shock was short-lived, and they fought back viciously.

Connor used his spear's length to keep the Talons, and any that slipped by fell to James's axe. Heimlan shot at one Talon and stabbed another through the stomach with a sword before kicking him off and using the blade's pommel to knock out a third. Farther off, James caught a glimpse of Shamus, who fought like a demon wind, while Paddy fired up at the wall.

Past the debris and flames, a greater number of Talons were cut off from the smaller force the rebels were fighting. Even in the chaos, James did some quick math and realized there were far fewer than they'd expected. Something wasn't quite right, but now was not the time to think about it as he narrowly escaped having his knee crushed by a sledgehammer. The Talon stumbled, off-balance from the hammer's weight, and James cut into his spine.

His axe was soon slick with blood and gore. In the back of his mind, however, he could keep the sense of unease from scratching its way forward. *The Claw* had *been expecting us to come here, right? Why, then, are they so unprepared?*

Distracted again, he only noticed a sword coming for his neck at the last second, and he ducked to the side. The tip of the blade dug into his right shoulder. The pain only made him angry.

Stop thinking and fight.

Grabbing the Talon's wrist, James pulled the blade out, swept the Cultist off his feet with a kick then dropped down on top of him. The Talon struggled, trying to get his sword arm free from his grasp until James planted a knee in the man's groin. The Talon gasped before vomit sputtered from his mouth. Then, James pinned the Talon's other arm with the handle of his axe. He reared his head back and smashed his forehead into the Cultist's face before finishing him off by cleaving his skull.

Breathing heavily, James wiped the dead Talon's vomit from his face as he got up and saw the Talons trapped behind the fire and wreckage had found a way to cross through it. He shouted a warning before pushing into the fray. Nathaniel was among the rebels fighting against the reinforcements. With sword in hand, the Crownsman kept several Talons at bay.

Catching one of the Cultists by surprise, James chopped at his back. The man gave off a startled and pained cry as he fell. Another, distracted by the fallen Talon, turned to see what happened, and Nate thrust the sword into his neck. The final one jumped at James while swinging a hand scythe. James trapped the curved blade with the handle of his axe and nearly lifted the Talon off the ground as he raised his arms. Seeing the opportunity, Nathaniel stabbed the Talon's exposed side at an angle, getting him right in the heart.

"You all right?" James asked.

Nathaniel gave him a nod, flicking blood from his sword. "They said I was too weak to be a Talon," Nate said and spat on one of the bodies. "How about now?" Sneering, he kicked the corpse.

"Well, mate, where would you be now if you'd been one?" James said. He pointed with his axe to where Ryan and the rest of the rebels slaughtered the Talons that made it through the debris.

James spoke aloud his previous thought. "This was far too easy."

"There were at least twice this number the last time I was here."

James suddenly felt disgusted. Was this some sick game to The Claw? Had he let these men die because they'd wronged him somehow? Trying to get some sense of control over the situation, he asked, "Where are the recruits kept?"

"Isolated in the barracks out back. They did... things to us. I don't know where these savages learned it from, but they know how to warp a man's thoughts. Make them think all manner of odd things." Nathaniel shivered, shook his head, and then squared his shoulders while looking up at him.

"Are you sure you're all right, you know, with being here?"

Nate gave him an annoyed look. "Yes, I bloody well am. Seeing this place torn apart has helped quite considerably."

GHOSTS OF THE PAST

After all the time spent working on the engine and planning the assault, James almost wished the battle had been longer. He also hoped it had just been luck, but questions continued to hammer inside his skull, and he looked for answers among the bodies until he eventually found a Talon that still breathed.

James slapped him until he came too. The Talon groaned and clutched at the ragged hole in his stomach. Even with the mortal wound, he somehow still clung to life. Once the Talon's eyes grew focused, James said, "There should be more of you. Where are they?"

A wet cough shook his body, and blood dribbled from the corner of his mouth, but Talon gritted his teeth and said, "Ordered away."

"Why?"

"The Claw commands… We obey." Eyes growing distant once more, the Talon's head lolled to the side.

James slapped him again until he looked back up. "Where did they go?"

With his last breath, the Talon said, "H-home."

James let the dead body fall back to the ground as excited voices drew his attention. Over by the wreckage, Nate and Ryan were helping pale; hairless men climb through. They shrank away from the rebels who welcomed them and offered them water, clearly unsure who they were and what they wanted. James approached, counting their numbers, and even with just those that had already come through, he estimated there were eight hundred at least. He hoped he could convince half of them to join his cause.

James spoke quietly with Nathaniel and Heimlan before addressing the wary, confused faces. Unlike Nathaniel, these weren't failed Talons. They had passed the Test but had yet to go through the training. Heimlan said, "Haven't earned their black sacrament yet. Got to keep them clean before they do. That's where the liquid convincing comes in."

The burning buildings did little to mask the stench of chemicals in the air. James told Nate, "Take a few men to the vats. I don't want any of it left for the Cult to use."

Nate nodded, his lips curling into a sneer. "Not a drop."

Finally, James turned to the gathered men. "You are all free now," he said in a firm voice.

They gawked at him.

"We've come to give you back your freedom."

A little, skinny man pushed through the crowd to the front and asked, "How do we know this ain't one of their tricks?"

James thought a moment and walked away, leaving them to whisper among themselves. He dragged over a dead Talon and dumped it in front of the scrawny one. "Does that look like a good use of resources?"

The man looked nervously at the corpse while poking it with his toe. When the body didn't immediately spring back to life, he said, "No, can't say it is. But it does raise another question, who the hell are you?"

James whispered a question to Ryan from the corner of his mouth. "You didn't tell them?"

Ryan shrugged. "Thought you should do it, yeah?"

"Pardon, but it appears introductions are in order." James cracked a grin, hoping it would put everyone at ease. "My name is James Barlow. And these"—he waved his arms to the left and right, indicating the rebels surrounding them—"are some equally minded gentlemen who have become tired of how the Cult runs things. We thought we'd stop by to see if any of you lads would like to join us and fight."

The scrawny man scoffed and said, "Fight? Fight who? The Dragons? What'd be the pint? They control everything."

Voices of agreement rose in the crowd.

From where he stood among the rebels, Connor called out, "Ain't controlling the Free States."

"Or bloody England," Ryan added.

"England?" someone asked from the crowd.

James said, "A country far across the ocean, where I, along with a few others, are from." He nodded to Ryan while patting his own chest.

Head tilted, the scrawny man asked, "You still haven't told us why we should trust you. What makes you so different from them?"

James took in the crowd silently until he had everyone's attention, then loud enough for those in the back to hear, he said, "Because we want nothing in return. You are more than a resource to us, and we don't want to become your rulers. When this is over, you'll be free to live how you want and where you want. From what little I've seen, there's enough empty land for people to live as they please here."

The scrawny man still looked skeptical.

"Listen, I've already lost one war, as well as my freedom. I know you think submission is the only way to survive, that the Cult is too powerful. But from where I stand, I see the ghosts of the past in all of you and the hope for the future. Everything is here, waiting for you, to live without fear. Good people are still here, and they want to make a difference. You'd be surprised where they show up," James said, putting a hand on Heimlan's shoulder.

"Some of us have suffered needlessly at the Cult's hand." He nodded to Paddy on his horse. "We're fighting to free this land. Make of it what you will. But make it *yours*. I want nothing more than for your people to be able to experience what true freedom has to offer. Now, is that not something worth fighting for?"

A few hopeful cheers sounded in the crowd.

The scrawny man appeared to have his doubts. "The Dragon never destroyed your country? This… England?" he asked.

Chuckling, Ryan asked, "You actually believe there's a dragon?"

"Course, there's a dragon. Just look around at the mess it's made." The man looked up to the blackened sky.

Taking a step closer to the crowd, James said, "Well, if you join us, you'll never have to fear a dragon ever again."

"Yeah? Why's that?"

"My friends," James smiled, "In England, we killed our dragons long ago."

The crowd, rebel and pale man alike, howled and cheered.

***

Only a handful chose to leave.

In the aftermath of the battle, James got a tally of their losses—close to two dozen rebels had been killed. The rest of the day was spent burying their dead while waiting for some counterassault.

While James secured the camp, Nate and some of the rebels had dragged the dead Talons into a pile behind a large platform built around four large iron cauldrons. Each one was deep and held hundreds of gallons of the chemicals the Cult used to torture the conscripts. It wasn't until Nate was already dumping the viscous liquid on the corpses that James came across the barbaric display. His senses assaulted; he swooned and had to hold on to something to keep upright.

The chemicals burned away the soot and grime from the dead Talons. Even the hair on their faces wilted and broke off. It bleached their clothing, leaving it brittle enough to fall away. Around him, the pale men spat at the bodies, and Nate was treated like a hero. Sickened, James left the gruesome scene.

Returning to the tents they'd set up just inside the gates, James sat with a groan. The adrenaline had begun to leave his system, and he felt all the aches and pains of the day. Beside him, a medic worked a bullet out of Shamus's bicep. Blood still trickled from his own forearm where the Talon had sliced in it during the chase.

As another medic prepared to suture the wound, James listened to Shamus hum a tune while the bullet was pulled from his arm.

"What's that?" James asked, more to distract himself from the needle passing through his skin.

"Eh?" Shamus said.

"The song. What song is that?"

With a wink, Shamus said, "Merely a ditty to keep the pain away."

James winced as the medic tugged at the thread. "You'll have to teach me sometime."

"Maybe when this is all over, we'll go on up and visit me ma and so she can teach you. Cor, I'll have to bring you along just so the clan'll believe I fought alongside a giant." Shamus slapped his knee and laughed. He looked at his arm and pointed at the bandage. "We about done here, lad?" Shamus asked the medic. Even before the medic nodded, Shamus was on his feet. "Right. Good luck with your scratch."

James stared after Shamus.

One of these days, I'll get that man figured out.

After the medic finished bandaging his arm, James went to find the scrawny man from before. He'd learned his name was Albert, the head of a small fishing village along the coast. The Cult had decided their quota wasn't met, and the Talons had come and taken all the men away.

"I'm not afraid of what happens to me," Albert said. "It's my wife… and the other women from our village."

James had noticed that there were only men at the work camps he liberated but had never given it any real thought other than that the Cult thought women were too weak for that kind of labor. There'd been a few women in the crowd at the Fighting Pen, Jessica back with Cutter Brian, and, of course, The Head. This was the first time he'd met someone from a 'disappeared' village.

"What about happens to them?" James asked Albert.

James could hear the disgust in the scrawny man's voice. "Taken to the Nests. To grow the Cult."

As James shouted for Heimlan, he could feel the revulsion wash over him.

The ex-Talon had been talking with Ryan by the twisted gates and took his time strolling over. "Yeah?" he said briskly when he arrived.

Rubbing the bridge of his nose, James asked, "What are the Nests?"

For the first time since James had met Heimlan, the former Talon seemed uncomfortable. Maybe even embarrassed. With a cough, he looked down and shuffled his feet. "Just hearing about them now?"

"He's putting on a sorry show," Albert said bitterly.

"Enough," James said after Heimlan glared daggers at the scrawny man.

"He's a Talon. Doesn't matter what that mark looks like. That means he's visited a Nest or two himself." Albert spat, matching the sharpness in his tongue to Heimlan's stare.

"I was born in a Nest!" Heimlan snarled. "It's my right."

James glared as he stepped between the two. "What are they?"

Looking away again, Heimlan said, "It's where we... I mean, the Chosen, er... the Cult keeps the women."

"For what?" James already knew, but he wanted to hear it, so his anger would be justified.

Scratching his ear, Heimlan muttered, "Breeding."

"You mean raping," Albert said.

Heimlan still couldn't meet James's cold gaze. "I was only with the willing... but..."

"Where are they?" James's words were clipped and soaked with barely contained rage.

Scratching the back of an ear, Heimlan said, "All over, really. There's one east of here, but the biggest is down in Dragon's Rest. It's where most hatchlings come from."

"Hatchlings? Never mind, I get it from context," James said irritably. He dismissed Heimlan and turned back to Albert. "We'll see what we can do about your village's women. Be ready to leave in the morning."

Albert nodded.

Next, James called Ryan, Nate, and Connor over and told them about what he'd just learned.

Both Ryan and Nate looked disgusted. Of course, there were brothels back home, but these Nests sounded like something far, far more sinister. Connor, clenching his jaw, said that he'd known about them.

Then James told them what he'd promised Albert.

Nate scowled. "Are you daft? We all need a rest, and here you are, wanting us to go marching right to the next battle?"

"Reckon the Talons know we're here by now too. Whole region has got to be swarmin' with them. Hell, they probably watchin' us right now," Connor snapped.

James said, "Look, we can't do this alone. We need more people to take a stand against the Cult. Freeing these women is a good way of inspiring others. If we're successful, we won't have to go looking for help. They'll come to us instead." He knew he hadn't entirely convinced them, but they agreed.

Ryan hung back after Connor and Nate left. Cautiously, he said, "We're doing this because it's the right thing to do, yeah? Not just to gain some support?"

James crossed his arms. "You know the answer to that."

Ryan nodded. "I remember."

So did James...

When they'd just turned twelve, he and Ryan were in a Crown-occupied village with his father. The squad had been hiding from a patrol when James heard a woman screaming and begging someone to stop. George Barlow had said there was nothing they could do, but James couldn't stand listening to her any longer. So, against his father's orders, he'd snuck away.

He found the woman, dress torn, in some dirty alley as she struggled to push the Crownsman off from on top of her. Tearful, pleading eyes locked onto his. James, so quick to help, had forgotten he carried no weapons. Unarmed children made great spies and scouts because they could say they were just out playing if caught.

The Crownsman had her pinned to the ground and grunted like an animal. She cried in pain with each thrust. James had felt so sick and weak as he watched. Then Ryan appeared next to him, carrying two heavy rocks. With a nod, he gave one to James.

That had been their first kill...

The two were quiet for a time before Ryan said, "All right, we help Albert and people join us. Then what?"

James watched the rebels and pale recruits going about their business. "Honestly, I just want to settle the score with The Claw. Whatever happens afterward is up to them."

"It all sounds so simple. But it won't be, yeah?" Ryan said, rubbing at the back of his neck.

James shrugged. "Only one way to find out."

"You're a loon. You know that?"

"Yes, but a loon with a plan." He gave his friend a slight grin and clapped him on the shoulder. "Don't worry, mate. There's always a plan."

Later that evening, James climbed up to the top of the walls where Connor was on watch. As he approached, the Black man stared out at the dark forest. James didn't bother with a greeting and just came out with what he wanted to ask. "What's bothering you?"

"How do you do that?" Connor muttered. "You a general *and* a mind reader now?"

James laughed gently. "No, no. Just observant. My father drilled it in me since I was barely old enough to walk. 'See the world for what it is. Keep your eyes open. Observe. Prepare for anything and be surprised by nothing.' Now, what is it?"

"My sister," Connor answered. "What if she ended up in one of them Nests? Here I've been feelin' sorry for myself, being locked up in that damn prison while she could be… I got to find her, James." There was guilt and anger in his voice.

"If the Cult has her, we'll find her. If I have to, I'll tear down every Nest with my own hands. I promise."

"Gonna hold you to that, Englishman."

James held out his hand and the two clasped forearms. "You do that," he said.

In the morning, they abandoned Hones and returned to the forest, following the tracks back south. Even with forward scouts, it was a harrowing march. Imagined ambushes and feared counterattacks put most of them on edge. More so when they found the dead Talons on the tracks were no longer there.

James slipped inside quietly as they passed the ruins where they found the engine. Lighting a lantern, he climbed down into the coal storage. The one-eyed miner was gone, and a small weight was lifted from his shoulders. He knew the miner had betrayed them, but if he'd been put in a similar situation—if his family was in danger—wouldn't he make the same choice? In a way, his being in America means he already had.

The army continued east for the next day while Albert did his best to guide them to where he suspected the women of his village were being kept. The scrawny man was not a fighter and had confessed he'd passed the Test by sheer luck. His Talon opponent had tripped on something and hit his head against a rock. So, dazed, it left an opening for Albert to finish him off. Though he lacked any martial skills, he said he could at least stitch up a wound or two.

By mid-afternoon, they arrived at an old warehouse which Heimlan confirmed was a Nest. Crouched behind overgrown bushes, James and Connor monitored the building for a long time. Even though no fires were burning in the area, James could still smell it in the air. A whistle from the other side of the building signaled no movement.

Everything about the place made James uneasy. "Did they know we were coming?" he asked.

Connor shrugged.

From where he leaned against a tree behind James, Heimlan grumbled. Catching everyone by surprise, he stepped out of the trees and shouted at the building to no response. Then he turned back and looked at James's gaping mouth. "You can learn a thing or two just by making a little noise." Spitting a wad of black sludge from his mouth, he added, "No one's here."

Was the Cult toying with them, or was something more sinister going on? James was beginning to grow frustrated with The Claw's games.

Inside the Nest, there was not a soul to be found or saved… or avenged. Just empty rooms cobbled together with wood scrap. The nicer ones had bare bed frames, but most had only piles of filthy rags in a corner. James felt sick when he found some had metal restraints fixed to the floor.

Heimlan had no idea where they could have gone, as was Albert. Others among the pale men had come from the same village as him and had hoped to free their loved ones. Now, they shuffled about, at a loss for words. Meanwhile, Connor had searched every room as he frantically looked for any evidence that his sister had been there but came up with nothing.

"What do we do now?" Ryan asked.

James sat on the edge of a cold, damp cot, looking at an old ring he'd found on the floor in his hand. A leak in the ceiling had rained orange, rusty water down into the room. "We head south," he said and pocketed the ring.

Ryan crossed his arms. "Is this still part of your plan?"

James sighed. He looked at his friend and said, "The plan remains the same. We just have to work harder to see it through."

"And what does 'work harder' look like?"

"People won't be flocking to us as I'd hoped. We're going to have to keep going to them."

"You really think they're going to follow you, yeah?" Ryan said. His shoulders were slumped, and he looked at James with tired eyes. The building was taking its toll on him, James knew, just as it was on everyone who knew what it represented. "Do we even want that? After seeing this place?" Ryan continued.

James stood, feeling an ache in his knees. "Of course," he grunted. "We need others to join us. A lot more than we've managed so far."

"That's not who I'm talking about."

Clearing his throat, James spat the bitter taste from his mouth and said, "I won't be responsible for genocide. That's what the Crown would want to do, not me. They'll get to decide what they want to do once we defeat The Claw. They can stay and help rebuild, or they can go and start somewhere else."

"Just that simple, yeah?"

Heimlan was waiting for them as they left the room, a strange expression on his face—bewilderment. He was bothered by what the empty building meant. But James knew what would help. He took a torch from a passing rebel and handed it to Heimlan. "Burn this bloody place to the ground."

By morning, nothing was left of the Nest except for smoking rubble and bent metal girders. Afterward, they returned to the forest and entered the hill country to the southwest. Again, there was the feeling of being watched with no sign of the watchers. It was a nerve-racking march, but most of them were used to it by now.

In time, they came across several empty settlements built within a region of ponds and small lakes fed by the runoff from the hills. Abandoned only recently, flies buzzed around rotting food left out on tables inside some of the homes. Riding through one village, James was reminded of the first time he set foot on American soil. And the mistake he'd made by knocking on Brian's door. He thought of the Cutter and his promise to save Brian if he got the chance. If the Cult has hurt him in any way... James would have to add that to the growing list of grievances he had prepared for when he met The Claw.

As they rode on, Ryan said to Paddy just ahead of James, "Guess they didn't hit their quota, eh?"

"I don't think so," James said quietly. He didn't catch Paddy's response as he was lost in thought again. None of the villages looked like the way the Talons 'disappeared' them. There was no sign of violence, doors kicked in, or buildings set ablaze.

The ground soon became rockier as they continued, and the ponds dwindled as they climbed further into the hills. At the top of one barren rise, James sat beside Ryan and Paddy as they got the lay of the land while the army rested down below. He could see dark clouds to the south through the ever-present brown haze.

"Probably wind blowing the damn smoke up from Phoenixville. Shit, I meant Dragon's Rest," Paddy said from his saddle, then grumbled, "Never got used to the damn name changes."

"Why is it called that?" Ryan asked, leaning against his horse and sipping from a waterskin.

"Because Jeremiah told us he once saw the Dragon resting on top of the factory." Paddy saw the smirk form on Ryan's face and quickly added, "Look, son, I didn't name the damn thing."

Steering the conversation away from the topic, Paddy said he remembered there had been a string of villages along the mountains to the west. "Last time I was out this way, Talons were camped all around here. But I'm not seeing any campfire smoking up the place. Not sure if that means the villages are still there or..."

James had a feeling they'd find the Talon camps only recently vacated. "Only one way to find out," he said.

Only a few reliable paths led to the mountains, and most of the next two days were spent cutting away at thick vegetation to make way for the supply wagons until they reached the range of mountains that Paddy said was called the Moosic Mountains.

Once they were in the shadows of the mountains, a new danger became apparent as well—the changing of seasons. With frost crunching underfoot, James guessed it had to be mid-October, and it was growing colder by the day. Aside from a couple of wagons carrying their food and whatever tents they had mustered up, the rebel force had only the weapons on their backs and little else. Most wore what they had on when they joined up, with no warm clothing. Shivering himself, James knew he had to get the men protected from the elements, and soon. Their only hope was the nearest mining village. Whether it was occupied or abandoned, it would hopefully offer some shelter.

Like everything else in this blighted land, a fire had swept through here at some point in the past, leaving the earth scarred. Flame-scorched buildings had become home to trees and creeping ivy, while lichen ate away at anything made of stone. To everyone's amazement, a small portion of the village had been spared from the inferno. Though they were far from habitable, a few buildings in the center of town had survived the brunt of the damage.

After sending the men to search the surviving buildings, James walked what had once been the main road but was now overgrown with thorny bushes and only found animal tracks in the frozen mud.

He looked up when the men started coming back out and dumping armloads of clothes on the ground. James hurried over as Ryan pawed through the pile. Most of it looked moth-eaten but serviceable.

"Lucky for us, it was getting warm when The Burn hit, or they might not have packed away their winter clothes," Ryan said. Sizing a thick wool coat, he stopped, looked at it thoughtfully, and added,

"Guess, maybe, it wasn't so lucky for whoever these blokes were, though, yeah?"

James shook his head and then helped pass out what they'd found to the eagerly waiting men.

There was more than clothing inside the few surviving buildings. Among the mildew and rot were discarded human remains. It wasn't easy to tell if they were victims of The Burn or just poor souls who died afterward. And as James laid awake, listening to the groans of wind blowing through the empty windows and fallen roofs, he had to remind himself that ghosts weren't real.

The following day, James stood at a cooking fire, eating a bit of venison brought back during the night. He was still amazed at the abundance of game around them and noted that humanity's suffering had allowed nature to thrive.

Is that the kind of day this will be? Profound thoughts on existence?

A shrill whistle pulled him from his meal.

A guard signaled from the end of the road leading into the old village as figures came out of the trees. Tossing the meat into the fire, James reached for his axe.

Ryan got there before he did and held his ground as the figures drew closer with their hands raised in a sign of peace. Both men and women approached, and James counted seventeen of them, but he couldn't be sure if there were more hiding nearby. Each one was dressed in fur clothes and armed primitively with thick, knotted clubs carved from branches, a few slings, and bows.

As James arrived, a woman talked with one of the guards, and he overheard her say, "—looking for the giant." A hood covered her head, but James could see a large scar running from her chin up past the edge of the hood.

"The what?" asked the guard.

"The giant. He's in charge here, right?"

James cleared his throat.

Turning from the guard, she grunted and said, "Guess that makes you him."

"In charge? I suppose, but…giant?" James asked.

Shrugging, she said, "That's what folks are calling you. Heard you were taller than a horse, and well…" She gave a low whistle as she looked him up and down.

"Thank you?" James said. "But who're they?" Putting a hand on the barrel of the guard's rifle, he aimed it away from her and signaled the others to follow suit.

Relaxing a bit, she lowered her arms and said, "Villagers, mostly. Words getting spread around by traders and trappers that'd seen what you've been doing these last few months. Some say the Dragons are dying from fright just by you showing up."

Brushing his red hair back, Ryan said, "If only it were that easy, yeah?" He stepped in front of James and held a hand out to her in greeting. "Ryan Lloyd, second to the, uh, giant."

Barely glancing at him, she clasped his hand firmly.

After she let go, Ryan flexed his fingers. "Hell of a grip there, Miss?"

"Gretchen. And I wasn't talking to you."

Cheeks flushed with embarrassment, Ryan frowned and moved out the way.

James did what he could to hide his laughter with another cough, then asked, "So, why are you looking for me?"

"Got some folks looking to join the fight, or whatever it is you've got going on here." She nodded to the camp as more onlookers emerged from their tents.

"Why?"

"Same reasons as the rest of you, I'd think. We're tired of the Cult and the Talons."

James crossed his arms and took in Gretchen and the people behind her. They didn't have the same frightened look he'd seen in the others living under the Cult's shadow.

"How many?" he asked.

"Couple hundred to the south. They're waiting in another place like this."

Ryan scratched his chin. "How'd you find us?"

The woman—Gretchen—rolled her brown eyes. "Before or after you started chopping down trees to make way for those carts you got. Which squeak louder than fingernails on a learning board. Don't forget you folks found a way to step on every twig between here and lake country too."

Ryan held a hand up and said, "Point taken." Seeing the furious look in her eyes, he turned from her and whispered to James, "She's right. The larger we get, the harder it is to hide our movements, yeah? Why haven't we seen any Talons since Hones? There's got to be a trap waiting for us."

"I'm sure there is, but it's only a trap if we aren't expecting it," James said.

"And what if this charming lady and her friends are part of it?"

James rubbed at his chin through his unruly beard, giving a side-long glance at Gretchen's people. He nodded to Ryan and then said so the rest could hear, "We'll have to search you all for brands."

Gretchen lowered her hood, revealing short brown hair, slicked back with something that gave it a sheen. Her scar followed along her jawline and stopped just below her left ear. She purposefully ex-tended her neck and flipped her hands over to show there were no brands. Then she tapped her forehead and said, "Don't have the gear to get one here."

"Gear?" James asked, knitting his brow.

Ryan muttered, "Think she means bullocks."

"Ah," James said.

That earned them half a smile.

The others with Gretchen did the same, showing their necks and hands.

One of the rebel guards said, "Could be branded... elsewhere."

Gretchen's face twisted into a scowl, and she spat out, "What? Are you expecting me and the rest of the ladies to get naked out here in the open for everyone to get a good look?"

"N...No," James stammered, his cheeks turning red. "We have a few medics that can check you in private."

Still scowling, she agreed only after he explained that a medic was another word for Cutter.

After he arranged for the medics to meet them in one of the build-ings, James put a hand on Ryan's shoulder to keep him from follow-ing them inside.

Ryan tsked in disappointment, then gave him a big grin. "That Gretchen's a pretty lass, yeah? I even like that scar of hers."

"We don't want to offend our new friends right away. Let them get to know us first. Then you're welcome to as much rejection as you can handle." James laughed.

Mocking a sour expression, Ryan could hold it for only so long before he laughed along with his friend.

The medics returned a short time later and reported that the women were unbranded, as were the rest of the men.

Later that morning, a table was dragged out of a building, and James took out a map he'd found on a dead Talon and laid it out. The map was marked up with the simple pictures the Cult used instead of writing, and with Heimlan's help, he could decipher them. On the other hand, Gretchen had no use for the map and said they only had to go south for half a day along the mountain chain.

"How were you able to get them there without the Cult knowing?" James asked.

Leaning back in a chair, Gretchen crossed her arms and looked at the many rebels moving about the camp. "How did you?" she asked in return.

She continued, cutting him off right as he opened his mouth. "Haven't been any Talons around here for weeks. All went south. Others on the westside of the range saw more come marching down from up north. If you ask me, they took the long way around. It'd been easier to come down on this side."

"Maybe they're tryin' to stay clear of us?" Connor said.

James nodded thoughtfully.

Across the table, Nate asked, "Do you know anything about the empty villages east of here? Where those people could have gone?"

At first, Gretchen had been apprehensive around the pale men, then angry that James had insisted her people be checked for brands when all the men from Hones had them and were walking freely around the camp. It took some convincing, but she begrudgingly accepted that, like her, the men were here to fight.

"Can't say," Gretchen said, not even attempting to hide her disdain. "Our people don't get along with the Lake Folk since they're true believers in the Dragon."

James looked up from the map and asked, "I take it you aren't?"

Gretchen spat on the ground and said, "In the Dragon? No such thing. We had elders from before The Burn that knew what happened. All long dead now, but their stories live on in secret. We've had to keep it to ourselves all these years because Talons are real good at rooting out any heresies."

Ryan nodded. "Very smart."

Her withering stare forced Ryan to look away. With a satisfied grunt, she said, "Nothing smart about it. Just fear, plain and simple. That's how you survive out here."

Before Ryan said anything else to upset the fierce woman, James quickly asked, "When will your people be ready to go?"

She slowly turned from glaring at Ryan and said, "Immediately."

The remainder of the meeting was spent figuring out where to go afterward. It was impossible to think that the Cult was unaware of their location, even though they let the rebel forces march unimpeded. If they were being given free rein to go where they please, Gretchen said the best route would be to follow the mountains southwest. She pointed out the villages and work camps along the way to Dragon's Rest, giving ample opportunity to add to their ranks. The meeting over, James ordered the others to be prepared to march by midday.

It was another long, cold march through the bleak hill country, but by late afternoon they came to a similar scene of collapsed hovels and fire-cleared ruins. However, Gretchen had been faithful to her word because groups of people were clustered around bonfires waiting for them. Like Gretchen's small band, they were clad in furs and brandished primitive weapons.

Astride his horse, James made his way through them until he was at the very center of the crowd. He didn't introduce himself, but by the looks on their faces, he didn't have to.

Here I am—The Giant.

The stares continued as he dismounted. Then James smiled and broke whatever spell was keeping them in place. They were a lively bunch that welcomed him with hearty handshakes and mugs of some strong-smelling drink that tasted of ashes and burned all the way down. It might not have been pleasant, but it warmed the body.

Downing a second glass, James belched before he loudly asked, "Take it you lot are looking for a fight?"

With weapons raised, the crowd howled.

James clapped a man on the back and held up a newly filled mug. "Well, a fight is what you're going to get. I can promise you that."

They applauded.

Then, ever so softly so only those closest had to strain to hear, he said, "But, I can't promise that we'll win."

People shouted for him to speak up, but James remained silent as he watched his words carried back into the crowd by harsh whispers. Voices filled with anger and disappointment flared as the crowd murmured among themselves.

At the peak of their discontent, James smashed the full mug on the ground and said, "Because winning will be up to you." He stuck his arm out and pointed to the circle, turning slowly as he faced everyone. "I can't win this war for you. It will take every single person here to bring these bastards down!"

Their response was deafening.

In a way, it felt like they'd already won, James thought as Gretchen's people welcomed the rest of the rebel force with open arms. He climbed back up on his horse and took in the nearly two thousand souls. A sense of power threatened to surface again, but only briefly. As intoxicating and seductive as that feeling was, it was quickly cast aside with the simple thought that he needed these people more than they needed him.

You are only a catalyst, a spark, nothing more.

With his head sorted, James joined the revelers.

SCARECROWS

The night was spent celebrating the union of the rebel army with the Mountain Folk, the collective name of Gretchen's people. Burnt wine, the local brew, flowed freely from kegs the Mountain Folk had brought with them. Having imbibed enough, James walked with Gretchen, who introduced him to a few of their leaders and told him the story of her people.

"Our elders came from these villages," she said when they passed a crumbling brick wall. "When The Burn came, they fled to the mountains to stay ahead of it."

"It would appear they succeeded," James said, distracted by a rowdy group of drunk men in a circle as two others wrestled in the middle.

"Wishing that were true. The Burn followed. There was no hiding from it."

James turned back from the match. "I'm sorry."

She shrugged. "It was before my time."

"So," he began, looking uncomfortable, "how do your people get by here?"

"Get by? You mean live?" She snorted a laugh. "Any way we can. Cut stone, hunt food, trade. Talons take most of it, but we've got some secret holdings further in the mountains they don't know about. That's where we keep the younglings. Got to hide most of the children, you know." Gretchen frowned. "Got to keep the Cult's recruiters from taking them all away."

"They never found it odd that you have no children?"

Eyes narrowed, she tilted her head and asked, "You heard me say *most* of the children, right?"

It took James a moment to understand her meaning, and then he took a step back to stare past her to the other Mountain Folk, seeing them in a new, more barbaric light. Dreading the answer, he coldly asked, "How do you choose who to sacrifice?"

She sniffed sharply and gave him a look of disgust. "Sacrifice? What the hell are you talking about?"

James blinked several times, unsure of how he'd gotten so lost in this conversation. "I... The Cult and its recruiters. I thought you gave them some children."

Her bitter laugh deepened his embarrassment. "Children got to believe to join. Our children don't. Doesn't stop those religious nuts from trying, though."

Wiping a hand over his face, James nodded. "Oh. I see. I'm sorry, I didn't know what you were getting at."

A thin smile formed on Gretchen's scarred face. "You always putting your foot in it? Or maybe it's something else...?"

"Let's just forget this even happened," James said, rubbing the bridge of his nose.

"Hard not to notice there's only men with you." Gretchen crossed her arms, the smile spreading wider. "Maybe you find us fair lady folk too distracting, eh?"

James started to defend himself, then realized she was only teasing him.

"You're going to fit in well here. I can tell," he said.

By morning, hangovers were prevalent around camp. Even before daybreak, James watched Shamus and Paddy head out to check in with the forward scouts, then prepared the camp for their next move. At the morning meeting, Ryan was noticeably absent. James, accompanied by Connor and Heimlan, cut the session short and went looking for him. It didn't take long before they found Ryan passed out on the ground outside of Gretchen's tent. Someone had been kind enough to throw a fur blanket over him.

James crouched down and slapped his friend's face until he woke up.

Groaning, Ryan pulled the blanket over his head, and his muffled voice croaked, "What?"

"What's all this then?" James asked. Connor and Heimlan, both grinning, did their best to keep from laughing at the fur-covered mound.

Ryan lowered the blanket and squinted at the early morning haze. He tried to sit up, but then laid his head back down on the rock he'd been using as a pillow. "Thought I'd have a nice chat with Gretchen, yeah?" He burped, then, with eyes going wide, covered his mouth.

The tent flap parted, and Gretchen, armed with an annoyed grimace, came out. "Don't go spreading no tall tales about me. The real story is he showed up last night, silent as could be. He stared at me, then passed out on the ground.

"It happens from time to time when the young'uns get into the wine. But I didn't want to have to explain why he froze to death on my doorstep, so I tossed a blanket on him. Now, can you get this idiot to leave? I've been trying all morning."

That burst the dam. Connor and Heimlan howled with laughter as James dragged Ryan to his feet and nearly carried him back to his tent.

"We'll be leaving soon," James told Ryan. "You might want to freshen up a bit."

The tall man snickered as his friend gave him a sour expression and stuck two fingers in the air at him.

Gretchen and the other Mountain Folk seemed to know which villages would be sympathetic to their cause. James was glad for that. It meant these people were hungry for change and had been talking about it well before he'd arrived. Each time they stopped, James would ride in, just as he'd done before, and give his resounding speech. It came to him easily now. After all, his father had shown him what to say years ago. The enemy might be different, but the emotions were all the same. Soon, they added twenty fighters. Then fifty. Then a hundred. It seemed that the closer they got to Dragon's

Rest, the more the people wanted to fight. Ruling by fear had back-
fired on The Cult.

It was a slow march over hills and through mountain passes; by
the second week, the sky was thick with smoke. Like snow, ash
floated in the air. It was in all their food and water. One had to drink
quickly or end up swallowing sludge. For days, it was all James
could taste. Like the Talons, everyone started covering their mouths
with scraps of cloth as best they could. But even with the added protection, James often spit out black muck.

Hoping to get out of the heavy ash, James led them to higher
ground and found it slightly easier to breathe. He was able to get a
better look at where they were going as well, and not far away, he
made out six enormously bright fires—the source of the smoke
they'd been breathing. It was disappointing, in a way. He'd hoped
the smoke had been a sign that they were near Dragon's Rest.

"How far are we from the capital?" James asked Heimlan.

"A day or two."

James sat back in his saddle and pointed at one of the bright spots
on the horizon. "What's that then?"

Heimlan leaned forward on his horse and peered at the tiny dots of
light just below the thick clouds. "Could be scarecrows," he grunted.

"Pardon?"

"You know, scarecrows. Probably trying to scare us away."

"Won't work," James said. Over his shoulder, he shouted, "You
lot scared?"

A resounding "No!" came from all who had heard him.

James nodded, feeling a swell of pride. Turning back to Heimlan,
he asked, "Which way from here?"

Heimlan pointed south-east. "You'll see it well before we get
there."

"Good," James said. He remembered the nightmarish city. The
flames that shot up into the black sky from giant smokestacks. The
mass of Talons and fear. The sadness. Embracing it, he rode on.

Deep down, James knew his bravado was a mask, albeit a neces-
sary one. It was something he had to wear to keep morale up, especially among the untested recruits. He'd made sure they received
training. But he'd already lost a quarter of the prisoners he'd escaped

with, and they were the best fighters he had. The men from Hones had barely begun to learn how to fight, though they had proven themselves capable of taking down at least one Talon. The most he could do was assign the escaped prisoners to lead the platoons and hope for the best.

The following day, curiosity got the best of James when they came near a hill with one of the bonfires. Burning this long could only mean someone must be feeding it. Not that he was looking for a fight, but it had been weeks since Hones, and he was a little tired of giving speeches. After calling for a halt, he tapped Ryan and Connor to join him, and together they rode up the dusty path.

Flames raged hot and bright. Even with cloth masks, the stench of oil and tar was suffocating. Soon, the three were coughing uncontrollably. The horse beneath James began to buck wildly, and it was all he could do to get off without breaking his neck. The animal ran off, and he lost it somewhere in the murky air. Wrapping an arm over his face, James lifted the axe from his belt. The roaring fire muffled other sounds around him; if anyone else was up there, he wouldn't be able to see them in the churning smoke.

And if I can't see…

"Let's stop playing games and get this over with already," he called out in a rasp.

He felt a pat on his arm and barely made out Ryan. The shape behind him must be Connor, he thought. Together, they entered the blinding smoke.

With a startled grunt, Ryan tripped over something in the smog. "Body," he said in a muffled voice.

Moving around, James found a man with one leg chained to a wagon-sized block of cut stone. By the way the blood was splattered against the surface, it was clear he'd been beaten to death. Looking through the bruises and swollen features, James recognized him as one of their scouts. James closed the dead man's eyes as he shook his head before it finally dawned on him. "How many scouts did we send ahead?"

"Six," Ryan said, smearing ash into his pants as he attempted to brush it off.

"Six scouts. Six scarecrows," James said. "When was the last time Shamus and Paddy were in camp?"

Amid a coughing fit, Connor managed to say, "Reckon... reckon about two weeks."

James bolted through the smoke to find his horse without waiting for the others. He came across it halfway down the hill and galloped hard for the next bonfire, where his suspicions were proven true. Like before, the scout had no way of escaping from the vicious pummeling that ended his life.

Both Ryan and his horse were panting when they caught up with him. Sucking in a breath, he coughed out, "There's only six of them, yeah? Not eight?"

James stood as Connor arrived and said, "It doesn't matter how many."

Ryan opened his mouth to say more, but nothing came out after James gave him a sharp look.

With a sigh, James turned from the fire and said, "Collect our dead. They deserve a proper burial." Later, he was glad to learn that neither Paddy nor Shamus was among their number.

At one of the graves, James faced the direction of Dragon's Rest and seethed with anger. This was a war. People died. But like this? Chained like a goddamn animal? He wasn't the only one boiling over with emotion. Those around him held nothing back. Everything from rage, grief, and despair was on display. And he felt pity for those that finally saw what could be in store for them if they continued to follow him.

What right do I have in giving them hope? These aren't even my people.

But, in a sense, they were.

Those who had joined his army wanted the same thing the resistance had fought for in England—a chance to control their fate.

But the men we bury today didn't die fighting...

He couldn't shake the guilt. More than that, he couldn't rid himself of the fury. Distracted, he'd missed Nate coming to stand beside him. The Crownsman was a different person than the one that had set out from England. Something still haunted him, but Nate had turned out to be a damned good fighter in the end. His presence was a good reminder that James wasn't the only that had suffered at the hands of the Cult. It was hard to remember everyone's names that had joined his cause, but they all had their list of grievances and pain.

Feeling less alone, James slid the axe back into his belt and picked up the shovel by his feet. Ryan was crouched at the edge of the grave with a grim expression. James gave him a nod, and they scooped dirt back into the hole.

Connor spoke quietly with a distraught woman at the foot of the grave, offering her words of comfort. The Black man had saved James's life more times than he could count. If he were the superstitious type, James might have thought it was fate that had brought them together in the Fighting Pen. That same fate had a real sense of humor when it came to Heimlan. The former Talon didn't even try to get along with anyone, but his loyalties were known, and that's all that mattered to James.

With the last shovelful done, James turned back toward Dragon's Rest. These people were counting on him to see this through to the end. But can he? Deep down, he knew their chances were small, but his father's words popped into his head again.

A lost battle can win a war.

"Even if we lose, it'll pave the way for the next bloke," James whispered.

After the funeral, James promised a proper memorial for their lost family, not just the six they today, but for all that had died for their cause.

"But for that to happen, we've got work to do," he said.

Beyond the fire-topped hills, they entered the hazy twilight of the Cult's homeland. Dull shafts of sun broke through parts of the thick cloud cover, illuminating the world in pale yellow. Under the smoke, nothing grew except for the toughest grasses and thorny vines. When night enveloped them in absolute darkness, they set up camp by torchlight, surrounded by ancient tree stomps of a forest cleared long ago. What little wood they could find was gray and brittle to the touch, but it still burned.

As James walked among them, he could feel the mood in the camp shifting. He did his best to keep their spirits up and offered words of encouragement when he could. But he also knew what was going on inside their heads. They were weighing their chances and wondering if they should stay and fight or take their chances and run away.

Only the Mountain Folk seemed unbothered by the impending battle. Sitting around campfires, they sang songs and ate. Either they no longer feared Talons or had never been to the capital and seen the horde as James had. He slowed to a stop when he saw Ryan was with them, talking to Gretchen. His friend had a stupid smile as he leaned close to her, whispering. And even though she was frowning, James could see her once ice-cold eyes had softened as she listened.

James smiled to himself and went to find some rest where dreams of war plagued him.

Crownsmen swarmed from every direction, and each rebel that died bore his mother's face. His brother Michael was pinned beneath every pile of rubble and burning wagon. As the world began to explode around him, he watched his father die again and again. And worst of all, lost and alone in all that chaos, he could hear his sister calling for him, but he could never find her. He couldn't save anyone. He couldn't even breathe.

James woke with a start. Still half asleep and coughing, he took in a deep breath. Then froze as a pistol hammer was drawn back with a resounding *click*. It was dark, but he could feel someone was inside the tent with him. "Who's there?"

Whoever it was had begun to breathe heavily but didn't answer him.

Slowly, James inched a hand over to where he'd left his belt but came up with nothing.

"No," said the familiar voice in the darkness.

"Nate," James said.

A match was struck, and Nathaniel Kitts lit the lamp beside him with one hand while the other aimed a pistol at James's head. Less than a foot away, the Crownsman sat with James's weapons behind him.

James eyed the shaking gun. "Why?" he asked and looked past the barrel to stare at Nate.

Dried tears stained the soldier's cheeks as his eyes darted between James and the gun.

Again, James asked, "Why?"

Nate licked his lips and whispered, "I want to go home."

"And this," James nodded at the gun, "will get you there?"

"I…" For a split second, Nate looked confused. Then his hand stopped shaking as his eyes grew cold. "I was promised," he said in a steely voice.

"By who? The Cult?" James already knew the answer but wanted to hear it from him.

"They have ships. They said they could take me home," Nate said, and his left eye twitched. James flinched when the soldier slapped himself and growled in frustration. He thought about trying to take the gun, but Nate stopped and focused again on him before he could.

"What the fuck did they do to you, mate?" James whispered under his breath.

Gritting his teeth, Nate jabbed the gun's barrel into James's forehead and said, "You know what they did to me. I told you. You think you're so smart, but you couldn't even piece it together."

"All right, all right," James said. Quickly, he went through all the conversations he could remember as he tried to make sense of what Nate was talking about. Then, like a flash, he saw Nate retching on the ground outside of Hones when he had described how they'd tortured him, and his words finally sunk in. *You'd do anything, agree to anything, just to make it stop.* James had thought the look he had given him then was one of fear, but now it looked more like a warning.

"You're right," he said. "You tried to warn me. I'm just a bloody muttonhead."

Saliva dripped from Nate's mouth as he sneered down at James. But there was no fire in his eyes, no anger. It was like looking into the center of a whirlpool, void of all emotion. Wiping his chin with a sleeve, Nate sat back, taking the gun from James's head but keeping it pointed at him. Emotions played across the soldier's face, revealing the battle inside his mind.

Then James asked, "How long have you been sitting there?"

Nate looked around the tent for a second as if trying to remember where he was before answering. "Long enough."

"You could have just killed me in my sleep."

A shudder passed through Nate's body as his eyes became glassy with tears.

"You don't want to, do you?" James said.

Nate shook his head and rubbed at one eye with the palm of his hand. The soldier's voice broke as he said, "I just w-want to g-go home." He blinked back the tears, but a few escaped and ran down his cheeks.

"I know, Nate, I know," James said. "Once this is over, we'll find Richard—" Nate, his face twisted in anger, struck James in the temple with the handle of the pistol. Seeing stars, James struggled to keep conscious.

Nate screamed, right up against his ear, "You sent him away!" He grabbed James's shirt collar and pulled while driving the gun barrel into his cheek with enough force that James feared it would pierce right through. "I can't do this without him." The anger dissipated, and Nate let go of his collar and sat back once more. As if he'd just realized it for the first time, Nate admitted, "I'm not strong enough."

James watched as Nate's gaze turned inward, and the gun lowered ever so slightly. "Bloody fool, you are," he said, and the soldier snapped out of it and stared back at him. "You're a goddamned Crownsman. A soldier in His Majesty's Army. You've been hunted and tortured, killed Talons by the dozens, and marched for hundreds of miles. If that doesn't make you strong, well, mate, I'd be afraid to meet the bloke that's stronger than you."

The barrel dipped even lower. "Richard was always the strong one. He had to be. Our father wouldn't tolerate anything less from him," Nate mused as he shed more tears. "He was right, you know. About me being afraid. I always have been. Even back home. I was afraid of the war, and then I was afraid the rebels would find a way to escape, and it would start all over again. But I was born a Kitts, which meant I had to join the army. I didn't want to." He cracked a smile. "I always wanted to be a writer."

"I was born a Barlow," James said. "And I've never had the chance to be anything else."

Placing the gun on the ground between them, Nate wrapped his arms around himself and lowered his head. James could hear him quietly sobbing as he rocked back and forth. He could also hear someone shouting his name from outside the tent, though it was far away.

"When were you supposed to kill me?" he asked Nate.

Nate wiped his face before he looked up again. "I was supposed to sneak inside the Fighting Pen and do it there. They thought since you knew me, you wouldn't expect it. But then I saw you outside the walls, and I couldn't do it."

James nodded and slowly sat up, glad to see Nate didn't reach for the gun as he did. "Why did you run for the Talons then?"

"I... I couldn't do it, but..."

"You were hoping the Cult would just be satisfied if you had the Talons do it for you."

Nate gave a pitiful nod.

"You've had plenty of chances to kill me since then."

Outside the tent, he could hear Ryan now, shouting for him and Nate. He'd be here in a matter of moments.

"We're mates now, aren't we?" Nate asked.

"Mates don't try to kill each other."

Nate frowned and looked back down at the gun. "What are you going to do to me?"

The flap on the tent parted, and Ryan stuck his head inside. "What's taking so long, Nate? I sent you to get his lazy ass up ten minutes ago." Then he paused, taking in the scene. "What's all this then?"

James picked up the gun and handed it back to Nate. "I must have been exhausted," he said, motioning for Nate to get up. The Crownsman took the pistol and slid it back in its holster with only the slightest tremor in his hand.

After the two crawled out of the tent, Ryan gave James a suspicious look and asked, "Sleep all right?"

James gave him a reassuring pat on the shoulder. "Before a battle? Never."

His friend eyed Nate. The soldier's face was still streaked, and he wouldn't meet either of their gazes. "He all right? Looked a bit jumpy earlier."

"He's fine. Aren't you, Nate?"

The Crownsman nodded meekly.

"He's just looking forward to all this being over. But," James put his other hand on Nate's shoulder, "we've got a lot more Talons to kill before then. Think you're up to it, mate?"

Nate blinked and stood a bit straighter. "Y-yes. I bloody well think I am."

"Glad to hear it," James said and let him go. "Now, why'd you send him to wake me up?"

Ryan reached back into the tent and handed James his weapon's belt. He shoved it into his chest and said, "Bloody right there is."

As he followed Ryan through the silent camp, James couldn't help but take in an orange glow from the south. The flames of Dragon's Rest. But that wasn't what Ryan had wanted him to see. In the distance, a dark mass slowly moved toward them across the blighted landscape.

Instinctively, James shouted, "To arms!" And regrated it immediately as the pain flared where Nate had struck him in the head. But the rebels had already gathered outside of camp, waiting for him. A bit embarrassed at his delay, he made his way to the front.

Ryan said, "Must be at least three or four thousand, yeah?"

Taking out his spyglass, James scanned the field to get a proper count.

It was an army, all right, and more than double their number. And it was being led by two men on horseback. James rubbed his eye and muttered, "They wouldn't." Then looked through the spyglass again.

"What?" asked Ryan.

"Shamus and Paddy are with them."

Details became clearer the closer they came to the rebel army. James didn't recognize the dark blue and gray uniforms they were all wearing. They were organized in regiments of foot soldiers and cavalry with supply wagons protected in the middle. When James got a good look at a few of their faces, his heart skipped a beat.

"Connor," James said, looking around until he found him nearby. "Take a look."

"What now, Englishman?" the Black man asked after taking the spyglass.

"Trust me."

After just looking for a few seconds, Connor's eyes widened, and he whispered, "Staters." Then let out a "whoop!" so loud it scared some of the horses.

When Paddy and Shamus arrived ahead of the Black army, word had already spread like wildfire. Paddy probably saw the confused look on James's face because instead of a greeting, he said, "Took a little longer than we thought. Our friends didn't know the way."

James said, "Friends?" And raised an eyebrow.

"Why're you so surprised? You knew we were coming, didn't you?"

James shook his head and told him what had happened to the other scouts.

Shamus growled fiercely at Paddy, "Told you, old man."

Mournfully, Paddy nodded. "That you did." Then to James, he said, "We knew we were being followed, but they left us alone, so we left them alone."

The conversation ground to a halt when the State Army soldiers arrived.

A man at the head of the column raised a hand and barked an order to halt. James could tell this was a general with all the tassels on his shoulders and the wide-brimmed hat. Clean-shaven except for a large mustache, he was older than James by about ten years and carried himself like a Crownsman officer. He climbed down from the horse and gave James an appraising look. "You must be The Giant we've been hearing so much about."

"Yes, I suppose. But I prefer my real name. James Barlow."

The general nodded and said, "Barlow it is." Then he held out a hand. "General Thaddeus Frasier of The Free State of Turner."

James grasped Frasier's hand.

General Frasier introduced Colonel Scott and Sergeant Favre next. As James reached out to shake their hands, a woman pushed through from the Stater ranks and shouted, "James!" Then wrapped her arms around him.

Confused, James carefully pushed the woman out to arm's length. For a moment, he couldn't believe who was standing right in front of him. "Liz?"

Wearing a sly smile, Elizabeth Stillman peered up at him. "It's only been, what? Five months? Do I look all that different?" She had cut her hair to just above her ears, and most of it was tucked under the cap of a Free State uniform.

"I... I never expected to see you again," he said.

James had been so focused on the rebellion that he'd thought little about what had happened to her. Now, seeing her here, it all came crashing down on him that his brother and the rest of the resistance back home might all be dead. He felt like he was about to faint and didn't notice when another man came to stand beside her, dressed in a similar uniform.

"What about me?" Okeny said, smiling.

Knees weak, James grabbed Okeny and pulled him into a hug just as Richard came over. The Crownsman's red uniform had seen better days.

"My god, you're all here," James said.

Suddenly, a pale figure shot past James and crashed into Richard. The soldier struggled, trying to pull himself free. But then, as he stared into the strange, pale-skinned man's face, he finally recognized who it was. With tears swelling in his eyes, Richard laughed and hugged his brother.

James held on to Okeny's shoulder as he asked Liz, "How did you get here? What is all this?"

Hands on her hips, Liz sternly said, "Pardon? Did you think you were the only one that could raise an army?" Then grinning, she explained how she had convinced the governor of Turner to send the army to aid James and his rebellion. Near the end of her story, she appeared distracted, almost as if looking for someone in the crowd behind him.

James felt ice in his veins as he realized who she was looking for. Eagerly, she asked, "Where's my grandfather?"

Placing a hand on her arm, he took Liz to the side and dropped to one knee. Her eyes brimmed with tears as he told her what had happened to the last of her family. Peter Stillman had known he'd only hold them back. He'd sacrificed himself so the rest of the crew might have a chance to escape.

Grief-stricken, she buried her face in her hands and sobbed uncontrollably.

James stayed with her as she cried, tears burning his eyes. In time, she looked back up at him and said, "I'd heard an old man was traveling with you. I… I… thought it was…"

"That must have been Paddy."

Wiping at her tears with balled-up fists, Liz sounded angry as she said, "He always had to get his way, didn't he? What a stubborn old fool."

He stood and, with a kind smile, said. "You're right. He was old and very stubborn, but Peter was no fool."

Liz nodded as fresh tears fell.

Nearby, someone cleared their throat. "Mr. Barlow," the general said from a respectful distance.

James touched Liz's cheek and said, "I'm sorry, Liz, but there's a war to win."

She nodded again and breathed out deeply. Liz trailed behind him as he went over to the waiting officers.

During the next few hours, James noticed she stood close to one of the officers. Occasionally, their hands brushed together when they thought no one was looking. Happy for her, James smiled inwardly.

Ready for this to be over, James and General Frasier made their plans to take down the Cult of the Dragon once and for all.

AND THE EARTH SHOOK

Beneath an angry sky, the two armies moved through a silent, dead world. As they marched, their feet kicked up ash clouds, and the horses snorted in agitation. Dense smog burned their lungs. Raw and red, their eyes felt like pebbles had been rubbed into them. The massive smokestacks of Dragon's Rest stood tall above the horizon, erupting in smoke and flames. It was a harsh and unforgiving landscape.

Then, drifting like the ash on the wind, came a sound that had struck fear in the hearts of many for so many years—the chant. Guttural, the very air vibrated with its primal rhythm. It was all some could do to keep from running, but the stronger among them gave them the confidence to keep going.

At the top of the last hill before Dragon's Rest, they found a field of stars that rose and fell in perfect unison. James saw that each star was a long, staff-like torch held by the Cult's true believers through his spyglass. Together, they beat the ground in time with the chant as they waited on the singed plain across the river from their capital.

James recalled the fear and panic he'd felt when the ironclad chased them on *The Ophelia*. He might have been afraid then, but he never let it cloud his judgment, just as he won't let it do today. Shaking his head to clear the dread from his mind, he knew it was more important to think logically if they were to win this day.

"The scouts were right," General Frasier said. The two had been riding at the head of the column together. "Got to be seven thousand down there. We'll be outnumbered, but not by much."

James nodded grimly. "I've had worse odds. But there's only one among them we need to be worried about."

"What if he isn't out here? He could be back in the city with his sister." The general had been dubious of James's plan. Putting everything on the line just to get James close enough to kill The Claw.

When The Claw dies, their will dies.

"He'll be here. Because, as they say, this is his use," James said.

The lines were clear, and the battle would be fought on this soot-stained field. The Talon army held close to the bridge that spanned the river, their only way back to the capital. The river continued to the southwest, flowing through a group of low hills. The rebels would have to take the bridge to seize the city.

The city itself had transformed into a fortress. Entire sections of the city had been torn apart to erect walls around the enormous factories and buildings. Dragon banners hung from the walls as if taunting the rebels. If James didn't look at it too closely, it almost looked like a romantic painting of a castle from the dark ages.

General Frasier shifted in his saddle and checked his pocket watch.

"See anything we haven't planned for?" James asked.

The general grumbled, "Not yet."

"Good," James said. "Let's go over this once more. The rebels will attack them straight on while you flank from the right. We hammer them hard and drive them away from the bridge, cutting them off from the city. It'll be easy enough to defend while we take control of the capital."

The general wiped the sweat from his face with a handkerchief before tying it back over his mouth and nose. "That's the sum of it, I reckon. Guess there's no more use putting it off."

"Let's hope fate is on our side," James said.

The two men shook hands and parted.

Returning to his troops, James took them down the hill. The chant grew deafening the nearer they got, and the ground shook beneath their feet. When they were only a hundred yards away, the Cultists suddenly fell silent. Calling for a halt, James continued alone for a few more yards, then waited. In the eerie quiet, James became very aware of the Dragon banners rippling in the wind and a steady machine thrumming from Dragon's Rest.

Ahead of him, torches parted, and a single rider emerged from the inky blackness of the sea of Talons. James didn't need his spyglass to tell him who it was. On the back of a black steed, The Claw approached. His eyes were hidden beneath the brim of the bowler he wore. And just like before, the rest of his face was covered by a black cloth that struggled to hold back his thick beard. The black material that covered the lower half of The Claw's face was lost in his thick, unruly beard. He still carried the same length of rebar on one shoulder as he guided his horse to James. In the torchlight, the metallic ribs on his vest gleamed as if freshly polished.

"Got yourself all gussied up for the occasion, yeah?" Ryan shouted from back with the rebels to a smattering of nervous laughter.

The Claw seemingly ignored the taunt and kept coming toward James.

No sense of humor. Pity that.

James nudged his horse to meet The Claw.

When they were within striking distance, the two reined their horses to a stop. Render Hollow lifted the brim of his hat a few inches and stared at James with veiny, green eyes that burned with cold rage. Quietly, they eyed each other. Then James, tired of waiting, said, "Should we even attempt negotiations?"

A rumble sounded from deep inside The Claw's chest that James assumed was a chuckle. In a deep voice, Render said, "What is there to negotiate? You've brought laborers and Southers while I have the power of The Dragon with me." The Claw raised his gauntleted arm, and the chant thundered once again. He lowered his arm, and the Talons fell silent.

James looked back at the determined faces of the men and women he'd gathered and said, "You know, you'd be surprised by what people can—"

An ear-piercing scream cut him off the rest of his words as James
found himself on the ground with his leg pinned beneath the twitch-
ing body of his horse. The Claw, placing the rebar back on his
shoulder, had crushed the animal's skull. Angry shouts came from
the rebel ranks, and they surged forward.

Render Hollow watched them for a few seconds, then looked
down at James struggling to pull his leg free. The Claw said, "Remember, Trespasser, you brought this upon yourself. The Dragon's
Chosen will live on well beyond this day." As if he didn't have a
care in the world, Render turned his horse around and rode back to
his men.

Rebels ran past James, kicking up dust as they went. Then Ryan
was at his side, and together they pushed the dead horse off his leg.
With his help, James stood. His leg ached, but it wasn't broken.
Again, he wondered if the Barlow Luck might actually be real. But
now was not the time to get philosophical.

With battle cries sounding all around them, Ryan picked up
James's axe and tossed it back to him. "Stop losing the bloody thing,
yeah?" he shouted before sprinting after the screaming rebels.

Groggily, James blinked, and Connor was there, pulling at his arm
until he was running. Even though James's head felt like it was full
of molasses, his heart beat faster as instinct took over. There was one
thing his body would never forget—how to fight.

Rebels crashed into Talons in a wave of violence. Torches fell as
weapons were drawn. The flames were trampled and snuffed out by
the press of bodies. Fighting ferociously, the Talons began to chant
again. Even in the face of imminent death, James wanted to understand the chant, but it was sheer nonsense sounds.

Then, he joined the fray.

Gripping the axe with both hands, James planted the blade in a
Talon's chest and kicked the dead body back, freeing his axe. Another Talon rushed and swung a chain at his head. James ducked below it and buried the axe in his side before the Talon could recover.
Out of nowhere, Heimlan appeared and shot the wounded Talon in
the head.

They exchanged nods.

As the battle grew more chaotic around him, James kept an eye out for The Claw but only managed to find Ryan with a circle of dead Talons around him. A few days before, Ryan had asked their blacksmith to add metal spikes to his cherished clubs, which now dripped with blood. James took his place and fought side-by-side with his friend.

James knew a straight-on assault would be dangerous, but even as the rebels fought hard, the Talons began to flank them. If the Cultists managed to close ranks, the rebels would be cut off from the Free State Army. After striking down another Talon, James looked past the flames and the fighting to see the better trained and better equipped State Army holding their own on the right flank. They'd have to merge their forces sooner than expected, he realized. He bellowed the order as he swung his axe.

The fighting was brutal, and it was all the medics could do to help the wounded. But it was nearly impossible to hold a man's guts in place while fighting off a wave of Talons. The horrors James witnessed made the war in England seem civilized by comparison. A boy, barely in the middle of his teenage years, clutched a severed arm to his chest. James watched as a Talon's sword struck a man's face, cutting through both eyes and slicing off his nose. Blinded and screaming in pure agony, the man still lashed out with his pickaxe and took the Talon down with him.

James pulled what wounded he could find to safety while Ryan covered his back. He heard the songs of the Mountain Folk as they tried to drown out the Cult's chant. Gretchen's people were fierce warriors who were stabbing and clubbing their way through the Talons. He even saw her break a Talon's knee with a knotted club before rolling onto his back and driving her knee into his spine. She got her club around his throat and jerked back, snapping the Talon's neck. For a moment, Ryan stood transfixed by how she fought, but James tapped his shoulder. With a blood-soaked grin, Ryan gave him a wink and then crushed another Talon's skull.

James, helping an older man drive back Cultists half his age, felt someone grab his arm and pull him around. Briefly, he'd hoped The Claw had finally found him but ended up disappointed when it was just another Talon. Then dirt was thrown into his eyes.

Blind and coughing, James was kicked hard in the stomach. Bending over, he felt a blade slice his forehead. Pulling back, James swung his axe wildly, hoping to keep the Talon at bay until his vision returned. Finally, blurry images coalesced into Shamus's back. His twin swords raised, the wild man had killed the dirt-throwing Talon, but two more now circled him. Shamus was a flurry of blades, stabbing and parrying as both attacked at once.

Not one to let someone else fight his battles, James rushed in and split the spine of one of the Talons. The axe had bit deep, and James struggled to pull it free while Shamus finished off the other Cultist.

"I think it's stuck on a rib," James said over the din of battle.

Shamus grunted, then unexpectedly darted past him. There was a clash of metal, and James turned. Shamus's blades were locked against a Talon's sword that had been meant for James.

Heaving with everything he had, Shamus sent the Talon's sword arm high and followed up with a vicious slash across the stomach as a second Talon came out of the mass beside him. James tried to call out, but the Cultist had already driven a jagged sword through the wild man's back. Uttering no sound, Shamus merely looked over his shoulder and backhanded the Talon. He then turned and stabbed him in the throat before falling to his knees.

James cried for a medic as he rushed over. Hearing James's call, rebels circled James to keep the Talons back, Ryan among them. Sword sticking out of his chest, Shamus's breaths came short and shallow. Down on his knees, James clasped the wild man's hands. Blood poured freely from the vicious wound as Shamus gave him a weak smile.

All James could think to say was, "I'm sorry."

"Bah. D-don't be." Somehow, Shamus was able to slap James on the shoulder and shake his hand. "This was a good death…" He let out a final gasp then his head fell to his chest.

Slowly, James got to his feet as his vision tinted red. He felt unbridled rage as he sprinted into the chanting mob and slammed his axe into every Talon in his way.

James's furry, matched with the rebels' determination, helped them edge their way closer to the Free State soldiers. The battle was just as fierce for the Staters as it had been for the rebels. Talons rushed firing lines and forced the army to fight hand-to-hand. Pressed on both sides, the Talons squeezed between the two armies and fought without abandon. Each one was a frenzied whirlwind as they chanted and fell upon swords. Teeth gnashed, and nails ripped even as they died. Gripping his axe tightly, James was more certain he couldn't allow the Cult to win.

The loony bastards can never be allowed to rule again.

There was no time for celebration when the rebels and Staters reached each other. The rest of the Talon army awaited them. The arched metal bridge lay fifty yards from where the fighting was fiercest. James still believed in the plan. They just had to clear the way first.

James searched for General Frasier among the officers but grew distracted by a bright streak in the air. He shouted in alarm just before the flaming barrel exploded among their ranks.

Burning rebels and Talons screamed in agony. The heat and stench of burning flesh were overwhelming. Among the chorus of painful cries, General Frasier's booming voice ordered to keep advancing, then he shouted for the cavalry.

"Take out those positions, Ms. Stillman. Now!"

***

Liz returned to the cavalry with blood smeared on her face. She reassured Richard and Okeny it wasn't her own.

"How did our scouts miss artillery emplacements?" Okeny asked. He'd been eager to join the fight, but the general had kept the cavalry in reserve.

Liz said, "I don't know, and I don't care."

It was a deadly oversight that was now raining down flames and death. A lump formed in her throat as she realized Thomas was out there. Was he even still alive? She didn't see him when she'd spoken with the general.

The original town that became Dragon's Rest resided in a shallow valley with hills on either side of the river to the southwest. The barrels were being launched from somewhere on top of those hills.

"Let's go," Liz said. "We've a job to do."

Another volley rocketed over their heads as they whipped their horses. Liz had a quick flash of memory of being chased and Collin's screams as he burned alive. She couldn't save him then, but now she could do something to protect everyone else.

Upon reaching the hills, they crossed through a small farm. A house and barn had rotted away long ago, and the fields were blighted with ash. At the eastern edge of the farm, Talons loaded a catapult beside a wagon full of barrels.

As they charged, Liz smelled her horse's sweat mixed with hers. With bullets whizzing by, she was amazed she could smell anything other than disgusting smoke. Pistols drawn, the cavalry returned fire. Caught by surprise, the Talons fell quickly. First to reach the catapult, Okeny pulled a knife and cut the ropes of the machine, dismantling it just in case the position was retaken.

"One down," Liz said.

At the next one, the Talons were waiting for them.

Barrels lay shattered after the Talons knocked their wagon over for cover. The viscous contents oozed on the ground. Liz shouted to Richard over the galloping horses, "Split off and flank the right. The rest of us will head left."

Richard nodded and took half of the soldiers with him.

Liz took the rest into a skeletal forest of thin, bare trees. Dismounting, they left their horses behind and went on foot. Heart racing, Liz waited. She'd stopped feeling guilty about killing long ago and began to wonder if that was good. But before she could continue that thought, Richard attacked, and Liz ordered the others to open fire.

After the initial barrage, the Talons left alive charged out from behind cover. One that came at Liz refused to die even as she emptied her pistol in him. Wide-eyed and snarling, he finally fell over mere inches from her.

Then the barrels exploded.

Debris ripped through the air as Liz was thrown backward and cracked her head against the ground. Her vision was filled with stars bursting in white patterns, and her ears rang. Sluggishly, she tried to move, but her head felt heavy, and she had a sharp pain in her chest. Fear took hold as she trembled.

There you are, Lizzy. I've got you.

Her grandfather's words were so clear in her mind. It was what he'd said when he'd found her hiding in the cabinet after her parents were killed.

Tears trickled from the corners of her eyes as she remembered him lifting her out of that basement.

Who'll save me now?

She knew exactly what he'd say if he'd caught her thinking that.

What? Is that how I raised you?

Groggily, Liz shook her head and wiped away the tears.

No. You're right. I'll do it myself.

Painfully, she rolled herself over onto her stomach and began to crawl.

Every part of her body ached, and the ringing in her head persisted. Ahead of her, the catapult was in ruins. Soldiers were moving around in the carnage, checking the bodies that lay like discarded rag dolls. Liz wished she could unsee the horses. Shrieking with pain, the suffering animals struggled to move while soldiers put them out of their misery. Fighting nausea, she willed herself to her feet to escape the dying creatures.

Liz walked through the wreckage in a daze until she came upon Okeny crouching over someone with bandages in his hand. In the glow of the flames, Liz saw Richard on the ground with his back propped against a dead horse. Covering her mouth to muffle her cry, she ran the rest of the way.

Okeny reassured the soldier that he would be fine, giving her some hope until she saw the extent of Richard's injury. Just below his left knee was a bandaged stump. Richard screamed in agony when Okeny tightened the belt around his thigh to slow the bleeding.

Liz knelt and took Richard's hand. She brushed a few loose strands of sand-colored hair from his damp forehead. With a grim expression, Okeny sat back on his haunches and wiped the sweat from his face with a bloody hand. He shook his head slowly.

Breathing in short gasps, Richard looked at Liz. "G-go. Finish this. I'll stay here and… and look after the h-horses." He laughed, then gritted his teeth in pain.

Liz held his hand tightly. "I won't leave you here."

Weakly, he pulled until she was close enough to hear him whisper, "If... if you ever get home, tell my father... Tell him I was a Crownsman to the end. Even if I... even if I-I didn't turn out the way he, the way he wanted. He was always so d-disappointed..." His voice broke, and he closed his eyes.

"I will," Liz said. Her tears dripped onto his hand as she squeezed it tightly. "I'll tell him you are the bravest soldier I've ever met. No matter what he thinks, nothing can take that away from you. But I want you there with me when I do."

Richard opened his eyes again and gave her a feeble smile. He took placed his other hand over hers and gently pushed her away. "Go. Others are c-counting on you." His head fell back against the horse's stomach, and his body went limp.

Okeny swore and put a finger to Richard's neck, then said, "He's alive, but he'll go into shock soon. We must hurry and be done with this; he needs a real doctor."

Liz knew he was right. The last of the catapults continued to launch barrels into the battle below. Taking off her coat, she draped it over Richard's chest to keep him warm and then stood. The surviving soldiers had retrieved what horses they could and waited for her command. No one had put her in charge, but they all looked to her. And why shouldn't they? They might not be her crew, but she was still a first mate after all.

"We've got to keep fighting. To the last man," she said to them. "Now get on those horses, shake your heads clear, and let's kill some dirt boys!"

As one, the soldiers said, "Yes, ma'am!"

ONCE AND FOR ALL

When the barrage came to a sudden end, the combined rebel and Free State armies redoubled their effort and successfully pushed the Talons away from the bridge. The Free State soldiers defended the bridge while James crossed over the river with what was left of the rebels and Mountain Folk. A small army of Talons was waiting for them, but most ran instead of taking them on.

Clearing a path to the city was far easier than James had expected. Even Ryan had noticed and said as he let go of the collar of a dead Talon he'd just clubbed to death, "These blokes seem different to you?"

James nodded. The fire was missing from their eyes. Some tried to keep up the chant and drive the more frightened Talons into the fight, but the will just wasn't there. James ordered the rebels to focus on the chanters and let the others go. Before long, the path to the city was open.

On the bridge, the Staters shot at the horde of Talons, leaving piles of bodies as an obstacle for the rest to contend with. Aside from the thrumming of machinery behind the walls, the city was quiet. Now, the rebels had to wait for General Frasier and his officers to arrive.

With no one left to fight, James began to feel the toll the battle had taken on his body. The worst was the gash on his forehead. The few surviving medics cared for people far more injured than he was, but Albert offered to help him with the wound. Albert had used up all his bandages and string during the fight, so all he could do was cauterize the wound.

"Nothing for it, I guess," James said and agreed.

Albert picked up a discarded torch and held it beneath a sword for several minutes. He tested the temperature by spitting on the blade, which sizzled loudly. Albert then gave James a piece of leather to bite down on before placing the searing steel against his forehead. This wasn't the first time James had smelled his own burning flesh, but that didn't make it any easier, and he ground the leather between his teeth.

When it was over, James went to touch his forehead, but Albert slapped his hand. "Leave it." And left him as horses approached from the bridge carrying the general and his men.

"This was almost too easy," the general said as James got up.

A vision of the sword sticking from Shamus's chest flashed in his head. James frowned. The general sounded as callous as a Crown officer. "Tell that to the dead," he said.

The general stiffened. "My apologies. Yes, you're right."

"The bridge?" James asked.

"Under control."

James nodded. "Good. I don't think they planned on us getting to the city. Paddy thinks we just killed a bunch of fresh conscripts."

"Where is that old man?" General Frasier asked.

James pointed a thumb at the bridge. "He went back to fight."

Something about being here bothered Paddy. When James had asked what it was, the old man wasn't ready to face the Hollow twins. He'd said, "They've got Jeremiah's eyes."

"And The Claw?" James asked.

Frasier shook his head. "No sign of him."

James thought that only left one place and looked back at the city. *Never took him as the hiding type.*

"Shall we then?" Frasier pointed to the looming eight-foot-high iron gate. Like their ironclad ships, the gate had spikes protruding in all directions except for the very middle, which had a red dragon symbol painted on it. Above the walls, smoke poured into the flame-colored orange sky. It was almost beautiful, like a sunset.

At least they're consistent.

Ryan had gathered the rest of the rebels by the gate and stood with Connor, Nate, and Gretchen as they waited for James to figure out how to get inside. He gave them a nod as he and the general approached.

"Got anything to get through that?" Ryan asked General Frasier.

Irritably, Frasier said, "I didn't think we'd be needing cannons."

Of all the people James felt closest with, Nathaniel Kitts was in the worst shape. Pale face covered in blood and dirt; Nate cradled a broken arm but refused to let anyone treat it.

"Gonna get yourself an infection," Connor said to Nate when James went over.

Nate shrugged, then moaned. He somehow looked even paler than he had before. "The pain helps," Nate said, "It keeps my head clear." Then his lip curled slightly. "And what would you know about fixing a broken arm? Are you a doctor now as well?"

"Hey, best be watchin' that tongue of yours," Connor snapped, then he gave James a wink.

Turning once more to the gate, James asked, "Should we try knocking?"

Others laughed, but James saw no reason not to try. He walked right up to it, but before he could knock, the gate slowly opened away from him. As the entrance widened, James saw people kneeling on the ground. Talons were behind each one, swords drawn and poised to kill. They lined the road up to the sculpture of the dragon's head outside the main factory. Flames burned in its eyes, almost as if it were staring into James's soul.

Sounding disgusted, Frasier asked, "What is this?"

"What does it look like?" The Claw's voice rumbled. He sauntered out from behind the gate, casually smacking his rebar against one palm.

James thought he looked too comfortable for someone who had just lost the battle. Sneering, he said, "Like you've taken hostages."

"Hostages?" Render Hollow scoffed. He went over to a woman dressed in filthy rags with a gaunt face and tangled hair. She looked blissful. "Are you a hostage, girl?" he asked.

"No, Lord Claw." Her cheeks flushed red, and she smiled.

Render bent down and gripped her chin, turning her to look up at him. If she was in pain, she showed no sign. "What are you then?"

The Claw looked to James as she answered him. "I am the Body of the Dragon. My work, my life, my purpose is to keep the Dragon alive."

From somewhere behind him, James heard Gretchen mutter, "Lake Folk."

The missing villagers.

But there were far more here than those villages could have housed.

Most of the ones by the gate had the same beatific expression as the woman, but those further back told a different story. Most were women, and many stared blankly at the ground, their lips quivering. A few looked at him with pleading expressions.

He realized who the rest of them were.

The Nests.

When his eyes fell on a young girl, not even twelve years old, with her face bruised, he drew his axe and took a step. But as he did, every Talon placed the tips of their swords at the side of a hostage's neck.

James finally saw what The Claw had planned.

His mind flashed back to that bridge in England, the one his mother was supposed to blow up. Her goal was to take out the parade of Crown soldiers; he'd never even thought about the cheering crowd. Not long ago, he'd called their deaths acceptable losses, but now he felt ashamed of that.

Then he remembered Peter's words, *"You can't save everyone. All you can do is try."*

Glaring at The Claw, James growled, "You god damn bastard."

Render's body shook as he laughed.

"You'd kill all these people?" James asked coldly. "Why?"

"I'm not the one that will kill them, Trespasser. You are." The Claw stepped away from the kneeling woman and leaned on his rebar like a walking cane.

"Remember," Connor said quietly so only James could hear him, "they play around with fate. You just got to figure out their rules."

James knew this was all a game to The Claw, like chess. But for James to get checkmate, he'd have to sacrifice more than just carved wooden figures.

"Let me guess what your plan is here," James said. "If we come in, you'll kill these people. But if we leave, you'll set them free."

Render lifted the rebar and waved it over the heads of some of the villagers. "Everyone, even these wretches, has their purpose. These ones are useful because they believe." Then he swung around and pointed behind James to Gretchen. "Unlike those ungrateful mountain dwellers. But we'll fix that in the coming quota." The Claw leaned to a strangely familiar-looking Talon and asked, "Ever bred one of their women?"

The Talon grinned even as he held a sword above a teenage girl, "No, Lord Claw. But I'd be eager to try that one." James recognized that grin immediately. It belonged to Jasper, the Foreman that captured *The Ophelia*.

Ryan struggled to hold Gretchen back as she bared her teeth at the Foreman. "You'd be dead if you tried!" she shouted.

James turned his back to the gate and locked eyes with her. "He wants us to make a mistake. Don't let him get inside your head," he said to her softly.

Gretchen spat toward the gate, then nodded to James. Ryan eased his hold on her, and Gretchen elbowed him hard in the chest. James waited to see if she'd try to make it past him, but she only sneered and waved him off, so he turned back around.

"Feisty," Jasper said, that irritating grin smeared across his lips. The Foreman looked at James and said, "Found yourself a whole mess of Southers now, didn't you?"

"Ain't gonna work, dirty boy," Connor said. "Move on."

James ignored Jasper. "I can't let you kill these people, but we won't just walk away. Do you have enough food in there for a prolonged siege? I doubt it." Crossing his arms, he leaned against part of the gate. "Look, mate, I'm not one to talk, but this plan of yours is truly piss poor."

The Claw squared his shoulders and took a single step toward James when a voice asked, "Brother, what have you done now?" And he froze in place.

The Third Head of the Dragon struck the hard dirt with her jawbone staff as she made her way through the tightly packed street. Talons pulled their hostages aside to make room, and all were extremely careful not to touch her as she passed. Sarah Hollow was hauntingly beautiful, and James was once more drawn to her emerald eyes. She barely gave him a second glance as she looked at her brother in irritation. "We asked you a question."

Giving her a dismissive wave, Render said, "I'm doing what needs to be done."

Her face, porcelain white with black paint on her neck and jaw, twisted in anger. "You've decided to waste all these people while they still have use?"

"This is their use. They're keeping these barbarians out of our city, *sister*." James could hear that The Claw was speaking through clenched teeth.

"Oh? Them?" Sarah Hollow looked beyond her brother to the city gate, scrutinizing each of James's companions before ending with him. Softly, she giggled and said, "You were the one who broke our brother's nose. The Trespasser."

James nodded, looking back and forth between the Hollow siblings.

Sarah took a few steps closer to the gate. "It seems you've met our friends in the south." The charms on her wrist sounded like tiny bells as she gave the general a mocking salute.

In response, Frasier stroked his large mustache and grunted.

Within arm's length of James, she stopped and gazed outside the walls. "You know, we've never once left our city." She lifted her foot as if about to take a step, but at the last second, she put it back down and shrugged. With a motion, she waved Jasper over and handed him her staff before facing James again. "Please, come inside. We have much to discuss."

Ryan whispered, "She's a loon."

Though he agreed, James shushed him. He found it quite difficult to follow her train of thought. Was she doing it deliberately to keep him off guard?

She must have noticed his hesitation because she again said, "Come in, please."

He knew that staying outside would just lead to a stalemate. Someone had to take the first step. So, he did. But the Talons again raised their weapons to the hostages, and he stopped.

Not even looking back to see why he'd faltered, she shouted, "All of you, stop!"

Many looked first to Render, but when he remained silent, they did what she asked and lowered their swords again.

With a tight smile, Sarah said, "See? Nothing to worry about." Then, much louder, she added, "Of course, if we find ourselves in harm's way, we might have to go through with our brother's threat."

James held up his hands peacefully and said, "There's no more need for bloodshed today, madam. I'm open to discussing your surrender."

Putting a hand to her chest, she scoffed, "Surrender?"

"You're beaten, Miss Hollow," James said, turning back to the battle at the bridge where the Talon numbers had significantly diminished.

Sarah laughed dryly. "That's up to interpretation. You've come into our kingdom, beaten our army, and now believe you should be handed the throne, yes?" With an upturned hand, she stopped James before he could respond. "To us, however, it seems you've forgotten the most important thing."

Incredulous, he asked, "And what is that?"

"Why we allowed you to come here at all."

James blinked, unsure what she meant.

"At least the Southers must have wondered why their journey was so easy, right, Mister...?" She looked to the general and his officers.

"Frasier. General Thaddeus Frasier," he said. Then quickly added at the end, "Ma'am."

"Our apologies, *General* Frasier," she said with an almost imperceptible sneer. "You heeded all the advice your little spy network

gave you, yes? Of course, after that, they did lose their usefulness..."
Sarah tapped her chin while her eyes drew upward.

James followed her gaze and felt a pit open up in his stomach.
While they'd all been distracted by the hostages, they'd missed seeing the bodies that hung from the buildings on either side of the gate.
All were Black men and women. General Frasier took off his hat and
swore.

Seemingly satisfied by the general's anger, she asked James,
"How was your march south, Trespasser? Peaceful, we hope."

The skin at the back of James's head began to tighten, and he felt
his *feeling* come, though far too late this time.

She bit her lower lip at first, then frowned as she said, "We'd
heard that some of your men didn't survive after they were captured.
For that, you have our apologies. You see, Lord Claw is like a boiler,
and if we don't allow him to let off some steam now and then, we're
afraid he might explode."

The wheels in James's head churned as he tried to make sense of
what she was saying. Was this all planned somehow?

Next, she raised an eyebrow at Nate. "Since you're still here, does
that mean our little soldier failed in his promise?"

At first, he flinched. Then Nate stood straight and stared back at
her with the steely eyes of a proper English Crownsman. Strangely
enough, James felt a bit of pride in that.

Sarah gave him a dismissive shrug before moving on. "Like bees
to a jar of honey, all those disloyal to The Great Dragon have
crawled out of the woodwork, or"—she glanced at Gretchen—
"should we say, stonework. And now that you are finally here," Sarah smiled and held her arms wide, "we have all our enemies in one
place."

"You're forgetting one thing, madam," James said, finding his
voice again.

"Oh?" she said.

"Bees tend to sting."

Laughing, she said, "Not if you put a lid on the jar and trap them
inside." Then she turned to her brother. "We hope this will teach you
to trust in our plans from now on."

Lowering his head, Render nodded even as he tightly clenched his fists.

James let out a long whistle as he slowly clapped.

Sarah had a bemused expression as she looked back at him.

Shaking his head, James stopped clapping and scratched the back of his shaggy scalp. "I once knew a bloke that would have loved to play chess with you. Unfortunately, he's dead now." He wondered if Reginald had taken the chessboard to his watery grave. "But I don't think you'd offer up much of a challenge." James winked over his shoulder.

Ryan laughed while Nate cracked a smile.

Sarah's emerald eyes seethed as he looked back. "Look, Miss Hollow, I don't mean to insult you, but this isn't going to end like you wanted."

With a voice like a frozen lake, and an even colder smile, she said, "We'll just have to see, won't we?" And then nodded at Jasper.

The Foreman let out a screech that bounced off the nearby buildings. From somewhere deeper inside the city, another screech responded. Seconds later, a red flare shot up into the sky, bursting above the smokestacks.

Bloody flares.

James asked The Head, "What is that for?"

Tilting her head back to the sky, the light from the flare made her eyes appear as if they were on fire. "The Dragon chose us to reshape the world. And we intend to do just that."

James felt a tap on his back and found Ryan pointing at the bridge just then. A second flare had burst above the Talons, who had ceased their suicidal attack.

What am I missing?

Mind racing, James tried to figure out what the Cult had planned. He whirled back to Sarah. "Are you surrendering?" He knew it was a stupid question even before he asked it.

The Head of the Dragon laughed. "Oh, no. Dear Trespasser, far from it." Then her eyes grew wide, and she said, "Ah, there he is."

James's heart sank as he turned back around. The sky burned red as hundreds of flares burst above the hills and plains to the north.

"I told you it was a trap, yeah?" Ryan sighed.

"Not now," James grumbled.

Pinpoints of light appeared on the hills at first but then spread across the landscape like a spark to a line of gunpowder. The lights danced to an unheard song, but James already knew the rhythm.

"Torches," General Frasier said, peering through binoculars.

James was suddenly so very tired.

There was a touch on his arm. Sarah, her body pressed close to his, had closed her eyes and tilted her head back. In a husky whisper, she said, "Theron is coming."

"Who?" he whispered back. Even with all the smoke, he could smell her. She smelled like flowers and coal. Sickly sweet. Like death itself.

Smiling blissfully, she said, "He brings the Dragon's Might. The end of all the unbelievers. Just as I planned."

James pulled away. How could he have been so wrong? He thought he'd been playing The Claw's game, but here was the real threat, in a deceptively delicate form. Has everything he'd been through, from killing The Claw's double to freeing the recruits at Hones, been part of her plan? Had he been a tool to bring the last of the dissenters of the Cult's rule here?

Connor tapped his spear against the ground, getting their attention, and said, "Seein' as it's gonna take them a while to get here, I reckon we might want to settle up here first. Maybe take a few hostages of our own."

Sarah opened her eyes and sneered at him with disgust. "Your opinion means little to us, Souther."

Connor grinned and leaned on his spear. "Might want to be careful with that kind of talk, Miss Head. Since y'all about to be Free State prisoners and whatnot."

"Prisoner?" Sarah scoffed. She turned back to James, and her eyes ensnared his. Reaching up, she placed a hand against his chest, just like she had done long ago. Achingly beautiful, she looked so innocent and sad as she seemed to plead with him.

James opened his mouth, but a roar cut him off, and Sarah was suddenly ripped away from him. The Claw held his sister in the air by her wrist. Struggling to free herself, Sarah's feet kicked at her brother to no avail. Then the knife she'd been secreting behind her back clattered on the ground. Staring at the blade, James realized it'd been meant for him.

Render's voice boomed, "You've taken everything from me! But not this! This. Is. Mine!" The Claw whipped her around and slammed her against a nearby building, shattering her deer skull crown. Sarah collapsed to the ground where she remained, unmoving.

In the shocked silence that followed, James thought, albeit briefly, that he should thank The Claw. That moment passed when he saw the rebar coming for his head.

Ducking, James drew the axe from his belt and raised it in time to keep The Claw from bashing in the top of his head. A resounding *crack* sounded as the two giants finally clashed weapons. With all his strength behind him, Render pressed against James, driving him to his knees.

"I'm going to break you," Render growled with crazed bloodshot eyes.

Both hands gripping his axe, James strained his muscles as he tried to get back to his feet. "You must have me mistaken for your sister," he grunted. James twisted the axe and heaved it to the side, getting out of the way.

Unbalanced, Render swung wildly as he stumbled forward. James avoided it and thrust the axe's handle hard under the Claw's chin before moving back to gain some distance. The Claw recovered in seconds. Locking eyes with James, The Claw smashed the rebar against the ground like a club. Then, as he started to circle, Render held his weapon at arm's length, pointing at James.

James pivoted with his axe raised, not wanting to let The Claw get behind him. The Claw stalked him like an animal, the circle he walked growing wider. Talons dragged their hostages out of the way to give their leader more room. When Render passed in front of the gate, James saw Ryan brace himself, and he knew what his friend was about to do. "No," James called out. "This is just between us."

Ryan didn't look happy about it, but he gave James a nod and backed down.

Taking advantage of the momentary distraction, The Claw moved in and attacked. James took a glancing blow on the shoulder as he tried to twist out of the way, and his whole arm went numb. Pulled by the force of his own swing, Render again stumbled uncontrollably. Hoping to break a knee, James kicked at his leg. But The Claw was far quicker than he had anticipated and grabbed James's foot and spun him around. Before he could get out of the way, Render had his arms around James and slammed him to the ground.

Disoriented and coughing, James rolled to one side and narrowly avoided having his face cracked open by the rebar. Instinctively, he wrapped his legs around one of The Claw's and moved again. Render fell hard. When his head hit the ground, his bowler was knocked off, tumbling away into the silent, awestruck crowd.

Quickly untangling his legs, James returned to his feet and raised his axe. But before he could deliver a killing blow, Render's heavy boot struck his ankle with an audible *snap*. James gasped and fell to his knee as sharp pain radiated up his leg, suddenly overcome with nausea.

There was little he could do to stop The Claw from getting up, and James barely had the strength to lift his axe to defend against the next assault. Again and again, the rebar hammered against the wooden handle, sending numbing pain through his arm with each blow. When they thought their leader was on the verge of victory, the Talons began to cheer for him, and Render redoubled his efforts.

Eventually, everything finds its breaking point. So it was for the axe handle, and it split in two with one last heavy blow. James had watched the cracks forming and knew there wasn't much time left, so when it finally gave way, he shuffled back onto his other knee. As James had seen him do twice before, Render was thrown off balance by his own strength. Taking advantage of this, James lurched forward and stabbed at his ribs with the broken half of the handle. It struck home but only resulted in a dull thud and glanced off The Claw's vest.

Render chuckled as he regained footing and knocked on his vest with a metal *clang*. "Learned from how you wasted Grayson," Render said and lifted the rebar above his head. James avoided the crushing blow at the last second by rolling toward Render and then buried the axe blade in The Claw's knee.

Letting the rebar clatter to the ground, Render bellowed and clutched at his knee. Blood poured from between his fingers as he grasped at the axe head. Shakily rising onto his good ankle, James struck Render's masked face with a haymaker. Looking up at James with pure fury in his eyes, The Claw grew silent before suddenly ripping the blade from his knee and slashing out at him. James hopped back to avoid it before moving in to grab the back of Render's head and slam his knee up under his chin. The Claw's teeth clacked together, and he let out a muffled groan of pain right before blood started to dribble from beneath his mask.

Render tore the black cloth off, revealing his face for the first time. While there were reflections of his sister, The Claw's features were filthy, and his nose had healed at an odd angle, which gave James more than some satisfaction. Blood gushed down his chin as Render spat out a piece of his tongue. James stared at the fleshy, pink thing just before The Claw let out a roar and tackled him to the ground.

Not thinking, James punched Render in the ribs and struck his hand against the hidden armor. As blood and spit rained down into his mouth, Render smashed him in the face once, twice, then James lost count. Baring crimson teeth, Render reared back and balled his fists above his head. But then paused and relished in the cheers of his followers. James's head was swimming, but he still knew enough to thrust his hips up and to the side and was able to throw The Claw off.

Landing on his split knee, a scream of agony burst from Render's throat before falling onto his back. Climbing on top, James put everything he had left in one final punch, breaking The Claw's nose in the opposite direction. Render spat blood in James's face and tossed him off.

Panting for breath, the two lay on their backs.

"Give up?" James gasped.

With half his tongue on the ground a few feet away, Render's response was difficult to make out. Though, James did get the gist of it when The Claw's bladed gauntlet landed within an inch of his head. James rolled to the side, and Render followed. The Claw was relentless, swinging his arm out each time he came around. Then James felt his back hit a wall and knew it was over.

But it was the wall that saved him. Instead of cutting him open, the blades bit deep into the bricks. James slipped out while The Claw tried to pull his arm free. Crawling, he made his way to one of the Talons watching on. Lifting himself to his knees, James punched the Talon in the groin, and with a high-pitched yelp, the Cultists dropped the sword he was holding. Knowing Render wouldn't be far behind him, James snatched it up and turned just in time to parry The Claw's attack before falling back on his ass.

Dragging his bad leg behind him, The Claw had retrieved the length of rebar and was pulling himself along one knee. James deflected the next blow and slid the sword down to cut into Render's hand, taking off a finger. Hand slick with blood, The Claw lost his grip, and James kicked the rebar out of reach. Getting up to his knees, James raised the sword above Render to end the fight, but then The Claw lurched forward and sliced open his thigh with a bladed gauntlet.

Clenching his teeth, James plunged the sword between The Claw's shoulders. Render gasped once, then went limp. The blade remained where he left it after letting go of the hilt. A dizzy feeling came over James as blood gushed from the wound on his leg. For some reason, he started to laugh even as he lost his strength. Faint cries followed him into the darkening world, but he ignored them. All James wanted was to rest.

LONG LIVE THE CLAW

Flares burned in the sky as Liz, with the remaining cavalry, tried to find a way out of the hills. The sound of the approaching Talon army had filled her with dismay, but when they had returned for Richard and found he still clung to life, Liz felt a spark of hope. Fashioning a sling out of their coats, the Free State soldiers carried the Crownsman carefully as Liz and Okeny led the way.

Down below, the fighting was over, and most of the remaining rebel and Free State forces were gathered close to the city. What was left of The Claw's men had retreated away from the bridge and appeared to be waiting.

Okeny asked, "Did they surrender?" They rode down the slope of the first hill, which gave them a good vantage point of the battlefield.

Liz gave a tired shrug. "We'll know soon enough."

Without warning, a woman ran out of the scraggy bushes and into their path. A bit younger than Liz, she wore a tattered black dress and had dark, greasy, messy hair. Sweat smeared the black paint she had around her mouth and neck, giving off the appearance that she was melting.

At first, the woman seemed surprised by them, but after a few seconds, she stood with her back straight and raised her chin. It reminded Liz of the duchesses back home, with all their grace and poise.

However, her voice was far from regal as she breathlessly said, "Oh good, we're... I... *I* mean, I'm glad to have found you."

Suspicious but exhausted, Liz put a hand on the empty pistol at her waist, hoping the woman didn't prove dangerous. "Who are you?" she asked.

"I've only just escaped from that horrible place." The woman pointed back to the city. "A man, I believe his name was James, said there would be people out here who could help me."

"Is that so?" Okeny said, sounding unsure.

Pulling a bramble from her hand, the woman said, "Yes. He's a tall man with an odd accent. Very similar to your own." She tilted her head curiously at them.

Okeny asked, "What exactly do you need help for, madam?"

"I must go south. I have certain... information that could help the Free States win this war." As if agreeing with herself, she nodded vigorously, then looked back at him.

Okeny exchanged a quick look with Liz, then asked, "What information would that be?"

Glancing over her shoulder, she wrung her hands together worriedly and said, "I can't tell you everything, but it has to do with the... the north! But I must get to... Turner, yes. As quickly as possible."

One of the few soldiers still on a horse said, "Don't know if you've noticed, ma'am, but we got a lot more dirt boys surrounding us now, and I reckon they'll be none too happy about us trying to get through them."

"That's all right." She reached into her sleeve and took out a scroll. Unfurling it, she held the paper up and revealed weird scrawling symbols across its surface. "I have a writ of passage. This will get us through, I promise."

"Who are you?" Liz asked abruptly.

Not meeting her gaze, the woman said, "I... I was The Claw's slave. He kept me as his pet."

Liz stared at her for several seconds. The strange woman's lips trembled slightly, and she kept looking over her shoulder. Leaning over to Okeny, Liz asked, "Wouldn't it make more sense for her to speak with General Frasier?"

Okeny shook his head and nodded toward the torches gathered on the hills behind them. "He might not be in the best position to get the information back home. None of us are."

Liz traced the line of flames that spread down the hills and across the plains, finally taking in the sheer number of Talons that surrounded them. If they attacked, there was no getting out alive. Quietly, she whispered, "What are they waiting for?"

"Who knows?" Okeny said. "I'm done trying to make sense of these people. I just want to get this over with." He looked tired, with new wrinkles around the eyes and a bit of gray at his temples. It made Liz afraid to look in the mirror to see what toll this had taken on her.

Liz rubbed the back of her neck. If this woman could help the Free States, they had to get her to Turner. Liz asked the soldier from earlier, "Can you get her back safely?"

He nodded and offered a hand to help the stranger up to his saddle. At first, the woman seemed reluctant, but then, with an almost imperceptible grimace, she took his hand and climbed up behind the soldier.

With her legs dangling to one side, she gingerly wrapped her arms around him and said, "You have no idea how much this means to me. We've much work to do, and I will be sure to remember this kindness once I get where we belong."

After the two had ridden off and the rest continued down the hill, Liz couldn't shake the nagging suspicion that she'd made a mistake. Doubt filled her head as they reached the plain, then she saw the bodies that littered the battlefield leading up to the river. It was a gruesome sight, made worse by the mound of dead Talons that had been cleared from the front of the bridge. But then everything was all right again as she spotted Thomas riding across the bridge to meet them.

Jumping off his horse, Thomas ran the rest of the way, and as soon as Liz's feet touched the dirt, she found herself enfolded in his arms. Holding her tightly, Thomas kissed her passionately. Liz's heart pounded in her chest. Then, despite telling herself she shouldn't, Liz closed her eyes, placed a hand on the back of his head, and returned the kiss. Electricity coursed through her body as she pressed against him. If this was to be the end, she would at least have this one moment of happiness.

It felt like an eternity, yet far too brief. His lips moved from her own, and his arms let her go. "Thom... Thomas, what?" she stammered, caught off guard. His warm smile was so soothing that she couldn't help but match it.

"Been wanting to do that for far too long," he said. Then with a sigh, he added, "But now ain't the time to dawdle. It ain't safe out here. We got to get y'all inside."

Clearing his throat, Okeny said, "Inside?" He looked uncomfortable. Almost like he had seen something he shouldn't have. "Does the general have a plan to defend the city?"

Hands still on Liz's shoulders, Thomas said, "Don't think we got to worry about any last stands. Least not right now anyway. Got sent to look for y'all by the new Claw."

Bewildered, Liz asked, "New Claw?"

"Yes, that's what I said. Now get yourselves across that bridge!" Thomas ordered. The soldiers carrying Richard obeyed immediately, moving as quickly as possible without dropping their load.

Okeny took both their horses' reins while Thomas escorted Liz across the bridge. There was blood everywhere, but Liz had become accustomed to such sights. It wasn't until they were almost across that she heard a voice shout, "Richard!" And Nate dashed to his brother's side.

The soldiers carrying the Crownsman carefully lowered him, and Nate knelt beside him, calling Richard's name repeatedly. Okeny passed the reins to another soldier and went over, easing Nate back. "He's alive," he assured and removed a coat covering Richard's missing leg. "If we can get him to a proper doctor, he'll be just fine."

Nate brushed Okeny aside and felt at his brother's neck with a shaking hand. He must have felt a pulse because he sobbed even as he laughed. "Maybe you'll find it harder to go on your own from now on." Then Nate shouted for a medic.

The soldiers picked Richard back up and carried him the rest of the way across. Once on the other side, medics shouldered past the pale Nate to get to his brother. He could only watch on as they assessed his brother, and he looked lost and helpless, hugging himself.

Liz gently rubbed his shoulder. "They're going to do everything they can to help him. Now, Nathaniel Kitts, would you care to tell me exactly what's happened here?"

He did.

And she ran.

***

"Where am I?" James croaked.

His blurry vision eventually revealed a familiar face, though it took him several moments for his mind to catch up to what he was seeing. Even after losing some weight and growing a thicker beard, his kind eyes gave him away. "Brian," James whispered.

The Cutter nodded and said, "Welcome to the infirmary, James. You almost bled out on us."

"How did I get here?" James asked. He tried to sit up, but the world went for a spin, so he gave up and focused on breathing instead.

"Got carried in by your friend and some Talons."

His throat dry, James rasped, "Talons? Why?"

"I'm guessing it's because The Claw is dead," the Cutter said, handing him a cup of water.

James drank greedily, and the rest of the small room came into focus. He was in a small room with a stained table at its center. But he wasn't on the table. He was lying on a stretcher propped up between two chairs. There was only one door out of the room, and two Talons stood just outside. His leg ached, and he looked down to see bandages tied tightly around his thigh. "So, did we win?" he asked.

As Brian was about to answer, Ryan hurried into the room. "Thought I heard your voice. Catch enough beauty rest, yeah?"

Putting his head back down on the stretcher, James was suddenly aware of all the scars and bruises he'd earned over these last few months. "Unfortunately, no."

Ryan went to stand beside him and clapped the Cutter hard on the back. "You had us all worried there with that fainting act of yours, yeah? Lucky for you, old Brian was still here."

James tried to sit up again but thought better and handed the empty glass back to Brian, who filled it up from a pitcher. Swallowing another mouthful of water, he asked, "What happened?"

Seemingly frustrated, Ryan slowly said, "We beat one Dragon army but got surrounded by a bigger one. Then you killed The Claw."

James closed his eyes and rubbed the bridge of his nose. "I know all that. But why aren't the Talons at the door trying to slit our throats?"

"Oh, them? I don't think they'd try and kill you after what you did."

James opened his eyes, the fog in his head beginning to clear. "What'd I do?"

Sitting back and scratching at his beard, Brian said, "You killed Render Hollow. Again." And gave him a wink.

"I'm painfully aware," James said. "But what are you getting at?"

Ryan grinned. "That makes you The Claw now."

James stared blankly at the two of them before sniffing the water to make sure it wasn't laced with anything that might make him have auditory hallucinations. Finally, he said, "What?"

Ryan said, "Not everyone's ready to accept the outcome, yeah? Some Talons think Render will rise from the dead. I heard them arguing after we brought you in, and one bloke said with Render's sister gone, he's going to stay dead." Then cupped a hand at the side of his mouth and whispered, "I still think they're a bunch of loons."

James started to laugh. How could he have missed something this big? Of course, every Cult leader had come to power by killing the previous one. He'd been so focused on winning that he never thought about what came after. Then he stopped laughing as it dawned on him that not all the leaders were dead. "Where is Sarah Hollow?"

Ryan shrugged. "She disappeared during the fight. General Frasier sent people out to look for her. But they can't go very far, yeah?"

The other *Dragon army.*

"Are the Talons still loyal to her?"

"No." Ryan shook his head. "Heimlan says that The Prophet never ran. He stayed and protected the children. She abandoned them."

"Is that why the other army hasn't attacked yet? They're under my control?" James said. Once again, the sense of power edged ever closer from deep inside. It would be so easy to give in. Then he looked at Brian and saw the sadness he tried to keep hidden just beneath the surface. The same sadness he'd seen in everyone since coming to America and knew where that power would lead.

Ryan said, "I don't know. Supposedly, they're from the south. Some bugger named Theron leads them. Paddy says they're made of tougher stuff than the Talons up here."

It made sense. Before his rebellion, all the Talons in the north had to do was keep the labor camps in line, while those at the border had to be prepared for war at any moment. He had a vision of all those flares in the sky and knew they had no chance of winning. "Hopefully, Theron is rational and will accept the change. But since coming here, I've learned nothing about this place is rational." Letting out a sigh, he asked, "What now?"

Ryan looked down at him, tilting his head. "You're the new boss, yeah? What do you want to do?"

"Sleep for a week straight. But," James groaned as he began to get up, "I think it's time I got to work."

***

The two men helped James out of the infirmary. At first, the Talon guards looked shocked as James passed, but then the shock turned into eager anticipation as if they were waiting for him to do something.

At the end of the hall, Ryan said, "I think they're expecting you to kill us, yeah? You know, for touching your holy ass or something."

James looked back over his shoulder and saw their disappointment. *Is that why you killed Peter? Because he touched you?* He wished Render would return from the dead so that he could rip him apart again.

The world outside hadn't changed much. It was still all smoke and darkness. There was tension in the air. James felt it right away once he stepped out into the street not far from where he'd fought The Claw. Talons had gathered outside the infirmary, but most had moved up near the factory with the hostages. The remaining rebel forces and Free State soldiers had come inside the city walls and taken up positions opposite the Cultists.

The looks of reverence James received from the Talons made his skin crawl. Not sure what to do, he coughed and gave them a slight nod before continuing. Outside the city, the torches still burned but had not come any closer. It was a harsh reminder that James still didn't know Theron's intentions. Turning his back to the gate, he headed to the large factory with the dragon's head on it.

In time, he'd learn the building was named the Den and was sacred. This was where Jeremiah Hollow had worked and where the Cult had been born. Inside, James went over and sat on the stairs at the back of the expansive room. People filed in after him. Not just Talons, but Lake Folk, rebels, and Staters.

General Frasier, his officers, and James's friends stood just at the foot of the stairs as the factory filled up. Noting some missing faces, James asked, "Where's Liz, Okeny, and Richard?"

General Frasier pulled away from a conversation and said, "Corporal Okeny, Miss Stillman, and Mr. Kitts were with the cavalry that dealt with the catapults. Since no one is currently raining hellfire down upon us, I'd wager they were successful in the endeavor and should be on their way back here."

"Send some people to look for them," James said. "They don't know what's happened here, and the last thing we want is for them to antagonize the southern Talons."

Frasier stiffened and ordered Thomas to take some men and search.

It was becoming stifling inside the large room as the crowd grew in numbers, and James felt strangely claustrophobic. A myriad of emotions stared at him. Anger, sadness, delight, resentment, envy, joy—all were on display. Even here, the people were divided, like oil and water. The Cult was on his left while the rebels and Staters were on the right.

"Probably should say something, yeah?" Ryan whispered to him through the railing.

Honestly, he just wanted to find a warm bed, but he agreed. Using the handrail for support, he got back to his feet, and the crowd fell silent.

Wishing he had some more water, James cleared his throat and began, "I can't predict the future." He let the words hang for a few seconds, drawing murmurs from the crowd, then continued. "I don't know what tomorrow will bring. Hell, I don't even know what will happen in the next ten minutes. But I do know that today didn't turn out the way some of you had wanted." He turned to face the rows of Talons. "The Claw has been killed, and The Head has abandoned you."

While many averted their eyes, others stared back at him in defiance. Even though they'd been disarmed, James knew he had to choose his words carefully. "I've been told since I'm the one that killed Render Hollow, I'm now The Claw of the Dragon. By your laws, you have to accept this."

Am I truly going through with this? What about England? What about Michael? There is an opportunity here, yes. If I had this army at my back and we set sail for England...

He rubbed a thumb on the railing and sprinkled brittle flakes of rust on the steps.

That war means nothing to them. I have no right to bring them into it. Hell, I have no right in being here. Let them choose. Be better than those that came before.

Angry voices rose while James stood there silently contemplating. He had to keep the peace. Reluctantly, he knew their faith would control them, and with little time to think of anything else, he shouted, "The Dragon brought me to this land because It saw the wastefulness here!"

Believers in the crowd flinched and bowed their heads.

He continued, "I proved myself stronger than Render Hollow. I bested him. Twice. First at the mine of Eck, and now here in the holy city of Dragon's Rest. Can any among you make the same claim?"

No one spoke.

"Now, we stand at the precipice of something new. Out there," James pointed at the great doors to the distant torchlight, "is a world that could be made better if each and every one of you is willing to work for it. But it can't just be us. We need to build relationships with our neighbors. Old prejudices must be buried deep and never shown the light of day again. You claim to be the Dragon's Chosen because you were spared from Its wrath, but you are not the only ones. Everyone alive today is descended from survivors of the most devastating catastrophe in human history. The people of the Great Southern Free States are no less special than you are, and because of that, we will gladly work alongside them."

The echo of his voice faded into silence.

He'd hoped his words would pacify the Talons, but he saw the fires of dissent begin to spread with each look of disgust. James steeled himself and stared into the flames.

"You are not prisoners here, and I won't force you to work against your will," he said. "If you do not want to make a better world for yourselves and your children, then you are free to leave. I will not stop you."

He paused a moment to let that sink in before continuing. "But before you go, just listen to what I propose. I've only known oppression my whole life. I fought battles, lost many, and was punished for my ideals. But after all that hardship, I finally know what I want. A world where we can grow and prosper without fear. A world where everyone has a chance to build a better life. Not just for themselves, but for the generations to come."

There was a smattering of applause from the rebels and a few Staters.

Ryan whispered, "Not your best work, yeah?"

A screech sounded at the center of the Talons, and a number of them made their way for the exit with a small portion of the Lake Folk following. Only a handful looked back longingly before leaving the Den. Of those that remained, James learned, many were recent conscriptions while more were Dragon-born Talons. Their belief in The Claw was unshakable, no matter who had the title. In the end, more of the Cultists stayed behind than left.

Ryan wore a wry grin. "Guess not everyone was happy with how the Hollows ran things."

Quietly, James said, "Seems that way." Then quoted his father, "'It is hard to take a new path when familiar ground is easier to tread.'"

James thought about what to say next when he saw Liz pushing her way through the crowd. Parts of her uniform were singed and completely ruined, and she looked just as battered and tired as James felt. Right behind her, Okeny appeared much the same.

Once through the crowd, Liz was prevented from coming any closer by two Talons. James told them to let her pass, and to Liz's surprise, they obeyed.

Looking up at him from the bottom step, hands on her hips, she said, "I suppose that means it's true then. You're The Claw now."

James shrugged. "I sort of fell into it. Honestly, I just wanted to kill the man that murdered a friend."

"I wish I'd been there," she said regretfully and frowned.

"It wasn't like in your story books," James said. "Nothing about it was chivalrous or pretty. I barely made it. Lucky for me, Brian was able to patch me back together."

Brian was near the stairs still but looked uncomfortable with the attention. With a warm smile, Liz nodded at him in greeting. Then her face went cold as she turned back to James and said, "What happens now?"

At the same time, James said, "Everyone keeps asking me that." A green flash caught his eye. Framed by the dragon's metal teeth, a single green flare arced in the sky. *Bloody hell, what now?*

He wasn't the only one to notice it as others turned to look. Furtive whispers grew until everyone seemed to be talking all at once. General Frasier looked agitated and began barking orders to find out what was happening. The only one not looking back was Heimlan. He spat and made his way to the stairs. For a moment, he hesitated before climbing the first step. Then, the former Talon continued until he was close enough for James to hear him over the other voices. "Theron don't agree with the change in leadership," he grunted loudly. "Green flare means retreat. Only Theron's got it." He crossed his arms and turned away.

With the railing's help, James hobbled down the stairs. Ryan and
Okeny were quick to lend him a hand at the bottom. The gathered
masses parted to make way for him as he looked at the flare in disbe-
lief. Liz followed behind him and asked questions that, if he'd been
paying attention, he wouldn't have had the answers for. He didn't
stop until he was at the gate of Dragon's Rest.

The Talons that chose to leave weren't far. They were marching
along the old road on their way to the bridge. One of them trailed
behind all the rest, seemingly transfixed by the green flare. Looking
closer, James recognized Foreman Jasper. The Foreman shook his
head once, looked over his shoulder, and spat, then continued on.

"What're we doing out here?" Ryan asked, his arm wrapped
around James's waist.

Resting a hand on his friend's shoulder for support, James muttered, "Hoping."

"For what?" Ryan said.

"Hush," Okeny said, holding onto James from the other side.

Sarah had said that Theron had brought The Dragon's Might, and
James couldn't think of a better way to describe it. It looked like a
wall of flame stretching for miles in each direction.

How could they have moved so many without us knowing?

Then it happened.

Starting on one side and then the other, the fires began to go out as
if extinguished by slow-moving rainstorms, until finally, only one
torch was left burning at the top of a hill. Even though it was impossible, James felt that whoever held that torch was staring at him.
Then it dropped and bounced down the hillside until eventually going out.

Liz broke the sudden calm that followed. "Is it over?"

"For now. It's time we bury our dead and plan our next move,"
James said.

With help, he turned around. The crowd had followed him to the
gate. No longer separated, Talons and villagers, rebels and Staters,
all mixed together. A Talon stepped forward and knelt in front of
James. Bowing his head, he held up a bundle wrapped in dark cloth.
Moving the fabric aside, James revealed the bowler Render wore. It
had been cleaned of dirt and showed no sign of their brutal fight.

James looked from the hat to the waiting, eager faces that watched him. And he realized what they wanted.

James picked up the old hat, turning it over in his hands. It appeared to be a perfectly normal bowler, perhaps a bit worn in some spots. But then, along the inner band, two initials had been stitched in red, *JH,* and he knew what made the hat so special.

Brushing back his hair, James placed the bowler on his head, and the Talons finally shouted their approval.

***

James spent a few days recovering in private. He took that time to lay the groundwork for the changes he hoped to bring to the Cult. The order was given not to go after Theron for fear of provoking him, but then a small patrol arrived from Turner and met with General Frasier. Afterward, the general looked bewildered as he came into the Den. "They're gone."

Sitting on the stairs, James asked, "Who's gone?"

"The entire Southern Dragon army. My boys said there was neither hide nor hair of them. It's the damnedest thing," Frasier said, his lips pressed together. James could just about see the wheels turning inside the general's head. "It's like they've done gone and vanished."

It would appear the general hated a mystery almost as much as James because he sent out scouts in all directions to find out what happened to the so-called "Dragon's Might." It was discovered that Theron had marched his horde west. Now, with the border between the Free States and Dragon Territory open for the first time since their inception, James saw an opportunity. Luckily, the general agreed with him. It took little persuasion for Frasier to offer aid to the people under James's care.

Like a bloodhound following a scent, Liz found Sarah Hollow's library. The collection primarily consisted of manuals for operating factories, treating ore, and repairing machinery, but there were also books on sociology, psychology, and far more fanciful stories. She was looking forward to spending days cataloging it all. That is until they found her grandfather.

The Free State Army had discovered the captain hanging from the wall with a second body. Both had become brittle from months of desiccation. It was a grisly sight, and James was glad Liz hadn't been the one to find her grandfather in this state. The second corpse had to be identified by Brian, who came forward and said it was Marcus, the young crewman from *The Ophelia*. He explained that Marcus had slipped into a coma soon after they were separated and never came out of it. Render Hollow had used the poor boy's body as a punching bag before stringing him up as a lesson to all who would defy the Cult's laws.

Liz had been gleefully organizing the library when James broke the news to her. Tears were shed, but she had mourned him once already. Holding James's hand, she said, "I'm glad I'll finally be able to say goodbye."

The next morning, a small funeral was held for their two fallen shipmates. James attended, along with Ryan, Connor, and Okeny. The bodies were placed on a pyre and set ablaze. As they burned, Liz said, "I want to take them to the ocean. It's where they belong."

James nodded and told Liz he'd be joining her. "I never told you this, but Peter knew my grandfather and told me stories about him. I wish I'd been able to tell him how grateful I'd been for that."

Tearfully, Liz smiled. "He knew. The captain liked you," she said. "He'd lost most of his friends to old age these last few years. I'm just happy he'd found one more before he…" She let the last words drift away as the bodies turned to ash.

After the funeral, James informed General Frasier that they intended to take one of the ironclads docked on the river and would be gone for a few days. The general wasn't happy, but he knew he couldn't stop him from leaving. Ryan and Okeny went to prepare the ship with the help of the Talons, and James went to the infirmary.

Richard was propped up on a bed. He wasn't alone, of course. James wasn't surprised that Nate was there, but he didn't expect to find Paddy as well. "Oh, sure. They found you a bed. Here I am, the bloody Claw, and all I got was a hard bit of wood," James said at the foot of the bed.

Richard smiled. "Nate wouldn't shut up until they brought me one."

Nate sniffed in annoyance. "If it weren't for me, you'd be lying in dirt. There's less chance of you catching gangrene on this."

Richard set his head back against a pillow and nodded. "Yes, as you keep reminding me."

Chuckling, James looked at Paddy on a stool across the room. "You doing alright?"

"Aye," Paddy grumbled. "Heard about the kid here. I reckon he might need help with his loss." He pointed at the missing leg.

James nodded. "That's kind of you."

"So," Richard said, "what brings the great and powerful Claw to the infirmary?"

James told them about taking the ship to scatter Marcus' and Peter's ashes on the ocean. He invited them to come along.

Richard said, "I'd be honored to go, but I don't think it'd be wise just yet."

"I'm going to decline as well," Nate said. "I should stay here."

"Paddy?" James asked.

"No, thank you," the old man said. "Lost my sea legs." He cackled at his joke.

"Fair enough," James said. "We won't be leaving until tomorrow, so the offer still stands."

Connor and Heimlan also stayed behind to help General Frasier keep order. Thomas also turned down the invitation. He wanted to give Liz time to mourn with her friends and said he'd be waiting for her when she returned.

To Ryan's delight, Gretchen was at the dock the next day, but only to see them off. Ryan made a show of kissing her on the cheek, which she returned with a punch to his gut. James caught the faint smile on her face as she stormed off. Rubbing where she hit him, Ryan watched her leave, then he winked at James and grinned.

Their first stop was *The Ophelia*. The ship was lost beneath the churning waters of the Delaware River, but it was enough to know she was there. Liz scattered a portion of the ashes over the sunken vessel. Liz brushed away tears as the dust dissolved below the surface. She only nodded when James asked if she was ready to leave.

Later that afternoon, James was below deck when the engines cut out. He guessed they'd finally reached the ocean and was about to get up when Ryan burst into the room. "What's going on?" James asked. He was immediately on edge and reached for the new axe he'd had made. This one was made for war, but he had hoped never to use it.

"Ships," Ryan gasped, then disappeared through the door again.

Getting the feeling under his skin, James limped up to the deck. He was right that they'd reached the ocean. It was a calm day, and the waves gently rocked the ship. But the serene view didn't put him at ease because everyone had gathered at the ship's bow. James joined them and finally understood what Ryan had meant. He saw sails and steam clouds rising from ships that stretched for miles along the horizon.

Okeny muttered, "Looks like they brought the whole bloody blockade with them."

Growing cold, James took out his spyglass. He identified warships, schooners, commercial ships, and fishing boats. Each of which flew the red, white, and blue flag of the United Kingdom. And aboard each vessel, he knew there'd be soldiers garbed in red uniforms.

Liz said, "I-I don't understand. I had only said we were in America."

One of James's Talon escorts asked what this meant, and he responded with, "The British are coming."

EPILOGUE: THE LOST ONE
COMES HOME

A soldier stood on top of the Great Northern Wall. These last few weeks, it had become a lonely post. The Crown had recalled most of the military for the expedition to America, leaving only a skeleton crew to man the Wall. He didn't see the point of being here, though. The overgrown wilds beyond the Wall had been empty for decades. It was almost peaceful here, except for the noise of prisoners splitting rocks on their side of the divide.

Then laughter caught his attention. He was drawn to the sound and found a few other soldiers pointing and laughing at something on the Scottish side.

He hurried to see what had caused so many to leave their posts. At first, he was surprised, then intrigued by what he saw below on a small dirt mound near the base of the wall. A young woman waved up at him. Tall for a woman, she was pretty with long dark hair. She wore a white sweater and a long wool skirt with a slit that ran up the side and showed part of her thigh. The men went from laughing to howling as she moved her hips suggestively from side to side and turned around, giving the soldiers a good look at her.

"Is that all of ye then?" the woman called to them in a strange accent.

"There's more here than you could handle, miss," one of the soldiers answered, and the others laughed.

She said, "Nay, I bet I could. But that's not why I'm here." She
placed her hands on her hips, and her demeanor changed. In a stern
voice, she said, "Got me brothers in there. Meaning to get them out."

"Oh?" a soldier snickered. "Who should we say is calling?"

"Name's Julia. Julia Barlow. But don't ye bother, I'll be looking
for meself."

"And how do you plan on doing that?" asked another soldier.

Sounding bored, she said, "By going through yer wall."

They laughed again, and one said, "Well, come now, Miss Barlow. Is that all?"

"Nay. Me Uncle and his boys would like a word with yer king."

"Oh, come off it. Really? The king?"

The laughter stopped when the men came over the hill pulling catapults and trebuchets.

"Aye, the king," Julia Barlow said, then drew a pistol and shot a
soldier square in the chest.

ACKNOWLEDGMENTS

This book has been a labor of love for the last four years. I'd like to thank my wife Laurie Moran for having the patience to let me just sit on my ass and 'write things down.' I also have to thank my friend Amber Newberry for re-sparking my love of writing and encouraging me by publishing some of my short stories. I should also thank my early beta readers: Kristin Harris, Scott Harris, Donna Moran, Brian Moran, and Adam Dziki. Their input helped to keep me going.

To the man who did the developmental edits, Tyrell Johnson of The Darling Axe (darlingaxe.com), thank you.

My cover artist, James T. Egan (www.bookflydesign.com) did a phenomenal job and brought my world to life.

To the readers, I hope you enjoyed reading this. If you didn't, that's fine. I'm not bitter. Well, maybe just a bit.

ABOUT THE AUTHOR

Dan Le Fever is a guy from Lynn, MA who puts one word after another in the hopes that they make sense in the end. His credits include PANIC, a horror story that appears in One Night in Salem by Fundead Publications, as well as Land of Promise, an American Gothic tale set during the Dustbowl Era, found in Exquisite Aberrations. Recently, he was published in Eerie River Publishing's It Calls From the Sea and on Dark Recesses Press.

CPSIA information can be obtained
at www.ICGtesting.com
Printed in the USA
BVHW031307260922
647986BV00017B/568

9 798985 036800